Last Dance
in
Havana

Rosanna Ley has written numerous articles and stories for magazines. A long-time creative writing tutor, she now runs writing holidays and retreats in stunning locations in the UK and abroad. When she is not travelling, Rosanna lives in West Dorset by the sea.

www.rosannaley.com

Also by Rosanna Ley

Bay of Secrets
Return to Mandalay
Her Mother's Secret
The Saffron Trail
The Villa
The Little Theater by the Sea

Rosanna Ley

Last Dance in Havana

Quercus

First published in Great Britain in 2016
This paperback edition published in 2018 by

Quercus Editions Ltd
Carmelite House
50 Victoria Embankment
London EC4Y 0DZ

An Hachette UK company

A CIP catalogue record for this book is available
from the British Library.

PB ISBN 978 1 78747 173 3
EB ISBN 978 1 78747 174 0

10 9 8 7 6 5 4 3 2 1

Typeset by CC Book Production

Printed and bound in Great Britain by Clays Ltd, Elcograf S.p.A.

For Alexa, with love.

CHAPTER I

Havana 1957

'Will you dance?'

The voice took her completely by surprise, so wrapped in her thoughts had she been. Elisa looked up and there he stood.

She had begged to come to La Cueva tonight with Pueblo.

'You're too young,' her cousin had scoffed. 'You're just a baby. Do you think anyone will want to dance with you?'

Elisa had tossed her head. 'I can watch,' she said. *I can pretend.* Though she didn't say that last bit. She was young, yes, but in a month or two she would be sixteen. And that wasn't so young.

'Come on then, little cousin,' Pueblo had said at last. 'But you'll have to look after yourself. I'm not going to be your babysitter all night.'

'I will.' And she was so thrilled by the prospect in store that she forgot even to be offended.

She borrowed the mimosa-yellow dress from her cousin Ramira and her mother pinned a white mariposa flower in her dark hair. It was the white ginger, the butterfly flower, and Elisa could smell the honeyed scent as she and Pueblo hurried through the dark backstreets of Havana to La Cueva.

When they stepped inside, Elisa almost lost her nerve. The walls were painted red and black and it was indeed like walking into a grotto; the lighting was low, a fug of smoke hung heavy in the air, and shimmering, perspiring bodies heaved and twirled on the dance floor to the salsa rhythm being played by the band. Elisa's jaw dropped open and she forced herself to swallow hard. She had grown up with dance – but not this kind of dance. It seemed to exude something she couldn't quite understand, a sensuality that was as yet unknown.

Her thoughts strayed to the boys she had grown up with – not just her cousin Pueblo, but the other boys who lived in her neighbourhood, the boys she'd gone to school with; who swam and fished for *pescado* from the beach with bamboo canes and catgut, who played tag on the shore or street baseball in the squares of the Old City of Havana. They were so familiar; they were like brothers: Miguel, Santino, Vincente and the others. They'd played together as children; their families all knew one another – some of them even lived in the same gritty old apartment block as she did.

Now, though things were changing. They were all growing less innocent; they were looking at each other in a different and less open way. Elisa and her girlfriends tossed their heads and conscientiously ignored these same boys they had grown up with as they passed them by on street corners. They would dance with them though – at parties in their families' apartments or in the balmy evenings when the music and the dancing spilled out of the city's bars and cafés and onto the pavements warmed by the hot sultry sun of Havana.

Elisa looked around her as she followed Pueblo through the sea of bodies in the nightclub. But they had never danced with the boys like this . . .

Pueblo found his friends and a chair in a corner for Elisa. 'Stay here,' he ordered. 'I'll fetch you a lemonade.' And he disappeared.

Sometime later, when she'd drunk it and when Pueblo had quite forgotten about her, and many more couples were entwined on the dance floor or draped over chairs at the bar and tables, Elisa noticed the boy. He was sturdy with a broad chest, short curly dark hair and full, sensual African features. He was about her height and not much older than her, she guessed, though he had an air of confidence about him that she couldn't help but envy. She looked at him once, then again, and the third time she looked, he was staring straight at her. She shivered. There was something so fixed in that look of his, so intense; it seemed to cut right through the people on the dance floor and hit her – just like the blast of heat from her mother's oven when she crouched down to open the door.

The drummers changed tempo and the singer began the introduction to a new number, vocalising syllables that made no sense. This was the *diana*, the opening segment of the rumba, sung in a strong voice that seemed to hold the ache of the Cuban people somewhere deep within. Elisa sighed. She was hungry to dance. But everyone here seemed so self-assured. She was just a young girl – and totally out of her depth.

The rumba was Elisa's favourite dance. It could be found

everywhere in Havana: on street corners on a Sunday afternoon, or in the evenings when a group of friends got together in somebody's backyard. And it was fun to dance it with the boys she knew so well. Safe too, because the rumba was the most flirtatious dance she knew. Elisa was well aware of its sexual symbolism and what the movements were supposed to mean. Miguel, Santino and Vincente could pose, preen and try it on as much as they liked. Elisa and her friends just laughed at them.

The version of the rumba she knew best, the most popular one in their neighbourhood, was the *guaguancó*. In this dance, the man would use *vacunaos* – kicks, flicks and thrusts – to catch or distract his partner. But it was a sexual competition. The woman would cover her groin with her hands or a fan to protect herself, even while she moved forward to entice. Elisa especially liked this bit. She smiled to herself, remembering the last time she had danced it with Vincente.

'You're such a tease, Elisa,' he'd hissed in her ear as the music got faster and faster, the heat rising. But she had only smiled, shaken her head and flounced away. It was just a dance, after all.

And how Elisa loved to dance . . . She sighed again. But to dance the rumba you needed a partner. She glanced across at Pueblo who was leaning close to a girl with long black hair. She was wearing the tightest and shortest red dress Elisa had ever seen, cut low to expose gleaming shoulders and breasts. No chance of dancing with him then; he'd forgotten she even existed. And for the first time Elisa longed for one of the boys she knew so well – Miguel, Santino or Vincente – to come along, to tease her, to pull her into the dancing with flirty eyes and a wide flashing grin.

'Will you dance?'

The voice took her completely by surprise, so wrapped in her thoughts had she been. 'Oh.' She looked up and there he stood – the boy with the intensity in his eyes. He held out his hand. He wasn't smiling like all the boys she'd ever danced with before.

Would she? 'Yes.' She got to her feet – gracefully, she hoped. 'I will.'

The melody began to wind its way through the sweet pulse of the drums as the other singers joined in with the song. Elisa waited. She knew how it worked. As the story is told within the song, the drums tell a story of their own: conversing, questioning, responding. Then the dancers would come in.

And so. The boy fixed her with that look of his and began to move, and on the exact same beat, Elisa did too; she seemed to know which way he was going, and she slipped effortlessly into the rhythm of the dance. She stepped to the left, placing her weight, she stepped to the right and shifted, rolling the balls of her feet on and off the floor; she moved her arms and she let her hips rock to the shakes and clicks of the percussion. She tossed her head so that her dark curls flew. Her shoulders relaxed, her knees bent; the music caught her, swept her into its intoxicating beat. It was a dialogue between dancers and drums; the drumbeat responding to their story; prodding and pushing them on.

The boy still didn't smile. His eyes darkened and he held out his hand to her, lifted their hands, which were clasped both together, like a wave as he pulled her closer, his other hand resting on her back. Elisa allowed her eyes to meet his; his gaze was hypnotic and for a moment she had no hope of looking away. They were almost touching, but not quite. Between them was a small space, and that space seemed to be charged with electricity. He kicked and he flicked and she responded in the tradition of the dance. But all the time she was thinking – *he means it, he really means it*. It had never happened to her before. She felt a lightness in her throat, in her breast; a giddiness she couldn't quite comprehend.

His hand was burning into her spine now as if he were branding her somehow. He made the slightest movement of his other hand and he spun her around and back, over and under, forward and through. He kicked in a fancy, counter-metric step, accented by the *quinto*, the highest, lead drum and Elisa arched delicately away from him. She swept the ends of her yellow dress together languorously – as if she were whisking the energy of him away, denying him. But in the rumba it was never so simple. They were the rooster and the hen. It was invitation and it was innocence. She let her upper and lower body sway in a contrary, sensual motion; opening and closing the hem of her dress in the rhythm of the wooden clave percussion and the clicking bamboo *guagua*. Under the dress she felt naked. He raised an eyebrow as if he were asking her a silent question. She looked at him. He must know. He had her.

The tropical heat of the dance seemed to thicken around them. Elisa was hardly conscious of the others on the dance floor though. It was just her and this boy, this stranger. She didn't know him but she seemed in this moment to know everything about him. His touch was on her back, her shoulders, her hands; his sweat had mingled with her own. His eyes, his intensity drew her in; his gaze seemed to wrap itself around her somehow. Together, they merged with the life pulse of the dance until she thought that they must take flight. But they stayed on the floor. And still with each chorus and each refrain, the rhythm rose and fell, faster and faster with a frenzy, driving them on to the shake of the maracas, to the clash of the *marugas*, to the powerful beat of the drums. And on to the final explosion when the rumba broke and they backed off, slick with sweat, panting for breath, from the dance floor.

He didn't let go of her hand. She saw the mariposa flower, the white ginger butterfly fallen from her hair, lying limp on the wooden floor, trodden half to a pulp by the dancers.

'Who are you?' Elisa whispered. The heat of his skin was still with her, still touching her. It was the flame of the rumba. And she didn't want it to ever go away.

'My name is Duardo.' He brought her hand to his lips, still looking at her with that intense dark stare, and he kissed it.

CHAPTER 2

Bristol 2012

Grace knew that her father had been drinking as soon as he opened the door of her old family house in King Street. His eyes gave it away – bloodshot and guilty. He'd been an attractive man once; he couldn't have caught a beautiful woman like Grace's mother without good looks and more than his fair share of charm. He'd captured Grace's stepmother, Elisa, too, she reminded herself. And now in his early seventies, his white-grey hair streaked with gold, though his figure rather more portly thanks to the booze, he still hadn't lost it.

Surreptitiously, Grace checked her watch. It was four in the afternoon. She could smell it on him too; the stale alcohol seemed to seep through the pores of his skin. But she said nothing as usual. Just felt the same old shiver of distaste.

'I wasn't expecting you, Grace,' he said. His hand trembled on the brass doorknob.

Clearly, thought Grace. She gave a little shrug. Back in the day, when she first became old enough to understand some of what was going on, when a slurred voice, shouting and tears combined with fast decreasing levels in a whisky bottle had begun to make sense . . . She had said something then. She had begged him to stop. Elisa had begged him too; Grace knew that. They had hidden whisky bottles, cried, cajoled, tried to make him face up to what he was doing, what his life had become. But nothing had made any difference. He was set on a pathway and he wouldn't listen. Grace wasn't even sure when it had begun or why. When her mother died? Earlier? She didn't know and she wasn't altogether sure that it mattered any more.

'Elisa asked Robbie to take a look at her laptop.' She held it out to him like an offering, but her father had already swung away from the door, leaving it open. Grace had grown up in this house, but since her mother's death it had never felt like home. The house in King Street had a grand entrance with a green painted door, a brass letterbox and a Georgian fanlight and once, she had loved it. Now, it left her cold. The truth was that after a while – a long while, she reminded herself – Grace had stopped trying to help her father. She'd become almost part of the pretence; another player on the stage of her father's alcohol dependency, she thought bitterly. On the surface, at least.

'Elisa's not here,' he called back to her as he strode up the hall.

Damn it. Grace would have waited for Elisa to collect it from hers, but she knew her stepmother was busy and Robbie had specifically asked her to bring it round. Grace hesitated. Sometimes she suspected her family of conniving to make her spend time with her father, as if they thought there would suddenly be some unexpected happy ever after reunion. This wasn't going to happen. Life wasn't a TV show. You couldn't simply take hold of a clean duster and wipe away the past. Once something had happened, it had happened.

Like that moment with Theo after the card trick three weeks ago, Grace found herself thinking. She pushed the thought away. It had happened, yes, but she wouldn't think about it, and especially not now. She and Robbie hadn't seen Theo for three weeks but there was sure to be a good reason for that – he was their best friend after all.

'Are you coming in?' her father called.

'Of course.' And Grace followed him inside the house.

Her heels clipped across the chequered Victorian floor tiles. 'Is Elisa working?' she asked him. Her stepmother had been officially retired for years, but she still gave occasional lessons in Spanish conversation and hosted parties where only Spanish was spoken. Then she had the regular meetings of her Spanish-speaking community group. Grace had attended those too. It was where she had first met Theo, before Robbie even.

Spain was close to Grace's heart. After Grace's mother had died, after the funeral and those terrible early months of loss, Grace had gone to stay with her mother's sister in Madrid. She was ten years old and had fallen for all things Spanish.

Not all things Spanish, she corrected herself firmly, thinking of Theo and that damn card trick again. But anyway, like Elisa, Theo was Cuban not Spanish; they also shared their Spanish roots and the language, though unlike Elisa, Theo had never lived in Cuba. His family had left when he was just a baby, he'd told them; Theo had been brought up in Florida, USA.

But as a little girl who had just lost her mother and didn't know where to turn, Grace had fallen in love with Aunt Mag, the city of Madrid and the Spanish language which had seemed so dramatic and flamboyant back then. It still did, actually. Spain had seemed like another world too, and that was exactly what Grace had been looking for. She wanted to live somewhere else and she wanted to be someone else – someone whose mother had not run into the road, someone whose mother had not been mown down and killed. But Grace couldn't – alas – stay with Aunt Mag forever; she was just a child and she had to return to her father and Bristol.

Even a child could make plans for the future though, Grace had thought. Maybe when she was older she could go and live with Aunt Mag in her cool, minimalist apartment with the clean white walls, flagstone floor and wrought-iron balcony overlooking a busy street. Grace had wanted to escape the clutter of her life, her home, her thoughts and her grief. This would be a good way. And so when she returned to the UK, Grace had persuaded her father to let her learn Spanish. *Aunt Mag says children should learn languages as young as possible . . .* She could still hear herself. And her father's sigh – because at that stage, only a year after Grace's mother's death, he was still trying to do what was right – before he found someone who gave private Spanish language lessons. Elisa.

Elisa had told Grace's father that she was Cuban. But her dark, olive complexion, raven hair and slightly haughty features reminded Grace of Spain. In her red woollen dress and with her shapely legs, she looked a bit like the flamenco dancer on Grace's mother's jewellery box, a present from her sister in Madrid. Grace had been irresistibly drawn to her.

'Why do you like Spain so much?' Elisa had asked her back then. 'Why do you wish to learn Spanish?'

Grace couldn't think how to reply. She liked Spain because it wasn't England. Because her mother's sister lived there and she seemed to be all that was left. 'Because it's warm,' she said, 'and I like the colours.'

'My family came from Spain – originally, I mean.' Elisa said. She taught Grace the names for the colours, one by one. And that's when Grace knew she had come to the right place.

Grace kept up with her Spanish, which was why she still sometimes attended Elisa's Spanish community group meetings in the church hall down the road from where she now lived. But not often, not any more. Now, there was her husband Robbie and their life together, now there was work and she had soon discovered that running her own business took up most of her time. Spain had taken a background seat in her life; even Aunt Mag, who now lived in a remote finca in the mountains of Andalucia, seemed out of reach.

'Elisa's always doing something,' her father grumbled, as he led the way into the kitchen. As always it was spotlessly clean and tidy, if a little old fashioned; as always making Grace aware of her shortcomings in the housewifely arena. Not that Robbie complained and, in any case, he was as untidy as she. But he earned more than Grace and worked longer hours and Grace had decided that they couldn't afford a cleaner. All in all, it was her responsibility.

She probably just wants to get away from you. But Grace didn't say it. She didn't want a row. There had already been too many.

The walls of the kitchen were yellow; on the floor were the original terracotta tiles. The old butler sink had never been replaced; neither had the painted metal bread bin. The wooden counter had the same burns and scratches that Grace had known all her life. The kettle and toaster were both new additions, but otherwise . . . This kitchen was so familiar to Grace that she felt she would be able to lay her hands on anything, even in the dead of night.

'Coffee?' He opened the cupboard and waggled a jar of instant in the air. Grace knew that Elisa only kept it there for when she wasn't around to make it properly.

She was about to say *no* – because what was the point in them spending time together when they always ended up arguing? – when she noticed the expression in his blue-grey eyes. There was a bravado there; always, there was bravado. But there was something else too. She blinked. It looked a bit like loneliness.

'I'll make it,' she said.

As her father sat down at the old farmhouse table that had also been there for ever, Grace busied herself with Elisa's percolator, filling it with water, adding the rich, strong coffee that her stepmother preferred – no doubt a legacy of her

Cuban days – and screwing on the top. She put it on the gas hob of the range cooker. It was only coffee. And he was, after all, her father.

How long had she been telling herself that? She felt a brief wave of affection for him, for the father he had once been. Turned round and caught him taking a quick slug from the bottle of whisky he kept in the pocket of his tweed jacket. Shit, she thought, what was she even doing here?

'How's work?' he asked when she put the coffee in front of him a few minutes later.

'OK.' She sat down opposite him but she was wary. Her father didn't approve of her new career direction. He thought it was beneath her – which was plainly ridiculous. He didn't say it in so many words. He didn't have to.

'Found any more clients?'

God, he made it sound so sleazy. How did he do that? Grace gripped her coffee mug a little more tightly. 'A few.' She was a massage therapist. A healer, she liked to think.

It had taken a while for Grace to find her way. She'd not done especially well in her 'O' levels, even worse in her 'A's – sometimes she suspected she'd done this on purpose to make a point to her father – but she'd worked in a bank and then an insurance company, and if the work wasn't thrilling, at least it was a friendly office and . . . The truth was, she'd always wanted to do something different. She'd said this to Robbie many times, half-hoping he would encourage her to give up her job, maybe even do a degree. *You're still young,* she imagined him saying. *It's not too late to start a new career, something*

14

more fulfilling, more creative perhaps. But Robbie didn't say any of these things because as Grace knew only too well, Robbie wanted her to do something else entirely.

And then one night about two years ago, she, Robbie and Theo had been sitting round the kitchen table and Robbie had complained of his shoulders aching.

'Let me.' She got up, kneaded out the knots he got from hunching over his computer all day.

'Oh, my God. That's so good . . .'

Theo had rolled his eyes. 'Please. Get a room,' he'd muttered.

Grace had playfully swiped out at him.

'You should try it.' Robbie flexed his shoulders. 'Go on, Grace. Give him five minutes.'

Grace had touched Theo many times without thinking. She had hugged him, she had kissed his cheek, he had even taken her hand to cross the street. But this felt different. She stood behind him and laid her palms on his shoulders. He was wearing a roughly woven cream linen shirt. Underneath this, his body felt warm.

She began to massage with her thumbs, gently at first and then, aware of a ripple of tension, she pressed. 'Jesus,' said Theo to Robbie. 'I see what you mean.' And they'd all laughed.

Theo caught her hand before she could take it away. 'You should train,' he said. His black eyes were serious.

'Huh?'

'Do it for a living. You've got the touch.'

Grace looked down at their hands and pulled hers from his grasp, with a light laugh. 'Sure,' she said. 'It beats insurance. But we have to pay the mortgage, don't forget.'

But Theo had been serious. He had leaned forwards in that way he had, intense and yet utterly relaxed, brow furrowed, sweeping his dark hair away from his face. 'If Robbie could keep things going on the financial front, you could train to be a massage therapist,' he said. 'Start up your own business. Work from home.'

'Massage therapist,' she echoed. The idea appealed. She looked across at Robbie.

'We could manage,' he said, 'if that's what you wanted.'

And she knew what he was thinking. This kind of change of direction was all right. It was safe. *It's something Grace can still do when we start a family* . . . They'd had the conversation monthly (yes, and Grace was aware of the irony) for more than a year. Grace was already in her late thirties. It wasn't as if she had a thrilling career that meant a lot to her. How long did she want to wait?

'It's a good idea,' Robbie said. And: 'Fancy a beer?' to Theo.

The moment passed. But the spark of the idea had lit something in Grace. She had investigated local courses and opportunities online to find out more. She'd given it a lot of thought. She even sometimes wondered if it had been in her background life for a long time simply waiting to be recognised. And now . . . She wanted to do it properly, she decided. She didn't intend to work in a beauty parlour; she wanted her work to have a more serious purpose, and if she really wanted to alleviate people's pain and stress, then she had to understand as much as possible about the process, how massage worked, how the muscles, joints, tissue functioned and responded to different methods.

The more she found out, the more she realised that she was stepping outside her comfort zone. But it seemed like something she needed to do. The course she chose – which fortuitously enough was right here in Bristol – was intensive and required a lot of studying, forty hours of massage practise, and a commitment – not just to the subject, but to herself. It included honest self-reflection, the keeping of a journal in which to express her own insights and experiences of her journey through the course, the study of anatomy, pathology and how the body systems such as the respiratory and digestive systems worked, and learning about the quality of touch.

But the more she thought about it, the more Grace liked the idea. She wanted to work with people and she relished the thought of doing something worthwhile. She was ready for the challenge. She wanted to develop as a person and become more self-aware. She wanted to use her sense of touch. There would be self-doubts of course. There would be times when her confidence would wane and the whole idea would probably seem a bit crazy. But Grace became determined to make it happen. She would build her practice and client base and she would make it her own.

Elisa approved too and it was only Grace's father who couldn't seem to get his head around the idea. Robbie and Theo both thought she was good at massage. Theo had said she had the touch. It was true that when she was working on Robbie's shoulders, she could feel the knots and the tensions; she almost sensed what needed to be done to make things right. A new career, a new life-direction was beckoning. And Grace decided to grab it. She did the introductory course as a taster and enjoyed it. It gave her the confidence she needed to go forward.

She called her business Equilibrium – since harmony and balance were what she was striving to achieve. Physical harmony with the body working as it should do, but mental harmony too; relaxation of the mind worked in conjunction with relaxation of the body, or so Grace believed. And the healing properties of touch. Some people experienced touch so rarely, and even for those who did experience it, how often was touch a communicator, a comforter, a healer – rather than a sexual touch? Touch was – had always been – integral to humanity. And Grace remembered the time in class when she'd done a foot massage for Cathy. When she finished, Cathy was so warm and relaxed that she hadn't realised for a full five minutes that Grace was no longer touching her. The powerful sensation of touch had remained . . . and Grace had felt proud.

She glanced across at her father. 'Perhaps you should come along for a massage one day.' She tried to make her voice light. Grace worked from their cottage in Passage Street but also travelled to clients' homes if necessary, to broaden her options and increase her client base. Sometimes it was good to offer a mobile service. No one had time any more. And that's what she was offering. Time given to oneself; in which to be nurtured and cared for. Time that everyone needed in this stressful and technological world they all lived in. *Or let me come to you,* she'd put on her website and business cards. And so far, her flexibility seemed to be paying dividends.

'Me?' Her father snorted in disbelief.

'Perhaps it might . . . help.'

But he looked at her as if she were proposing something unmentionable. 'I don't need any help,' he growled.

Even so, she saw something in his eyes. Fear perhaps? And again she softened. He was from a different generation after all. She blamed him for so much, but in the end he was still her father and she still cared for him. She put down her coffee cup and leaned towards him. 'I know it's not exactly what you wanted me to do with my life,' she said. She wanted to tell him that it was a good thing, despite what he thought. She wanted to tell him that he was mistaken in the assumptions that he'd made. She wanted him to take her in his arms and hold her in the way that a father should. But there were so many barriers between them. His attitude, the blame Grace had laid at his door. His drinking, her mother's death, his guilt. All these things seemed to stand there like sentinels, determined not to let her through.

'It's not, no.' He gave her a look – unusually serious and direct. 'But it's your decision, Grace. It was important to both of us, me and your mother, to give you a good education, that's all.'

Grace could scream. And then he had to bring her mother

into it. 'But I've used that education,' she said, forcing herself to stay calm. She should show him her APP work. The study of anatomy was complex, the work had always been challenging. Plus there was a huge responsibility on the therapist's shoulders. The client trusted his or her therapist to make a difference. And if the therapist didn't deliver in a way, they'd failed. 'I have a foundation degree, Dad. I researched the courses and I chose a good one. Why can't you see? Massage therapy is a serious profession.' Her name was on an accredited register and she was bound to keep her skills up to the mark through CPD, continuing professional development. But she shouldn't even have to explain all this to him.

'Call it what you like, it's still what it is,' her father muttered. His left eye had started to twitch. It was a sign she'd learnt to recognise. 'We've had massage parlours since time immemorial.'

'I don't work in a massage parlour.' Grace was aware that her tone was crisp and dispassionate. She put down her coffee cup. She wouldn't rise to the bait. She wouldn't give him the satisfaction. And she could get upset later. But it was so bloody infuriating. Yes, she did get the occasional call from prospective clients who imagined massage therapy was a euphemism for something more intimate. But she had her speech already rehearsed. And she wasn't telling her father about *that*.

'I just wanted you to have every academic opportunity,' he said sadly. 'I pictured you as a teacher or even a lawyer. You're a clever girl, Grace, you always were. I didn't imagine you doing this, that's all.'

This. 'Your picture, Dad,' she said. 'Not mine. Your expectations. Not mine.'

He nodded. 'I tried to teach you to aim high though, Grace,' he said. He sounded injured now, self-pitying. That, she knew, was the drink speaking. He had taught her other things too. Like how to destroy someone. Like how not to bring up a child and how to take your child's mother away. Valuable life lessons. Let's talk about those, she thought.

'Your mother . . .'

Don't. Grace pushed back her chair. She went over to the sink to rinse the cups, balanced herself by gripping onto the rim of the butler sink, just for a moment. Even the white porcelain smelt of alcohol, lying just below the surface cleanser as if he'd tipped a glass of whisky down the plughole when he'd heard her knock on the door. *Let it go . . .* Grace forced her grip to relax. How did Elisa stand it?

'Sorry, love. It's just that . . .' He sounded confused now. But Grace had lost the moment of sympathy. She was back in the past. What had her father done to make her mother run across the road all those years ago? She had a good idea.

'My mother might have understood,' she said coldly, not turning round to face him. 'My mother might have wanted me to make my own choices.' Grace wasn't sure though. She blinked fiercely. The white of the old porcelain seemed too bright, too brittle. And Grace's memories of her mother were blurred around the edges. She remembered how beautiful she was — but she had a photograph in their bedroom to remind her of that. And she remembered her mother's perfume, floral and sweet, and her smile — slightly wistful, slightly vague. She remembered bedtime stories read in her mother's soft voice, early-morning cuddles in her parents' bed, and odd details of the clothes her mother wore: a silk scarf in crimson and cream, the zig-zag pattern of a favourite mini-dress. She remembered her hair, which was ash blonde and flicked out at the ends. But oddly, most of Grace's early childhood memories were of her father. Had she blocked out her mother to lessen the pain of loss?

'Oh, yes.' His voice hardened. 'Don't come here talking about choices.'

'I won't.' She kept her voice clipped. *Because I won't come here*. Though even now, she wouldn't say it. But she did turn around.

'I'm sorry, love.' Her father's expression was contrite — so suddenly — almost stricken, and Grace knew that this was how the drink took him. Abrupt bursts of anger and irritation followed by apologies. This was the moment when Grace was supposed to tell him it was all right, that she wasn't upset, that she didn't mind.

Her eyes filled. 'I enjoy my work.' And despite everything she believed about human touch, she stopped herself from going to him, from putting her hand gently on his shoulder. 'And you're wrong — what I'm doing is important. It helps people.'

'I know, Grace. I shouldn't have said all those things. I'm just a stupid old man. Please . . .'

She stomped into the hall to fetch her jacket. The anger had started to creep up from her toes. It was always the same. Grace tried to be conciliatory, then he said something to make her mad. Something inflammatory. But the real reason why they couldn't be nice to one another . . . That, she thought grimly, was as buried as her mother was.

CHAPTER 3

'Well, Theo,' said Elisa, 'where have you been hiding?'

'Hiding?' For a moment his dark eyes held an expression she couldn't read, and then he was smiling that broad smile of his and the impression was gone. 'You know what they say, Elisa.'

'I certainly don't.' Elisa continued to smile, wave and nod goodbye to people as she spoke. She suspected that Theo too was eager to be gone, but how could she tell? He was always a restless soul.

He leaned closer towards her. 'They say that magicians are better than anyone at keeping things hidden.'

Hmm. They were certainly good at being enigmatic and nothing less than excellent at preventing you from knowing what they were thinking. These were not Cuban characteristics and so she could only suppose that yes, they belonged in magician territory. 'It's just that I haven't seen you for a while,' she contented herself with saying. He came and he went, but Elisa had always had a special bond with Theo. Partly because of their shared nationality, partly because he was so friendly with her stepdaughter and Robbie, but also because Elisa was fond of him. Theo was a young man who liked to tease, but she sensed that his heart was in the right place.

'You missed me, huh?' And there was that smile again.

Elisa clicked her tongue. 'Of course. You always have an interesting contribution to make to the meetings.' At least he was the only member of the group who spoke Cuban Spanish with an American accent.

He laughed. 'In that case I'll make an effort to come more often.' He kissed her lightly on both cheeks.

'Hmm. Good. *Hasta luego.*' And she watched him lope away. He hadn't come by car then; he was heading towards Castle Park and it was a long way home. But he was young and the young had boundless energy. Those were the days, eh?

Elisa continued to walk past the imposing church with its tall tower and Gothic windows. She didn't attend church herself. Her parents had held to Catholicism throughout their lifetime but Elisa's religious fervour had never been strong; it had dwindled when she was a teenager back in Cuba and nothing she had seen or experienced since had persuaded her to rekindle her faith. She let her gaze stray over the golden stone of the building. In comparison, the little community centre attached seemed very small and meek, but it served a good purpose, not just for her Spanish-speaking community group, but as a crèche, a mother and toddler group and more besides. If there was a god, she might not have lost her man, she found herself thinking. Could that be true? Religious faith was a support; some preferred to go it alone. Not that there hadn't been times when she'd been tempted . . .

She walked across the spindly grass of the churchyard and on to the street, ready to walk back to King Street, which wasn't far. It had been a lively session. They were a decent bunch of people and Elisa saw it as her duty to make them feel at home here in the UK. Some of them were British and simply wanted to brush up on their Spanish conversation skills, but most had come here to make a fresh start. Like Elisa had – back when she was just eighteen years old. It was, she thought now, as she crossed Tower Hill, almost too many years ago to remember. But she did. Not that she'd had much choice in the matter, mind. And little had she imagined when she first set foot on English soil that she would still be here now, doing what she was doing. No, indeed. It had never seemed like a permanent arrangement.

She made her way over Queen Street and past the little pub on the corner. For a moment she imagined she glimpsed Theo's dark head by the window, but the next instant it was gone. Seeing things, she thought. Whatever next? There was a guitar shop and a sandwich bar and then of course Grace and Robbie's little house. She paused. Should she knock on the door, stop for a chat with Grace? She could pick up her laptop while she was at it, and she knew that Robbie was away at some conference or other. But there was no light on, so Grace must be out. Maybe she'd even gone round to King Street. She quickened her steps. It was beginning to look like rain.

Although it was supposed to be spring, it was cold. Elisa thought of the warmth of the Cuban sun. Such a long way . . . It would be cold here until April or May when a stuttering British spring would jerk into an unsettled summer: one day sunny, the next bringing cloud and drizzle. You never knew where you were with British weather – no wonder people talked about it so much.

Elisa shivered despite the coat with the fur collar she had been wearing all winter, despite her leather gloves and the fleece-lined boots she wasn't quite ready to put away until November. She stepped gingerly down towards the wharf, made her way along the path under the archway, watching a yellow ferry boat as it idly chugged by. She was growing old. She felt the cold much more than she had at eighteen. Sometimes she felt she could no longer imagine the heat of that Cuban sun – the way it warmed your bones, relaxed your muscles, lit your heart. And sometimes she felt as if it – Cuba, Duardo, the last time she had danced the rumba with him in Havana – had happened only yesterday.

After that first rumba with Duardo in La Cueva, back when she was only fifteen years old, Elisa had gone home in a dream. She had lain in her narrow bed in the crowded apartment the whole family shared, pushed aside the flimsy shutters to watch the stars in the night sky and relived every moment of the dance. She had heard again the music drumming in her head, felt again his body press against hers, half drowned in the intensity of those eyes. And the next day he had found her.

They started seeing one another – it was easy back in Cuba in the late 1950s – people were more worried about having enough food to eat than what their kids were getting up to.

Elisa and Duardo walked halfway round the city during those days, among the hawkers, the carriages and the street traders – not in their own neighbourhood but further afield where no one would recognise them and ask questions. And they spent hours down at the *malecón* – the jetty – sitting together on the beach, heads close together or watching the brown pelicans diving into the churning waves. That was where they were when he kissed her for the first time – gentle to start with, as if he were searching her out, then more demanding, the passion breaking over them like the very waves upon the shore.

Elisa shivered once more at the memory. Many years ago, it might have been, but sometimes it was clearer than yesterday. That was also where Duardo had told her all his dreams and ambitions. Duardo, as she had guessed from the first, was no ordinary boy. He believed in the Cuban revolution, in their country's fight for true independence.

'Did you know,' he asked Elisa one day, his dark eyes burning, 'that when the treaty of Paris was signed in 1898, when Spain gave Cuba her independence, that it was the US flag not the Cuban flag that was flying over Havana that day?' He wore his hat usually at an angle so that part of his face seemed always in shadow.

She shook her head, almost scared to comment on this fact that so angered him. But she knew already that Duardo wanted nothing more than to fight with the rebels, with Che Guevara and Fidel Castro. He was ready to sacrifice himself for the cause. He had told her so.

'And what then?' Elisa asked him. In those days she had

little interest in politics. She was fifteen years old and head over heels in love for the first time. She wanted to hear about love and romance. What did he feel for her? That was what she wanted to know.

'Then our lives will get better,' Duardo said. He stretched out his legs, picked up a pebble and tossed it towards the water.

'You mean we'll have more food?' Elisa couldn't see far beyond this. She hugged her knees and looked out towards the faintly purple horizon. Her family, the Fernandez-Garcias, had been relatively wealthy once – her father still mentioned this frequently. Elisa's forefathers had run a sugar plantation in the countryside east of Havana until the Americans came over with their expensive machinery and their newfangled ideas and more or less forced them to sign over the land, by inching them out of the market. Elisa's family simply couldn't keep up. The industry was changing and they had no way of competing with the US plantation owners. Elisa's father – who might have been expected to inherit the plantation – had become instead a bell boy in a swanky hotel in Havana serving the Americans they all hated. It must be a terrible humiliation for him. But that was their life and Elisa had known nothing else. At least her father was working – unlike so many. At least they had a proper roof above their heads. At least they could eat.

'More food, yes. But more importantly . . . freedom,' Duardo said. He tossed another pebble and she watched it skip over the waves. 'We'll be free, Elisa, think of that. We will be free.'

'And will we be free to be together?' she asked him shyly. She shielded her eyes from the sun as she looked at him, at his chiselled African features, at the sensuality of his full lips, the slight gap between his front teeth. She was only young but this was what she wanted more than anything.

'Oh, yes,' he said, and he turned the intensity she adored back on to her again. He took her by the shoulders and kissed her hard on the mouth until she felt she would dissolve right there into the pebbles and the sand and be taken away on the tide. At last he drew away. 'We will be together, Elisa, you can count on that.'

But it hadn't been so easy, Elisa thought now as she walked towards Castle Park. There were many obstacles in front of them and back then they didn't know the half of them. They were just a boy and a girl from totally different backgrounds who wanted to be Cuban and to be free. A boy and a girl in love. Elisa shook her head sadly. That was all they were.

In Castle Park in front of her was another church – St Peter's – which was just a ruin these days. There were so many churches in Bristol; it was a wonder they managed to fill them – if indeed they did. Elisa nodded hello to a passer-by and patted the golden retriever bounding along beside him. She was feeling cheerful still. Her Spanish community meetings always brought her pleasure and these days, of course, it was also a relief to get out of the house. Her expression changed and she knew her smile had faded. She took the shorter path alongside the water.

Philip was getting worse, no doubt of that. This curtain of

darkness – it showed no signs of lifting. But apart from her need to get out of the house, the meetings were a way of keeping in touch – not just with the Spanish language, its idiosyncrasies, its rhythms and its cadences, but with a small community of Spanish speakers, who found themselves here.

Elisa let her gaze scan the waterfront and thought again about those obstacles. Being from different backgrounds had been just the first obstacle that she and Duardo had had to overcome.

Elisa's father had disapproved when an aunt reported who his daughter was spending time with and her mother had remonstrated with her too. 'It's not who he is,' she had insisted, 'but how young you are.' But they had nothing on the way Duardo's mother had reacted when the truth was out.

Elisa shook her head. And it was ironic that after everything that had occurred, here she was now in Bristol. Bristol was a port with a long and historical association with the trades at which Cuba had excelled, and it was a cosmopolitan city in which to live. Yes, many traders here had sent out slave ships – heavens, at one time Bristol had apparently been the busiest port in Britain, at least when it came to rum, sugar and slaves. And you only had to wander around the Old City to see some of the architecture built from the proceeds of those trades. But Elisa believed in putting things in context. Her family too had once owned a sugar plantation in Cuba; her family too had once owned slaves. She was not proud of it. But slavery – brutal and inhumane as it was – was part of their history. And Duardo's too. The world though had moved on, or so Elisa would like to think.

She hurried along towards the main road and Bristol Bridge, the wind whipping at her fur collar. Duardo's mother hadn't thought the world had moved on. She had done everything she could to break up the relationship – and succeeded for a while. But . . . Elisa smiled to herself. There would always be a 'but' when it came to thinking about Duardo. They had climbed that obstacle and they had done what thousands of lovers had done before when faced with parental opposition. They had run away together.

Elisa walked on. She couldn't run now if she tried. There were always plenty of people strolling along the pathways of Castle Park; drinking coffee at the little kiosk in the piazza outside the church, sitting on the blue benches to admire the view of the waterway and the old warehouses and brewery building beyond. Naturally, the people who came here now from abroad felt alienated to some degree, just as Elisa had, and as she still did from time to time, even after all these years. Speaking the Spanish language ensured that it stayed alive; the language was a thread that kept Elisa connected to the land of her birth. It had been a hard life, but in so many ways, a good one.

Her Spanish-speaking community group held unusual little afternoon gatherings. Sometimes they talked politics, often they drank strong coffee or even English tea, or someone would bring in a musical instrument – such as a Spanish guitar or a conga drum and some maracas and they would sing in Spanish, smiling at each other, for music was a direct tunnel to the soul and nourished it like nothing else on earth. It was a strange mix of English, Spanish, Cuban and South American customs, Elisa thought now as she crossed the road towards Welsh Back. Today, a Spanish girl who taught flamenco had brought in tapas, someone else a silky rioja and they had sat around sipping the rich oaky wine and talking food. She smiled. It had been a pleasant afternoon.

There was a new Cuban restaurant opening in Bristol; they were speculating on how successful it might be, how tasty and authentic the food. Cuban food was vastly underrated, in Elisa's opinion. British people who travelled there came back complaining about hotel fare, about the paucity of the choice available, the plainness of the cooking. Elisa frowned. This made her mad because nothing could be further from the truth. Cubans managed with so little – which was a skill in itself – but what they could do with some rice, a few chickpeas, a free-range chicken and some black beans . . . She herself still cooked many of the dishes Mami had cooked before she passed away – still mourning, or so Elisa believed, the warmth of Cuba, the loss of her family and a life that had never been the life she expected or desired. *Que frigo,* she had muttered when she first set foot in England. *How cold* . . . And *que frigo* she had continued to mutter until the day she died.

Papi had soldiered on, never admitting how disappointed he was in their new life – if indeed he was. He had struggled with the English language, but had mastered it sufficiently to gain employment on the railways as a guard and he was proud of this; it was not quite what he'd predicted, but it was a decent job and he was paid a fair wage for it. There was certainly more work here in Bristol – though much of it was unskilled and meant long hours. Immigrants were coming to Britain from other countries too, Elisa learned – her father had not been alone in his ambitions. There was a better standard of living here. In the United Kingdom it seemed that the people in government were sensitive to the potential problems of poor social housing and they didn't want to encourage ghettos and segregation. Capitalism though proved to be part of a more complex world and Elisa could see her father struggling to get to grips with the more competitive aspects of this new life: the bureaucracy, the fact that here there was no turning to the state – everyone had a responsibility for his own future and the future of his family.

He tried. But poor Papi's heart was not in his new life once Mami was gone, and he too died young, leaving Elisa alone here in England when she was only a little younger than Grace was now. Elisa had felt old before her time, for sure. Was it possible that your youth could be for ever trapped in the place you had left behind?

It had been the most difficult time. Should she go back? She had certainly considered it. Elisa still had relatives in Cuba – her mother's sister, Aunt Beatriz and some of her cousins. No doubt there were friends too, though they had all lost touch.

But by then Elisa had a life in England. She had studied the

English language and she had gained teaching qualifications through the college here. She had worked both in schools and privately teaching Spanish, and she earned a reasonable living. She'd had boyfriends too – though none of them had come even close to matching Duardo – and she had her Spanish-speaking community of friends and compatriots. She kept abreast of events in Cuba, but she wasn't sure she should go back. Life would be much harder there. The truth was, that Duardo's shadow still loomed over the city of Havana. They say that the city where you first fall in love will for ever have a hold on you . . . If she went back to Cuba, she wasn't sure she would ever be free of him.

And how ironic was that – given what happened soon after? Elisa grunted just with the effort of walking, for although it was less than a fifteen-minute walk from the church hall to King Street, she had been on the go for most of the day and now she was growing weary. Once, she had worked all day and cooked and cleaned all evening; once, she had danced all night with Duardo in La Cueva . . . But her dancing days were over. She knew that now. Yes, she was growing old.

She wondered if she could persuade Philip to try the new Cuban restaurant. Perhaps. But could she risk even going out with him? His drinking was spiralling out of control, dragging him deeper in; these days she was never sure when he might get irritated or angry, when he might burst into tears or simply get awfully, slovenly drunk in a way that Elisa detested. She tried to feel sorry for him, but her sympathy was wearing thin. Whatever he felt after his first wife's death, it was too long ago for him to still be ruining his own life – and hers. She paused for a moment on the other side of the road, looking down and across the waterway, at the house-boats moored here, at the restaurant boats and in the distance the row of pastel-coloured houses on the quayside.

He had deceived her. Years ago, not long after Elisa's father had died, when she first met Philip Hendon, when he first brought his daughter Grace to Elisa to learn Spanish, he had deceived her. He had drawn her into his world and before she knew it, the door had closed behind her and she was trapped. Ah, Philip. You should have let me be, she thought. But then, of course, she might never have returned to Cuba. And she had not been blameless – far from it.

Elisa walked along the cobbled street of Welsh Back. She liked this street with its big trees and black railings and she liked the way it bordered the water. You had to be careful, mind, on the cobbles when they were slick with the drizzle which had just started up, but then, some might say that nothing was worth doing if it had to be done carefully. She smiled to herself. Duardo would say that. There was certainly no room for caution in the rumba.

Ah, Duardo. Elisa turned into King Street. How often she still thought of him . . . She walked past the cream and green almshouses, the theatre and the pubs. And yes, their house – Philip's house – was one of those Georgian villas which had been built with the profits from the sugar houses. Philip had owned it when she met him. It had been in his family for generations. He had lived there with Grace, and with Nancy, before the terrible accident that had torn his family apart.

Elisa let herself into the house. 'Hello . . .' It was how she always greeted her home. A home which had never – quite – felt like her home, populated with the ghost of Nancy as it was. What was she saying? *Hello, please let me in, please let me be part of this?*

She had wanted to be a part of it at first. She had been looking for something, she supposed. Someone to need her perhaps, now that her family were gone? She had walked right into that world and let its darkness surround her. She thought she could help; open a few windows perhaps and let some light in. She thought she could make things right. Philip had made it clear from the start that he had no intention of selling the house. It had been in his family for too long, he said. But she changed what she could. The heart of the house hadn't changed though – that went a good deal too deep.

Philip was sitting at the mahogany dining-room table, head in hands. On the table was his whisky tumbler – empty, she noted – the bottle of Jack Daniels beside it. He hadn't even bothered to hide it in his jacket pocket as he usually did.

'What's wrong?' she asked him.

He looked up, bleary-eyed. 'Grace came round.'

'Ah.' Elisa spied the laptop. 'Did she stay?'

'Not long.' He shrugged.

'Did you argue?' While she talked to him, Elisa slipped off her coat and hung it on the hook in the hallway beside Philip's dark overcoat.

'Not really.'

Which meant yes. 'What about?'

'Nothing. Oh . . .' He sighed. 'I might have said something.'

'About what?' Elisa's heart sank. She was tired. She still had to cook supper since Philip wouldn't have prepared anything. Did she really have the energy to sort this out?

'That job of hers,' he growled.

'Oh, Philip.'

'Well, I don't like it.'

Honestly. 'What do you imagine she does?' Elisa put her hands on her hips. She knew she could be quite fierce when she put her mind to it. Sometimes she'd had to be. She loved Philip in her own way. But he had not been fair to her and he knew it. Yes, she lived in his smart Georgian house. But she had also prevented his world and Grace's world from crumbling into pieces – more times than she cared to remember.

'Does?' he echoed.

'Massage.' Elisa came to stand behind him and began to knead his shoulders. She hadn't touched him like this in a long time. Under her fingers his shoulders felt bony and fragile. 'It eases aching muscles, it loosens stiff joints, it aids relaxation.'

He ran his fingers through what was left of his thinning gold-grey hair. 'Yes, yes, that's what she says. But before I met Nancy, when I used to go up to London . . .'

'I know.' Elisa patted his shoulder and moved away. 'You were lonely and you found postcards in phone boxes and women offered massage which meant sex.' In Cuba you were brought up to say what you meant. Sex was out in the open.

People weren't coy about it and this made the whole subject more honest somehow.

He stared at her. She supposed he still hadn't comprehended the fact that she knew him inside out. Sometimes she knew what he was thinking. Often she knew what he was about to do or say. Occasionally, he surprised her.

'It's not like that now,' she informed him, as if she were an expert on the London prostitution scene. 'Things are more transparent in some ways. Massage therapy does what it says on the tin.'

'You watch too many adverts,' Philip said, with a touch of his old humour.

She smiled. 'Massage is more like physiotherapy. Only not so technical.'

'But Grace –'

'Knows what she is doing.'

'Perhaps.'

His head hung, and she felt sorry for him again as she always had. He had a way of tugging on her heartstrings.

'But I can't help it, Elisa, love. I look at her and she's so distant. She gets closer to all those clients of hers than she does to me – she doesn't come near me, these days. Everything's so different from what I imagined. And we used to be so close. I worry about her and it all comes out wrong.'

The booze makes it all come out wrong, Elisa thought but didn't say. She knew that Grace blamed her father for her mother's death – but why should she? She would never say. And it was so long ago. Wasn't it time to forgive?

'Did you upset her?' Elisa asked him.

'Probably.'

'I should go round there.'

'Why should you?' Defiantly, he refilled the tumbler. 'I'm the one who did it. I'm the one who always says the wrong thing. Look at me. I'm a disaster.'

And I'm the one who always picks up the pieces, thought Elisa. 'You're in no fit state,' she said instead, casting a knowing glance at the whisky bottle, refusing to acknowledge the self-pity that so riled her. That was why he was a disaster.

'She's a grown woman. She's married. She'll get over it.'

But Robbie was not at home and Elisa knew how vulnerable Grace could be where her father was concerned.

'I might go,' she said. 'Just for half an hour.' But oh, she was tired. And she couldn't ask him to drive her – he wasn't capable.

'Leave her be.' Philip got awkwardly to his feet, lost his balance, regained it and somehow sent the chair crashing down behind him. 'Leave her be, Elisa.'

Elisa hesitated. She watched Philip stagger into the lounge. He would collapse into an armchair and in five minutes he'd be asleep, snoring loudly, till past bedtime. This was her life, she thought. This was what she had come to.

Compromise. Elisa was good at that. She went into the hall, picked up the phone and punched in Grace's number. It rang and rang and then the voicemail cut in. Either Grace still wasn't in or she didn't want to talk to anyone.

Elisa left a brief message: 'Hello, darling. If you want to

talk, give me a call.' It was almost like a code they had. Then she picked up her laptop and took it up to her room – the room on the first floor which she could call her own, which had begun as a study and workroom and which now also housed a small bed and an armchair. She wouldn't bother with cooking supper for a drunken man whom she wouldn't have a hope of waking, and she'd had enough tapas this afternoon not to bother for herself.

She opened the laptop, switched it on and located the document immediately. No, she thought. It was this that was her life. This was the story of a young girl who had left her homeland and travelled to England with her family. A girl who had settled here but who had often longed to return. And once, she almost did. Elisa wiped a tear from her eye and settled into her writing position. It was called Last Dance in Havana.

CHAPTER 4

Grace indicated, turned into Passage Street and parked the car; luckily there was a small space just outside the house. She climbed out, ducked round the black railings, bottle of red wine in a carrier bag hanging on one arm, her keys in the other hand. It was still chilly for early March but at least the evenings were getting lighter, thank heavens. She probably shouldn't have even gone round to King Street, she thought. It had left her feeling depressed and angry. Her father had left her feeling depressed and angry. And there was no Robbie at home to make her feel better. She and Robbie had been a little at odds for the past few weeks, but right now, Grace didn't want to be alone.

She let herself into the tiny two-bedroomed cottage she shared with her husband. It was small but it was theirs and Grace had adored it on sight; loved the blocks of pale-honey-comb stone, the way it squatted by the steps that led down to the quayside as if it would secretly like to jump into the canal. And that was the best thing about the cottage – it overlooked one of Bristol's veined waterways; colourful and steeped in history.

She dumped the carrier bag down on the 60s Ercol table she'd paid far too much for in a local antiques emporium just after they moved into the cottage five years ago, shrugged off her jacket and hung it on a hook by the door. Robbie had driven up to Gloucester for a weekend conference and Grace had been quite looking forward to some time alone. But now . . .

She pulled the wine out of the carrier bag. Seeing her father had sent her into a tangle of frustration, confusion and little-girl fury. She was thirty-nine years old and she hadn't been a little girl for a long time. Sometimes she felt as if she never had, as if her childhood had been snatched away from her along with her mother. Even so. He was her father. He was supposed to be the one she could lean on. And she had never, since she was nine years old, been able to.

'And I never will,' she told the pot plant in the corner – a Christmas cactus which looked like a limp, giant spider all year, before flowering in a brief rush of glory in early November, ensuring its blooms died well before the festive celebrations for which it had been named.

She shouldn't dwell on this latest falling out with her father. She never liked seeing him when Elisa wasn't around; her stepmother was a buffer that stopped them grating each other to pieces. And Grace was sick and tired of examining why he made her feel this way. Oh, she knew what she had against him, of course. She knew what she blamed him for; what she would always blame him for. For a brief moment a picture swam into her vision; her mother's body sprawled in the road, her blood . . . Grace closed her eyes, repressed the shudder.

Damn it. She swore softly and went into the kitchen to locate the corkscrew. But equally, she had learnt to put the blame to the background of her mind, to feel sorry for him even. Her father had not physically pushed her mother into the road; her mother had run. And despite everything, her death must have hit him hard, though at the time Grace was too young to be aware of that. She could hardly conceive her loss, let alone anyone else's. But her father had been affected too. Look at him now. He drank. He was losing his grip. So why was he determined to make things even harder? Why did he always try to rile her? She wanted to love him, but how could she love him when he wouldn't stop drinking? How could she love him when she held him responsible for her mother's death? How could she forgive him for that?

As she came back into the sitting room, Grace glanced briefly outside towards the old terracotta warehouse opposite. She liked to imagine Bristol in its busy heyday, smoke billowing from the breweries, the tobacco factories and sugar houses. But then again . . . It was probably a lot nicer to live here now. And the way in which her father's family – her family – had made a small fortune back then, was a way that no one, including Grace, would approve of now.

She opened the bottle and poured herself a large glass. She took a sip, then another. That was better. She had wanted some me-time and that's what she had got, so she would put this afternoon right out of her head. She hung on to the chair back and slipped off her shoes. She had wanted some me-time because things had been oddly difficult with Robbie ever since Theo had pulled off that ridiculous card trick. She shook her head. *Find the lady, indeed* . . . Not that Robbie had even been aware of it (she hoped) but it was in her head now, that was what mattered. She watched someone clattering down the steps to the waterfront. This thing with Theo – it was all a bit confusing. And dangerous, she told herself.

The level in her wine glass had already gone done quite alarmingly, so Grace went into the kitchen to do something about supper. She opened the fridge. There was salad – the nice organic stuff from the food market with properly large beetroot leaves and orange nasturtium flowers – and some fresh ravioli. That would do. She filled a large saucepan with water and put it on the gas hob to boil; checked the messages on her mobile but there was nothing from Robbie yet. He'd text later and phone before she went to bed; Grace knew his movements better than she knew her own. She supposed that hers were more unpredictable – which worried her sometimes.

And her father worried her too. Grace took another slug of her wine, aware of the irony. She was drinking pretty fast tonight. Did that make her her father's daughter? She went back into the kitchen and prepared a dressing for the salad from olive oil, balsamic and Dijon mustard and shook it up in her baby kilner jar. Back in the sitting room she laid a single place at the table. Stared out towards the small square panes of glass in the huge arched windows of the warehouse opposite. Poured herself more wine.

★

An hour later, Grace was still sitting at the table, her plate half empty, the wine bottle more so. She was vaguely aware of the light outside dimming, of the fact that she should shake herself up, clear the table, stop mooning around with no sense of purpose just because –

There was a sharp rap at the door.

Grace frowned. She wasn't expecting anyone. For a moment she considered not answering – there were no lights on in the house, so no one would know she was at home – but it might be Elisa, and a chat would lift her spirits. When she thought of her stepmother, Grace always felt a warmth. What would she do without her? How could she ever have coped these past years?

She got to her feet, automatically glanced in the mirror on the wall. Even in the dim light she looked exhausted. Yes, Elisa would know by now that Grace had been to the house in King Street and probably she'd also know that her father had upset her. Elisa knew that Robbie was away because Robbie had promised to look at her laptop before he left. So . . . Grace ran her fingers through her long dark hair. Her stepmother had so often provided the lifeline that kept her going. Sometimes, Grace even wondered if that was why . . . But before she could articulate this thought, she recognised the shape outside. It wasn't Elisa.

Grace took a deep breath and opened the door.

CHAPTER 5

'Theo.' He stood there, tall and uncharacteristically adrift.

'Evening, Grace.' He looked at her, but didn't look at her. At least not like he had before. Black eyes. Was he remembering? Because Grace was. She couldn't help herself.

She waited for him to say something else although none of them had ever been stuck for something to say. Their relationship wasn't like that. Theo was one of her and Robbie's closest friends. He *was* their closest friend. He'd never been left waiting on their doorstep since Grace had known him. Behind Theo, the contours of the monstrous office block on the other side of the street collided aesthetically with the black railings and old stone wall outside the cottage. She always noticed that. Theo's presence just added to the collision of opposites.

'Robbie's not here.' It was of course an odd thing to say. Whether Robbie was there or not had never had any bearing on anything. Grace hung on to the doorframe and wondered exactly how much wine she'd drunk. She wondered also, briefly, if Theo had known she was alone. But, no. That wasn't his style. He was only deceptive in the magic he practised. Or so Robbie had said that night. *Find the lady . . .*

'Ah.' He nodded, as if this explained everything. 'Sorry.'

For what exactly? For the trick he'd played three weeks ago? For the look he'd given her? For the look she'd given back? She shrugged.

'Has he . . . er . . . ?'

'Haven't you seen him lately?' Grace had been dying to ask Robbie if he'd heard from Theo. But his name hadn't been mentioned, which was odd as well. Theo hadn't come to the cottage for three weeks, which was a long time for someone who used to drop by every few days for a coffee or a low-key supper, a drink or a laugh. He was the kind of friend with whom you could just kick off your shoes, put your feet up and watch telly; the kind of friend for whom you didn't have to put on make-up (although usually, Grace reminded herself, she did). The kind of friend you could confide in.

'No.' He shook his head to emphasise the point. 'I sent him a text to tell him I'd be away for a while.'

'Oh. He never said.' Grace frowned. *Was it possible . . . ?* But, no, how could Robbie have known what had happened? When nothing had.

'So, where . . . ?'

'He's at a conference,' she told him. 'In Gloucester.' Behind Theo, two girls passed by, walking along the pavement, one of them sending a curious glance their way. What did they look like? Grace wondered. Two acquaintances exchanging small talk? The close friends they were supposed to be? Or something else?

'At a conference,' he repeated. 'Ah.' He scrutinised her more carefully, she could feel it, his magician's black eyes taking in every detail.

She shivered and pulled her cardigan closer around her.

He frowned. 'Are you all right, Grace?'

What was he asking exactly? *No*, she wanted to shout. Of course she wasn't all right. Things had not been right with Robbie since that bloody card trick and before that even. He wanted them to have babies; she didn't. And now things were not right with Theo either. Her father was an alcoholic and today he had practically accused her of running a sleazy massage parlour. So, no. She looked straight at Theo, this man who didn't seem to be quite the friend he'd been before. She was not all right.

'Should I come in?' Theo suggested. 'You look as though you could do with some company, Grace.'

Oh, she could. But not Theo's. 'I'm fine,' she said brightly.

'The thing is . . .' He hesitated. 'I've had a few beers. So I guess I was hoping to cadge a coffee.'

Grace summoned up every ounce of willpower she possessed. 'I'm a bit tired, Theo. It's been a hard day. And . . .'

'And?' He raised an eyebrow.

'And it's probably not a good idea to be honest.' Because they should – shouldn't they? Be honest? And if he'd had a few beers that made it an even worse idea. 'Where did you go?' she asked weakly.

'To the pub down the road.' He pointed. Grace found her gaze riveted to his hand. Nimble magician's fingers with

49

square-cut nails. Olive-skinned hands. She knew what his hands felt like, what his skin felt like even.

'Really?' It wasn't the kind of pub she, Robbie and Theo would normally go to. And it was only a few doors away. Which must mean . . .

'Plucking up courage.' He shrugged.

'Courage?' she echoed. Somehow the door had opened a little wider.

He held out his hand and Grace half expected a pound coin to materialise in his palm. He'd done *that* before. 'Courage,' he confirmed.

'But . . .' Grace tried to stay firm but he was making it very difficult. And it wasn't just a question of courage, was it? It was far more complicated than that.

'We're not friends any more, is that it?'

'Of course we are.' Grace wondered how convincing she sounded. She looked away, down the road past the trees and towards the church where Elisa went to her community meetings. Why hadn't Theo come here for three weeks? She knew why.

'Then, what? I can't see you? Is that it?'

'If Robbie were here . . .' Her words hung in the cool evening air. If Robbie were here he'd be wondering why Theo was still standing on the doorstep. Theo wouldn't be still standing on the doorstep, he'd be inside in the living room with a drink in his hand by now.

'Are you scared of me, Grace?' Somehow, he'd moved closer. He was only inches away. She could almost feel his breath, see his chest rising under the blue cotton shirt and the open jacket he wore, smell the scent of him, which was resonant of red apples, pepper and something vaguely Caribbean. Theo may not have been brought up in Cuba – but Grace sensed that the country was there, somewhere inside him.

'Course not.' She laughed but even to her own ears it sounded strained.

'Then you should be.' He lifted her chin so she was forced to look at him. 'Let's not pretend.'

'OK.' She mouthed it. If she didn't say it aloud, perhaps she hadn't said it at all.

'I can't lose you two,' he said. 'You're too important. Both of you. That's why I haven't been round lately.'

'Cold turkey,' she murmured.

'That's it. I thought I could let you go, but . . .'

Grace felt sure that any second her legs would stop supporting her; she almost sensed them weakening with each word. He was right. He was their best friend. 'You should come in,' she said. 'We can't talk about this on the doorstep.'

This. The first time she had given it a name. The first time she had acknowledged it and made it exist. 'No tricks, mind.'

For a moment he looked serious and then he smiled. She couldn't help liking it when he smiled. His mouth was a bit too wide; when Theo smiled, he beamed. She couldn't help remembering that old Billie Holiday song Elisa used to listen to: *I'll Look Around*. Until I find someone who smiles like you, she thought.

'No tricks,' he said.

Grace stood back. She felt him brush against her and she let out the breath she'd been holding and closed the door. But instead of going straight through to the living room as he always did, he was still standing behind her in the tiny hallway when she turned. There was nowhere to go. Nowhere to hide.

'Grace,' he said.

He'd said no tricks. She looked back at him. *Let's not pretend.* She had known this would happen since three weeks ago. She had known even before that, when she placed her palms on his shoulders to give him a shoulder rub, when he took her hand to cross the road that time when Robbie was walking on the other side of him, the first time he fooled her with one of his card tricks. Every time he smiled. She'd known it from the first time she'd met him in Elisa's community group. And finally, she'd known when Robbie had said one day when they were first together: 'Hey, Grace you've got to meet my best mate from uni.' She had looked up with a friendly smile to see Theo. And she had almost lost her nerve. It was summer time, they had met in the park and a certain slant of early evening light was falling across his face.

She had known when Robbie said, 'Grace, this is Theo. Be nice to me and he'll love you for ever.'

It seemed like somewhere inside she had always known.

CHAPTER 6

The following morning, Elisa tried Grace's number again. It was early, Philip was still sleeping it off – in bed now – and Elisa had already made breakfast and cleared the kitchen. She felt restless and she wasn't sure why. Was it the thoughts she'd been having about Duardo and Cuba? Was it Grace?

Her stepdaughter picked up the phone; she sounded unusually subdued.

'Is everything all right, Grace?' Elisa asked her. 'You're not upset?'

'I was, yes.'

'And now?' Grace didn't sound herself. But Elisa couldn't put her finger on the difference. She wasn't an easy girl to understand, never had been.

'Can I call you back in five minutes?' Grace hesitated. 'I just have to . . . do something.'

'Of course.'

Elisa stayed by the phone, distracting herself by giving the directories and address book a quick tidy. She straightened the coats, sat down on the little cushioned bench and waited. She could remember so clearly the day they had first met, the day she first saw Grace standing in front of her with her serious grey eyes, her nut-brown hair braided in two neat plaits.

'She's only nine,' her father had said.

'Yes.' But with the eyes of a sixteen year old, thought Elisa. She smiled at the girl encouragingly. Why would a child of nine look so sad?

'It seems she's desperate to learn Spanish.' He laughed – perhaps at the unlikelihood of this idea.

'And why not?' Elisa had looked at the girl's father properly for the first time. He looked sad too. He wasn't old – only in his forties – but already his shoulders were bent as if with a burden, the skin around his blue eyes bruised with tiredness.

He seemed determined to explain. He spoke of his wife's sister in Madrid, a tragedy in the family (here, Elisa's attention was caught by the lowering of his voice and his apologetic glance at the child, but Elisa was diplomatic enough not to probe) and a wish to give the girl as wide an education as possible. 'So she can do something with her life,' he concluded.

Elisa raised an eyebrow. 'Spanish is a good way to begin,' she said mildly.

She'd expected the girl to lighten up after a few weeks; most of her pupils were nervous to start with, but it didn't last, she could always put them at ease. This little one however, was different.

Although she had a way of frowning in concentration and although Elisa did not doubt that she wanted to learn, she seemed to find it difficult to keep her attention focused. Her eyes would glaze, she would stare out of the window, and then she would come to with a jump when Elisa altered the tone of her voice, and she'd begin to concentrate again. And it was almost impossible to get a smile from her. So what was this tragedy that had occurred in their family? Why was the girl so sad? Elisa decided to find out.

It took half a term of after-school lessons before she finally did. They were speaking in simple Spanish about the girl's family. *Do you have any brothers or sisters? Who lives in the house?* And so on. Very basic stuff. When the girl burst into tears.

'Grace. My dear.' Elisa had reverted immediately to English. 'What is it? Please tell me.'

And out it had come. An accident. A death. A girl with no mother.

Poor child. Elisa's heart had gone out to her there and then. Her own loss of her family was still close, her own emotions still bruised – though they had felt that way for so much longer. Coming to England with her parents twenty years ago, at a time when she had still been heartbroken, to a strange place where a different language was spoken and the customs were often hard to understand, had made the three of them form a secure little unit. When she lost her parents so close together, Elisa had felt her support system crumble. And so it must be for this girl who had lost her mother so young. Elisa knew little of the father who picked her up at the end of the lessons but now she watched him more carefully and she saw his pain.

Elisa grew fond of Grace; she was a sweet girl and it was a

challenge to bring a smile to that serious face. Elisa produced morsels of Spanish tapas as an after-school treat and she introduced her to Cuban music. Once, six months into their lessons, she even taught her some steps of the rumba . . . but that was no good. The rumba was dead and gone for Elisa. She couldn't think of it without a terrible sadness settling on to her heart.

Elisa couldn't have explained what it was about Grace that drew her. It wasn't simply the shared bond of maternal loss. The girl had a way of reaching out to her, and Elisa couldn't help but respond. Something was not right at home – that much was clear – and there was a need in her that Elisa recognised even though she could not give it a name. Perhaps Grace was igniting some maternal instinct in Elisa that had never been aroused before. Or perhaps Elisa sensed that she was giving the girl more than just Spanish lessons, even perhaps that she was fuelling a dream.

Grace's father remained an enigma. He was polite, even charming; he was always dressed in a well-cut suit, which made Elisa guess that he was a businessman and probably a successful one, but Elisa felt he hardly noticed her, this woman who taught his daughter Spanish. He loved his daughter though, of that much she was sure. His eyes would skim over her tenderly when he came to pick her up. He would hold her hand and stroke the girl's nut-brown hair. But something wasn't right. And Elisa sensed that this was in Grace herself. She did not flinch from him, but neither did she show any sign of affection. And you would think, would you not, if a girl had lost her mother . . . that she would cling all the more to the father who remained?

Still. Elisa looked now at the photograph of her stepdaughter on the table next to the phone. She picked it up and scrutinised it more closely. Grace had been about twelve when it was taken; still serious, but growing up. The braided hair was shorter now, her features more defined; she had lost the roundness of childhood. And now? Some would call her beautiful. She certainly had a serenity which was most striking. Thank goodness she had learnt to laugh. Back then Elisa had had no idea that this family would become her family. She hadn't known how they would help her, how she would help them, or how they would inadvertently stop her from going where she desperately wanted to be . . .

It was easy now to see how it had happened. Elisa sighed and glanced at the phone, but it remained stubbornly silent. So she allowed herself to think back to that time.

It was coming up for Christmas in 1983 and Grace had seemed even sadder than usual. Perhaps it was the time of year her mother had died? Elisa had questioned her gently. 'What is it? Is something worrying you, my dear?'

And it had all come out. On Christmas Day it would be just Grace and her father. It would be so lonely. Grace couldn't bear the thought of it. And then, as if she had suddenly had a bright idea. 'You'll be on your own too, won't you, senora? Would you come and have Christmas dinner with us?'

'Oh goodness, no.' Elisa had laughed as she declined, but she had felt flattered. They had grown close the two of them.

During their weekly sessions they often chatted about their lives and Elisa felt she was beginning to understand Grace at last.

'Why not?' Grace's huge grey eyes had filled with tears. 'Are you going somewhere else?'

'No, but . . .' She couldn't really think of a satisfactory 'but'. 'I am not part of your family, my dear. Your father certainly would not want me there. Especially not on Christmas Day.'

Grace had looked at her for a full moment and she seemed to accept this. But the next day came a phone call – from Grace's father. He soon came to the point. Would she consider joining them for Christmas lunch? There would be just the three of them. It would be difficult for Grace, because . . . Well. It would be easier if someone else were there, someone Grace enjoyed talking to. 'I'd be honoured,' he said. 'Grace has really taken to you. I know it's an unusual request, but the circumstances . . .'

'Very well. Thank you.' Elisa was aware that the circumstances were unusual. And even then she had felt that she couldn't let Grace down. Perhaps if she'd had a child of her own . . . But as it was, Grace appeared to have usurped that empty space in Elisa's affections.

So she went to what had seemed like a very grand house on King Street and she had helped cook the Christmas lunch – Philip had been so funny, wearing a flowery apron, struggling with an over-sized turkey and a massive array of vegetables, as if he were trying to make up to Grace for his shortcomings

in other areas – or something. The meal had been delicious; afterwards they had played a few old-fashioned parlour
games which Elisa had certainly never come across before,
Elisa and Philip shared a bottle of wine, and yes, he had been
very attentive, very entertaining. Grace had seemed happier
too; laughing as she exclaimed over her presents. Almost like
a normal little girl on Christmas Day, Elisa found herself
thinking.

The wine, Elisa supposed, had loosened them both up and
there was none of the awkwardness she had feared. When
Grace finally went up to bed, Elisa got up to go and Philip
showed her to the door. He helped her into her coat and
offered to call her a taxi, but she refused. It was Christmas
Day. She would prefer to walk.

'It's been wonderful having you here,' he said.

Wonderful. It was quite a word. Elisa looked back at the
sweeping staircase, the parlour and the kitchen of this elegant
house. It was very lovely, but didn't he and Grace simply rat-
tle around in here on their own? She smiled and nodded and
busied herself doing up the buttons of her coat.

'Thank you so much for coming. I do hope we can do it
again.'

Again? Elisa was embarrassed. What exactly was he expecting from her? 'I enjoyed myself,' she said honestly. 'Thank
you for asking me.' Though they both knew it was Grace
who had done the asking.

And so it began – though Elisa couldn't quite have explained
what 'it' was. It was certainly unlike any relationship she'd

ever had before. Elisa's small kindnesses to Grace were rewarded – with a dinner, with a box of chocolates, with a bouquet of flowers. Soon there were regular lunches at the house in King Street on a Sunday (such an awful day to be alone, Philip said). Once Elisa mentioned a film showing at the colourful local hippodrome and Philip offered to take her, and one summer Sunday the three of them took the train to Weston-super-Mare – a journey which reminded Elisa with some poignancy of her father.

That autumn, Aunt Beatriz had telephoned from Havana. Things in Cuba were so bad, she said. She had tried everybody else. 'Could you help us?'

'What with?' But of course, Elisa knew. The family needed money. Two of the cousins had no work at all and another had a new baby to support. Things were tough in Cuba. Naturally they had turned to their relatives to help out.

Elisa began to send small sums of money. Aunt Beatriz was a good woman; she wouldn't ask unless she needed. But Elisa didn't have much, as she told her, and it was true. The rent on her small studio flat had just gone up again and she had recently lost two of her private clients.

Next, her cousin Ramira rang to tell her that Aunt Beatriz had leukaemia. She didn't have long to live. She had received medical help of course – this was freely available in Cuba, and was one of the great things the revolution had achieved for its people in Elisa's opinion – but now her aunt was going home to die. The family were still struggling financially – and now there was this new loss to contemplate. They were at their wits end. Aunt Beatriz had asked to see Elisa and they hated to tell her 'no'. Was there any way . . . ?

Elisa wanted to help ease their money worries and she'd love to be able to visit her aunt before she died – but she couldn't possibly afford it and there was nothing left to sell. She couldn't see what she could do.

That Sunday at Philip and Grace's she was just dishing up the potatoes (fortunately Grace was outside playing in the garden) when Elisa thought of her mother and then Aunt Beatriz, and before she knew it there were tears fizzing into the hot oil in the roasting pan.

'Elisa, my dear.' Philip grabbed an oven glove and took the pan from her. He led her to the big farmhouse table and made her sit down. He poured her a small glass of wine and handed her his own handkerchief, a large white cotton square with an embroidered PH, an act which had seemed almost unbearably personal. It was so old-fashioned too and he was being so kind – which made her cry all the more.

'We're friends, aren't we?' he said. 'Tell me what's wrong.'

And out it came in fits and starts. How Elisa wanted to help her family but didn't have the means. How she yearned to go back and see them one last time before her aunt died. How she missed her parents. And then, oh heavens . . . 'I feel so alone,' she'd cried.

'There, there.' He had patted her awkwardly on the shoulder, and even at this small touch she realised how little physical contact she had with human beings these days – and how much she missed it.

A few minutes elapsed while Elisa brought her emotions under control. She was being foolish. If she couldn't help, she should simply tell them. And they would understand perfectly when she told them she couldn't afford to come and visit. They were her family but she had a different life now. She shouldn't get so upset over it. But she knew it wasn't just that.

'Do you know what I think, Elisa my dear,' Philip said, stroking his chin. His blue eyes were troubled but kind.

Elisa shook her head. But sometimes she longed for someone to think for her, to be on her side for a change; someone to lean on, she supposed.

'I think you need someone to look after you,' he said.

Elisa was so surprised that she just stared at him.

Philip dropped to one knee on the terracotta floor tiles.

Oh, my heavens. Elisa put out a hand. 'Please don't. Philip, please don't.'

'I'm older than you,' he said. 'But I have a daughter who already thinks of you as a mother.'

But that was not reason enough . . . Elisa made to speak, but he silenced her with a raised hand. 'I can assure you that she does,' he said.

'And is that the only reason, Philip?' Elisa couldn't believe this was happening. She hadn't imagined, she certainly hadn't encouraged.

'Naturally not. I like you very much indeed,' he said. 'Perhaps you like me too? Just a little?'

Elisa nodded. 'Of course,' she said primly. 'I *like* you,

Philip.' But she couldn't help but think of Duardo. This was so far from his passionate declarations that she almost wanted to laugh. But she must not laugh at this man who was being so thoughtful, so generous. 'But that is not enough for what you seem to be suggesting.'

He nodded. 'But marriages are not all alike, dear Elisa,' he said. 'We have a large house. But it has become an empty one – apart from the days you are here.'

'Oh, really –'

'You see we have been adrift, Grace and I,' he said. He gave a wistful smile. 'And then we met you.'

'Philip.' Elisa laid a gentle hand on his arm. 'That is not enough. I am sorry. But it is not.'

'I'm lonely.' And it was true that he often still looked sad. 'And I think that sometimes you are lonely too.'

Which was also true, but . . .

'Grace and I – we need you. And I want to help you. I want you to have an easier life, not to have to work if you don't wish to, to go to Cuba to visit your relatives. And to see your aunt before she dies.' He sighed. 'That is, as long as you come back here to us in Bristol.'

'But, Philip . . .' *But I do not love you,* she was about to say.

'I know I haven't mentioned the word "love",' he said. 'But I do think that love can grow. And if not . . . Then life has taught me that something else is more important than love.'

'Something else?' Elisa could not imagine this. What could be more important than the kind of love she had shared with her Duardo?

'Friendship.' He took her hand. 'Also trust. Loyalty. Companionship. Please at least think it over, Elisa. That's all I ask.'

And so she had. She had thought of Cuba and Duardo and she had thought of her family who remained there. She thought of Grace and Philip. And finally she thought of her life here alone in her little studio apartment. One day, two weeks later she almost surprised herself by saying 'yes'. She did not love this man – at least not yet. But she was fond of him. And he was right. Friendship was important and love could grow.

At last the phone rang. It was Grace.

'He is who he is,' she said without preamble, picking up the thread of their conversation where they left off. 'And he is *what* he is.' An alcoholic, she meant. 'I keep trying to persuade him to get help,' said Elisa. 'But he has to want to. Maybe you –'

'I'm sick of trying.'

And Elisa wasn't sure, but she thought she heard tears just below the surface.

'But – why?' Elisa wasn't thinking of why Grace might be sick of trying, she was wondering why he had started drinking in the first place. 'Why is he so miserable? Is life so bad?' Sometimes she wanted to bang her head against a brick wall in pure frustration. He should go to Cuba. Then he would find out how hard life could be. 'Is it me?' she asked. 'Is it my fault?' He was drinking before they married, though she never knew it at the time. In those days it was easier for him to keep it a secret and in those days he had the control. Now, the whisky had control over him.

'Of course not.' Grace's voice was flat. 'He's punishing himself.'

Elisa paused to let this sink in. Grace had never said such a thing before. She had always just shrugged and talked about weakness and addictive personalities. Many people found life hard, Elisa knew. For those who had no religious faith to turn to in times of trouble, there were other things. Some could fill their lives with interests and hobbies. She thought of the room upstairs. For some, the intensity of work was enough of a challenge, and for others a close family unit provided the support that was needed. But for others . . . Gamblers, drinkers, addicts of food or drugs, they would turn to a substance, an activity which could become addictive, which could take over their life and their identity. Which could help them forget.

Elisa sighed. She had looked it up on the internet. She might not be young but she had taken to the technology like a duck to water and Robbie had advised her on buying a laptop and taught her everything she needed to know. Many studies had been done on the subject of addictive personalities – she'd even found a page on Wikipedia, and she had discussed it with Grace on several occasions. But this? This was new. 'What for?' she whispered. 'What does he want to punish himself for?'

'Guilt,' said Grace, 'is a powerful thing.' And then her voice changed abruptly. 'Look, Elisa, I've got to go, I've got a friend coming round and –'

'Yes, yes, of course, my dear. I'll see you soon.' Guilt? Elisa put down the phone.

She had helped Grace and her father – of course. But they had helped her too. They had provided her with a different life. Look at her now with her laptop and her community meetings and all the friends she had made that way. And then there was Grace; the special relationship with her stepdaughter was one that she cherished.

But something wasn't right with Grace and she knew it, just as she'd known back when they first met. So she would go round there at the first opportunity, Elisa decided, and find out exactly what it was.

CHAPTER 7

'Hey, Gracie!' Robbie swept into the house with his weekend bag, laptop and flowers.

Grace forced a smile. 'Hi there, you.' She had never felt so bad. *If he knew* . . . The heating was on quite low for a chilly spring evening, but she felt her hands go clammy.

This afternoon, she had walked through Castle Park, trying to make sense of things. As if anyone could. Not of her father's drinking – as she'd told Elisa this morning, she'd long ago given up on that one. But her and Robbie. And Theo. She was also hoping the brisk wind and the wan sunshine might numb what she had done. What she and Theo had done. But it didn't. And her body was a traitor. It still felt warm from his touch; some pulse of her he'd found still flickering.

Even while she was walking along by the floating harbour and up the slope towards the ruined church of St Peter's, Grace found herself checking her phone for a text message. What was he doing? What was he thinking? But there was nothing to give her any clue. She'd composed twenty texts to him this morning. *We shouldn't have. We can't. We mustn't. We did. Never again.* And sent none of them.

The planting in the park was coming into spring growth. There were pockets of white and violet crocuses and daffodils in bud under the trees. A time of change, Grace found herself thinking. A time of hope and growth and . . . Oh, hell. There was no one she could discuss it with either. Robbie and Theo were her best friends. Her other friends were Robbie's friends too. They would be shocked and horrified. Elisa would be shocked and horrified. Elisa knew Theo even better than she knew Robbie. He was her compatriot; they'd shared a friendship before Theo and Grace had ever met. Shit. So there was no one she could talk to. She had to deal with it alone.

She trudged up the hill until she got to the pink and grey jumble stoned church. So – what? Was she looking for some sort of redemption? No. Because the truth was that Grace too was shocked and horrified. She couldn't believe it had happened. It should never have – oh, God, she was going round in circles – and yet when Theo had kissed her in the hallway, she hadn't even wanted to push him away.

Grace held up her face now for Robbie's kiss. You traitor, she thought. This kiss was tender, soft and very different. And even the thought of that difference sent a streak of desire running through her. She choked it back. Would Robbie feel it? That her lips had touched another man's lips? Would he guess her treachery; their treachery? She had to stop this.

Theo. She couldn't have pushed him away. He had felt dear and familiar and the only place she wanted to be in that moment was in his arms, her fingers threading through the dark waves of his hair, feeling his grip on her shoulders, his need. His lips felt just as she'd known they'd feel – warm and full, his eyes closed. Grace gave herself up to it, to him, with a moan of longing. And it wasn't a trick. It had been inevitable.

Grace went through to the kitchen to check the dinner was under control. She was almost surprised she had any – control, that was. Robbie was all nervous energy, charging around the living room, putting his bag on the pale pine chest in the corner, his laptop down on the Ercol table, his coat on a chair – as if he were claiming back his territory. She could see him through the wide hatch that separated the two rooms.

Grace came back into the living room. 'Do you want some tea?' She glanced at her watch. It was six p.m. 'Or wine?'

'Wine please, Gracie, it's been a hellishly long day. And mmm . . .' He pushed back his specs, lifted his nose and pretended to follow the scent into the kitchen. 'Roast beef?'

'The very same.' Their conversation, she thought, was that of an old married couple. Talking in shorthand, joking around, not head to head, eyes locked as Grace and Theo had talked yesterday night.

'What shall we do?'

'I don't know.'

'Oh, Theo.'

'Grace, I –'

'How long have you known?' (*About us,* she meant).

'Forever.' And he'd blinked – as if he'd suddenly been hit by daylight.

In the kitchen, Robbie was rubbing his hands together. 'That's my girl.' Oh dear, thought Grace.

Well, it was Sunday. And it wasn't just because she was feeling guilty. Grace was glad to see him. He was her husband. She loved him. She'd missed him. She came up behind him and gave him a fierce hug. Why, oh why, had he had to go away?

'That's nice.' He turned around and took her in his arms. 'I should go away more often.'

'No,' she whispered. 'Please don't.' He was shorter than Theo, she found herself thinking. He was fair while Theo was dark. Robbie was solid. Rock solid. He wasn't going to dematerialise in front of her eyes. Theo was an enigma, elusive as a dream. Grace let her head rest on Robbie's shoulder. He was her reality. What had she done to him?

After that kiss and the next and the next, Theo had held her face in his hands for a long moment, gazing his black-eyed intent. He sighed. There was a moment when she was sure he would leave. And that's when she grabbed his shoulders and pulled him back to her. *Don't go*. Then he had taken a shallow breath and pulled at her clothes and she had pulled at his, and . . . Grace looked across at the sofa. She swallowed. She had put the throw in the wash, plumped up all the cushions. Tried to make it look like just a sofa again.

Grace moved away towards the kitchen and Robbie grabbed a bottle of wine from the rack. He fetched a corkscrew from the drawer by the cooker and opened the bottle with a few deft twists and a sharp pull.

'So how did it go?' she asked him, putting two glasses on the counter.

And she listened to the story of his weekend conference, breaking away to baste the meat, turn potatoes, check the vegetables; only half-listening really, but wanting him to talk because it stopped her thinking, made her feel that nothing had changed. Grace and Robbie; a team. She knew the story well enough from other conferences to smile in all the right places, to ask the right questions, to look sympathetic if anything hadn't gone quite according to plan. But she felt terrible.

He broke off abruptly. 'What did you do this weekend?' he asked.

Grace jumped and burnt her finger on the side of the roasting pan. 'Oh, nothing much.'

'Did you see anyone?'

'Dad.' She put the potatoes back in the oven. Oh yes, and Theo.

Robbie let out a sympathetic groan. He was a family man. She'd known that when she married him; it had even been part of the attraction. He'd grown up in a happy and well-adjusted family environment – the opposite of Grace's – and nothing really bad had ever happened to him. Until now, she thought.

'How was he?'

She gave him a, 'I don't want to talk about it' look. 'Not great.' And took a sip of her wine.

'And?' Robbie had already finished his first glass.

This was the moment. Grace's hand gripped the stem of the wineglass so tightly she thought that it would snap. Or she would. This was the moment when she could tell him that Theo came round. When she *should* tell him that Theo came round. Because apart from anything else (her wedding vows, she reminded herself; her determination to love Robbie and be happy with Robbie; her loyalty to the man she'd married) someone might have seen him. Anyone could have seen Theo standing there on the doorstep – she'd kept him there a while – and might mention it casually to Robbie, as people did. And the next thing . . . But Grace couldn't contemplate the next thing.

She forced herself back to the conversation. 'No,' she said. Because she couldn't bear to talk about Theo even though it was the thing she wanted to do most in the world – say his name. 'No, I don't think so.' She put her glass back on the counter and drifted back to the cooker. *As if you could forget Theo.*

They hadn't even decided on a story. He had simply kissed her gently on the lips and walked out of the door.

'I went to the park,' she said. She had stood on the flagstones by the rosemary bushes, leaned on the dark turquoise railings above the stone wall, inhaled the scent of wood, pine and mint and tried to think. Not about Theo but about what she should do. What she could do.

In front of her, people with uncomplicated lives – or so she liked to imagine – wandered along the quayside. From her vantage point, beyond the silver birch trees, she could see the office blocks and the old warehouses and even her own house in Passage Street. She heard a siren, the constant drone of traffic going over Bristol Bridge. Grace sighed. She wandered back beside the lavender beds, past the old wooden benches with their broad arms. She touched a brown stone jutting from the higgledy-piggledy wall of the church and watched a pigeon strutting in the spring sunshine. It was no use. She couldn't clear her mind. It seemed he was rooted in it.

Robbie was talking about his mother now. Why was he talking about his mother? Grace frowned. She whisked the meat out of the oven and tested it with a skewer. 'You spoke to her?'

He gave her a funny look. 'Yes, dreamboat, I just told you. I rang her Friday evening.'

'And how are things?' Grace put some foil over the pan. The beef needed to rest. She closed her eyes for a moment. She needed to rest.

Yes, Robbie was a family man. Still close to his parents who lived in West Sussex and to his sister, Nita, who had given their parents no less than four grandchildren – with the help of her husband, Alex, of course.

Grace fetched plates from the kitchen cupboard; she'd warm them in the oven. She pushed her hair back from her face. Her forehead felt hot. She hoped she wasn't going to pass out. You'd really think four grandchildren was sufficient, but no, this was not enough for Tony and Liz, who (especially Liz) wanted one or two – or heavens, maybe four – from Robbie and Grace too.

But Grace was not ready. She wasn't sure she'd ever be ready.

'Mum's fine. Natalie's at nursery school now, so she's got a bit more time on her hands.'

'That must be nice,' said Grace. Because she liked Liz, she really did. And Nita and Alex's children were very sweet.

Robbie's mother had welcomed Grace into the family with open arms; none of that 'mother/son, no woman is good enough' nonsense. Grace pulled the roast vegetables out of the oven. Almost there. She put the pan on for the gravy and had another quick swig of wine as she passed. Oh, there might have been a bit of an atmosphere in recent years as time went by and Grace failed to produce the requisite amount of grand-children needed to fill her mother-in-law's life . . . *Stop it, Grace,* she thought again. There was no need to be cruel. It was normal to want children – and grandchildren too. It was Grace who was childless, not family-minded, apparently somewhat peculiar . . .

'You'd think so.' Robbie was pouring out more wine. 'But she misses it. Doesn't know what to do with herself.' He smiled fondly.

Grace burnt her fingers on the pan again. 'Perhaps she should get a life of her own,' she said, before she could stop herself.

'Grace!' She could see he was shocked.

'Sorry.' But she'd meant it. She added the browning and stirred. It wasn't good for anyone to live their life through someone else. And Liz was putting pressure on the rest of them along the way.

'What she'd like . . . What would really make her happy . . .' Robbie swirled the wine around his glass. 'Would be if we –'

'I'm dishing up.' Not the baby conversation, Grace thought. Please, not today. 'Can you carve?'

And thankfully, with a thoughtful glance across at her, Robbie pushed his glasses up his nose again and came over to give her a hand.

But at the dinner table, when they were halfway through their meal and Grace had realised she wasn't remotely hungry, he brought it up again. Round the houses, that was Robbie. He tried to be subtle but Grace could see it coming a mile off. He waited until he'd demolished most of his roast, then a certain look appeared on his face.

'Jack was at the conference.' He speared a carrot.

'Jack,' she repeated. That would be Jack with two toddlers. Jack, whose life had changed out of all recognition and who loved every minute of fatherhood. 'Oh, yes?'

'He showed me some photos on his phone.' Robbie laughed – with a sudden joy that almost brought tears to her eyes. A knee-jerk reaction. She put down her knife and fork. If I could be someone different, she thought. *If I were able to give him this.*

'Photos of the kids?' Of course, of the kids – what else? Something Grace had discovered about her friends of thirty something. When they had children, they could talk of little else, or so it seemed. Their lives focused down to a narrow world. A family world.

'It changes everything,' Robbie said.

Grace glanced across at him, surprised. It was as if he'd been following her own train of thought.

'Your mother wouldn't be able to look after our children,' she said gently, taking another sip of wine. 'She lives too far away.'

'We could move.'

Grace stared at him. She thought about moving – to the small village on the South Downs where everything was quiet and safe and everyone knew what you were doing, when and why. She thought of Liz looking after her children – their children – and of how happy that would make Robbie. She felt a kind of terror clutching around her heart.

'But what about your job?' And what about Theo, she thought. 'What about Dad and Elisa?' She could hear her voice rising. *And Theo.* 'What about my work?' She was gradually increasing her client base. She was still learning – perhaps she'd never stop. There were strokes and techniques she'd favoured from the start, but she was keeping her repertoire broad and she still found herself inventing new ones. It was a marvellous feeling – forming a new touch because it just felt right; moving to an area instinctively in a new way. Which meant she was still developing the sensitivity of understanding what was under her fingertips, Grace realised. And best of all, she was enjoying the work. It was hard, but satisfying. When a client came in and said – 'I felt so much better after the last session, you wouldn't believe' – she did believe and it gave her a warm glow. She was truly a massage therapist. She was helping people. *Yes, and what about Theo?*

'I could easily commute to the London office from there.' Robbie pushed his plate away and grabbed her hand.

'But then you'd hardly see the children,' Grace moaned.

'What children?'

'Our children.'

His face lit up. Just the thought of imaginary children could do that.

'I know you'd miss Elisa,' he said, 'but we could visit.'

Oh my God, he really means this, she realised.

'And your dad . . .' He didn't need to finish the sentence.

But Grace felt responsible for her father. And as she thought this, she knew it was true. She couldn't leave Elisa to manage alone. 'And my job?' she asked. He seemed to have it all worked out.

He grinned. 'You'd give it up, wouldn't you, if we had kids?'

'Why should I when your mother's itching to look after them?' Grace retorted. And then there was this thing called childcare. But she couldn't believe they were even having this conversation – it had never gone this far before. She realised it would turn into a row; it already had.

'You could still do your massage part-time,' Robbie soothed. 'You could build up a client list there just as easily as here.'

'Except I've already started.'

'We'd work it out,' he said. 'We'd work everything out.'

But not Theo, she thought. They wouldn't work that one out.

'I'm still not ready,' she said quietly. She'd tried to explain to him many times. 'After what happened to me . . .'

Robbie got up out of his chair and went round to her side of the table. He put an arm around her shoulders. 'It won't happen to our children,' he said. 'Nothing bad will happen to our children.'

Grace couldn't bear it. He was too nice. 'But I don't want any children,' she said. And then when she felt his reaction, the stiffening of his body beside her. 'Not yet,' she amended. 'There's plenty of time.'

Robbie took his arm away and paced over to the window. He stared outside into the darkness; slowly and deliberately drew the blind. 'You've been saying that for years, Gracie,' he said. 'You're thirty-nine. I'm not sure we still do have plenty of time.'

Grace got up to clear the table. *And I am not a baby machine.* That was what her husband didn't seem to understand. She couldn't click her fingers and make her life different, make herself someone else, make herself want a baby. She was herself. Grace. Her own woman. And – oh my God – she was terrified that she was falling in love with another man.

CHAPTER 8

It was coming up to one p.m. and Grace's late-morning patient had just departed, seeming very satisfied with her full body massage – an absolute necessity after her extremely tense weekend, she'd said with a sigh. Grace chucked the drape into the laundry bin and replaced the sheet of paper on the massage bed. She sat down for a moment with her consultation pad and made a few notes on what she had done and what aftercare she had advised.

She had felt the woman's tension from the outset; it was easy for clients' emotions and nerves to be transferred, which was why it was important to set the scene and atmosphere as far as possible with good lighting, warmth and soft classical music, to create a relaxing vibe. She'd found the music also helped prevent any potential awkwardness from the silence (some people felt compelled to fill it) and in practical terms, it enabled Grace to know when she should be moving on to the next area of the body. If the client wanted to talk – and some did, as if they expected Grace to provide a counselling service while she was at it – then Grace was fine with that. This, for some, was another part of the unloading. She would listen, but she tried not to allow it to interrupt her focus, the movement of her hands, her rhythm. And as for tension – after the weekend Grace had just experienced, she had every sympathy.

This client hadn't gone into details, which was probably a good thing. Grace didn't need to know why, she just needed to make it better. Checking that the client was comfortable, that nothing was hurting in any way, that the pressure was OK, was all that was needed. And in a longer session like this one, Grace found that she could get fully involved, almost lose herself in the massage and what needed to be done. When she had first started her practice, Grace had resisted scented body oils – they were too associated with beauty therapy for her liking and seemed to detract from the seriousness of her intent. But she had found that many clients wanted them and so last year she had studied aromatherapy to add an extra dimension to her practice. She had found that they didn't detract in the slightest; massage therapy and aromatherapy seemed a marriage made in heaven. Now, she couldn't imagine working without them.

She had used a fairly deep pressure throughout, working mostly on the upper back and shoulders around the scapula where this client seemed to hold a lot of her tension, pressing on the shoulders, using one of her favourite knuckle strokes down both sides of the neck, followed by a stroke of her own invention, taking her thumbs slowly down the spine, leaning down into the forearms to cover the whole of the back, sweeping back in and up to the shoulders and the side of the neck; finally finishing with her usual heart hold.

Grace slipped out of the white cotton tunic she wore for work and pulled on a loose sweater over her leggings. It had been a good session and she'd been relieved that her hands had their usual flow and had not been stalled by her own preoccupations. And as for the client – by the time she left, she looked radiant.

Someone rapped on the door and for a second Grace's heart jumped. But it wouldn't be Theo. Not in the middle of the day. Not when Robbie could walk in at any moment – he did sometimes come home for lunch after all. She wound up the blind and glanced out of the window. Cold callers she could live without. But it was Elisa standing by the black railings, a tiny figure wrapped in her huge coat with fur collar, her black patent-leather handbag on her arm.

'Just coming,' called Grace. She signalled that she was on her way to the front door.

Robbie wouldn't be coming home for lunch today though. This morning he had not been happy. He had kissed her goodbye but with a disappointed look on his face, as if she'd misled him in some way. Grace pulled her soft house-shoes on to her bare feet; she always worked in bare feet – it made her feel more relaxed and grounded. She didn't think she'd misled him. They hadn't really talked about babies or how they felt about having children – not in their early days. Grace hadn't given it a thought back then. She supposed they'd only been concerned with each other. But after they got married – that was when Robbie had started the baby conversations. *When did Grace think they should start trying for a family? When did she think she'd be ready?* Never *Do you want to?* Only ever *when?*

Grace pulled the door of the therapy room closed behind her and went to let her stepmother into the cottage. 'Hello, Elisa.' She stood back. 'Come on in.'

'Are you free?' Elisa stepped into the tiny hall and nodded towards the closed door. It used to be their dining room and was small, but just about big enough for Grace's requirements. Although she offered her mobile service, in practice she'd found that many people preferred to come to a different environment where Grace had tried to create a calm and tranquil atmosphere, with her oils, her candles and her music.

'One client's just left and the next one's here at two thirty. That's it for today.' Grace kissed Elisa on both cheeks. 'It's lovely to see you.' Which was almost true. Even more true was that she worried her stepmother knew her rather too well.

'That's good. You're quite busy then.' Elisa held out a Tupperware box. 'I brought lunch.'

'Two clients in one day, I know.' Grace took the box. 'But this is nice.'

'And it's still early days,' Elisa reminded her.

Early days, Grace thought, would be about all it was, if she and Robbie moved to West Sussex. Had he already talked to someone in his London office? She wouldn't put it past him. She could imagine Robbie presenting her with a fait accompli and expecting her to be delighted. It wasn't that he didn't know her. He knew her. But sometimes he just didn't think.

Grace took the Tupperware box into the kitchen and Elisa followed her. Grace opened the lid. 'Mmm.' Meatballs in tomato sauce with rice. She'd always loved her stepmother's cooking; she just wished she was hungrier.

Elisa took a bowl from the cupboard – she seemed to know this kitchen as well as her own – and emptied the contents into it. She opened the microwave and put it in. Grace filled the kettle. They were used to cooking together, the two of them; they worked well as a team. When Grace had switched it on, she turned around to find Elisa looking straight at her, hands on hips. Help, she thought, she knows.

'Grace. What is it?'

'Um . . .'

'I know something's bothering you.' She sighed. 'Is it your father?'

Grace shook her head. So she didn't know. She thought of Theo. No text. No phone call. Would they ever see one another again? Was it cold turkey – again? How could she go back to what she was before? And yet equally, how could she go forward?

'It's Robbie,' she said with some desperation. And it was – partly. 'Same old. We had the baby conversation.'

She saw Elisa frown as if this hadn't been quite what she meant, but her stepmother soon recovered and swooped into the cupboard to retrieve two plates. 'Maybe you should think about it, my dear,' she said. 'There's nothing wrong with having a family.'

For the first time, Grace wondered if Elisa would like to

have grandchildren. She'd never said; she always insisted that Grace should do what she wanted. But what did Elisa want? She wouldn't be a grandmother by blood, but she was all Grace had, and she'd be as good as. Robbie hadn't considered that, had he? And so even if Grace were to agree to having children, why should she deprive her stepmother by moving to Sussex? 'I have thought about it,' she said. Yes, and discounted it.

Elisa shrugged. 'Sometimes in life we have to compromise,' she said. 'We have to please not just ourselves, but also the person we love.'

Wise words. Elisa had always been good with those. And Grace had mostly appreciated them. How much had Elisa compromised in her marriage to Grace's father? Grace wondered. A lot more than she'd bargained for, she guessed. She wouldn't have reckoned on being married to an alcoholic.

Grace got the cutlery out of the drawer and when the microwave pinged, Elisa removed the bowl and put it on the table. Grace poured out sparkling water and they sat down to eat.

'The thing is, he wants us to move, as well,' Grace told her. She picked up her fork and tasted the tomato sauce. It was good.

'Move?' Elisa looked less thrilled about this.

'To West Sussex. Where his family live. But don't worry.' Grace reached out to put a hand on hers. 'I'm not going.'

'Even so, he is your husband,' Elisa said. 'If he has to move because of work . . .' She began to eat, slicing a meatball with her fork, dipping it in the sauce, scooping some rice up around it.

'It's not because of work.'

Elisa watched her. 'You don't want to go?'

Grace thought of Theo. She took another mouthful and chewed thoughtfully. It would be an answer – of sorts. If she moved to West Sussex it would be a new start, away from him. She could have her own family maybe, spend more time with Robbie's family, devote herself to the family . . . She felt the panic wrap around her again. 'No I don't,' she said. 'My life's here.'

Which was what she'd said to Robbie last night. *My life's here.*

'What about our life, Gracie?' he'd asked, apparently forgetting that his life was here too, that it was his parents and his sister's family whose life was somewhere else.

'This *is* our life,' she'd said to him.

Elisa was looking thoughtful. 'And yet your life is the two of you and what you make it,' she said. 'I don't want you to move away, my dear. But your life together could be built anywhere.'

'This is our life,' she said to Elisa. 'Here. Now.'

Elisa jumped.

'What is it?' Grace paused, a forkful of meatball in mid-air.

'Nothing really,' she said. 'It's just that I've been thinking a similar thing lately.' She smiled ruefully. 'For me it's different though. I'm old and you're young. You have plenty of choices ahead of you.'

Plenty of choices . . . So why did Grace feel she was being backed into a corner? Again, she reached out for her stepmother's hand. Between them, she and her father had given Elisa a hard time. But if she could make it up to her . . . She pushed her plate away. She'd lost her appetite lately.

'Did you never want children?' she asked Elisa. Her stepmother had only been in her late thirties when she met Grace's father. And what about before that? Grace was pretty sure there had been someone. She'd seen the shadow of him sometimes in Elisa's expression, in her voice when her stepmother talked about her past. And then she noticed the look on Elisa's face right now. Utter sadness and loss.

'I did,' she said. 'Want children, that is.' She smiled, but it was a wistful smile. 'I longed for a baby.'

'You did?' Grace frowned. 'Wasn't there . . . ?' *Someone*, she was going to say.

'Yes.'

'What happened between you?'

Elisa shook her head. 'We were young. Other things in life got in the way. Politics. War. I lost him, Grace, that is all.'

'Did you want to have children with him?' Grace asked. Sometimes she was terrified that it wasn't so much that she didn't want to have children, it was that she didn't want to have children with Robbie. Didn't want to form the kind of happy family unit that he longed for. Which was awful – if it were true.

Elisa took a small forkful of tomato and rice. 'We didn't quite get to that stage, my dear.'

'And with my father?' Grace couldn't quite leave it. 'Didn't my father want to have any more children?' Maybe that was it. She realised that this was something that hadn't really occurred to her before. That she could have had a half-brother or sister; that she might not have been an only child.

Elisa glanced across at her and Grace held up a hand. 'Sorry. I didn't mean to pry. It's none of my business. I just . . .' her voice faltered, 'wondered.'

'We hadn't been married very long,' Elisa said. Her voice took on a more distant quality. She too pushed her plate away although at least she had managed to eat more than Grace. She hesitated. 'When I became pregnant.' Her voice was so low that Grace barely caught the words.

'Oh.' Grace tried to remember. 'I don't . . .' What had happened? Why didn't she know anything about it?

Elisa looked down. With a fingertip she traced a pattern on the wooden surface of the table. 'I lost the baby, Grace.' She sighed. Her eyes filled with tears. 'I had a miscarriage. It was in the third month. Very early on, but even so . . .'

Grace didn't know what to say. It had seemed an innocent enough question to ask her stepmother but she'd had no idea that Elisa had lost a baby and now she was totally unprepared. She felt bad too for being so selfish and not wanting one of her own when Elisa and her father had been through such a loss. She recalled those early years when Elisa had first married her father and moved into their house. She'd felt relief more than anything – that she had someone to turn to, that Elisa would be there in the house cooking for them, taking her to school and just being there; that she wouldn't have to be alone with him any more. But this . . .

'I'm so sorry, Elisa.' How little she knew her, she thought. How little she knew of her stepmother's life with her father. 'I didn't know.'

'It was a long time ago.' Elisa looked up, gave another small smile that didn't reach her eyes. 'The sadness is still there, but I can at least talk about it.'

Grace squeezed her hand. 'But to have a miscarriage, to lose your baby . . .' She felt inadequate now as well as guilty. 'How awful for you.' She tried to imagine how it must feel to lose a baby – a baby you had wanted and longed for. 'It must have been so traumatic.' And then she thought of her father. If Grace had had a sibling, her life would have been so different. And maybe her father would have been different too.

'It was,' Elisa conceded. 'But as I said, my dear, it was a long time ago. Sometimes these things are not meant to be. And perhaps that is how it is with you and Robbie.'

'Perhaps.' But she and Robbie hadn't tried – not yet. On the contrary, Grace had been taking the contraceptive pill religiously ever since they first met. Maybe she wouldn't be able to conceive – it happened. Or maybe Robbie would have a low sperm count or something. But Grace wasn't prepared to risk it. 'The difference is that you and my father both wanted a child,' she said. They must have – even if she hadn't been aware of it. 'The difference is that you and my father both wanted the same thing.' Grace got to her feet and started clearing the plates away. And that was the problem in her marriage, she realised. They didn't want the same things. 'Robbie wants us to have a baby. But I don't.'

She stopped short as she noticed Elisa's expression. Her stepmother didn't say anything at first. Then, 'It wasn't quite like that,' she said. Her gaze drifted. 'Sad to say.'

Then what was it like? Grace frowned. She was struggling to understand something that remained unsaid. But it was there, lying behind Elisa's eyes. 'Even so,' she said softly, 'I would have had a brother – or a sister.'

Elisa said nothing. But again her gaze drifted. As if, thought Grace, she'd simply slipped off to another world. Grace thought of Theo and looked at her stepmother sitting at the table, so lost in thought. Whose world was Elisa in? What secrets was she hiding? How Grace would love to know.

CHAPTER 9

Elisa thought about this as she walked back to King Street – Robbie wanting one thing; Grace another. Which way would it go? Grace was stubborn, like Elisa had been when Duardo had wanted to go off to fight. And so she hoped that Grace wouldn't – what did the English say? – bite off her nose to spite her face.

She paused as she got to the merchant navy memorial to men lost at sea in the two world wars Great Britain had lived through in the twentieth century. Many men had died and yet to her mind Great Britain had experienced nothing in comparison to the things her compatriots had lived through in Cuba. Even so, she liked the solidity of the giant capstan and compass base, the individual brass plaques on the metal seating that snaked over the cobbles. It showed respect and she felt that too, whatever cause or country a man was fighting for – presuming that it was a fair one. Elisa walked on. She thought about her stepdaughter and her husband. Elisa liked Robbie. He was good for Grace and she hoped they could work it out.

As she turned into King Street, Elisa saw a young family sitting on the wooden benches outside the dark red façade of the Old Duke pub. They were laughing together, the father ruffling the hair of his son, the mother helping her daughter with her glass of lemonade. The sun seemed to catch the blonde hair of the little girl and almost light her up. Elisa smiled. She thought of what she'd told Grace about her own pregnancy. As she'd said, it was a long time ago now and Elisa had stopped feeling pain every time she saw a young child or a baby, every time someone she knew told her they were pregnant, every time someone became a grandmother even. But even so . . .

She nodded hello at the family as she passed by and her pace slowed as she recalled that unique sensation – of being alive, not just for one person but for two. Such a remarkable feeling; to be carrying such a precious burden. She stopped walking. Until you realised. *This wasn't how it should be.*

There was so much more that Elisa could have told Grace – she could sense her stepdaughter's curiosity and she had certainly been less than honest with her. But why bring up old pain and loss? They were past. Sometimes in life it was simply time to move on.

Elisa lingered outside the theatre, looking to see what was playing although she knew she would not be going with Philip. She had been sad to miss *Swallows and Amazons* but . . . Last time they had gone to this theatre on their doorstep it had been to the Bristol Proms and he had drunk too much in the interval and fallen asleep – rather embarrassingly and noisily – in the second half. She did not much want to go home, she realised. What was there for her at home?

Elisa was no fool. She knew perfectly well that the row with Robbie was not the only thing bothering Grace. The timing was wrong for a start. Grace had sounded out of sorts well before Robbie arrived home. And she had looked different this morning – raw and jumpy. But again, silence was her prerogative. Grace was old enough to know her own mind. And she knew where to come when she needed a friend.

Elisa let herself into the house. She divested herself of her heavy coat with the fur collar and exchanged her boots for fleecy slippers. She made coffee. Philip was out – she did not know where. Lately, he had taken to going on long walks. She just hoped he was thinking about something productive. Because surely it was not too late, she told herself, sitting down in the armchair for a few minutes with her coffee. Their life could be so much better.

After she'd drunk her coffee and had a bit of a rest, he still wasn't back and so Elisa got her ironing board out from the cupboard under the stairs and fetched the dry laundry from the spare bedroom. She had always found ironing therapeutic. Like walking, it was good thinking time too.

At the community meeting this week Elisa had been talking to Theo about Cuba. This wasn't unusual; Elisa liked to talk of her homeland and Theo seemed to like to listen. He'd never been back there; perhaps this was why. His parents had left for the US when he was a baby, he'd told her, as so many had in those so-called freedom flights, and so he had no memories of the place. After the borders had closed it had been impossible to go back; so many families had been separated for decades this way. And when the borders finally opened again. . . By then, Elisa supposed, many people had laid to rest their previous lives in their home country. Some would never return.

'Pop only ever wanted to get out,' Theo had said rather ruefully. 'And Mom would go wherever he wanted.'

Elisa nodded. 'It was like that in my family too.'

Theo laughed. 'Things have changed a bit between men and women, Elisa, hmm?'

'It seems so.' Elisa thought of Grace. She wasn't prepared to follow Robbie to West Sussex – although Elisa suspected this was partly down to his reasons for wanting to go. Was that a good thing or bad? She wasn't entirely sure.

'But your people must have had family still living there,' she said to Theo. Family – that was always the link. Family had drawn Elisa back to Cuba in 1984 and when she'd arrived in Havana it had almost felt as if she had never been away.

'Most of the family left too.' Theo shrugged. 'It was a mass exodus. To all intents and purposes we became American.' He clicked his fingers in that way he had. As if it had been that easy. 'But . . . .'

'But you'd like to go back there one day?' she guessed. 'To visit?'

'It's a dream I've had for a while.' He nodded. 'And I guess I will go back. But I don't want to be disappointed. I've been dreaming it for so long, Elisa. I want to get the timing right.'

'You won't be disappointed.' She smiled. He was a good man. And it was natural to want to find out about your history, visit the place in which you'd been born, go back to your roots.

'And you?'

'Me?'

'You know what I'm saying.' He fixed her with that dark gaze of his that reminded her so much of Duardo. 'Would you ever go back to Havana?'

Would she? Elisa was ironing her red blouse. She ironed methodically – the right front, then the back, then the left. The sleeves were puffy so a light touch was needed if they were not to crease. Poppy red, she thought. She had taken to wearing these colours again in her sixties. That was the freedom to getting older. Poppy red, canary yellow; the colours of Cuba and her girlhood.

She had been wearing a canary-yellow dress when she first met Duardo. With a white butterfly flower in her hair. She had been wearing a yellow dress on the day they ran away together too, the note she'd left her parents tucked under her mother's pillow where she knew she would find it only when they'd had a chance to get far enough away. She was only just sixteen and so was he. Elisa had thought this was just the start of their life together but it had not turned out that way. She had not reckoned on him not finding work, she had not reckoned with being so hungry. Six months into their lives together and all he could talk about was going off to fight with the rebels. Going off to leave her – alone, abandoned. She couldn't bear the thought.

She had clung to him at night and railed at him in the

daytime. Everyone had a pathway. Elisa believed that she and Duardo had chosen the pathway of love, but now he wanted to choose a different pathway – one made up of blood and tears. She watched his expression change when he looked at her, and she thought: *What are we becoming?* And yet still he insisted on fighting.

'I can't stand by and watch other men die for the cause,' he said. 'I would have to live with the consequences for the rest of my life, Elisa, can't you see?'

No, she wanted to shriek. No.

He put it off once, twice, when she begged him not to go.

And then there were political meetings. 'How many men want to finish off Batista?' he demanded of her, when he came back from those meetings with leaflets in his hands and that fire in his eyes. *Death to the Tyrant*, she read. *Long Live the Revolution*.

And then at last he left as she had known he would and all she could do was regret that she had not been more supportive, that she had not given him her blessing before he went.

He left to go and join the rebels, his head held high and that intensity burning in his dark eyes. Elisa was left in Matanzas, miles from her family, miles from her friends, at sixteen years old with no food and no work and no man to care for her. What had she done? She cried herself to sleep more times than she could remember. And then one day, she walked to the highway and found her way back to Havana, taking lifts in a truck carrying fruit and with a man who tried to have sex with her in the back of his car.

It was a good question that Theo had asked her though, Elisa thought now. A lot had happened since she had been in Havana. What would she do? Would she ever go back there?

Philip entered the house and broke into her reverie. Elisa came to with a start. She had ironed two blouses, three of his shirts and one pair of trousers without even being aware of it.

He stood in the doorway. 'I'm sorry, Elisa,' he said. 'I know I've let you down and I'm sorry.'

She blinked at him. It was rare for Philip to talk candidly these days. What had brought this on?

'We made an agreement when I asked you to marry me and I failed to give you the full facts.' He leant on the doorframe as if otherwise he might fall.

'That was years ago,' she said lightly. They had got together because of Grace and agreed to marry because of Grace and their loneliness. But, of course, not just because of that and not just because of Philip's promise to help her visit Cuba one last time. There had been something between them. There must have been, because despite everything, they had stayed together. Perhaps she needed him as much as he needed her. They had stayed together, despite Philip's drinking and despite Cuba, even after Grace left home – which she had done fairly soon after she met Robbie, as Elisa recalled. And Elisa couldn't blame her. It was no longer a pleasant house to live in. Once Grace had left, Elisa could have left too. But she never did.

'I'm sorry too,' she said. He knew what for. They both did.

It was an olive branch and he took it. When she'd finished the ironing he took the pile of laundry upstairs to the airing cupboard and then he came back down and folded the ironing board, putting it back in the understairs cupboard. Elisa had to smile.

'How was Grace?' he asked.

She fixed him with an unequivocal look. Might as well take advantage of this honesty, this peace-making, she thought. 'You should talk to her, Philip.' And she didn't mean in order to criticise Grace's career decisions. 'Really talk to her about things.' He knew what things.

'But when I do . . .' he began.

'You should talk to her when you're sober.'

This was his cue to slump into the nearest chair. To walk out of the room. Or reach for the whisky bottle. Any excuse.

This time however, Philip surprised her. He came up to her and he put his hands firmly on her shoulders. 'I can't bear it, Elisa,' he said. The look of sadness she had always known, that she'd recognised the first time she met him, that had disappeared only briefly from time to time in the past thirty years, was there again in his eyes.

Elisa realised that he was shaking. That would be the booze too. He needed a drink. She understood that it wasn't easy. 'What?' she whispered. What couldn't he bear?

'The way she looks at me.' He sighed.

Elisa waited for him to go on. She recognised a turning point when it was in front of her. You could only hide your head in your hand for so long before . . . Well, you either came up for air or you suffocated.

'She hates me. She's my daughter and she hates me.'

It was stark. Was it the truth? Elisa wasn't sure that it was quite so simple but she didn't deny it. She had thought once that she could make things better between the two of them, but it had proved beyond her. Grace wasn't the only one who was stubborn. She had inherited the trait from her father, it seemed.

'When did it start?' she asked. Because clearly it hadn't always been like that between them.

'When her mother died.' His expression grew thoughtful. 'We were close once. Very close. You'd never believe it.'

'Oh, but I would.' Elisa had seen a great deal. She'd believe most things.

'And it gnaws away at you. It really does.' His eyes strayed to the whisky bottle on the sideboard. Elisa realised she should have poured it away while she had the chance; she'd assumed he'd taken it out with him; hadn't even noticed it sitting there like some evil eye all the time she was ironing.

'Yes,' she said. 'I do understand.' And she also understood that every alcoholic could find an excuse for every drink. That was probably how it started. Wanting to relax, wanting to feel more confident before a party or social occasion, wanting to feel better after a bad day at work, wanting help to make a decision. Feeling sad and wanting to cheer up, feeling happy and wanting to celebrate. Losing the boundaries of not drinking till past six o'clock, of not drinking at lunchtime, of just one drink or two or three or four. And then needing a drink in order to do almost anything.

Philip took a step forwards.

'I'm going to make some tea,' Elisa announced.

'Tea?' Philip stared at her. 'You never make tea.'

'Never say never.' Elisa loved English sayings. There was one for almost every occasion. 'We are going to have a cup of tea together, Philip,' she said. 'And then . . .'

She had never asked before. Philip was a very private man and she had preferred to let him share his confidences when he was ready. But this had gone on for long enough. It struck her from the way he was speaking that these events were connected in a way she didn't understand. And so she should get to the bottom of it. There was, she thought grimly, no time like the present. 'And then you are going to tell me,' she fixed him with another of her looks, 'exactly what happened when Nancy died.'

By the time Philip had finished talking, the teapot was stone cold and Elisa's limbs had stiffened up from sitting in the chair for so long. 'I see.' She got to her feet with some difficulty. Keep moving, that was the thing. It was so much more than she was expecting. But also, rather less. Why hadn't he told her before? Had he been afraid it would turn her against him? Had he been ashamed – or was it just plain old-fashioned embarrassment? 'I'm so sorry, my dear,' she said. 'That must have been hard.'

'It was.'

'And did you love her? All the time you were married? Even when . . .' She sighed. 'Did you always love her?' Elisa had always believed that Nancy was the love of Philip's life and this story seemed to confirm it. She had never thought that it mattered – after all, Duardo had been the love of *her* life and she had never tried to pretend otherwise. Which was why, she supposed, it had been so hard for her to love again. Love, for some, was a once in a lifetime experience. But you could still have . . . something.

'Yes, I always loved her,' Philip said. He too got to his feet, but thankfully he went nowhere near the whisky bottle. Instead, he fetched a shawl from the back of the sofa and placed it carefully, tenderly, around Elisa's shoulders. 'It was a shock, of course. But none of it mattered, you see. She was everything.'

His words moved her, and so did the simple gesture. It was the sort of act of kindness that had first made her appreciate Philip, that had persuaded her to marry him. And naturally he had loved Nancy. He was protecting her even now.

'But she didn't make it easy,' he added.

'No, I see that.' Images flickered in Elisa's mind. Not that she had seen any of them in reality. She had of course never even met Nancy. But what had Grace seen, she wondered. What did she know – or think she knew?

'Shall we have some more tea?' Philip asked. He clearly didn't know what to do with himself.

When you are addicted to a substance, Elisa remembered reading during her intensive research into the subject – you have to break your routine in order to break its hold over you. Drink tea instead of coffee. Change your diet. Have dinner at a different time. Start a new hobby. Go for a walk when you'd normally sit and relax. See it as a lucky escape rather than a deprivation. Elisa wondered whether to say any of this to Philip. Probably best not. He hadn't even said that he was going to try to quit.

'Or is it time for dinner?' Time for something stronger, he meant.

'Coffee,' she said firmly. 'And perhaps, a snack.' If and when he made the decision, it would be his decision. And it would mean small steps.

She packed the filter with the strong Arab blend she pre-ferred and put the percolator on to simmer. All the time she watched him out of the corner of her eye. He was nervous and twitchy, one minute wringing his hands, the next shov-ing them into his trouser pockets and jingling the small change, as if it were impossible to keep them still. She knew where they wanted to go; she knew what would still them. But was there another way? What else would help, she wondered.

'Does Grace know any of this?' she asked at last. Just to make sure.

'Of course not.' His eyes widened. He looked shocked, as if telling his daughter the truth hadn't even occurred to him.

'Then I think that you must tell her.' She nodded, fetched the milk out of the fridge and set some in a pan to warm. That would be a start at least. That would do some good.

'How can I?' The tone of his voice surprised her. She turned around to see him standing, shaking. He slammed a fist down on the sideboard and the whisky bottle rattled. 'Nancy was her mother. She loved her. I couldn't possibly destroy Grace's memories like that.'

His voice was strident, but she was used to that. Elisa turned back to her coffee. *Or Grace's illusions*, she thought to herself. 'Even so,' she said. 'It would help if she knew how things really were.' Yes, and listen to her, who had so often kept the truth hidden.

'Never.' Philip shook his head and tightened his lips.

Elisa repressed a sigh. He was still protecting Nancy

now – even at the cost of his own relationship with his daughter. It was the kind of man he was; loyal to the end. 'It wasn't your fault, you know,' she said.

He looked as if he couldn't quite believe her. 'It was my fault she ran into the road that day,' he said. 'And Grace knows that.'

'But . . .'

He shot her a warning look. But he needn't worry. It wasn't for Elisa to tell her stepdaughter. Elisa would keep Philip and Nancy's secret, just like she had kept her own.

'I have loved you too, Elisa.' Philip stood behind her now. He placed a trembling hand on her shoulder. 'I honestly have.'

She reached up to cover it with her own. Wondered if his words could be true. They had separate rooms now; separate lives. They ate together – when he was sober. But they no longer went to the cinema or took the train to Weston-super-Mare.

She took the pan from the hob and poured the warm milk into a jug. The coffee was percolating and she turned down the heat to prevent it bubbling too fiercely.

'And when we were first married,' he said, 'I thought we could build on what was between us. I really did, you know.'

Elisa nodded. But she thought back to before they were married, when Philip had encouraged her to go to Cuba to see Aunt Beatriz one last time, to see the cousins Elisa had left so far behind her. She thought of how generous he had been with the money he had given her for her family. And of how he had made her promise to come back.

'Of course I'll come back,' she'd told him. It had not entered her mind not to. Even if not for Philip, she would always have come back for Grace's sake. Though she'd had no idea at the time, that her visit to Cuba would turn out to be such a test . . .

But she had come back to Bristol and they had married – not in church but in the local register office as they both wanted. It wasn't as if it were a love match. At the time, Philip had made it sound more like a marriage of convenience. And yet after they married, it was true that, despite everything, she and Philip had become close – for a while.

Elisa whisked the milk so that it would froth up. Had he loved her? She remembered the first time they had made love, tentatively, him so afraid of not pleasing her, thinking she would shrink away from him in revulsion.

But she had never felt revulsion for Philip. How could she? Oh, his body was very different from Duardo's – long and pale with a sprinkling of acorn-coloured freckles and a slender build. Like Grace, he was willowy; he almost seemed to bend in the wind. But she had made her decision and she was determined to make the best of it. Every other possibility had gone. She had committed to Philip. She liked him and she had respected him – until she'd found out the truth about his drinking.

Elisa poured the frothy milk into the cups. Philip had been pacing the room, but now, at last, he sat back down in the armchair. She'd smelt alcohol on his breath more than once in those early days; that rancid smell of stale whisky, and she'd found his stash – four large bottles of Jack Daniels tucked away at the back of the sideboard behind papers, photographs, an old food blender that no one ever used and other assorted paraphernalia. She'd stared at them – discomfited. It wasn't normal, was it, to have so much whisky in the house? She knew he had a small bottle he drank from regularly. And now, she began to watch. She realised it was usually in his jacket pocket – to hand whenever he needed it. And she realised that he refilled it – often.

'Why do you drink so much, Philip?' she'd asked him. They had been married just a few weeks. She'd been hoping to get it out into the open. In Elisa's experience you couldn't even begin to tackle a problem until it was acknowledged.

'To forget,' he said. He spoke without thought, without consideration.

Elisa looked into his eyes. 'To forget Nancy's death?' she asked. If it weren't for Duardo, she would have almost begun to think that she could love him – one day at least. They had grown closer, he was kind and their lovemaking had become more natural, more tender. She had made the right decision, she was sure, the only decision she could have made given the circumstances. Grace was happier too. But Philip . . . He had stared back at her, blank and remote.

Now, Elisa poured the coffee and brought the cups over to the table. She got out a small dish and shook in some almonds, toasted sunflower seeds and a few dates. Over the years, she would become accustomed to that stare. It meant that, for him, she wasn't really in the room. It meant he had been drinking and that meant he didn't care.

'To forget everything,' he'd said.

She had never let him know what a blow that had been. To her self-esteem, to her hopes. And so much for bringing a problem out into the open. What had she done, she thought again – for the second time in her life. Had she made another dreadful mistake after all?

Elisa settled herself back into her own chair. Philip wasn't watching her. He was fidgeting and ill at ease. She repressed a sigh. Was that when he began to drink more? Was that when Elisa first began to realise the nature of his deception? And yet there had been no written contract. He was what he was. Perhaps she should have opened her eyes from the start and seen it.

Thinking back, Elisa was no longer confident that she could answer any of these questions. But, yes, Philip had deceived her. He hadn't told her who – or what – had the real control in their lives; who – or what – would rule them. He hadn't warned her that he wasn't just the nice man who had invited her for Christmas dinner and invited her to be part of his and Grace's life before helping her family in Cuba in a way that had made it impossible to leave him. He hadn't said that sometimes drinking could make him fly into a temper, or make him burst into sudden hot tears. He hadn't even told her that he'd had a breakdown after his first wife's death which had led to him losing his job. He hadn't mentioned that after Elisa went to Cuba there would never be enough money for her to go again. And he hadn't told her the truth about Nancy. All these things – bar Nancy – emerged gradually in the early months of their marriage. And the deception cut into the vulnerable shoots of Elisa's growing feeling for him and killed it stone dead.

But she too had played her part, she reminded herself. She had done the unforgiveable.

'Thanks, love,' Philip said now. He stirred his coffee with a trembling hand. 'Perhaps if I could have stopped drinking before we got married.'

'Then why don't you stop now?' Elisa leaned forwards in her chair. She willed him to look at her but tears were in her eyes half-blinding her. 'Why don't you stop now, before you destroy us any more?'

Philip looked across at her. She knew what he was thinking. 'Philip. Listen to me,' she said. 'Perhaps it is not too late.'

The following morning, Robbie was late for work. He couldn't seem to find anything – a clean shirt, some paperwork he needed to take in, his keys. Grace had never seen him so flustered.

'There's a meeting,' he told her.

'You didn't say.'

He paused. 'We haven't been saying much, have we, Gracie?'

'No, we haven't.' They didn't often row; when they did, they'd always made it a rule to make up before bedtime. 'No bad dreams,' Robbie would say. 'No bad connections. You and me. Back on.'

But this time they hadn't. Which meant, Grace realised with a dull kind of certainty, that it mattered. It had become a Big Thing. Instead of making up, instead of shouting at each other or flouncing out of rooms, there had been an awful and stilted politeness between them. Grace hated it. It cut into her much more than out and out plain hostility. And there had been no contact from Theo. It was as if he and what had happened between them – so vital, so electric – had been a mirage, like one of his illusions. Perhaps she'd been wrong about him, Grace thought. He was a magician. Perhaps he'd always intended to deceive.

'Look, Gracie,' Robbie said. 'Can we talk later? Properly talk, I mean?'

'Of course we can.' She took a step closer and so did he. He held out his arms. 'Truce?'

'Truce,' she agreed and stepped into them. It was a very easy place to be. Crazy, crazy girl for risking losing this, for imagining there could be anything better than this out there.

He kissed her lightly on the mouth.

'Robbie?' There was a buzz from the direction of the door, where her leather handbag was slung over the brass hook.

'Hmm?'

'Oh, nothing.' Grace glanced towards her bag. He was right. They should talk later.

'Text for you,' he said. 'And I've got to go.' He looked into her eyes. 'I'm sorry, OK?'

It wouldn't be Theo. Theo wasn't going to contact her, she felt sure. 'Me too,' said Grace. She was sorry for being unkind. But not sorry for what she felt. She couldn't help what she felt. She'd just have to try to make him understand.

She saw him out of the house and into the car, waved him down the street. And when she was sure that he had really gone, she ran to check her mobile.

The message was from Theo. *Can I see you?* it read. No kisses.

For a moment, Grace simply stared at the screen. Then her fingers flew over the keys as if of their own accord. *When?*

Half a second. Knowing she wanted to prolong even a text conversation. Knowing that she'd been fooling herself. The pulse of desire was still there. It could spring into being from four words in a text. So what in God's name would happen when she actually saw him?

They arranged to meet that afternoon in a coffee shop at the bottom of the Christmas Steps which was far enough away from the house and from Robbie's office, and was the kind of place they were unlikely to run into anyone they knew. And even if they did, she reminded herself, they were just friends meeting for a coffee. To everyone else, at least.

Grace moved swiftly down the steps of the cobbled alleyway. It dated from the mid-nineteenth century and included many little independent shops that helped give this area in the Old City its character: the stamp shop, the cider shop, Flicks Videos, the brass and woodwind instrument shop and Harry Blades with its posters and stickers – the coolest hair stylists in Bristol. At the very bottom of the steps was the café. Grace took a deep breath and pushed open the door.

Inside, it was warm and steamy and smelt of fresh coffee and almond biscotti. Friends having a coffee, yes. But Grace sat down away from the window so she wouldn't be spotted by anyone. Already, it was starting. The practice of deception. What was it Robbie had said? *What a tangled web we weave* . . .

Theo appeared from nowhere and slid into the seat opposite her. 'Thanks for coming.' He took her hands.

She felt the warmth, the jolt. It hadn't gone away then. She gave a little shrug. 'I couldn't resist.'

He nodded. 'Me too.'

Grace let this sink in. She guessed he had been at the hospital where he spent an hour most afternoons entertaining the kids in the children's ward. It was good practice, he'd told Grace and Robbie; it gave him a chance to hone his skills for adults who were harder to distract and keener to catch him out. But Grace knew it was more than that. It was a nice thing to do. People talked about children in need, many gave money to children's charities. Theo gave his time and his skills. He made them laugh just at the time they needed it most.

'But I wondered if guilt would have kicked in,' he said.

'It did.' Grace looked down at their clasped hands; at her pale skin next to Theo's, which was toffee coloured. He had clever hands. Sensitive fingers. Hands that could perform many a trick and illusion to keep people guessing – at weddings, private parties, at ice-breaker sessions and at company events in trust-building and team-bonding exercises. Trust building, she thought. That was a joke. Theo still only worked at his magic part-time, but he was well known – in Bristol at least – for his magician's repertoire which, combined with his more than personable good looks – dark wavy hair, full mouth, sloping cheekbones and those black eyes– made him pretty desirable. And Grace, apparently, was not immune to his charm.

'But you still came.' And he was still watching her.

'I wanted to hear what you would say.' She extracted her

hands from his. 'I thought you would text earlier. When you didn't, I wasn't sure . . .' *What to do? What to think? How to deal with it?* Truth was, Grace hadn't been sure of anything really. He had knocked her world sideways. She was as off kilter as she'd been at nine years old.

'You thought I was backing off.' Those eyes drilled into her. She nodded.

'I'll be honest with you, Grace.'

Good, she thought.

'I would have if I could have.'

'Me too.'

'But I wasn't. I just . . .' He paused. 'Wanted to think.'

Grace on the other hand had been trying not to. She didn't need to ask him what he had been thinking about but she did want to know his conclusions.

'Coffee?'

'Please.'

He got to his feet, light as anything for such a tall man and went over to the counter. She watched him. He didn't even need to ask her how she took her coffee, Grace realised. He knew her so well.

He returned with two flat whites and put them on the table.

'So what was the result of all the thinking?' she asked him.

He frowned. 'Grace.'

She loved the way he said her name. She drew her coffee closer to her and took a tentative sip.

'We need to approach this problem with logic,' he said. He steepled his fingers.

'Logic!' Grace laughed without humour. She hadn't been expecting that. 'This isn't a mathematical equation, Theo.' She took a more reckless gulp of her coffee and this time it scalded the roof of her mouth. 'This isn't a client trying to get out of paying a tax bill.'

Theo's other occupation (even more surprising, in Grace's view, than being a member of the Magic Circle), the job he'd been doing for a firm in Bristol until he started to make money from magic, until he was able to go freelance and take part-time hours, was that of an accountant. Grace had never quite been able to get her head round it. She supposed she'd made certain assumptions about men who worked with figures – at least until she'd met Theo.

'Accountancy's not so dissimilar from magic, you know,' he had told Robbie and Grace once, ignoring their raised eyebrows and shrugs of disbelief. 'It's also concerned with logic and observation, patterns and likelihoods. It's analytical. It requires patience and practise.'

'And deception,' Robbie had added.

'On the contrary.' Theo had flicked his wrist and produced a black handkerchief which sat flat in his palm. 'Tax deception is illegal, but tax evasion is simply common sense.'

'And magic?' Grace had asked.

'Magic implies something you will not believe or understand. A special power, if you like.'

Robbie snorted but Theo ignored him. 'Such a power suggests that what you think you see you will not have seen, that your eyes will deceive you.' He closed his palm, opened it and the black handkerchief had vanished. 'So it can't be true deceit. True deceit can only happen when you don't make others aware it's going to happen.'

'Clever words,' Robbie had said. 'Otherwise known as bullshit. "Oh, what a tangled web we weave" and all that.'

'Huh?'

'"When first we practise to deceive." Shakespeare, I think.'

'Sir Walter Scott,' Grace had corrected.

True deceit, she thought now.

'I know.' Theo took hold of her hands again. 'This concerns our emotions so you don't like to use a word like "logic". But it's still a problem – isn't it, Grace? And we still need to find a solution.'

'Yes.' She'd give him that. But logic was far too rational.

He gave her hands back. 'My position. I love you and I love Robbie.'

'I know.'

'And what you also need to know is . . .'

She waited. Did she want to hear this?

'That I don't regret what happened between us.'

She blinked at him. 'Really?' Neither did she. It was an awful thing to think, but if she had the chance again, she'd do it again. Simple.

'It's changed my life.' His gaze was dark and dense and yet she trusted him. He was a magician, and Robbie said he deceived people, and yet she trusted him. 'You've changed my life. Hell, Grace, you've changed the way I want my life to be.'

Crikey, this was big stuff. Terrifying and exciting in about equal measures. But Grace wouldn't have expected less of Theo. Even so. 'But I'm married,' she said. She stirred her coffee and took another gulp. 'And to Robbie.' Because as they both knew, this made it so much worse.

'Exactly. And that's what makes it a problem.' Abruptly, he got to his feet, swilled down his coffee in one hit. 'Let's walk.'

Grace followed him out of the café, having to stop herself from taking his arm. The awful thing was that when they were just friends, she could have taken his arm. So now it felt more than weird. He made to walk along Lewin's Mead, hesitated, then retraced his steps back towards Colston Hall, keeping to the back streets, she noticed, already exercising caution even while they were both flinging it into the wind.

They walked side by side going west, getting closer to city hall and she wondered if he could feel it. Their bodies, bending towards one another as if of their own volition; the way she wanted to cleave against him, fit into him, make herself one with him. Oh, dear.

'I want you,' he muttered. 'I need you.'

Grace gulped.

'How long do we have?'

What did he mean? Her mind was frantic. Days? Weeks? Months?

'When do you have to be back?'

Grace understood. 'Just over an hour,' she said as if she'd thought about it, already calculated it. That would give her fifteen minutes before Robbie got in from work. Fifteen minutes in which to have a shower and get ready for pretending. Grace couldn't believe she could be so callous.

'Good.' Theo had manoeuvred them down a side street and then another. Then they were in Jacob's Wells Road and Grace realised they were going to his place. Of course. What did she think?

Next thing, his key was in the door of the cottage that was painted as bright as sunshine and they were inside. It was smaller than she remembered and, my God, she could hardly breathe, it even smelt of him. She'd been here once or twice before, and she knew Robbie used to hang out here a lot, but these days, usually Theo came round to theirs.

The moment the front door closed, she was in his arms and he was kissing her. Any doubts dematerialised and it swept over her just like it had before. Theo.

'Theo,' she said.

'Grace.' He took her hand and then somehow they were in the bedroom, where she had never been before. And then . . . And then.

It was slower than before; they took more time. They drank in the sight and the feel of one another's bodies and they explored. Grace ran her fingers over his caramel-coloured skin and she kissed his neck, his shoulder, his chest, his belly until he groaned at her to stop. When at last he took control, she could bear it no longer – she wanted to scream his name. But in the end she only whispered it – again, as if it held everything dear, 'Theo.'

Afterwards, he made tea and they drank it sitting up in bed. The afternoon sky was already darkening, but this just made the room more cosy. Grace felt as though she could stay here, lying in his arms for ever. The curtains were open and the cottage was on a hill, so she could see the rooftops and chimneys opposite and the rather grand independent school for boys which used to be Queen Elizabeth hospital. She didn't want to leave this little haven and step back into the reality of the outside world but she knew that she had to. Afternoon delight, she thought. She should feel wicked. But. She trailed her fingers across his back and as she closed her eyes, she could almost feel it all again. Playback time. Every detail.

'Don't.' He grabbed her hand. 'Or I'll have to have you again.'

She narrowed her eyes at him. 'You could try.' But they both knew there wasn't time.

Instead, she got up to use the bathroom. She couldn't help examining the products on the shelf above the sink; everything that had been as close to his skin as she had, the shaving foam, the aftershave cologne, the coal-tar soap. She came back and sat on the side of the bed. On a chest of drawers by the bed was a picture of a young boy with a magician's hat perched on top of dark curly hair.

She laughed, delighted. 'You?'

'Me.'

'Was that how it all started?' She leant across, twirled a finger through a strand of his hair.

He nodded. 'I guess it was. My uncle gave me a magic set one Christmas,' he said. 'It had a magic wand in it and everything.'

'And everything?' she teased. 'Sweet.'

He pulled a face. 'Apparently I was hooked right from the start. I used to give family performances every weekend. During the week I spent time perfecting my technique.' He flexed long brown fingers and raised an eyebrow.

Grace could just see him. She started pulling on her clothes so she wouldn't be tempted to jump back into bed with him again. 'What was the attraction?'

His eyes grew dreamy. 'I guess I just wanted to impress people.'

'And were they? Impressed?'

'You bet they were.' He laughed. 'But more than that . . .' He sighed. 'I wanted to make things different. I wanted to see how far I could take it.'

'It?' Grace knew she should go. She'd be late. But it was hard to tear herself away.

'Illusion,' he said. 'How much could I make people believe, make people see.'

Grace was still for a moment. 'And now?' she said.

He shrugged. 'The same.'

'I have to go.' She rose to her feet.

He got up too, grabbed a towelling bathrobe from the hook by the door. 'Grace,' he said, 'when's your next free afternoon?'

Her heart leapt. She felt as though she could fly. Ridiculous. 'Thursday,' she said. She didn't need to think about it.

'Can I see you?'

She didn't need to think about that either. 'Yes,' she said.

They still hadn't talked about what they would do, about the problem and about the logical solution. She had promised to talk to Robbie tonight but Grace couldn't think about that. She couldn't think about any of it. Not when her body was still pulsing from his touch. Not now.

CHAPTER 12

Elisa was on her way to the community centre – taking a different route down Queen Charlotte Street today as she needed to get some fabric from the market. But she was thinking not of her new cushions but about Philip.

After their discussion, after he had told her about Nancy, after she had told him that it wasn't too late to stop drinking . . . He had got up and come to stand beside her.

'I'm going to try, Elisa,' he had said.

She had eyed him warily. 'Are you sure?'

'I'm sure.'

She let out a breath she hadn't even realised she had been holding. 'But why now?' She almost couldn't believe it; it had been so long. But then it had taken him so long to tell her about Nancy. And perhaps telling her had released some of his burden.

'I went to the supermarket earlier,' he said.

Elisa nodded. It was only round the corner. They didn't bother much with big shops these days.

'I was just . . .' His voice trailed.

Buying whisky. He didn't have to say it. He hadn't asked her if they needed anything. She guessed that he alternated various supermarkets with the off license so that people wouldn't guess. As if cashiers and shop assistants noticed how many times a week a man bought a bottle of whisky. 'And what happened?' she asked.

'A woman backed away from me.'

'What?' Elisa frowned.

'It's true.' He hung his head. 'She was walking up the aisle – a woman about your age, well-dressed, expensive jewellery, nice hair. I smiled at her, just a half-smile, being polite, like you do . . .'

'Yes?'

'And she smiled back.' He nodded. 'She looked friendly. She was buying a bottle of vodka; looking at the labels as if she wasn't sure which brand to choose. But when she got close to me . . .'

Elisa frowned. She thought she knew what was coming.

'She flinched,' he said.

'Flinched?'

'Yes. She sniffed and flinched, and then she backed away. She actually backed away. And the look on her face, Elisa.'

'What sort of a look?' She reached out, put her hand on his arm.

'Disgusted,' he said. 'She looked at me with disgust.' He shook his head. He seemed horrified. 'In all the years that I've been drinking, that has never happened to me before, Elisa.'

'I see.' And she did. It was the moment that sometimes came from nowhere when you first saw yourself as others saw you. Like the moment you glanced, carelessly, into a mirror and glimpsed your old age, your mother looking back at you. Or the moment when you overheard two people talking about someone who didn't sound at all familiar or pleasant, and suddenly you realised they were talking about you. That moment. Self-realisation. When the bubble of your self-image was pricked and you saw what was underneath. What other people saw. 'Poor Philip,' she said.

'I hared out of the shop,' he said. 'I couldn't buy the whisky. I couldn't stay there. I walked and I walked. I thought of you and I thought of Grace and I thought – *you selfish bastard.*'

Elisa nodded. She understood now why he had been in such a strange mood when he'd arrived back at the house. She understood also why – when she'd pressed him – he'd been able to tell her about Nancy at last. It might seem random, that a stranger in a supermarket could have such an effect, that she could have succeeded where his wife and his daughter had failed. But that was life. And it had indeed been a turning point.

She gripped his arm. 'It won't be easy,' she said. 'I'll help you, but it won't be easy. You may have setbacks. But . . .'

'There's support available,' he said. 'I'll join AA. I'll do whatever I have to do.' And he had broken down there in front of her and wept, his whole body shaking. 'I don't want to be an old drunk and I don't want to die a drunk either. I want to make a new start with you, Elisa,' he said. 'And with Grace too.'

Elisa had been a bit wary of leaving him this afternoon, but she had to give him the responsibility of it; she couldn't carry that for him, she could only support. And she would keep her expectations low, she decided. It wasn't that she didn't think he could do it. And it wasn't that she didn't long for him to do it. But she knew it would be a long road. They had both decided not to tell Grace, at least not yet – because what if he raised his daughter's hopes and then slipped back again? Even more damage might then be done. And Elisa had to protect herself too.

St Nicholas Market was busy and Theo was already at the hall when Elisa got there with her little parcel of bright red and yellow Indian cotton. It wouldn't transform the sitting-room, which in her opinion was more than a little dull and old-fashioned, but it might help.

'*Buenos tardes*, Theo.' Elisa slipped immediately into Spanish. '*Como esta?*' She was a little surprised to see him here again so soon after his last visit, even though he had said he would try to come more often. He was always busy, even more so since he was no longer just an accountant. Elisa smiled. She guessed a man like Theo would always need more magic in his life than the kind you got from figures . . .

He bent to kiss her cheek. '*Hola*, Elisa. I'm very well, thanks. And you?' His dark eyes were grave.

She shrugged. 'I am well.'

He hesitated. 'And your family?'

Elisa thought of Philip. 'Oh, there's always something. Family problems, you know?' She hesitated. She mustn't forget how friendly Theo was with Robbie and Grace. And she didn't want to be premature on this one. Grace's problems with Robbie were her own affair and they would wait before they told anyone about Philip.

'Family problems?' Theo frowned. 'Nothing too serious, I hope?'

'Ah, no. I'm sure it will all be fine.' She hoped. Because it was all very well to manage her expectations, but if only life could be different . . . Elisa began to busy herself with chairs and Theo helped her.

'You shouldn't be moving furniture around,' he said.

'Ha! You think I'm too old?'

He laughed. 'You're a woman. And yes, you should leave it to all the strong young men you surround yourself with.'

Elisa rolled her eyes. 'I wish, Theo, oh yes.' She noticed him take a glance at his watch. Ah, so he was not here for the duration, she thought. 'So what brings you here today, Theo?' She had the feeling that he wanted to ask her something. A couple more people had drifted in but they had ten minutes.

They sat down in two chairs facing the door.

'I don't have anyone else to ask,' he said, the words coming in a rush. 'You've always been, well, a bit of a mentor for me, Elisa.'

'There are worse things,' she murmured. At least he hadn't said 'mother figure'. 'And? Spit it out, Theo.'

'What would you do?' he said thoughtfully. 'If you wanted something very, very badly, but you know it's wrong?'

'If it is wrong, maybe you should not be wanting it so very

badly,' Elisa said. 'And who says it is wrong? You or everyone else?'

He drummed his fingernails on the side of the chair. 'Oh, everyone else,' he said. 'No doubt about that.'

Elisa thought of Duardo. 'And is that some*thing*, Theo?' she asked. 'Or someone?'

He glanced at her. She could see him making a mental calculation. That was what magicians did, she supposed. Calculated the odds. Distracted you. Made you think something was another thing or in another place entirely. Diversionary tactics. She was far too old to be fooled by that sort of thing. But what had the odds been for Duardo back in the days of the revolution? How many comrades had been killed fighting for their freedom against Batista's men? He was young, but she couldn't say she was surprised when she heard the news, when Francisco came knocking on her parents' door and told her breathlessly that her worst fears had come true, that Duardo had been killed in action – in almost the final battle before victory. 'There was a fire,' he said. 'Nearly everyone was killed. We found his name tag . . .'

'I'd be grateful,' said Theo, 'if you'd care to just answer the question.'

Fair enough. 'I would always follow my heart,' she said.

Time was when everyone was against them – her and Duardo. But they'd still come through. *Would have come through*.

She had been devastated. She'd cried 'no' and she'd pressed Francisco for more details but he just shook his head, tears in his eyes. And he'd given the name tag to Rosalyn, to remember her son by.

Elisa thought of Rosalyn, of the expression on Duardo's mother's face when Elisa had raced round there, looking for some sort of confirmation of what she couldn't bear to be true. Rosalyn was a strong woman and she had not always been kind – she had wasted no time in sneering at Elisa for running back home to her parents, for not waiting for Duardo in Matanzas like his woman should. But she loved her son, no doubt of that. And so Elisa had to believe it was true. He had really gone. He would never be coming back. She would have to live the rest of her life without him.

Theo was looking at her now a little strangely. Elisa wondered if her emotions had shown in her face or if she had spoken aloud without meaning to. 'So?' she said.

'Ah, nothing.' He smiled though he still had a grim look about him. 'I thought that's what you'd say. Gotta run.' And he was up from the chair and out of the hall before you could say Jack Rabbit.

Elisa watched him go. That young man had so much energy. Suppressed inside, some of it, which wasn't always a good thing. 'Just so long,' she added, 'as you are not hurting anybody along the way, mm?' But it was much too late. Theo had gone.

CHAPTER 13

Havana 2012

Rosalyn picked up the framed photograph of her husband, Tacito. Her dear Tacito. How she missed him still. The silver-plated frame was tarnished and split, the photograph slightly out of focus. But his dark eyes still shone from the sepia image as warm and gentle as she remembered them.

Tacito had been born in the same village as Rosalyn. As children, they had played together, climbed the same hills and swum in the same pool, and as they grew into adolescence, many a time had she felt his brown-eyed gaze upon her, searching, as if he would know her every secret. She had laughed it off. He was too serious and Rosalyn had no time for it. Besides, in those days she had no secrets. But even so, that look of his seemed to creep inside her and when he was not around, she found herself instinctively casting her eyes round, watching out for him.

She held the framed photograph for a few moments next to her breast and closed her eyes. A tear slipped from them and she brushed it away with her free hand. The time for tears had long gone. Sometimes it felt as if her beloved Cuba was built on tears. And in the event, what had the tears achieved, hey? So much, her blessed *abuela* grandmother had said. So much, yes, to a woman who had been a slave, who had worked all her life for others, back-breaking work sometimes, not for personal gain but simply to stay alive and to ensure her family stayed alive too. Rosalyn was not so sure. So much, Tacito had said too, for he had been the son of a poor baker, pushing a hand cart around to sell his father's bread for a meagre pittance that barely gave them enough to live on.

Oh, he hadn't said that when Rosalyn first knew him. Back then he had been just a boy, throwing rocks and chasing lizards. But at least he always knew where he was bound. He was a baker's son. That was his pathway. Not so Rosalyn. Her father died when she was twelve years of age. Her mother was exhausted and old before her time, worn down from poverty and the struggle to get enough food for her family. There was no pathway for girls like Rosalyn. Or so it had seemed.

But they had seen changes. Her beloved grandmother had seen liberation; the end of one kind of slavery, even while her granddaughter Rosalyn had been forced into a different kind. And Tacito's family no longer lived in a shack in the slums where families huddled together, sleeping at night side by side on mats on the floor while children ran barefoot and splashed in dirty puddles.

Gently, Rosalyn replaced the photograph in its place on the sideboard by the radio – she had lost count of how many times that old radio had been mended. Her Tacito . . . She smiled. It was Tacito who had saved Rosalyn from her particular kind of slavery, and for that she would always be grateful.

She was a young girl of fifteen in February 1938 when they came for her – an aunt and an uncle on her father's side who had the ear of one of the nightclub owners in Havana. What had they told him? That she was pretty? That she was a virgin? That she had big brown eyes and curves in all the right places? Even at fifteen?

Black skin too – he would have been asked, because as Rosalyn knew, the mulatto girls were considered the most attractive and certainly were the most sought after. Black skin, they would have said, because Rosalyn was African Cuban through and through and proud of it. Who wouldn't be proud of a generation who had been brought to Cuba on slave ships in appalling conditions, bought and sold as if they had no more value than a mango? And they worked in that sugar plantation – they had to. There were worse owners, Rosalyn's grandmother had told her that. Owners who were cruel, who committed atrocities she would not mention. But all owners were owners. Every kindness was another way of saying – *You belong to me; I will decide how good your life can be.*

Rosalyn didn't blame her mother. Her mother hardly knew where she was being taken nor why; she had no voice in the matter. She wasn't to know that sexual gratification had become the main business of the city of Havana.

'She'll be better off with us,' her uncle had said. He wore

an old felt hat and had jutting ribs and an arrogant way about him that made Rosalyn unwilling to trust him. 'We'll see you right.'

At fifteen, Rosalyn was the oldest child. There were other children to worry about. Her mother no longer had a husband to protect her family. She had to take what she could when the chance was offered.

Rosalyn had never been a political woman. Tacito had not been political either – though he could recognise injustice when he saw it. So how she and Tacito had come to raise such a political son . . . Rosalyn shook her head, distracted for a moment from her thoughts of the past. She had no idea. She only knew that her Duardo had fire in his eyes from the moment he was born. He had opened his eyes and looked at her and she had seen it. He was always going to fight, that boy, and the woman was foolish who thought that she could prevent him, who thought that she could tie him down and stop him trying to change the world. Not Rosalyn. She did not want to lose her boy; she shuddered at the thought of losing her boy. But she always knew what he was and what he needed.

So fifteen-year-old Rosalyn was taken that afternoon to the city centre frequented by bootblacks, pimps and lottery sellers and into the nightclub to be shown round the place. To be more accurate, *she* was shown; the nightclub owner came to inspect her as a farmer might any working animal. Rosalyn didn't know much about this kind of city life. All she knew was that the nightclubs in Havana meant Americans and that

Americans meant money. Later she learnt that Americans had wanted to make Cuba the 'Paris of the Caribbean'; a place where hedonism was all and morals could go hang. Cabarets, nightclubs, sleazy strip joints and bars; gaming and gambling from night till dawn – these things were the name of the game. And Cuba became the whorehouse of the Caribbean, with most of its people living in poverty or slums.

'She'll do,' the owner said. He tipped Rosalyn's chin so that she was forced to meet his gaze. 'Can you be nice?'

Rosalyn didn't reply. She knew her eyes were growing wider. Still, she didn't have much idea of what they expected of her. Was she to clean the place? To serve drinks?

'She can be nice, all right,' her uncle replied. 'She just ain't had no practice, if you get my drift.'

The nightclub owner nodded. 'Start her tomorrow night,' he said. 'We'll see.'

And so Rosalyn supposed that whatever the test was, she had passed.

'You can earn good money here,' her uncle said. 'And you'll give it to me. I'll see your family are looked after. And I'll see you have your own bit of pocket money too.'

Her aunt nudged her. 'But you have to be friendly.'

'Friendly?' Rosalyn asked.

'You'll see.'

Something about the conspiratorial glance they exchanged made her scared. *Mary, Mother of God . . .* She sent up a silent prayer. How exactly was she to earn all this money – a girl like her? 'I don't want to,' she told her aunt and uncle. 'I want to go home.' Home was poor but it was safe. She did not belong here and she didn't like the nightclub owner and the way he had looked her up and down as if she were a side of beef. His stare had resounded in her head and met the voice of her beloved grandmother. And what she had heard had frightened her.

'You can't. You'll be living with us now.' Her uncle pinched her cheek, his thin dark stare lingering over her shoulders and her breasts, just like the nightclub owner's gaze had done. 'You're a lucky girl and don't you forget it. We'll get the money to buy you a few dresses. And we'll get you a room.'

'A room?' Her eyes widened once more.

'But yes,' her uncle said. 'Of course, a room. It won't be anything smart, mind. But it'll be a place you can take –'

'Don't be a fool,' her aunt whispered to her. 'This is how you can help your family. They'll get their share just like we told you. And it's only for a year or two . . .'

'A year or two?'

'Jesus!' Her uncle swore. 'All she can do is repeat everything. She has no wits about her, woman.'

'She has no need of wits.' Her aunt looked away. 'She has what they want – at least for a while. And we must take advantage of it while we can.'

And so it was settled. Rosalyn was installed in a cheap and tatty room but she could have a meal with her aunt and uncle before she went out each evening. She was told that she must not try to see her family. Every night she must go to the club.

She would be given a drink or two and then she must wait – to be picked up by some fat cigar-smoking American who wanted a tasty morsel on the side. This was not what her aunt and uncle told her; this was how she told it to herself, when she got there, when she finally realised exactly how it would be.

Rosalyn remembered the first time. One of the other girls sitting at the bar took pity on her and gave her a cigarette, told her how to smoke it. 'And don't sit like that, honey,' she added. 'Sit up straight, put your legs to one side like this. Shoulders back – don't hunch.' But these girls scared Rosalyn almost as much as the men did – with their glamorous made-up faces, their low-cut dresses and the jewellery that glittered at their throats and on their fingers and wrists. They looked like rich women. They acted like rich women. But Rosalyn saw them sashay over to the men's tables when they were called for, and she knew that they were whores.

The girl who gave her the cigarette had more tips to offer. 'You ain't never gonna get chosen looking sullen,' she said. 'Take that moody look off your face is my advice.' She took her to the cloakroom too and painted on some eyeliner and brows. 'Unavailable is fine,' she said. 'They like that because they know it's not true. But you gotta have some glamour.' She tweaked at Rosalyn's faded cotton dress and sighed at the sight of the cheap sandals on her feet. 'You've got a lot to learn, girl.'

They returned to the bar and pretty soon the waiter tapped her on the shoulder. 'Come along this way.'

Rosalyn felt the dread settle on her stomach. She had been waiting for this moment, feeling more nauseous by the second. She got up from her barstool, almost stumbling. No way could she do that sinuous walk that the other girls made look so easy.

'I bet he thinks she's a virgin,' one of the more bitchy girls sitting at the bar said in Spanish-Cuban. 'Why else pick a girl like that?'

Why else pick a girl like that? Rosalyn followed the waiter over to the far side of the room. Seated at a table was a morose-looking man, wearing shades and old enough to be her father, she guessed.

'Can you speak English?' He looked her up and down just like the club owner and her uncle had done.

'No, Mister.' She gazed down at the floor – it seemed safer.

But he patted his knee. 'That's good. Tonight, honey, all you gotta do is dance.'

Rosalyn could dance. She had always been able to dance. Everyone in Cuba learned to salsa and to shimmy from the time they first learnt to walk – they were used to a mother dancing a cha-cha-cha across the kitchen or a father singing a bolero as he strolled home from work. And the rumba was part of the culture of Rosalyn's forefathers; the rumba of the *cajón* and the kettle drum, the rhythm of her people. It was a way to keep their truth, her grandmother had told her; it became a protest – though little good that did those who were bound in slavery. But it was also a way of expressing their identity – and not even the slave masters could take that entirely away from them. Rosalyn's grandmother also talked about music played on a wicker *marímbula*, a deep-voiced drum that some said was a voice from the grave – though the blacks on the plantation would probably have stayed up half the night dancing the rumba if they had ever got the chance.

The music here in the smoky nightclub was a different sort of music, but it was one Rosalyn had been brought up with. At first her limbs were stiff and unresponsive to the American's touch but as the band played on, as the drumming vibrated through her body, as the trumpet player let loose and the black female *artista* sang . . . Rosalyn danced the *merenga*.

When they left the club he hailed a cab and that's when he tried to kiss her, in the back seat of that big black Cadillac. Rosalyn turned her face away. His lips were thin and unattractive, his skin glistening with a film of sweat, his eyes red from drinking. What little hair he had was greasy and fair and clung to his scalp in skinny wisps. A dot of saliva had dribbled from his mouth to his clean-shaven chin and she tried not to stare at it.

'Don't be scared, honey,' he said. 'Is it your first time?'

She looked away, over his shoulder. She didn't know what to say or how to be.

'I'll show you,' he promised. 'You got nothing to fear.'

Before he left in the morning he tucked several dollar bills under her pillow. 'See you soon,' he said.

But Rosalyn never saw him again. Instead, she saw a string of other men, a different one every night: some quiet, some loud; some kind, some not; some gentle, some rough; some mean, some generous – with money and with jewels.

She understood then where the women's jewellery came from. She understood why they needed to be chosen when they sat at the bar which was no more than a showroom for female bodies and what they did to be chosen. Because if you weren't chosen, you didn't earn money, and then it was all for nothing. If you weren't chosen . . . She had thought at first that this was what she would do – look miserable, down at heel and unattractive and ensure that no man wanted her.

But the girl who had first befriended her put her right. 'Anyone that's left at the end of the night,' she said, 'gets given to the staff for free.' And she'd looked over at the bartender who shot her a saucy wink. 'If you get my drift.'

Rosalyn got it. There was no way she was doing this for free. So she learnt how to put her hair up so that her cheekbones were more pronounced, how to use make-up to enhance the width and slope of her eyes, the fullness of her lips. She asked her uncle to buy her more dresses – which showed off her assets – and some high-heeled shoes. And she learnt how to walk in them – sinuous and silky, each step a curve and a promise. She learnt how to laugh too, how to listen, even how to flirt. She was still only fifteen. In Cuba, she learnt, anything goes if you have enough dough. But she hated every second of it.

She began to save. Most of her money went to her uncle and aunt for her room, payment for this precious opportunity they had given her in life. They said they gave some to her family too but Rosalyn had already begun to doubt it. She realised that her uncle had no way of knowing how much she was earning and that some clients were both reckless and generous. She knew that her uncle regularly checked the room to ensure she wasn't keeping a stash, so she was wily; she kept it near the pan in a place she knew he wouldn't look. And the stash was growing. He didn't take her gifts of jewellery either – seeing these as an investment which would attract richer clients, she guessed – so she sold some of them when she had the chance and when she thought he wouldn't notice.

One day, when she had been working for several months and just after her sixteenth birthday – which she had celebrated under the body of a fat American sailor who had drunk too much rum to be able to do his business but not enough to stop him trying for over an hour – she secreted some money in her underclothes and went back home. She took a taxi back to a place near the street where her family lived, taking care to wear no make-up, to dress modestly, to cover her head with a scarf. She listened to the shouts of the scissor sharpener and the fruit seller, the hooting of horns from the main road and the clattering of hand carts on the cobbles. She picked her way through the puddles. How much her life had changed, she thought. Who was the creature she had become? She hardly knew her. She didn't wish to know her.

She found her mother inside, cooking a meagre stew with black beans and a few scraps of pork. Nothing seemed to have changed. And yet it was a world that now she had no place in.

'Oh, my dear, my love.' Her mother cried. She reached out her arms and she held her. Rosalyn allowed herself to be held, but she recognised her own coldness. She didn't blame her mother for allowing them to take her away; she even understood. But nevertheless, she could not feel the same way about her any longer; some bond between them had snapped and died. Besides, Rosalyn had no tears. Her tears were all dried up inside her; she wasn't sure she would ever cry again.

'Are you well?' her mother asked her. 'Are you safe?'

What could she say? 'Do not worry about me.' That was all she could manage.

But there was another thing. Rosalyn kissed her younger brothers and sisters. Her sister Amelia was fourteen and growing up fast. Already Rosalyn feared for her. 'Have you been given money?' she asked her mother.

'A little.' Her mother looked down. 'But if you are well...'

Once again, there seemed nothing she could say. So Rosalyn gave her mother the money she'd brought and watched her eyes widen in disbelief. 'Take it,' she said. 'It is mine. Use it wisely. And do not let Amelia go where I have gone.'

Her mother shook her head. She was still crying.

When Rosalyn left the shack, she saw Tacito in the street, selling loaves. She tried to avoid him, hurrying away in the opposite direction. She was so ashamed. She didn't think she had ever been so ashamed. She really could not face him.

But she heard him calling her name. 'Rosalyn! Hey, Rosalyn!' She ignored him.

But he had caught up with her. He must have left his cart of bread behind, because he was there, pulling at her arm. 'Stop,' he commanded her.

She stopped.

'Where are you going?' He did not let go of her arm.

She was silent. She couldn't look at him.

'Where have you been?'

Rosalyn shook her head.

'Rosalyn. Where?'

'Let go of me.' She tried to pull free but he was stronger than her. 'You do not want to know,' she said at last.

'Where?' And she saw from his face that he was not giving up.

'The city,' she said. 'Havana.'

He nodded. 'They said you live with your aunt and uncle now. They would not tell me where.'

She shrugged.

'But I tell you this.'

At last she felt compelled to look up at him.

'I will find you,' he promised.

She shook him off. 'Do not bother,' she said. She was spoiled for ever. There was no point. Her life was over so far as that went.

For a moment he wavered. 'If you ever need me,' he said. 'If you need a friend . . .'

'I will not.' And now she really did shake him off and she ran. Because she wanted to tell him, but how could she? She wanted to feel his arms around her, protecting her, as once he had tried to do – once, when she had just laughed and pushed him away. She wanted it but she could not have it – not any of it. She was a different person now.

CHAPTER 14

For so long, Grace had ignored it, her growing feelings for Theo. The attachment. If she didn't acknowledge it, how could it be there?

'He's like the brother I never had,' Robbie had said once.

'Me too.' But in truth, Theo had never been much of a brother figure for Grace. More of a soulmate. He just seemed to get her.

Not that she'd ever imagined . . . She'd taken care not to get too close, not to let these thoughts cross her mind. She'd taken care not to look at him for too long, not to laugh with him too long, to keep their kisses light and on the cheek and their hugs brief. Very brief. And he had colluded. She could see now that he had colluded.

That night, after the text from Theo, after that afternoon in his flat, she and Robbie had talked.

'Just think about it, Gracie,' Robbie had said. 'The baby thing. Please just say you'll think about it. Until then – we won't mention it again.'

'Really?'

'And we don't have to move to Sussex. You're right. Our

life is here. We have family here – your family. We have Theo and all our friends.'

Theo. His name on Robbie's lips. Grace had to repress a shudder.

'But you have to accept one thing, Gracie.' He didn't seem able to drop the subject.

'What?'

'You're almost forty.'

'Yeah, I know.' *Thanks, Robbie.*

'So . . .' He ran his hand through his fair hair. 'What if you get to forty-five and you desperately want a baby?'

'Then I'd go for it,' Grace said.

'But what if it's too late and you can't have one?'

'I don't know.' She had thought of that. But it was hard to transport yourself forward even five years and know how you would feel. People change.

He moved closer. They were sitting at either end of their sofa, a cushion parked between them as if it were marking a boundary. Robbie's persistence, his downright stubbornness had made him the loyal problem-solver Grace had fallen in love with. But at the moment that same persistence was driving her pretty much demented.

He took her hand. 'What if we just let nature decide?'

She stiffened. 'What do you mean?'

'You know.' He played with her fingers, almost speculatively.

Grace wanted to snatch her hand away, but she forced herself not to. 'No, I don't.'

'Stop taking the pill. See what happens.'

'That's not making a decision,' she said. And now she did pull away from him. 'Or at least it is. And it's an irresponsible one. No one should risk getting pregnant if they're not even sure they want the baby.'

'For heaven's sake, Grace.' He got to his feet and paced the room. 'We're married. What's irresponsible about doing what nature intended?'

Grace could see where this was going – again. 'Robbie.' She put up a hand to stop him from saying more. 'You just said I could have time to think about it,' she reminded him. 'You said you wouldn't mention it again till then.'

'Of course.' He let out a deep sigh and picked up the TV remote. 'If you promise you will. Think about it, that is.'

'I will.'

He pressed the standby button and a newsreader popped on to the large screen.

Grace relaxed. It was a reprieve. So at least she had time. And time was all she needed. Every problem could be solved with time (and logic, according to Theo). Everything would become clear. She had to trust in that. And meanwhile . . .

'When did you know?' she asked Theo, on Thursday afternoon, when she was at his house in Gorse Lane. There had been no pretence this time of having coffee first. This time they needed every minute for themselves. 'Really know?'

They were in bed. He traced a fingertip down her spine,

smoothing over the knotty bits. Clever fingers. It wasn't any recognised technique, but it was nice all the same.

'You know when I knew.'

Grace wriggled. She knew when but she wanted him to say it.

'Find the Lady,' he whispered. 'My downfall.'

Hers too. That card trick. Hers too.

It had started innocently enough that night. The three of them had had supper – Grace had cooked prawns with caramelised garlic and aubergines served on linguine and they'd probably all drunk a little more wine than usual. They had these suppers fairly frequently – once a fortnight or so. Occasionally, over the years, Theo would be seeing someone and Robbie would say – bring Jane or Rosa or Annie. But Theo never did. And the women – pleasant though they were – tended never to stay around long enough to become an established part of their little unit.

'Don't know what's wrong with you, mate,' Robbie would say about Rosa or Jane or Annie. 'She was a nice girl. What happened?'

And Theo would shrug and say: 'It just didn't work out,' or, 'She wanted more than I could give,' or, 'We just didn't have that spark, you know?'

Unlike most people Grace knew, he never allowed a relationship with a woman to drift into anything remotely comfortable. With Theo it was all or nothing. And just the thought of that made her shiver.

On the night of Find the Lady, Theo was sitting on the

sofa practising a card trick with Robbie, who always got frustrated when he couldn't see how Theo was doing it – which was most of the time.

'Damn it,' he said. 'How did you get it from there to there? It's impossible.'

'Nothing's impossible,' Theo said. He lifted his glass of red wine to his lips. Grace watched him, feeling safe in the companionable semi-darkness, for the only light in the room came from the art deco lamp on the wall and the flickering flames in the woodburner. *Nothing is impossible*, she reflected. Only clearly some things were.

'You should be more like Grace,' Theo said, and she realised he was looking straight at her. 'More trusting.'

'I'm not trusting,' she demurred.

'Really?' Robbie pretended to be upset.

'I just accept the trick.' Grace poured herself more wine. 'That's not the same as being trusting.'

Theo raised an eyebrow.

'I don't need to see how it's done.' She sipped her wine slowly and considered. 'I know it's a trick. But I don't want to be a magician. So why would I need to know how it's done?'

Theo laughed. 'My perfect audience. She appreciates but she doesn't question.'

Robbie frowned. 'Nothing wrong with a little curiosity,' he said.

'And persistence,' said Grace.

Theo turned to Robbie. 'It's just another version of Find the Lady, that's all.'

'Find the Lady?'

'I'll show you.' Theo selected three cards from the deck – two black aces and the queen of hearts. 'It's the oldest con in the book,' he said.

'Yeah?' Robbie leant forwards. Grace could see his determination to work this one out.

'OK. Your street magician plays with a couple of accomplices. They're in on it; part of the show.' Theo flicked the three cards around between his fingers as he spoke. 'Their job is to find the lady – identify where the magic man has put the queen.'

'Sounds simple,' said Robbie.

'It is – relatively. They lose some and they win some; but they're not very good. So when the mark comes along, he watches them and he thinks he can do better. It's human nature.'

Human nature, thought Grace. Like Robbie, needing to win.

'Yep. All he has to do is watch the lady.' Theo glanced at Grace. She hoped her expression was in shadow. There was something different about tonight. Robbie seemed genuinely put out and Theo . . . Theo had a devil-may-care look about him. If he was playing poker, he'd be going all in. 'But as you might guess, the magic man is controlling the game.' Theo showed the three cards, one by one and then placed them face down in a row. He began to switch them around, slowly at first and then gaining pace. Grace could feel the intensity of Robbie's concentration. Anyone would imagine it perfectly possible to get this right.

Theo sat back. 'Find the lady,' he said to Robbie.

Robbie frowned. 'In the centre.' He pointed. Grace could see that he was confident he'd chosen correctly. She was equally confident he'd be wrong. It's a trick, Robbie, she wanted to say. Don't forget that.

Theo turned over the card. It was the ace of clubs.

Robbie swore under his breath. 'Let's have another go,' he said.

Grace sighed and shook her head.

'And so that's how it works,' Theo said.

'The mark wants another go because he keeps wanting to beat you,' Grace said.

Theo nodded. 'And he's confident that he can.'

Grace smiled. 'The trick's beginning to annoy him. He thinks it should be easy.' And Robbie was playing the part to perfection.

Theo nodded again. 'Like I said, it's human nature. We all want to win. None of us wants to be fooled.'

'Unless we're Grace,' said Robbie.

She pulled a face. 'I'm just a realist.'

'And I want another go.' Robbie looked expectantly at Theo.

'Human nature,' Theo said again. 'We all want to believe the evidence of our own eyes.'

Grace shifted slightly in her chair in the corner. Eyes, memories . . . What could you believe in, if not in them? Unbidden, the images pulsed into her brain and she felt herself flush into panic. A crash, a thud, a scream, the sound of a man running. His voice. 'Nancy. Oh, Nancy. I pushed her into this. She'd never have run . . .' Another voice. 'Take the child away. For God's sake.' The calmer voice of Amanda's mother. 'Come with me, my dear.' And a woman. A woman standing by her father's side. Frozen and unmoving. A woman smelling of lily of the valley and of death.

'Grace?' Theo was looking across at her. His expression was concerned. 'Are you OK?'

'Yes.' Grace should never have witnessed the moments following that awful accident. She wasn't even supposed to be there, she was supposed to be having tea with her best friend Amanda; only Amanda had felt sick and Amanda's mother had taken Grace home. They had arrived only seconds after it happened.

Over the years, Grace had often asked herself who that woman standing by her father's side could be. She wasn't some passing stranger. She had come out of the house behind Grace's father and she had stood there staring and immobile. In shock, Grace supposed. There was only one explanation Grace could come up with. No, her father had not physically pushed her mother into the road. Of course he hadn't. But as he'd said himself, he'd pushed her into running. There was only one thing that could have made her run like that. Her mother had walked in on them. She had come home early and she had seen them together. Her husband and his mistress. The shock had been too much. She had rushed headlong out of the house and on to the road without looking. And . . . her father and the other woman had followed behind.

Theo was still looking at her. Was it being a magician that made him so observant, so perceptive? Or something else?

Robbie, on the other hand, was still glaring at the cards as if they were trying to make him look stupid. The male ego, she thought. He was doing it to himself.

'This one,' he said triumphantly.

And yet your eyes could be mistaken. Your memories could be blurred, altered, fragmented with time.

'Sorry, mate.' Theo sounded anything but. He turned the card to reveal the ace of spades.

'Damn it,' said Robbie again. He sat back. 'OK. So how do you do it?'

Theo shrugged. Sometimes he wouldn't tell Robbie his secrets. He had to protect the rules of the Magic Circle, he said. He wasn't allowed to give everything away. But this time, 'It's as old as the hills,' he said, 'but there are different methods. All involving sleight of hand.'

'Is that it?' Robbie looked cross.

'It has to do with the way the cards are held and the way you toss them on to the table.' Theo demonstrated. 'The magician can use a double lift, a triple lift, a false take.'

Grace watched his fingers, skilful and deft, moving the cards so fast that if you blinked you'd miss it.

'But I have my own version,' Theo told Robbie.

'You would.'

'There are four cards, not three. And I took the chance that you'd be able to follow.'

'I don't think that I do.' Robbie shook his head.

'In my version,' Theo said, 'the magician always has the lady. She's never actually available or out there. He keeps her hidden in the palm of his hand.'

The magician always has the lady. Grace had looked at Theo. Theo had looked at her. Poor Robbie was oblivious, still trying to work it out. And that's when it passed between them. The knowledge. That was the moment that had led them to this. That was when.

CHAPTER 15

Havana 1939

Tacito found her though. Somehow, he found her. One night, Rosalyn was coming out of the club with an American she'd been with all evening. The man was already getting frisky and instead of hailing a cab right away, he dragged her off down the street, laughing. He pulled her into a doorway and leaned forward to kiss her.

Rosalyn never kissed them. That was one thing she would never do. So she pushed him off. 'Wait, mister,' she told him.

'I want you now,' he growled. 'Right here and right now, dammit.'

She took a step away. He wrenched her back towards him. Ah, he was going to be one of the rough ones. Rosalyn had known a few. But the odd slap meant nothing to her, not now – she almost wanted them to hurt her; it was all she was worth.

And then Tacito stepped out of the shadows. She didn't recognise him at first, his face was so black, his eyes simply glittered. 'Leave her.'

She gasped.

The American glared at him. 'Who the hell do you think you are?'

Tacito stood up straighter. 'I look after this woman,' he said.

Rosalyn looked from one to the other of them in despair. Tacito had no idea. He did not belong here. This was her world and he was no part of it.

'You're her pimp, is that it?' Already the man was reaching for his wallet.

'No.' Tacito stood his ground. 'I said I look after her. I protect her.'

'Is that right?' The American rocked back on his heels. 'So what are you trying to say?'

Rosalyn knew what she must do. 'Leave him, mister,' she said, forcing herself not to look at Tacito. She struggled to find the words the American would understand. 'He is nothing.'

'Nothing, eh?' The American was still appraising him. He stuck one hand in the pocket of his trousers, still holding her arm with the other. 'Hear that, boy? My girl here says you are nothing.'

Blushing with shame, Rosalyn looked down at the pavement. That wasn't what she had meant. But she had to get Tacito out of here somehow and away. It wasn't safe. He could end up getting hurt – and so could she.

'She ain't your girl,' Tacito said.

'Is that right?' Once more, the man scrutinised him. 'You had her once is that it, eh? Well surely there's enough here to go round? Maybe some other night she'll come to you, huh? She ain't fussy, I can see by looking at you that she ain't fussy.'

Rosalyn wasn't sure what happened next. But Tacito must have hit him because the American was on the ground squealing with pain and Tacito's eyes were gleaming as he stood over him.

'What the hell are you doing?' she shouted at him. 'This is my work. This is what I do.'

'In that place?' He nodded towards the club. His lip curled.

'Yes – in that place.' But Rosalyn wondered if she'd be able to work there again. There were other clubs. She knew all the names: the Tropicana and San Souci, Lucky Seven and The New Capri. But . . . She glanced down at the fat American groaning on the sidewalk. Word would get around. Who would want her now? And what else would she be fit for?

'Why, Rosalyn?' Tacito asked.

She shrugged. 'Isn't it obvious?'

He held out his hand. 'Come with me.'

'Why should I?' she asked. But she took a step away from the American on the sidewalk. One step and then another.

'Because there is a better way. Because life has to be better than that.'

'My life doesn't,' she told him. And that was the truth.

'It does now,' he said. 'You have me now.'

She narrowed her eyes at him. Didn't he know it was too late? 'Why would you want me?' she whispered.

'Because I always have,' he said.

His hand was still outstretched. 'Come,' he said.

And so she did.

Rosalyn took down her hair and changed her dress and stayed inside the shack to which he had taken her. There was no one else there, he said, his father had died; it was theirs now. The first night she had taken off her clothes, half-expecting him to be like all the rest, but he had shaken his head and said, 'No, Rosalyn. I will wait.'

They talked and little by little, day by day, she told him of what had happened to her and how she had felt – how she felt still.

Tenderly, he touched her face. 'That is not the life for you,' he said. 'I am here. We will share a different life together now.'

On the fifth day she broke down and cried and it was as if her tears had somehow washed her clean. He held her then and soothed her and that afternoon he took her to her mother's house.

If her mother was surprised to see her she didn't show it. If her aunt and uncle had visited, demanding to know her whereabouts, she said nothing.

'I can't give you money,' Rosalyn told her mother. 'Not any more. But you mustn't let them take Amelia. It's wrong. You must promise that she'll stay here with you no matter how bad things get.' Because there was no death worse than that one, night after night in a different man's arms.

'I won't.' But her mother looked frightened.

'And if anything happens,' Tacito added. 'Come to me.'

She nodded. 'And Rosalyn . . .'

'I will look after Rosalyn now,' he said.

And he did. Rosalyn had never imagined that she would feel desire for a man, but eventually, she did. And that was the day she kissed a man for the first time. Her Tacito.

CHAPTER 16

Grace was walking back from Theo's, a circuitous route she'd devised early on, a route which gave her time to think, and in which she could even perhaps become a different person again – the Grace who was married to Robbie. She could have gone to Theo's place by car, but cars could be easily recognised if they were parked in a road nearby. That's how devious she had become, she thought. But also, Grace needed this walk back home. She needed to lose some of that adrenalin that was still humming round her body from his touch. The walk took less than half an hour and she wanted to feel the fresh spring breeze reminding her of the reality of what she was doing. She didn't want to feel cosy. Because this wasn't cosy. Not at all.

She saw him most afternoons. They walked over and round Brandon Hill because it was close by, because it was pretty and because there were narrow, undulating pathways and small private niches – usually with a bench and spectacular views – where for minutes at a time they could be alone. At the bottom of the steps that led to the Cabot Tower was a pond and a belvedere look-out point where they often lingered. The place was so stately, seemed so superior and sure of itself, and it felt so peaceful; they would sit on one of the dark turquoise benches and look down on the trees, terraces and spires and the open countryside beyond the city, and it would feel – really feel – as if they were in another world. Perhaps that was what made it seem justifiable, Grace thought. This feeling that what she had with Theo was another life, that where they were was indeed another incarnation, another place. Perhaps that was how she could do it at all.

They talked about everything imaginable. Theo told her about the way he'd been brought up in Florida; there had been a Little Havana in Miami – men still played dominoes and sold cigars and people still talked politics and knew what was happening in Cuba. But no one, he said, had much time for Fidel. Theo told Grace why he had wanted to come to England after his parents died, to see a place that had so much history, and how he had never intended to stay, but found himself loving the Somerset landscape, English eccentricity, the history of the buildings in Bristol.

Grace talked about her childhood too, told him how she had felt after losing her mother, how she met Elisa and about the difficult relationship she had with her father. 'I've decided to stay away from him for a while,' she confessed to Theo. 'It's the drinking – I can't stand seeing him that way.' They talked politics, they talked books, they talked about countries they had visited and where they might go to next. But they didn't talk about who they might go there with. And they didn't mention Robbie. That subject was out of bounds.

They walked, they talked, they took crazy risks, because as

they walked and talked he would reach down and kiss her, or throw his arm around her, or they would hold hands and any-body . . . anybody, Grace told herself, might see them. But she couldn't help herself. Moth to a flame. Her wings might get burned but she was past caring. And as they walked along the top of the hill they could see the bright yellow-painted house in Gorse Lane, shining like a beacon. They would walk down and it would get closer and closer . . . And they both knew what was waiting for them there.

Other times, perhaps if it was raining or if they couldn't bear to wait, they simply stayed in and made love; long lan-guorous afternoons in bed, which Grace never wanted to end. She loved the way his mind worked and she loved his body – the feel of it, the touch of it, the connection that they had. He was her closest friend and he had become her lover. It was the best time. But she also knew that it was stolen time. She couldn't see how it could ever be anything other than that.

Now, Grace made her way again up the steps to Brandon Hill – this time on her way home. There was a wildlife trust on the corner; at this point she always glanced back the way she'd come, back to Gorse Lane and the high terraces of Clifton, before taking the shady path and heading home. It was her turning point. This afternoon she noted the daffodils about to bloom under the trees on the undulating hill, heard the birdsong so sweetly trying to outdo the sound of distant traffic – and succeeding, against the odds. She passed the pond bordered with willows. It still looked lifeless, murky and overgrown with brambles, but Theo had told her that in the summer it was a hive of activity with yellow flag irises, marsh marigolds, frogs, toads, newts and glittering damselflies skimming over its surface. Now, there were mainly just grey squirrels and birds, but later in the year there would be butterflies and bees attracted by the heathers and meadow flowers. Would she be here in the summer? Grace couldn't say. She walked on until she could see the terrace of grey and lemon three-storey Georgian houses on Queens Terrace. She headed down towards Brandon Steep. She couldn't say because she just didn't know.

She had stopped taking clients in the afternoon. She supposed Theo's work was suffering too. He still went to the hospital, he still did all his weekend and evening events, but he was looking tired and drawn. There was a gauntness to his face that hadn't been there before; he had a hunted look about him. They were drowning in each other. Grace passed the mullioned windows and royal blue door of Brandon Cottage and glanced at the plaque. *Home of the Bristol Savages 1907–1920*. It sounded vaguely threatening, but Theo had told her it was an art club founded by painters in 1904.

Grace didn't like that hunted look of Theo's. She didn't like what was happening. It seemed too much, too extreme, a madness which couldn't go on. It wasn't real life, she told herself again as she passed the high stone wall with the odd, quirky sculptures of mermaids and fish that someone had fixed on to it, the little wooden door. Like *Alice in Wonderland*. It was unsustainable. But all the time and despite this, she craved his look, his voice, his touch. She craved it now, even as she was walking away from him. And it did go on. It seemed that they couldn't get enough of each other.

Grace walked round to the front of city hall, to the impressive piazza that housed not just the elegant arc of city hall itself, but the library and the statuesque cathedral. In the moat and waterfall outside city hall, pigeons were bathing, shaking their wings. People milled around the cathedral entrance; there were always tourists in Bristol and Grace liked the feeling that she lived here, that she could lose herself among them. *That's an illusion, Grace,* she told herself sternly. She was doing a Theo; just trying to pretend.

Sometimes – times when the future loomed so scarily that she slipped into panic – Grace asked him: *What shall we do?* He was the one who had always had a logical answer for everything. But he would just shrug and say, 'I don't know, Grace. I just don't know.' And so it went on.

After supper, Robbie jumped to his feet to clear up. He put a hand on her shoulder. 'You stay there,' he said. 'I'll do it.'

That's what was happening now; Robbie was being nice to her – which was awful. Especially because of the reason. He was being nice to her because she was always ill. Or said she was. She couldn't make love because she had a headache or a stomach upset. Like Theo, she was losing weight. When she looked in the mirror her eyes seemed almost hollow and while she'd always been slim, now, her clothes were practically hanging off her. She tried to disguise it, but it was hard. She wasn't eating. She wasn't eating because . . .

'Thanks, love.' And it was true that Grace's adrenalin had now entirely evaporated, leaving her feeling drained. She couldn't believe the energy she'd had all day, but she knew it would be the same tomorrow; the thought of Theo driving her on.

Grace glanced warily at Robbie as he cleared the plates. They had kept to their uneasy truce. Families and babies had not been mentioned, much to her relief. And she couldn't say that the subject was uppermost in her mind.

Robbie came back into the room. He frowned at her.

'What?'

'You have to go the doctor, Gracie,' he said. 'This has been going on for weeks. You're not well.'

'A doctor won't help.' What could a doctor tell her? Her problem was that she was in love with a black-eyed magician who happened to be her husband's best friend. Any pills for that, were there?

'How do you know? At least he could take a look at you. Do tests or something. Come and sit down.' He tugged at her hand and took her over to the sofa.

Grace allowed herself to be led. 'It's just some virus,' she said. 'I'll feel better soon.' But she knew that she couldn't fob him off for ever. Something had to change.

Later, in bed, Grace was almost asleep; Robbie just getting undressed. 'And another thing,' he said suddenly.

'Mmm?'

'A really weird thing.'

'Uh?' She opened an eye.

'I saw Theo.'

'What?' Grace sat up in bed. This was it then. He'd seen them. He knew. Grace felt it in the pit of her stomach – the rumble of panic.

'Yeah. Well, you know he said he was going away for a while?' Robbie took off his glasses. He always seemed so much more vulnerable when he didn't have his glasses on.

Grace nodded.

'Which was odd because I've tried calling him but it seems he's not just away but incommunicado as well.'

'Um.' She waited.

'Well it turns out he's back.'

'Back,' she echoed. 'Oh . . . Good.' What was she supposed to say? Suggest they invite him round? She couldn't even begin to imagine how awful that would be.

'And yet he hasn't come round to see us. No text, no phone call, nothing.' Robbie pulled off the black trousers he wore for work. He hadn't bothered to change when he got home tonight. He got into bed quickly and reached out for her.

'Maybe he hasn't got round to it yet,' Grace mumbled. She settled into his arms in her usual comfortable spot. She almost preferred it when they were arguing. At least it was more honest.

'Yeah, but . . .' Robbie shook his head. 'I've called. I've texted. Bloody hell, Gracie, it's like he's blanking me.'

She lifted her head to look at him and he looked so miserable that suddenly Grace wanted to cry. She'd done this to him. 'Maybe he's just busy,' she said. 'Maybe he's seeing someone.' It was awful to lie to him. She just wanted to make him feel better.

'I don't think so,' he said. He stretched out and switched off the bedside lamp.

That was better. At least now he couldn't see her face. 'You saw him?' she asked carefully.

'Yeah. Near the cathedral.'

What were you doing near the cathedral? she wanted to shriek, because that was her route home. But she held back. All at once the happiness of all three of them seemed to be hanging by just one thread. And she didn't know what to do about it.

'Did you speak to him?' she asked instead. Her voice was so flat you could iron a shirt with it.

'I tried. I was driving. I yelled out of the car window. I don't think he heard me though. There was a lot of traffic.'

'Did you stop?' she asked.

'Course I did. I parked the first chance I got and went back to look for him.' He paused.

'And?'

'And he was gone.'

Grace turned over, away from him. The magician, she thought. Always so good at the vanishing act. Theo and Robbie hadn't talked – but they'd have to eventually. Theo couldn't just drop his friendship with Robbie. And yet . . . how could he not?

'I don't know what's going on, Gracie,' Robbie muttered. And he too turned away to go to sleep.

Thank God. She didn't think she could talk about Theo any more. But she'd have to do something. She'd tell him what had happened and they'd think of something. They had to. Or . . . She closed her eyes.

'But I'm going round to his place,' Robbie muttered into the darkness, 'and I'm going to bloody well find out.'

CHAPTER 17

The next afternoon, Grace almost didn't dare to go round to Theo's. But she had to. As she climbed the slope of Brandon Hill she didn't feel the usual sense of anticipation, the thrill of what lay ahead. For once, her mind was skipping on to what she would say to him and the cravings of her body were still. She looked from left to right as she walked briskly up Jacob's Wells Road, checking behind her as she turned up and into Gorse Lane. She hated that. But still, the yellow house with the stained-glass door seemed to smile at her.

Theo answered the door and she slipped inside and into his arms. For a moment she couldn't breathe and then she smelt that reassuring scent of red apples and pepper that seemed to be a part of him, and she felt herself begin to relax for the first time since she'd been here yesterday.

'What is it, Grace?' He kissed the top of her head. 'Why are you so strung out? What's happened?'

She lifted her face and looked at him. 'Robbie saw you yesterday. He can't understand why you haven't been in touch. He said he'd been sending texts and trying to call you.' She waited for him to explain.

'He has, yes.' He stroked her hair.

'You didn't tell me.'

'I didn't want you to get upset. Like this,' he said.

'But what did you do?' she asked him.

'I ignored them.' He sighed. 'What could I say? I can't see you, Rob, I'm sorry. I'm busy having a relationship with –'

'Don't,' she said.

'Come and have some tea.' He took her hand and led her into the kitchen.

The room had become familiar to her in the past month: the green tiles, the cream-coloured stove, the Shaker-style kitchen cabinets and the jazzy mosaic worktop. There was a small wooden table with two chairs and Grace sat down on the one nearest the window. She looked out at the small flagged courtyard with the stone wall behind.

'When it gets warmer,' he had said the other day, 'we can sit out here in deckchairs and drink cocktails.' She had laughed and said she couldn't wait, loving the picture his words created in her mind. But how could they do any such thing? How could they even contemplate the future?

'But what if he comes here, now, this afternoon?' Grace felt a flare of panic.

'Relax. We just won't open the door.' And he smiled. It wasn't a happy smile though – the smile he used to have, when he'd come round to see them, spent evenings with them both. It was his new, hunted smile. A sort of – yes, this is awful, but this is the best I can do – sort of smile. And Grace hated it.

'Anyway . . .' He grabbed the kettle, filled it and switched it on; dropped tea bags in two cups – green tea with mint for her, Assam for him. 'All that matters is that you're here, this moment. If we didn't have that . . .'

'Oh, Theo.' Grace twisted her hands together. 'It's no good. We can't do this, can we?'

He came over to the table and sat down opposite her. 'What are you saying, Grace?'

She reached out to him, touched his mouth. 'We have to stop seeing each other,' she said softly. It was the only way. She and Robbie could move to West Sussex to be near his family as he wanted. She would have the baby he longed for. And in time she would forget Theo and the way he made her feel. She had to.

He grabbed her hand and kissed it, not taking his eyes from hers. 'Because you can't see any other way out of our situation,' he said.

'You're right. I can't.' Her voice was low and miserable. 'Can you?'

Theo held her hand now between both of his. She felt warm and enclosed. Safe. 'I've lost Robbie,' he said. 'Whatever happens now, I've lost him.'

He didn't need to say it. If she left him, he'd have lost her too. So either he lost them both or Robbie lost them both – and she was the one who had to choose between them. Which wasn't a choice at all, as far as Grace was concerned.

'But you could repair your marriage – yes? Do you think you could do that, Grace?'

She couldn't look him in the eye. 'Maybe.'

'*If* he never finds out about us,' Theo added.

'If he never finds out about us,' Grace agreed. If he found out about Theo he would never forgive her – and she wouldn't blame him.

'You could go back to where you were before? You could go back to Robbie and forget about me? You could be happy?'

Grace wasn't at all sure that she could. She watched him; his dear face, the curve of his jaw, the slant of his cheekbones. And she saw his hurt. 'We'd have to go away from here,' she said. 'But I think we could make a go of it, yes.'

'But you'd lose me.' He gripped her hand harder. 'You know that we could never be just friends again?'

Grace trembled. Yes, she knew that. But she didn't know yet how hard it would be. 'I can't see any other way,' she said. 'Theo, I just can't hurt him any more.'

Theo was quiet for a moment, his gaze fixed somewhere behind her. 'You could always come away with me,' he said at last.

'What?'

'We could leave Bristol. Set up somewhere else. You and me, Grace.'

She stared at him. 'Leave Robbie, you mean?'

'It's an option,' he said. 'Marriages break up. And it's not as if you even have any children. If you love me –'

But already she was shaking her head. It was mind-blowing; she couldn't even begin to consider it. If she began to consider it, she'd be too tempted. 'Theo, I couldn't do that to him. You and me? It would destroy him, you know that.' It

167

was unthinkable. When Robbie found out . . . It would be too awful. 'And you and I would never be able to live with ourselves afterwards. Can you imagine? We'd be so consumed with guilt we wouldn't even be able to enjoy what we have.' She was almost crying now.

He let go of her hands. 'Then go,' he said.

'But . . .'

'Go.'

Grace stumbled to her feet. So this was what it would be like without him. If she had ever known she'd feel this way, she would never have let it begin. 'When Robbie comes round . . .' she began.

'I won't open the door.'

'Thank you.'

Outside the house, Grace took a deep breath and automatically began to walk towards home. She took her usual path over Brandon Hill, walked towards College Green and realised that she was doubling back again towards Clifton. She couldn't go home yet – she just couldn't. She walked and she walked. She walked for an hour and found herself up on Bellevue Terrace above the steps that led down to Gorse Lane. She ran down to Theo's door.

He opened it. He didn't seem surprised to see her.

'I can't leave you,' she said. And she stepped back inside.

CHAPTER 18

With Robbie's help, Elisa had printed out some leaflets advertising her Spanish-speaking community group's crafts and cuisine day at the end of June. This was a regular event. It served the purpose of advertising their existence – to people who had recently moved to the area, who might feel as isolated as Elisa once had and who would like to spend a few hours a week speaking Spanish and mixing with a multinational group – and it retained their connection to their homelands. It also brought some ethnic products to Bristol and made a profit to put towards the costs of room hire.

They had started small, but apart from a few British people learning the language and interested in Spanish culture, they now had several representatives from South American countries such as Argentina and Mexico, two Cubans – herself and Theo – a couple from the Canary Islands and several Spaniards. Their native languages had differences and idiosyncrasies but generally they could all understand each other very well. The crafts and jewellery sold at the event were either made locally or at source, often using recycled materials, and the cuisine was particular to whichever area they came from.

Elisa looked at the neat pile of leaflets on the desk in front of her. She had chosen a bright shade reminiscent of mango flesh; another sign that daily she still attempted to bring more Cuban colour to her world.

But she had adapted.

For some time at the end of the 1950s her parents had talked about leaving Cuba. Many had gone before them; no one – except perhaps Duardo and his comrades fighting the revolution – could blame them. People were struggling – for food, for work, for decent habitation. Look at her father. A Fernandez-Garcia whose family had once run a thriving sugar plantation – although the sugar industry had in fact been a rollercoaster of dips and surges from all accounts – was working as a bellboy in a hotel in Havana. Elisa, of course, had not contemplated the idea of leaving at first. Naturally, she would wait for Duardo to return. She would miss her family, of course, but although Duardo had gone off to fight, he was still the driving force. She ached to see him again.

But once she knew that Duardo was lost to her, that he had been killed and was never coming back, she was forced to think again. She was still only sixteen years old. She would have to leave with her parents to wherever they decided to go. What choice did she have?

'Bristol,' her father declared one night when they were at home in their crowded apartment in Havana. 'That is where we will head for. To Bristol in England.'

'What is there in Bristol?' Elisa had cried. Oh, she knew all about the grand Hotel Bristol on San Rafael Street in Havana. But what was that to her? Her father might as well have said Timbuctoo. Bristol sounded horribly alien and lonely. And she was heartbroken. Didn't they understand she was heartbroken? She had lost the only man she would ever love – or so she had imagined at the time. She was young. She didn't want to go to England at all.

Papi's face had darkened. 'We have links with the place,' he said. 'Don't you know that Bristol was once the centre of the sugar industry in England?'

Oh, sugar, sugar, when was he going to forget about sugar? Elisa could scream. 'And why England?' she asked. Though she knew the answer to that one. Hotels again. He worked in the Hotel Inglaterra and although some would say his job was demeaning, it seemed that the hotel itself made him proud. It also transpired that over the years he had met various Englishmen travelling in Cuba and he had been impressed by them. Even Winston Churchill had stayed at the Hotel Inglaterra when he was a young journalist in 1895, so her father liked to tell. Papi had come to the conclusion that England was the place to be.

'England is a land of plenty,' he said now, thus proving her point. 'Everyone says so. It's a land of opportunities. It is a place where there are jobs. People work hard and are paid for it.' Which, Elisa had to admit, was very different from Cuba, where everyone was poor however hard they worked and got very little in return.

She thought of Duardo. So often she thought of Duardo.

'But everything will change here now, Papi,' she said. 'The rebels have been victorious. Now that Fidel Castro has gained power, he will look after us. I know it.'

Sadly her father shook his head. 'If only it were so simple, my dear,' he said. 'But you know it won't end with these recent battles for independence. It never does. The Americans will never give up. They will plague us and they will punish us. We will stay poor and we will never be free.'

Elisa didn't reply to this because she didn't know what to say. If Duardo were here, he would know. But he was gone and she had to accept that. And besides, what did it matter if she went to England if she had no chance of seeing his dark eyes again?

'What is wrong with America, though, my love?' Elisa's mother had asked her husband gently. 'That is where everyone is going, you know.' And it was true that a few of their relatives on both sides were already in Miami. Thousands of Cubans were in Miami. They had left on small boats and on rafts; many had perished, Elisa knew. America had treated their country badly, yes, Elisa had heard this from her father, but most of all from Duardo, who had given everything to Castro's revolution. But they *knew* America. It was close and it was familiar. Not so England. England was so very far away – from her hopes, from her dreams, from what might have been.

'How can you even ask?' Elisa's father had thrown his hands up in despair. 'After they took our plantation, our livelihood, our sugar?' He paused as if to mourn the loss, although in truth it had never been his personal loss for it had happened to his family years before he was even born.

'If we stay we might get it back,' Elisa put in. She had heard that Castro was now returning land once taken from Cuban plantation owners by the US when their puppets had been in government and their citizens growing rich on Cuba's sugar. Castro might not give them much, because Duardo had told her that true communism frowned on ownership and profits; land was for the good of all; no one should be so poor they could not feed their children or get health care for their sick relatives. But they might get something restored to them. A way of life. A small living.

'After they made prostitutes of our women . . .' Elisa's father continued to rail on as if she had not spoken. 'And destroyed our most beautiful city with their gambling, their drunken debauchery, their filthy goings on. Cuba has been a plaything for them, I tell you. A plaything.' His face was red. Even Elisa took a step towards him but her mother was already ahead of her.

'Don't fret, my love,' she soothed him. 'England it will be.'

Elisa shook her head. Her father had never realised how closely his views had mirrored Duardo's. If only, she thought. Though it would make no difference now. She looked out of the window at the narrow street below. Nothing seemed to have changed and yet everything had changed. She sighed. How she wished she had supported Duardo more in the days and weeks before he left her to fight. How she wished she hadn't struggled against him and tried to make him stay.

It had done no good and his last memories of her would be not of love, but of how she had let down the cause, tried to prevent him from doing what he had to do. 'But –' she began.

A stern look from her father silenced her. With Duardo by her side, Elisa had found a strength she had never had before. A strength that had enabled her to find her own voice, rather than unthinkingly accept the dictates of her family. But without him . . . perhaps she would never have that voice again.

'This is for you, Elisa,' her father said. 'In Cuba you will stay hungry.'

She knew he was right. She had known hunger while Duardo was away and it had scared her. She never wanted to feel that way again. They had all hoped the revolution would bring better things. But would it? At this moment it seemed unlikely.

And so they had begun the preparations for leaving. Elisa's father had been saving the tips from rich American and English tourists for some time. He had sold all their family heirlooms too, from back in the days when to be Spanish Cuban was a matter of prestige; he'd sold much of Elisa's mother's jewellery, some of which she'd had since she was a girl. They had enough for their passage and a bit more besides. They packed a few things and gave the rest away to the family that remained. They would travel via Spain. It was all decided, all planned. And so they said their goodbyes and began the gruelling journey to a place they knew so little of.

★

Elisa snapped herself out of her reverie. She knew that it was the writing she was doing that was bringing all this back into the forefront of her mind. Every day she would spend an hour jotting down reminiscences of her girlhood in Cuba – of places and people; of fragrances and colours. She smiled and looked again at her leaflets. This shade of orange would certainly catch the eye. A few people had volunteered to distribute them and she had also hoped to give some to Theo at the meeting yesterday, but he hadn't turned up.

Elisa frowned. Hopefully he had sorted out whatever was bothering him. She wasn't worried about him exactly; Theo was more than capable of looking after himself. But . . . She glanced out of the window. The sun was trying to shine and it promised to be a bright afternoon. Philip was at a meeting with his counsellor. And it was only three thirty. So.

Perhaps she should go round to Theo's house and take some leaflets with her? She could do with some fresh air and it would be a good excuse for her visit – he'd promised to drop some off at the hospital, the community care centre and the library, which would be a good start. The more Elisa thought about this idea, the more she liked it. Theo usually worked from home and was likely to be in once he'd finished his early-afternoon stint at the hospital. She didn't think he would object to a short interruption.

She fished her mobile phone from her black patent-leather handbag. She didn't use it often, but as Robbie had said, it was useful for calls to mobiles and so many young people nowadays didn't bother with landlines. She found Theo's number and pressed to call, but it went straight to voicemail. It would though if he was working. Should she leave a message? She decided against; she'd never enjoyed talking to machines.

Elisa scooped up her bag, picked up a small pile of the mango-coloured leaflets, placed them in a transparent plastic wallet and took them downstairs. She put on her coat, gloves and scarf – it might be spring, but it was still not what she would call warm – checked her watch and let herself out of the house. There were regular buses from the Centre, just round the corner from King Street, up to Triangle West, and from there it was simple to walk down to Gorse Lane. She might even do a bit of shopping in the Triangle first. She and Theo could have a coffee together and a chat. Perhaps she could be of more help in whatever might be troubling him.

As Elisa sat on the bus that headed up through the Old City, past the museum and art gallery and Berkeley Square and on towards the busy area of Triangle West, she let her mind drift to Philip. The counsellor had been Elisa's idea; she felt strongly that Philip could not do this alone, and she was not sure that she was the right person to help him. It had only been a few weeks. But he was doing well; really well. He seemed determined to face up to things at last, and during the past weeks she had felt a growing sense of companionship with her husband. Of course, he would never be Duardo . . .

Her shoulders drooped just slightly but immediately she straightened them again. That had been something special. A once in a lifetime thing. Philip needed her and she supposed that she needed him. They knew one another; they had familiarity and thirty years spent together on their side. She hoped – how she hoped – that he would see it through. Then, at last, she might get at least part of her life back.

Elisa got off the bus at Triangle West, lingered for a while at the shops – she was looking for a new blouse, a bright turquoise perhaps? – before glancing again at her watch. She should get on with her main purpose. She walked briskly towards Clifton Hill, the folder tucked under her arm. From Bellevue Terrace she could actually see Theo's house – it was distinctive, being painted bright yellow and she smiled approvingly – and of course she had been here before when Theo had hosted a pre-Christmas drinks evening for their group a few years ago.

She stopped short. The front door was opening. Someone was coming out; a woman. Elisa paused, curious. The door shut behind her and the woman didn't look back. Instead, she looked swiftly from left to right and then she walked fast, head down, away and out of sight. No wave. Theo hadn't stayed in the doorway.

Elisa hurried to the top of the steps so that she might have a clearer view. But she knew already that it was Grace, she could see that it was Grace, even though her stepdaughter was now at the corner. And then, once again, she was out of sight.

Elisa frowned. Something was not right. Grace was a friend of Theo's. There was no reason why she shouldn't visit him. But. The way she had been walking had told another story. The way she had left and not looked back. Even the way the door seemed to have shut so rapidly behind her. Had they argued? No, Elisa did not think so. And then she thought of the way Grace had been lately – jumpy and on edge, losing weight, a flush to her cheeks, a light in her eyes . . . How could Elisa have been so blind?

Grace was in love. And Theo also was in love. Elisa wasn't so old that she couldn't recognise the look of love – and remember.

CHAPTER 19

Elisa stayed in the same position, standing on Bellevue Terrace, as if riveted to the spot. The look of love. Oh yes, she could remember that all right. Yesterday afternoon she had begun writing about the time she returned to Cuba in 1985 after Philip had asked her to marry him. That time. It could have been such a turning point in her life, but in the event . . . Sometimes you didn't recognise turning points – or at least only in retrospect. Other times you couldn't help but see . . .

Returning to Cuba had not been an experience devoid of anxiety for Elisa. She had been worried about her aunt. It had been so long. And . . . Well. The final reason was somehow connected with Duardo and what they had experienced together back in the day. Elisa was awfully afraid that returning to Cuba would hurt . . .

Cuba 1985

It was strange, she found herself thinking on the plane, but although she had left the country over twenty years ago, Cuba was as fresh in her mind as if she had left it yesterday. As for Duardo – he had never gone away; she could see him as clearly as she ever had. His hat worn at an angle so that part of his face seemed always in shadow, the dark, liquid, serious eyes, the full lips, the warm chocolate-coloured skin. The way he'd held her when they danced that first rumba – as if he knew her already; the shape of her body, the way she would move. The first brush of his lips on hers – soft as a summer breeze, but holding the promise of a storm to come. The joy of him; the life. It seemed branded into her soul and she wasn't sure she could escape it, no matter that the life had long since left him, no matter how old she was or how much time had gone by.

The plane touched down at last – Elisa had traced the patterns of her beloved Cuba from her porthole in the sky; the jewelled blue of the Caribbean Sea around the island edging into turquoise and green by the white sand shores, and last of all, the jumble of buildings and squares that made up the city of Havana – its *centro historico*, its half-derelict buildings, its grand American boulevards. Elisa made her way into the terminal building, queuing with the tourists, almost feeling like a tourist herself in this smoky atmosphere of laid back officialdom. It had been a while. But she was home, and her feet knew where to tread.

Outside, she cut through the throng and hailed a small yellow taxi. She told the driver the address, lapsing immediately into the Cuban Spanish she had not spoken for so long – fast and casual, dropping words, forging a rapid bond with the female driver.

'You have been away a long time?' the woman asked, as they reached the outskirts of Old Havana.

'Over twenty years.' Elisa sat back in her seat and looked around her at the horses and carts, the American cars and *camellos*, the slow and dirty buses that crawled over the cobbles, at the colourful people in the streets contrasting with the general air of decay, the crumbling plaster of run-down buildings. Old Havana had suffered over the years and even if she had not heard about the problems from her family, she could see them for herself right now. Things had been bad enough when she left, but she had hoped the revolution would have led to more improvement than this . . .

'But now I am back,' she said. 'For a while.' Which would be long enough, she hoped, to spend some quality time with her family before her aunt's health declined still further, to give them the money Philip had given her, to make things better for them. It felt like making amends. 'And now it does not seem so long at all,' she told the woman driver.

The taxi pulled up close to Plaza de Armas. At first sight, the place seemed mostly unchanged. There had been some attempts at restoration, but building and social housing would not have been the government's first concern, she guessed. Making amends, she thought again. Because she had gone away and deserted them – the rest of her family, her beloved country, and yes, even the memory of her Duardo. She looked around at the familiar dilapidated buildings – blackened and peeling with broken shutters and balconies, at the lush vegetation in the square, the fountain and the ceiba tree with its bark like elephant hide. And she felt a throb of emotion deep in her breast. She swallowed hard. Time enough, she thought, for that.

Elisa had been back in Havana for twelve days when she decided to go and have a coffee in the plaza. This felt rather like a betrayal, but there were times when you needed to get away from your family and think.

Times in Cuba in 1985 were harder than she had thought they'd be; there was a worsening crisis and people were short of both food and living accommodation – crammed together in houses where one floor had to do for one family. Shops were almost empty and it seemed there was nothing to be had. The Hotel Inglaterra that had been so close to her father's heart was still going and still grand, but the Hotel Bristol had long since been abandoned and fallen into disrepair. She'd heard its former employees had lived there – perhaps they were there still – using the empty cracked rooftop swimming pool as a kitchen. Elisa had been right in her first impressions. And yet so many men, including Duardo, had given their lives for the revolution. So what price freedom? And if this was freedom – struggling to make do with no running water, little food and hardly a roof over one's head – then had it been worth it at all? There was subsistence food, yes – white rice and black beans – and Elisa could almost hear Duardo's voice reminding her of how things had been before supply shops ensured that every family had at least some food to live on. But it was not enough. Her aunt and her cousins had told her it was not enough and now she had seen the evidence with her own eyes.

Her family was one of the luckier ones. Tucked away, just off the plaza, there were only six of them in a large apartment and they were struggling, but surviving. Two of the cousins had work and so although even Elisa was shocked at how little they earned, they could at least buy food – when it was available that was. Even so, when she saw how little they had and she thought of Philip's grand house in King Street and the food they ate in England without a second thought, she had to repress a shudder. If her father had not been so determined to leave Cuba, if Duardo had not died fighting for the cause, how different Elisa's life would have been.

'Tell us about England,' her cousin Ramira's children had clamoured, their eyes wide. 'What do you eat? Where do you sleep? What do you do?'

Elisa had laughed and talked of her teaching. She had even told them about Grace. When she mentioned Philip, there was a lot of joshing and raucous laughter.

'You sly thing,' said Ramira. 'You kept that quiet. So you have found a rich Englishman, eh? Lucky Elisa. Lucky Elisa to have left when you did.'

Which made Elisa remember how unhappy she had been, how reluctant to leave. She had never felt lucky at all.

'Do you miss him?' asked Ramira's daughter who was almost grown up herself. 'Do you miss your Englishman while you are here with us?'

Elisa smiled. She knew they wanted some romantic story of love and a handsome English prince. But the truth was that she hadn't missed Philip. As soon as she was back in Cuba, it was as if she had never left. This saddened her, but was not exactly a surprise. After all, they had never pretended to be love's young dream. They had both known love before; they had married for different, more practical reasons. But Elisa did miss Grace. And she missed the peace of England; the tranquillity she had created in her own life. Here it was always so noisy – music playing, voices clamouring, always somebody wanting to be heard. 'Of course I do,' she said lightly. 'But I am happy being here with you.'

They touched her clothes and tried on the few bits of jewellery she had with her. She had brought cosmetics and a few small luxuries as gifts, and these they grabbed, fighting for the best items. Naturally they wanted to know about the food in England, so Elisa told them about the roast dinners with Philip, tactfully playing down the different types of meat available and the amount of vegetables. 'But I still cook Cuban food,' she said. 'It remains the best.' She made a kissing motion with her fingers on her lips. When the ingredients were available, that was.

The family seemed to find this both hilarious and hard to believe. 'Nothing is better than rice and beans?' they demanded. 'I bet. You have gone a bit crazy in England, I think, Elisa.'

'It's simple food,' she said, 'but it tastes good.' She longed to be able to provide them with more chicken, more vegetables, all the things they lacked. 'And you cannot drink fresh fruit juice as we do here.'

'Why not?'

'It's cold in England,' Ramira replied for her. 'Mango and papaya hate it there.' And they all laughed.

Which was lovely, Elisa thought to herself as she sipped her hot, strong coffee in the plaza. Because Cubans could stay sunny no matter what they went through, no matter how hungry or desperate they were. They saw the bright side and they stuck together. Even so . . . there was no disputing that not only was Elisa's a different life, but that her new life had made her a different person.

'You have finished, senora?' the young waitress asked her.

'Yes. I was only thinking,' she replied, not even quite sure how long she had been sitting here in the café facing the square. 'It's a long time since I lived here in Havana.'

'Oh?' The girl hid her evident surprise that Elisa was not a Spanish tourist; she probably could tell from her accent as much as anything she actually said.

'It's possible to go away,' said Elisa. 'It can be a really simple thing. But you know, it is never so easy to come back.' Because for years she had wondered how she would feel when she set foot on Cuban soil. And now she knew. The noise drove her crazy, but the place was answering something deep within. The pain of her loss was here too, but somehow it comforted her. Times were hard but the Cubans were still making music and dancing. When she thought about returning to England, she already felt homesick. There was something here that she had been missing – maybe lots of things. She had committed herself to staying in England with Philip and Grace – that was how she had been able to come back here and help her family. And so. She had no choice. And Duardo was gone. But she supposed that Cuba was still in her blood after all.

She glimpsed the young man walking across the square from the pitted grey temple-like building of El Templete, the spot where the city of San Cristobal de la Habana had first been founded. He was walking past the majestic ceiba tree and towards her. She stared at him until he was lost somewhere in the vegetation of the plaza, and then he reappeared.

Elisa caught her breath. There was something about him, the confident swing of the hips, the brown arms held loose by his side, the way he wore his hat – tilted at a roguish angle . . . that reminded her so sharply of Duardo. She reached for her bottle of water from her bag and took a desperate draught. How ridiculous she was. Look at her. A woman over forty, staring at this boy of, what, twenty or less, when she was old enough to be his mother? Even so. She thought of Philip, conscious of a sense of betrayal. There was an effortless confidence in the manner of Cuban men which still appealed to her. A certain rhythm in the way they walked – as if they might suddenly break into a salsa or a rumba. She smiled at this. Then shook her head, despairing of herself once again. Well, those days had certainly gone.

She got to her feet and left the café, her gaze not leaving the male figure as he crossed by the stone fountain. His walk was loose and easy. He wasn't in any hurry. And as he drew closer she realised that he was whistling. Mother of God. Even his whistle sounded like Duardo's.

The boy was almost level with her now and he moved aside to let her pass, touching his hat as he did so. Charming, she thought. So charming.

'*Hola*,' she said, on a whim.

'*Hola*, senora.' He didn't seem surprised at her greeting, but of course Cubans talked to strangers all the time – it was how they were. 'You are enjoying your day?' He grinned.

Oh my. Even his grin was Duardo's. Though his eyes were quite different, with much more of a teasing sparkle and less of Duardo's seriousness, and his hair too was much shorter and more curly. He was taller too and leaner. Elisa took a breath. Here I am, she thought, talking to a young man and imagining my dead lover from twenty years ago. What kind of a fool am I?

'I am,' she said. 'It is good to be back in my home country.'

'You're Cuban?' He raised an eyebrow. 'I thought so from your voice. But . . .' He looked at her. 'You dress like a European – if you don't mind me saying so, senora.' Again, he grinned.

Elisa was sure that most people would forgive him anything. She looked down at her red and yellow cotton dress. In England, she would be dressed like a parrot. Here, her dress was not short enough nor tight enough and possibly not even bright enough to pass muster. She smiled back at him. 'I left many years ago,' she admitted. 'I went to England with my family.'

'Is that right?' he said. 'I know a lot of folk who took off to America. But England – that's real exciting, huh?'

She laughed at his enthusiasm. And thought of how lonely life had been at times – especially after the death of her parents. How grey England had often seemed. How dry and devoid of the joys of home. 'It has its moments,' she said dryly. 'But I miss so much.'

He cocked his eyebrow at her again. 'Such as?'

'Such as the people,' she replied. That was easy. 'The sunshine. The rumba.' Because the rumba was Cuba; simple as that.

'Ah, the rumba.' He eyed her more curiously now.

And she supposed it had been an odd thing to say. Had she hoped this handsome young man who reminded her so much of Duardo would sweep her off her feet into a rumba? Hardly. He was friendly – but not crazy.

'And you still have family here in Havana?' he asked.

'Some.'

'From the Old Town?'

'From the Old Town.'

'That's nice.' He nodded. 'Well, enjoy your stay, senora. It was good talking to you.'

'And to you,' she said.

After he had left her, Elisa walked around the square taking in the familiar sights. On the opposite corner to El Templete was the Castillo de la Real Fuerza, dating from the sixteenth century with its broad moat and angular ramparts, and on the next corner was the old palace of the generals which had a statue of Columbus and two towering royal palms in its grand courtyard. Leaving Cuba had given her perspective though, Elisa thought now. It had made her think about her country's history, from the conquistadors to the revolution. It seemed there had always been someone trying to take over.

It had been an interesting *encuentro* with that boy. She walked slowly through the plaza, past the white statue and another knobbly-barked ceiba tree, and back towards the café. His face had stayed with her; his smile and the tilt of his hat. There was a second-hand bookstall selling magazines from the 1940s and 1950s and newspapers from the time of the revolution. Elisa paused and leafed through one of these. She didn't want to remember, but . . . She put the newspaper back down again. It's past, Elisa, she told herself. She had expected to feel some sort of displacement coming back here. But still the place felt like home.

She turned, about to make her way back to her aunt's tenement building when she heard someone say her name. It was an oddly familiar voice. She spun back around.

'Elisa,' said the man. 'It is you.'

Elisa thought about how nearly she had bumped right into Grace. It was fortuitous, perhaps, that there were two ways of approaching Gorse Lane – from Jacob's Wells Road and from the steps which led up to Bellevue Terrace. It was fortuitous, perhaps, that Elisa had not chosen to walk the other way. She clicked her tongue.

And what now? She walked down the step towards Theo's flat and rang the doorbell as long and as fiercely as she possibly could.

CHAPTER 20

There was no answer. Not a sound from inside. But Elisa knew Theo was there. He must be there. She opened the flap of the letterbox. 'Theo!' she called. 'Come to the door, will you?' Nothing. She knocked again. 'Theo?' Louder now. 'I know you are —'

'Elisa?'

She spun around. And yes, now Robbie was standing beside her, a bemused expression on his face. 'What are you doing here?' He pushed his spectacles up his nose. 'Is he in?'

'I came to deliver some of those leaflets,' she stammered. The plastic wallet was in her hand. *Oh, my Lord.* 'No, he isn't here.'

'Oh? I thought you were talking to him through the letterbox.' He put his head to one side.

Elisa thought quickly. 'No, no, I was simply calling out to see if he was in.' She laughed uncertainly and then grabbed Robbie's arm. 'Could you possibly give me a lift home, Robbie? I came by bus, but now, you know, I am not feeling so good.' And it was true that all of a sudden she felt weak-limbed, as though she might fall.

'Of course I can. Are you all right, Elisa? What is it? Do

you need to sit down?' He looked so concerned, poor love. *How could they?*

'I think I am all right, yes.' But she wasn't. She was suffering from shock. She must be.

But Robbie seemed reluctant to leave. 'You're positive he's not around though? If he's in you could sit down for a minute.' He hammered on the door. 'Theo?'

'No, he is not in,' she said firmly. She pulled at his arm. 'Can we go, my dear? I am so sorry to be a nuisance.'

'Yes, we can. Sorry.' He glanced at the plastic wallet of leaflets she was still holding. 'They've come out pretty well, haven't they? But aren't you going to put them through the letterbox or something?'

'No. Oh, yes. Yes, of course.' With Robbie's help, she did so. She heard them give a little slide and a thud as they landed on the mat inside. But all she wanted to do was get Robbie away from here. His wife was no longer inside, but she still needed him to go.

'Come on then.' He took her arm. 'Lucky I turned up when I did. The car's only just round the corner.' He pointed up Jacob's Wells Road in the direction Grace had been heading.

My goodness, Elisa thought. How had he not seen her? She had the unsettling sensation of everything moving too quickly as if life were on fast forward. Was she right about Grace and Theo? She must be; she felt it in her bones. And now she came to think about it, she could see . . .

As they got to the main road Elisa peered around, but

Grace was no longer in sight. She would have got to the bottom of the hill by now, Elisa supposed, or cut through the park. At any rate, she was safe. She leaned more heavily on Robbie's arm and tried to think what to do, what to say.

Robbie kept up a stream of casual chit chat on the way home in the car and Elisa replied as best she could, trying to sound as if nothing was wrong. Hopefully, he would simply think her tired or unwell. He would not suspect this, of that she was sure. Elisa shivered.

'Thank you, Robbie,' she said when he finally pulled up outside the house in King Street. 'I'm very grateful. And funnily enough I feel a lot better already.' Though this was certainly not true.

'No problem.' But he frowned. 'So, have you seen him lately?'

'Him?' she asked weakly.

'Theo. Seems he hasn't been around. And now he is, but he's not.' He smiled ruefully. 'If you see what I mean.'

'I do, Robbie, but I'm afraid I have no idea.' What could she say? 'He might have been away, but . . .' She let her voice trail.

'OK. Hang on a sec.' Robbie jumped out of the car and went round to open her door.

'Thank you.' Elisa swung her legs round, eased herself out and smoothed down her coat. 'Would you like to come in for some coffee, my dear?' It would be difficult, and she had no idea what to say to the poor boy, but it was instinctive to be polite.

'Thanks, but I'd better be getting home.' He was already back round the driver's side.

Elisa hesitated. 'How is Grace?' She'd known she was off colour but she still couldn't believe she hadn't recognised the signs.

'Oh, you know.' He was quiet for a moment. 'She's a bit run down. Some virus, I suppose. She'll be fine.'

Elisa nodded. How soon could she get to her? How soon could she talk to her? 'Give her my love,' she said.

'I will.' He opened the car door and climbed in, giving her a final wave.

Elisa made her way inside and flopped into her favourite armchair. It was a minute or two before she could even summon up the energy to take off her coat.

Philip was in the kitchen. There was quite an unusual smell coming from in there, but Elisa couldn't think about that now. Whatever hobby Philip chose to take up to distract him was better than him drinking.

'Are you all right, love?' he called. 'What is it?'

'Nothing,' she said. 'I'm fine.' He came to the doorway looking concerned. But she couldn't tell him – not after what he had been through with Nancy.

'A cup of tea then?' he suggested.

'Lovely.' Elisa sighed. 'And how did it go this afternoon? With Ruth?'

'Very well.'

She listened as he bustled about in the kitchen, putting on the kettle, making tea, telling her what he and his counsellor had talked about this afternoon. Though truth to tell Elisa's mind was half drifting. Back to Grace, back to the Plaza de Armas in 1985, back to the look of love.

'And I've been thinking.' He placed the tray carefully on the little table in front of her. 'I think I'm ready to talk to Grace. I think it might help.'

'Talk to Grace?' She stared at him. 'What about?'

'I want to tell her I've stopped drinking. I want to ask her forgiveness. I want us to try to start again.'

'Oh, Philip.' Elisa reached out to put a hand on his arm. 'That's good. She'll be . . .' But her mind went blank. What would Grace be? Would she be pleased? Would her head and her heart be so full of Theo that she wouldn't give her father the reaction he deserved?

'She hasn't been round here for weeks,' he said. 'And who can blame her?'

Elisa had noticed. 'Are you sure you're ready?' she asked him.

He nodded. 'I am. And it might help. I can't let her down again, Elisa, can I?'

She shook her head. No, he couldn't do that. But she must talk to Grace herself first. She mustn't waste any time. And to Theo. Someone must stop them. And as far as she could see, she was the only person who could do it.

Later, Elisa sat at her desk and closed her eyes so that she was back in the Plaza de Armas in Havana in 1985. She tried to make her breathing even and slow.

'Elisa,' he had said. 'It is you.'

She had stared at him, stupidly. All she could think was – *but you are dead*. And yet clearly he wasn't dead. Duardo – an older Duardo with lines on his face and creases around his eyes, with an older man's stature, an older man's look, an older man's frown, was standing in front of her. Older, but very much alive.

'But . . .' she stammered.

'You have been talking to my son.' He took a step towards her and he reached out his hands. There was something so familiar about the gesture that she felt her heart catch. It reminded her so sharply of her roots, of Cuba, of home. 'You have been talking about England and Cuba. About your family here in the Old Town. About sunshine,' He sucked in a breath. 'And about the rumba.'

Elisa was still taking in every detail of his face. His lips, the slight gap between his front teeth, the serious look in his eyes. Of course, she thought, his son. She had not been so foolish then. She would have known. Only . . . I thought you were dead,' she told him.

His eyes clouded. 'Elisa,' he said. And then she was in his arms and it was hard to think of anything at all.

CHAPTER 21

Havana 2012

Rosalyn was queuing at the supplies shop. Duardo had told her time and again that she did not have to do this. 'Send someone else with the *libreto*, the ration card, Mami,' he would tell her. 'Stay in the *casa*. Rest.'

You are old – that was what he was saying. And it was true that these days she felt it. She would wake in the morning confused from her dreams – always of the past and always including her Tacito; a much younger Tacito, a man who laughed and smiled and made her do the same. But as he reached out to touch her, just before he did, she would wake, and there she was in the same bed without him. No dark, curly head of hair on the pillow next to her, no warm strong arms to wrap around her and keep her safe. She was once more alone.

So Rosalyn would sigh and get up. And, oh, Mother of God in heaven, how her joints would ache – every last one of them it seemed, and her eyes would be bleary and she would remember. Tacito was dead and she was old. But she did not want to be, so she would go into the kitchen and she would prepare food – Duardo's woman hardly bothered; she was worse than useless. Sometimes her grandson's wife would work with her though and they would chat of this and that. Unlike the others, young Benita did not tell her to sit down or rest; she accepted Rosalyn as she wanted to be seen – still capable. Nevertheless, it was Benita's brisk hands that would get the rice rinsed and the chicken or pork prepared, the cassavas and yams peeled and ready, so Rosalyn hardly needed to lift a finger if she did not choose to.

The apartment they lived in now was much smarter than the one in which she'd lived with Tacito and Duardo when her son was small. That building had been so ramshackle; the balcony so unsafe she hadn't even been able to hang out her washing on it. Downstairs, an old man had lived in squalor and darkness with only his chickens for company and the stench had drifted up along with the sewage on the street to become part of every day. But Duardo had worked hard. Now, the building they lived in was still old – each layer of paint revealing its history – but it was not so damp and not so cramped either. There was running water – although the plumbing could still be unreliable at times – and a good stone sink and gas cooker in the kitchen. Compared to many, they lived well.

After Duardo had told her to rest and gone off to work to drive or tinker with that taxi of his, Rosalyn would get ready to go out and head for the supplies shop or the fruit and vegetable stall. She'd be damned if she was going to stop moving. Life had to be better than that. Which was what Tacito had said to her once a very long time ago – *life has to be better than that.*

'Shall I come with you?' Benita would ask her. She was always willing, but Rosalyn knew that she had her own chores to do.

'There's no need.' And Rosalyn would give her a reassuring smile and be on her way. This was her independence. She preferred to go alone.

She walked along the crumbling pavement past the men huddling in groups, the mangy dog lying corpse-like in the middle of the road and past the rundown buildings and tenement blocks. Just down the road on the opposite side of their apartment was a bizarre sight, though she was used to it by now – the building nothing but a slice of fancy baroque plasterwork of crumbling stucco, held up by bits of ancient decaying timber. It said a lot about their country, in Rosalyn's opinion.

Rosalyn collected their food supplies and set off for Plaza de Armas to buy vegetables and fruit. To one side of the square some boys were playing football. Rosalyn didn't trust those boys. They were not from her immediate neighbourhood and she didn't know their families. Once, Havana had been a safe city in which to wander, boys had been polite and respected their elders. Now, she saw a nasty gleam in the eye of one of the boys – a tall youth wearing a baseball hat (how she hated baseball hats; she had always discouraged Duardo, Federico and Luis from wearing them; a straw hat had been good enough for her Tacito and was good enough for the rest of their family too).

So because of the gleam and because she didn't want a

football to be shot at her legs when she was least expecting it, Rosalyn skirted the makeshift pitch and kept close to the blue shuttered coolness of the hotel Santa Isabel instead. There were tourists around of course, but tourists were safe enough. Sometimes they asked Rosalyn how to get to the Plaza de la Catedral or the Museo del Ron and she took great delight in sending them off in the wrong direction. She might be old, but there was still room for some pleasure in her life . . .

The bag was heavy on her arm. She passed the second-hand bookstall, glancing at the books and posters on sale. The image of Che Guevara was never far away. If Duardo were here he would carry the bag for her. She shifted it over to her other arm. Federico or Luis too, though her great-grandson was always at his studies and Federico . . . Well, even Benita did not always know where her husband could be found.

Duardo's woman Jaquinda never offered to go shopping for the household. Rosalyn clicked her tongue in disapproval. She had been a mistake for Duardo – a big one. Rosalyn didn't blame her son. He had come back half-dead from fighting and with his woman gone (Rosalyn skipped over this in her memory; it was convenient sometimes to be old and to forget the details of the matter) he had grabbed the first half-decent female he saw. Jaquinda had undeniably had looks – once – now she was fat. She had given him a son too, but other than that she was a lazy good for nothing who loafed around, ate them out of house and home, and who had taken her favours – though not her appetite for food, Rosalyn noted – elsewhere.

She sighed. It was humiliating for Duardo, though he pretended not to care.

Rosalyn paused by the café. She didn't bother to watch the rich tourists; they were nothing to her. But she couldn't help noticing how divided the city of Havana had become. There were tourist bars and there were local bars; there was tourist money and there was her money. El Templete on this very plaza was where their city had been founded. Tourists flocked to gawp at the fancy colonial buildings, but colonialism wasn't Cuba; it was what had been done to Cuba. By others. She looked around the square at the *castillo* and the palace and compared them to her own faded and dilapidated apartment building. That was what her son's precious revolution had done for them – pulled them out of a system where the rich were rich and the poor lived in slums, and planted them in another where they could survive, but barely.

She thought of her great-grandson Luis. They had education in Cuba – but nothing worthwhile to do with it. They could try to better themselves, like Duardo, but it seemed as if the very system was against them. Or they could be lazy like Federico, and just let it all go on by. The truth was – and this was a truth she was unable to speak to her son – it hadn't worked. Rosalyn shook her head and looked down at the basket she was carrying. She thought of the special period, the nineties, with some bitterness. No meat, no vegetables, just rice. Queues for grain, oil, salt, sugar, toothpaste and soap. Queues that snaked so far along the road that they seemed never-ending. '*Quién es ultimo?*' people would ask as they joined the queue. *Who is last?* Because that way people could mill around and maybe sit down and still know who to follow. But when you got there – who knew what might be left?

They didn't have much – though most people owned some American-made electrical appliances left over from the fifties, functioning now thanks to Russian parts. And they could get hold of even less thanks to the US embargo. Housing, electricity and water were almost free, yes. But even a humble teabag had to be shared between four people. Some people – like Rosalyn's sister, Amelia – did not survive the hardship. And Rosalyn had often wondered where it would all end.

Things were better now and Duardo earned decent money too. But for many, like Federico, there was little incentive. They pretended to work just as the government pretended to pay. And that was about it.

Rosalyn stomped off again towards the fruit and vegetable stall on the corner of Obispo Street. She wouldn't buy much; a nice watermelon perhaps or a few mangoes; she could come back for more tomorrow. She would hide them from Jaquinda until the men came in. That woman didn't deserve fresh ripe fruit. Rosalyn shifted the weight of the bag once more. She had always hoped that Duardo would find someone else. Not someone like Elisa Fernandez-Garcia, who hadn't been right for him because of who she was and what she was, and not someone like Jaquinda, who was greedy and failed to look after him properly. But the woman he deserved. The woman who could give him a relationship like the one Rosalyn had enjoyed with Tacito. That was what Rosalyn had wanted for her son. Was it too much to ask?

As Rosalyn approached the fruitseller, she saw a woman she recognised on the other side of the square, just walking round from Calle O'Reilly. It wasn't the first time she'd seen her. She was old too, though not as old as Rosalyn. She was always smiling – what was so amusing, Rosalyn had no idea – and she always nodded to Rosalyn as if she knew her. It was extremely irritating. Rosalyn braced herself. And sure enough the woman nodded to her.

'*Hola*,' she said. 'It is a good day today, I think.'

Rosalyn ignored her as she always did, barely bothering to make eye contact. A good day for what? she wondered. Perhaps the woman was not quite right in the head. There must be something wrong with her for her to smile all the time like that.

Rosalyn knew who the woman was, of course. She was the older cousin, another Fernandez-Garcia. And Rosalyn ignored her for many reasons, not least because she didn't want to be reminded of the woman's cousin Elisa, who had run away with Rosalyn's son many years ago and then run away with her family to England. She was the reason Duardo hadn't found a decent woman here in Havana – he was still mooning over that one.

Rosalyn nodded to the fruitseller, put down her basket with a small 'ah' of relief and took her time examining the goods on offer. The quality of the produce wasn't consistent. Today for example, the bananas were too black and the mangoes too hard. She poked one experimentally with her finger; shook her head in despair.

And what mother in her position, she asked herself, would have done differently when it came to Elisa Fernandez-Garcia and Duardo? No one could blame her, surely? It hadn't even been a lie; more a twist of the truth. The end, she liked to think, justified the means. Only the end had not turned out quite as she had imagined.

Rosalyn selected some fruit and paid the fruitseller. Now, she had an even heavier basket but not far to go home. She set off, recalling Duardo's earnest face when he first told her. *I have met a girl.* He had been so serious.

Rosalyn had pulled back in alarm. 'But you are so young, my son,' she said. Much too young, she thought in her heart, although she knew of course that both men and women were never too young for love.

'He will move on,' Tacito had said, soothing her later that night. 'Don't fret. Our son is not stupid. He's young, yes, but he knows what he's doing.' But Rosalyn had known even then that Duardo would not move on. He was serious then and he was still serious now. When he loved, he was like his father. He loved for ever.

'Who is she?' Rosalyn asked him a few days later. She didn't mean her first name for he had told her that already and it meant nothing to her. Elisa. Who was Elisa? What was important was – who were her family? She couldn't be from round here, for Rosalyn would know her. 'Is she one of us?'

Duardo told her Elisa's family name and Rosalyn had to

hold on to the tabletop for support. She sat down heavily, put her head in her hands. Fernandez-Garcia. She knew that name rather too well.

'Mami?' She heard the anxiety in Duardo's voice. 'What is it? Are you unwell? Should I fetch my father?'

'No,' she had said. And: '*Mi madre.*' Mother mine.

'You cannot go on seeing her.' Rosalyn had lifted her head and stared straight at him. 'It's impossible.' And then she had told him why.

Rosalyn still often heard the low and sing-song voice of her dead *abuela* in her dreams and thoughts, just as she had heard it when she was a girl. She spoke to Rosalyn often about her life on the sugar plantation in those days before she died. She told her about the mill, the *cachimbo*, how the cane was cut and how cane sugar was made into muscovado. She told her how they lived – in barracoons, hot as furnaces with almost no ventilation; with dirt floors, whitewashed on the outside and padlocked at night, which was no surprise, for there were plenty of runaway slaves. And she told her that her grandfather had escaped to the forest wanting to be a *cimarrón*, craving a freer kind of life.

'Many Africans were afraid of the shadows in the woods,' she said. 'They imagined them full of evil spirits. But not him.' And her voice was proud. 'That man was determined to escape. He didn't want to be chained to no slavery.' But he was found by the slave catchers, the mean *guajiros* who the master sent after runaways with their hunting dogs, trained to catch blacks. He was brought back to the plantation after a few days and that was when they had got together, the two of them, finding some comfort that way.

Rosalyn imagined how her grandfather had felt when he escaped to the woods. How scared had he been of the shadows? How fearful of the consequences of being caught? 'What did they do to Grandfather?' she asked. 'When they caught him?' She had never known her *abuelo* for he had died years before she was born. But she could still feel his pain.

Her grandmother's face darkened. 'Whipping,' she said. 'Enough to strip the skin, it was. Though he was lucky he weren't put in the stocks for a few days. Men were.'

When Rosalyn's mother heard *abuela* talking that way, she tried to stop her. 'She's young,' she said. 'Things are different now. She don't need to know all that.' But Rosalyn thought she did need to know. And she thought of her grandfather's skin, leathered and black as earth, torn by the whip of the overseer.

'We had herbs,' her grandmother said sagely. She put a bony brown hand to her greying head in remembrance. 'We knew how to make things better with tobacco leaves, urine, salt . . . A lot of the women used witchcraft even.' She seemed to shake that thought away.

Rosalyn had moved closer, eager to find out more.

'Your grandfather, he used to say that women were good for dreaming,' she said. 'We had to dream, we had to take ourselves away from how we were living sometimes.'

Rosalyn shivered, imagining yet again the back-breaking work, the poverty, the disease and the appalling conditions that her grandparents had lived through. She hadn't had much when she was growing up, or even once she'd moved in with Tacito, but she'd had a lot more than that. But since her days and nights in Havana, Rosalyn could identify with that need for dreaming. Sometimes it was the only way for the spirit not to be crushed.

'It wasn't all bad times, my little one,' *abuela* would continue in her sing-song voice. 'We had each other.' She began to rock slowly from side to side. 'We had our *conuco*, our little garden. We even played games, you know.'

'Games?' The young Rosalyn couldn't begin to picture that. Working those sort of hours in those conditions, how had they ever found the energy for games?

'*Tejo.*' *Abuela* smiled and explained how it was played with a cob of corn and a stone. 'Singing and dancing too,' she murmured.

Rosalyn nodded. She knew already about the makeshift instruments and the dancing. 'What did you grow in the garden?' she asked.

Her grandmother shrugged. 'Sweet potato, squash, corn, beans, taters. We traded for milk. Milk cleans you out and clears infection. We drank cane juice as it ran, straight from the press. We did our best. We was a community.' Again, she sounded proud.

And it was that pride, that dignity, that touched Rosalyn more than anything. She knew that her grandparents had started working in the fields when they were still only six years old. But not her mother. Rosalyn knew too that by the time her mother was born, slavery in Cuba had been abolished. She was lucky. If she'd been born a few years earlier she would have entered the world in the plantation's infirmary and she could have been sold off to another plantation as so many were, like animals, never to see their parents again.

Rosalyn saw a faraway misty expression in her grandmother's dark eyes as she thought back to that time. 'But bodies wore out quick,' her grandmother sighed, 'and that's the truth.'

Now that Rosalyn too was old, she did not think back to the bad times as her grandmother had done; she had never talked of them to Duardo, only Tacito. When she was buried, those times would be buried with her. But it still was the truth. Bodies wore out quick. And Rosalyn shifted the weight of the basket once more as she drew closer to home.

But she wouldn't accept that other burden, even if sometimes she had to forget what Tacito had said to her. She had done what any mother would have done. And now it was too late for anything to be done differently. Some things, she thought darkly, could not be forgiven. It was a matter of pride. Her grandmother's pride. Some people had to atone.

CHAPTER 22

Grace was still in the shower when she heard Robbie arrive home: the slam of the door; the faint, 'Hello?'

What had happened at Theo's? Had he seen him? She'd have to find out. Grace switched off the water and stepped out of the shower. She grabbed her towel, closed her eyes for a moment and thought of what had happened this afternoon. So much for good intentions. Which left them . . . where?

'I'm in the bathroom,' she called back and began to towel herself dry briskly, afraid that Robbie would come in and . . . What? Touch her? He hardly dared to these days since there was always something wrong with her. But she'd better get used to it – if she was going to do what she'd told Theo she could do and make a go of their marriage. She wanted to be able to. But could she? She hadn't been able to leave Theo today.

Grace peered into the steamy mirror. Was it written on her face? Where she had been? What she had done? She had walked and walked; she hadn't meant to go back there. But the thought of being without him . . . Even now, the thought of it made her legs buckle. Grace gripped the towel rail. How could people sustain affairs for months, years even? It was beyond her. When did an affair stop being so . . . all consuming?

Since Theo, she'd used every excuse known to woman not to make love with her husband. She'd felt cruel and she'd felt guilty and she'd gone on and done it anyway. It seemed that good intentions, loyalty and truth – all the qualities she'd held dear – had flown from the window of her life that night Theo had come round to her house. It wasn't fair and it wasn't right, but that was what love had done to her.

She was not cut out, she knew, for loving two men at the same time. And after what had happened to her mother . . . She had simply not believed it possible that she could do what her father had done. Had she thought herself above it? Stupidly imagined that she would never be tempted? And that if she were, she would exercise a hell of a lot more self-control? Look at her. It was pitiful how much she wanted Theo. It was written on her face. She was like a teenager in love and she wasn't proud of it.

'I can't do it,' she had whispered to him when he let her back into the house on Gorse Lane. 'I can't leave you.'

'I know.' He held her face and looked into her eyes.

What made him so sure? Was it because that was how it was for him too?

They had gone upstairs and made love almost frantically. And Grace didn't want to think – *as if it were to be the last time* . . . but there had been something desperate about the way they had clung to one another, the way they kissed and touched and . . . She covered her face in her hands, reliving it. Mind blowing but so terribly painful.

Grace heard Robbie moving around outside. She still loved him. She still wanted to make a go of their marriage, she just wasn't sure how. And when she thought of how close they had come this afternoon to Robbie finding out . . .

She'd spotted his car coming up the hill only a few minutes after she'd left Theo's house, which was a minor miracle considering her state of mind. She had dodged behind a tree, bent down to tie an imaginary shoelace, thinking, *if he sees me* . . . Fortunately, she was already on the other side of the street by the steps that led to Brandon Hill and the road was quite busy.

He couldn't have seen her. He would have stopped the car. He would have called out to her. Said: *Grace? What are you doing here?* She could almost hear the curiosity in his voice, sense the moment when he understood. Instead, he had driven straight past. Silently, she cursed her own weakness. When she walked away from Theo the first time – that had been her moment, her chance. She should have just kept going.

If Robbie had seen her . . . Something inside her dipped in pure panic. It would be awful. But what she felt for her husband wasn't the kind of love she'd experienced this afternoon – it never had been. It was a different kind of love. It was warm and comfortable and even exciting at times. But it had never been desperate and it had never been wild. It had never seemed inevitable.

How could she expect to respond to Robbie, when the taste of Theo's skin was still so fresh on her lips? When she could still feel the hardness of his body pressed against her? Something inside her still seemed to hold him. And no amount of showering could take that away.

Robbie was in the bedroom getting changed. He looked as if sex was the last thing on his mind.

'Good day?' She kissed him lightly on the cheek and went round to her side of the room, collecting clean clothes from her underwear drawer on the way. Waiting.

'Not specially.' Robbie frowned. 'I went round to Theo's.'

Grace tensed, although of course she knew that. She pulled on her knickers and fastened her bra. 'Was he there? Did you speak to him?' She tried to sound casual. What had happened?

'No.' He shook his head. 'But someone else was.'

Oh my God. Grace pulled on a loose cotton top and turned round to hide her face. So he *had* seen her.

'Oh?' Her voice came out in a squeak.

'I saw Elisa.'

'Elisa?' Grace heaved a sigh of relief. 'What was she doing there?' She pulled on her jeans. Then she thought – *oh, shit* – if Elisa had been around . . . What if her stepmother had spotted her? But wouldn't she have said something to Robbie? Unless . . . Grace's mind was spinning.

'Delivering leaflets apparently.' Robbie had also changed into jeans and a T-shirt. He ran his fingers through his fair hair. 'She didn't even seem to know that Theo had been away.' He shook his head, clearly baffled.

'And Theo didn't answer the door?'

He gave her a strange look. 'Well, I assumed he wasn't in,' he said. 'Even if he's blanking me for some reason I know nothing about, he wouldn't be blanking Elisa too, would he?'

Grace thought of Theo on the other side of the door at Gorse Lane. First Elisa and then Robbie. Now that Robbie knew he was around, what would Theo do? He couldn't avoid his best friend for ever. Everything was spoiled – their friendship, their easy relationship. Everything was a mess. Everything. It was a sobering thought. She twitched open the curtain and stared out towards the old warehouse. She gazed down into the water below which looked faintly ghoulish in the light of the street lamp. No answers there.

'Elisa was acting a bit strange though,' Robbie added. 'You finished up here?'

She nodded and followed him downstairs. She must start cooking supper. She must carry on acting as if everything was fine. 'In what way strange?' So she had seen her. And she hadn't said anything to Robbie. Which must mean . . . *Damn it*. Her stepmother had guessed what was going on.

'She was a bit unsteady. She asked me if I could give her a lift home.'

She wanted to get him away, Grace thought. She knew all right. So that was it. Their secret was out. And how long would it be before Elisa came round and asked Grace what the hell was going on?

CHAPTER 23

Elisa spent a troubled night. Everything that was happening with Grace seemed too close. She tried not to dwell on it and in the morning, she retreated upstairs to her laptop and her story. She wanted to write some more. She wanted to write about Duardo and the way in which she had found him again.

Havana 1985

He seemed to hold her for so long. *As if you'll never let me go*, she thought. She closed her eyes. The scent of him surprised her since it was so familiar – the faint tang of tobacco, the warmth emanating from his skin, the faintest hit of sweet mango. He held her for so long. And yet it was not long enough.

He came to his senses before she did. He gripped her upper arms and stepped back and away – which told her a lot. He dropped his hold, his hands now hanging by his sides and they stared at one another in shock. A thousand emotions flew through her mind but Elisa had no idea which one to run with.

'Duardo,' she said at last. 'How are you here? How can it be you?' To her own ears she sounded breathless, almost a naive girl once again, the girl who had first met him in the dark recesses of La Cueva.

'I live here,' he said as if she were some crazy woman. 'How are *you* here, Elisa?'

'My aunt is sick.' She couldn't look at him any more so she looked down at the grey cobbles instead. 'I came back for two weeks to . . .' She hesitated. 'Help.'

'Two weeks?' he echoed. '*Por Dios* . . .' he muttered.

Elisa heard a note in his voice she didn't understand. 'I leave tomorrow.' It was so final. But she didn't know how else to say it. She could have left, she realised, and not known he was still alive. Had her aunt known? Her cousins? They must have. And if so, why had they not told her? Elisa could guess. Best to let her be, they must have thought. It was never the right match. *She has a good life in England*. Yes, thought Elisa. Sending them money . . . Though this was unfair, of course; she should not think that way. And then she had come here talking of Philip . . . Her mind raced. Had her parents known? Years ago, when they first moved to England? At a time when she could have gone back to him? She thought not, but she couldn't be sure.

'I see.' He nodded. But she didn't think he saw at all.

'I thought you were dead,' she whispered.

Around the plaza people were going about their business as if nothing had happened. This seemed astounding to Elisa. A few were eyeing them curiously.

Duardo seemed to realise this at the same moment as she, for he took her arm and led her towards the seclusion of one of the little gardens. There was no one there bar a friendly Cuban blackbird pecking for grubs in the earth.

He let go of her arm again and eyed her gravely. 'Is that why you didn't wait for me?'

'How can you wait for someone who is dead?' But even as she said it, she realised that you could and that in fact she had.

'But as you see . . .' He spread his hands. Those dear familiar hands. 'I am very much alive.'

'But . . . Francisco,' she named the compatriot, the friend who had come to her that day, 'said that you'd been killed.' She did not understand how this could be. 'And your mother . . .'

'What about my mother?'

She saw him bristle and, miserably, she shook her head. 'Nothing.' What did it matter now?

'Did Francisco say that he had seen my body?' he asked.

'No.' Elisa could remember his exact words. *He must be dead. There was a fire.* 'But they had found your nametag,' she said. 'Everyone assumed . . .'

'We fled into the mountains,' Duardo said grimly. 'It was hard. We did almost die. But you did not wait long for me, Elisa.'

Once again, her instinct was to look away. But, no. She looked back at him and met his gaze head on. She had been young and she had been foolish, but that was who she had been. She could not change it. 'I was frightened,' she admitted. 'After you left me in Matanzas, I was hungry too. I had no food. I had no friends near me, no family. I didn't know where to turn.'

'So you ran back home to your mami?' His tone was harsh.

Elisa hated that. She stood up straighter. 'Yes. I ran back home. I was sixteen years old, Duardo. Hardly more than a child. You left me to go off to fight. I felt abandoned. What was I supposed to do?'

His lip curled. 'I was not a coward, Elisa.'

Elisa was reminded of all the rows they'd had when they had first run away together to Matanzas. They had escaped, they were together, they had what they had longed for. And yet how they had argued, hot and angrily, about Duardo going away to fight. 'No,' she said, 'you were not a coward. But you had another responsibility. You had me.'

They were silent for a moment as if reassessing that time. Elisa was still trying to take in the fact that he was alive. And Duardo . . . Well. She sneaked a glance at him. He had moved a pace or two away from her and was leaning against the knobbly grey trunk of the ceiba tree. He was a proud man, he always had been. It was in the set of his jaw, the tilt of his head. He had been too proud not to fight. And he was too proud now to give her an inch, even to try to understand how it had been for her.

'You left Cuba,' he said at last, the accusation in his voice, his eyes, the straight set of his shoulders as he took a step closer to her. 'After all we fought for.'

'My family left Cuba,' she said. 'I had no choice. I couldn't stay here alone.' And she remembered how she had pleaded with them. 'And I wasn't like you. I was never political. I was never brave. How could I have stayed here? My heart was broken. I thought you were dead.'

He seemed to soften towards her at last. 'Let us sit for a moment.' He indicated the marble bench behind them.

Obediently, she sat. 'Did you ever try to let me know that you were still alive?' she asked him.

She saw his expression change and she knew immediately what his mother would have said to him. *She has run away. She is weak. She did not love you enough. She did not wait for you, my son.* Elisa thought that she understood Rosalyn. Duardo's mother would have known all the right buttons to press to stop him from trying to contact her. It wouldn't have been easy to get a message through but Duardo could have gone to Elisa's aunt. He could have begged her for their address in England. He could have done something.

'What would have been the point?' he said slowly. 'You chose not to wait. You had left to search for a better life, even while I was fighting for independence for our countrymen and women of Cuba. Why should I try to drag you back here when you couldn't wait to be gone?'

It wasn't like that. Elisa wanted to shout it. But it wasn't just she who had been young. Duardo had fought in many battles and skirmishes and he had endured tremendous hardship for the sake of the revolution. And she admired and respected him for that. But he too had been young.

Elisa took his hand. 'It was a waste,' she said. 'I loved you so.'

His eyes darkened, but he said nothing. Even so, she thought, he had come to the plaza to find her. He had talked with his son and had thought it could be Elisa with whom his son had spoken. And he had come to find her. The thought made her heartbeat quicken.

'You are married?' she asked him, somewhat shakily.

He shook his head, looked at her long and hard. 'And you, Elisa?'

She too shook her head. But very nearly, she thought. Very soon, she would be. 'But there is a man.'

His smile flashed and then was gone. 'And there is a woman,' he said.

'Of course. You have a son.' She nodded. 'He's lovely, Duardo. So like you. That was why I spoke to him.'

He gripped her hand more tightly. 'You have children with this man?'

'No.' She thought of Grace. 'Although there is a child. His child. She depends on me.'

Duardo looked away into the distance of the plaza. 'Naturally, you will have a life,' he said. But she could hear the bitterness in his voice. 'Naturally, we will both have a life without the other after all this time.' He looked across at her. 'But what kind of a life? That is the question. What kind of a life, Elisa, eh?'

Elisa had no idea what to say to this. She didn't even dare to think about it. 'Tell me about your life,' she whispered instead.

He said nothing for a long moment. And then he

sighed – again, in a way she remembered from before. 'Will you spend the evening with me, Elisa? For old time's sake? And then I will tell you.'

Elisa thought of her aunt and her cousins. They would be expecting her to spend her last evening with them. 'Yes,' she said. It was impossible to refuse him.

'Good.' A slow smile spread across his face. 'We will eat and we will talk. And we will go to La Cueva. And perhaps we will dance the rumba – one last time, eh?'

And Elisa smiled too. She couldn't resist. Something amazing was happening to her today. She had found the love of her life, the man who she'd believed to be dead all these years. He was still here, still alive, and nothing else seemed to matter right now. 'One last time,' she said.

Elisa and Duardo went to a local bar behind La Bodeguita del Medio in La Habana Vieja some streets away from his neighbourhood. Elisa understood that Duardo wouldn't want to see anyone he knew – especially not the woman he lived with presumably – and neither did she. Her aunt had guessed who she was meeting, before she even said a word. Was it some new sparkle in her eye? She wouldn't be surprised. But she couldn't help it. He was really alive. And she was seeing him tonight. It ought to be a dream and she kept pinching herself – but it hurt, so it must be true.

'Don't be a fool, Elisa,' her aunt had said from her sick bed before she left. 'Don't jeopardise this new life you have. What do you think you are doing? Leave well alone.'

What *was* she doing? Elisa didn't much care. But she knew she had to do it. So she batted away her aunt's anxieties. 'I will do what's right, *tía*,' she said, attempting a casual tone very far from what she was really feeling. 'Don't worry.'

'And what's right? Is risking everything you have, right? Eh?'

If her aunt hadn't been so poorly, Elisa might have lost her temper then. And what was it to Aunt Beatriz anyway? What did she know of what Elisa had? Elisa was so tired of everyone trying to control her; first her parents and now her aunt, when she had come all this way to help her. 'I can make my own decisions, *tía*,' she said quietly. 'I'm not a child. I'm not going to do anything crazy. But even if I was . . . even if I was –' She broke off. Because even meeting him was crazy, for sure. 'It would be up to me.'

'Oh, lah di dah.' Her aunt pulled a face, as if she were in pain. 'No girl of my sister's is too old to be told a thing or two by her elders and betters. If it was my girl and your mother was alive, bless her, I'd expect her to do her best to stop my girl making a fool of herself . . .'

She was still talking as Elisa left the apartment, slamming the door behind her so that the walls shuddered. It had only been twenty years, but she'd forgotten how much they all *talked*.

In the café, Duardo and Elisa ordered beer and a modest *ropa vieja* with fried plantains, which was very tasty.

'So tell me,' Elisa said carefully, 'about the woman. Your woman.' She didn't like this thought, but she'd lost all right to him.

He eyed her gravely and took another mouthful of the *ropa*. He chewed slowly. 'She was around when I came back from fighting,' he said. Subtext: *You weren't*. 'She was cheerful.' He paused. 'And willing.'

Elisa raised an eyebrow. Was that all it took? 'Why didn't you marry her?' The woman had, after all, given him a son.

'Only one woman I wanted to marry.' He stopped eating, pressed a warm hand on hers.

The sudden gesture – and his words – surprised her. She was silent for a moment. Then she withdrew her hand and took another forkful of stew. 'Even when she gave birth to your son?'

'Even then.' He shook his head. 'And nothing's changed.'

'But you still live together?'

He frowned. 'She's got nowhere else to go. We manage.'

Elisa watched him. She'd always loved the seriousness of him. He wasn't like other men. Around them some of the locals were drinking rum, talking loudly, laughing at one another's jokes. The bartender was telling some story about a guy who'd been drinking in the bar the night before, the tale accompanied by loud guffaws and the occasional thump of his palm on the counter in front of him. It was good that there was a lot going on around them. No one paid any attention to Elisa and Duardo. No one was listening to their conversation.

'You don't love her?' she asked.

'Elisa.' He put his hand on hers once more. 'You know how things are in this country.' And just for a moment she heard there the layers of hurt, his feeling about the regime he had fought for. 'We slept together, we had a son, we lived together, we stayed together. I was lonely when I met her and I was less lonely for a while. Now . . .'

'Now?'

He shrugged. 'She has a lover.'

Elisa tried to take this in. The noise was still going on around her and someone had put some money in the old juke box and some strange old Spanish-style rock and roll was playing. She knew the situation Duardo described wasn't so unusual. Cuban people were fairly promiscuous by European standards. They also tended to live together for longer – even when they had stopped having a sexual relationship. Sometimes – the housing situation being what it was – they had no choice.

'Do you mind?' she asked him. 'Do you still love her?' Because he hadn't answered this question yet. Perhaps she had no right to ask him these things, but she so desperately wanted to know.

'She's the mother of my son.' Duardo pushed his empty bowl away, 'but she can do as she likes. Sometimes she cooks for us – although my mother does mostly. Jaquinda cleans, when she feels like it. She's a good mother to our son. She's not a bad woman, Elisa.'

'No.' Jaquinda . . . Of course she wouldn't be a bad woman, not if Duardo cared for her even a little. Elisa sat back in her chair, let the sounds of the café resonate around her. He didn't mind then that she had a lover. Perhaps he had even driven her to it, or perhaps he too had strayed and was straying even now. But he still hadn't quite answered Elisa's second question. She waited.

'Not in the way you mean,' he said heavily. 'I never did love her. Not in the way you mean.'

And Elisa thought that she should have been glad to hear this. But she felt sorry for the woman who had been second best just as Philip had been. And she didn't want Duardo to be unhappy . . . So she wasn't glad. She pushed her half-eaten *ropa vieja* to one side. Besides, what could Elisa offer him now?

They left the rowdy bar soon afterwards and strolled side by side, close but not touching, towards the *malecón*. Their old stomping ground, thought Elisa. The place where they had fallen in love. They passed an almost empty shop window displaying not much more than one of the usual posters of Fidel Castro, and Elisa felt Duardo pause. She realised that he was looking, not at the poster, but at a bust of the revolutionary poet and philosopher José Martí, labelled with a line of his poetry: *Our wine is bitter, but it is our wine.*

She let out a small sigh. Duardo said nothing, but he gripped her arm more tightly as they walked on to the *malecón*, and towards the pale stones of the Castillo de San Salvador de la Punta, listening to the musicians who busked here, pausing to watch the occasional evening fisherman trying his luck. There were other couples too, walking hand in hand or sitting on the low wall staring out into the Bay of Havana with the city behind, for this was a popular spot for romance. Elisa glanced over at the grand buildings she'd hardly noticed as a child. Now, their decorative façades had faded: pink, yellow and grey pillars slowly crumbling in the face of the sun, the salt air, the wind. Elisa and Duardo moved swiftly away from the wall, along with the other promenaders, because the wind was beginning to whip up, catching at Elisa's dark hair, sending the first wave crashing over the sea wall and on to the wide promenade.

'My grandmother would have said that Yemayá is angry,' Duardo said wryly as they looked out to sea, keeping their distance this time. The ocean was dark and grey-green in the evening light, the tide bucking like the back of some prehistoric animal.

'Yemayá?' Elisa watched the white waves curling, the spume flying up into the evening air. She held her hair away from her face with her hand. As a child she'd loved it when there was a storm in Havana. She and her friends had always wanted to come down to the *malecón* to taunt the sea and run away from the rising tide before they got soaked to the skin.

'The sea goddess.' He smiled and turned to her, touching her windblown hair.

'Ah, Santería.' This religion, emanating originally from an African faith, was, for some people, an important part of their national identity– and over the years it had blended almost seamlessly with Roman Catholicism. Elisa had always known of the rituals – the music, the flowers, the offerings but her family had been Catholic through and through. She glanced at Duardo. 'Do you . . . ?'

He shook his head. 'But I know that the lady Yemayá wears

blue and that like most women she is capable of great sweet-ness and great anger.'

'Hmm.' Nothing new there then. Elisa wondered again about the woman he lived with, Jaquinda. Was she capable of sweetness and of anger? And what would she say if she could see them together now?

Duardo's mood seemed to have lightened since they left the café and he continued to chat, mostly about his work, his family and his ambitions. He told her about the car he drove, how Francisco had let him have it for a low price when he left the country, how Duardo had worked on it until he got it running again, using some ingenious means, a bit of Russian machinery and a new foreign motor.

'So you have a car?' she teased.

'Not just any old car. An American car.' And he told her about his plans to get into the tourist industry, because that was the place to be in order to earn the best money, money that didn't always have to be declared and which couldn't be taken away. 'I will start my own business,' he said proudly. 'When I get the chance.'

'With your son?' Elisa thought of the young man she'd met in the Plaza de Armas who had seemed not to have a care in the world. He had reminded her of Duardo and yet he was so very different.

Duardo let out a snort of derision. 'My son isn't interested in working as a driver.'

'Oh?' Though she wasn't surprised.

'He plays in a band of musicians – when work is available.

Mainly though, he does nothing. He is good at that, you know.'

Elisa smiled. She knew Cuba. She could imagine.

'He is lazy,' Duardo went on, 'but he will have sons too. And then we will see . . .'

Elisa believed that Duardo would do what he said. He had fought for this life and he was going to make the best of it.

They were walking along the *caleta*; the beach where the *habaneros* flocked on Sundays to play beach games, swim, socialise and drink rum, though it was almost deserted now. She remembered how they had come here as young lovers; it was a place where they could be relatively anonymous. It struck Elisa that throughout their relationship they had been looking for places where they could remain anonymous. Perhaps in a way even this had bonded them and set them apart.

She waited for him to ask her about Philip. But he didn't. Instead, they headed away from the *malecón*, past San Lazaro and into the backstreets again, passing shabby bars and lodgings, making their way to La Cueva. It would bring back painful memories, but Elisa didn't want the evening to end.

They arrived almost before she knew it. They stepped inside and Elisa was immediately transported back to when she was fifteen years old and had come here for the first time. The walls were still painted red and black, a band was playing – a guitarist wearing a cream linen suit with a gardenia in his buttonhole, drummers and some percussionists – and the dance floor was already heaving. The atmosphere was loud, hot and electric; the place smelt of smoke, of rum and of body heat.

Duardo pushed through to the bar to buy beer and they managed to find a table in the corner. When they spoke to one another they had to lean closer in order to make themselves heard above the music. But mostly they just sat back, watched the dancing, looked at one another and smiled. The memories were almost overwhelming.

At some point – Elisa wasn't sure when – Duardo took hold of her hand and showed no sign of letting it go. Elisa did nothing to stop him. She liked the feel of it, she always had. Philip never held her hand; he put out the crook of his arm, wordlessly inviting her to tuck her arm in his, which she invariably did. It was rather sweet and old-fashioned and anyway, she wasn't sure she wanted to hold Philip's hand, which was pale, soft and slightly moist to the touch; the hand of a man who probably hadn't done a day's manual work in his life. Duardo's hand was nothing like that; how could it be? It was dry, firm and calloused; the hand of a man who had dug land, who had fought in the revolution and lived in the mountains and who had tinkered with car engines for hours at a time. It was the hand of a man so different to Philip – the man she was going to marry – that she couldn't quite accept the incongruity. It was a hand that felt so familiar and right.

Later, after the colourful energy of the salsa, the lights dimmed and the drumming began from the three conga players. Elisa caught her breath. It was the rumba. Time was when they had played on *cajones*, she thought, just wooden boxes.

Rumba was the recreation of humble people back in the day; people who owned very little – but what they did own could be used as percussion: a wooden drawer played with spoons perhaps, the surface of a table, a bottle, a pair of sticks, even the wall of the house. It sounded random, but in Elisa's experience, it wasn't. She'd heard these ready-made instruments many times when she was a child and they produced an astounding variety of timbres and pitches, each seeming to fill a clearly defined rhythmic role.

She watched the musicians taking centre stage now. Traditional rumba was still all percussion; the guitarist with the gardenia in his buttonhole had taken a break. Rumba was about the rhythm. She began to tap her foot; it was instinctive. The *diana* began – a kind of chant from one of the singers in a nasal timbre, picking up the pitch from the third drum, the *quinto*. The *diana* was just meaningless syllables really, nothing you could understand. Even so, it was hypnotic and it began to seep into her. The percussion joined in – the harsh dry sound of the *guagua*, a hollowed-out piece of bamboo, the grainy shake of the maracas – the rhythm of the dry seeds – on the main beat, the metallic *marugas* worn on the wrists of the drummer of the *quinto*, the bright click of the wooden claves interlocking with the pace and timing of the *guagua*. The melody began – sinuous and inviting.

Duardo got to his feet as she had known he would. He held out his hand. 'Will you dance, Elisa?' he said.

As soon as she was up and facing him, Elisa let herself begin to absorb the music; she let the rhythm come in and take her.

She bent slightly at the knee, relaxed her shoulders and took her first few delicate steps, her body trembling. They moved in time, side to side, not touching at first, placing their feet and shifting their weight, hips swaying, each one absorbing the tempo of the song, each one silently watching the other. Two more singers joined in with the first refrain in an effortless harmony, raising the melody. And once again, Duardo held out his hand, as brown as the earth and as grounded. Elisa lifted hers to meet it like a wave; his other hand rested on her back, he pulled her closer into him and now, the dance had really begun.

The lead singer seemed to be improvising; the lyrics passed over Elisa as if they were part of a dream; the beat of the drums penetrated her being and became a part of her, pulsing inside. The rumba seemed to meld the cultures of Cuba together, or so Elisa had often thought. Here, Spanish Cuban and African Cuban were as one forming a new cultural and common identity. She and Duardo had not danced together for twenty years and yet his body knew her body and her body knew his, and she knew where and when to turn, to twist, to bend, to spin. He leaned into her and back; he pulled her closer and away. He explored, she denied; he supported her, she leant on him. They paused, they placed; they took, they gave. And once again the flame of the rumba was possessing her; the dance was setting her free.

Duardo's hand moved down to the small of her back; she felt the press of his fingertips into her spine. Then his hands were on her shoulders; the brush of his palm on her neck. His legs kicked in the *vacunao* as he tried to catch her; she spun, bringing her skirts together in the traditional gesture of protection, as if she were whipping the sexual energy away from her body. As if . . . The rhythm intensified, the heat built inside her, Duardo's eyes grew darker and they pressed together, their bodies slick with sweat and the sensual heat of the dance. He spun her round, he seemed to let her fall, he caught her and held her head cradled in his hand, his fingers caressing the nape of her neck. Elisa stared up at him into dark, glittering eyes, hardly able to breathe. And the rumba broke.

They stayed in La Cueva drinking beer and *canchanchara* until the small hours. The crowd on the dance floor had thinned by then, the guitarist was back and the tempo of the music was seductive and slow. The harmonies of the rumba were still lingering in Elisa's head just like Duardo's touch on her skin. Drinks had been spilled on the wooden floor and heels and soles were sticky with deposits of rum and fresh fruit juice. The lights were low, a fug of smoke hung in the room, a few men sat or slumped by the bar, half-empty glasses beside them. In the far corners of La Cueva where it was darkest, a few couples were wrapped in each other's arms, oblivious to the people around them. Elisa felt it too, that old throb of excitement and sensuality that came from the music, from the dance, from Duardo. They were dancing again. He held her close now, her body cleaved to his; there was no distance between them; it was as if they were dancing as one body, or maybe one soul. And Elisa felt as if all her senses were on fire.

A woman came on stage – a black woman whose cinnamon-coloured eyes seemed older than her years. She wore a long dress shimmering with silver sequins; her arms were like polished ebony, her hips undulated in time to the music. Elisa recognised the musical introduction; the melody was familiar. It was '*Noche de Ronda*', a song about the moon and a night watcher, about a man waiting for his woman to return. The singer began, soft and slow, singing with genuine soul as if she were singing not for the last people left in La Cueva that night but for herself. There was no sentimentality in the way she sang, but her voice was mellow and oily and the lyrics seemed to sink into Elisa's head.

She looked at Duardo and she could see what he was thinking.

'Let's go,' he murmured in her ear. 'It's late. There are no more *cantos*.'

No more songs? But she thought she understood him. Reluctantly, she drew away from his side, went to fetch her wrap.

Outside La Cueva, he turned to her. She thought he would kiss her – how could he not kiss her when she felt as if they had made love through the dance already? But he did not. Instead, he held her face between his two hands as if it were all he wanted. His dark eyes seemed to be slowly drinking her in. Elisa held on to his shoulders, felt the moist heat of his skin burning through the cotton shirt under her fingers.

'I must have you, Elisa,' he said. '*Por Dios* . . . I must make love to you. *Te quiero*.'

Her body seemed to turn to water. *He wanted her.* 'But . . .' They had nowhere to go. This was all she could think – that they had nowhere to go.

'But?' He tilted her chin. He wouldn't allow her to stop looking at him.

'Yes,' she said. Because she wanted it too. She couldn't think about her life in England – not at this moment. All she could think of was Havana, Duardo and the seduction of the rumba. 'But where?'

'I know a place.' He turned and grabbed her hand. 'Come with me. It is where I work.'

'Where you work?' A garage? It was a bit of a come down after the atmosphere of La Cueva.

He shrugged. '*Cuba e Cuba,*' he said.

She smiled. It was a common catchphrase of the Cuban people. Cuba is Cuba. Yes, and it always would be. It was ambiguous and a little crazy and nothing was easy. But . . . They hurried along the backstreets and at last arrived at a run-down shack in a yard. It was *madrugada*, that special time between midnight and six a.m. And Cuba was Cuba. It might be a bit of a come down but Elisa hardly hesitated. She'd go with him anywhere. She'd trust him with her life.

Duardo groped in his pocket for a key and opened the door of the building. 'Come.' He stepped inside, but Elisa stopped in the doorway. She'd been right. It was a garage. An American car – she couldn't make out the colour or the type – took up almost every inch of available space.

'Where?' she asked him. Was he crazy? Probably, but so

was she. He could almost have taken her there and then in La Cueva and she didn't think she would have stopped him. He'd always had that effect on her since the very first time he'd stood in front of her, since the first time he held out his hand and asked her to dance.

He unlocked the car and gave her a little nod. She remembered that nod from before. 'In here, Elisa,' he said. 'It's the only place. A good place.'

Oh, my. But she laughed and climbed in to the back of the car. The interior smelt of tobacco and old leather and was surprisingly comfortable — more comfortable than the bed she'd been sleeping in at her aunt's place. 'Ah.' She leaned back and arched her eyebrows at him as he climbed in beside her. She felt sixteen again.

He put an arm around her, gently stroked back her hair. '*Besa me, mi amor,*' he said. And at last, he kissed her. The soft brush of his lips on hers. Moving away. Moving back. Harder now, more demanding. It was like the dance itself. It felt good. It felt very right. Elisa wrapped her arms around his neck and pulled him closer. She could hardly believe it, but it felt just like it always had before.

'Duardo,' she breathed. She kissed his neck, twined her fingers in his soft, African hair, breathed in the hot, damp scent of him. Now, she really had come home.

CHAPTER 24

Havana 1985

Later they slept, right there on the back seat of the car, his jacket and an old blanket creating a makeshift pillow that they shared. At least Duardo slept. Elisa felt as though she'd been awake all night, thinking.

As an early dawn light was creeping through the cracks round the door, she did eventually drift off into a fitful doze – and woke to find him staring down at her.

'Elisa,' he said softly and she turned to him again as he pulled her towards him, her dark hair falling on to his chest.

They had breakfast in a small local café an hour or so later. 'What will you do, Elisa?' Duardo asked her as they drank their coffee. He seemed as serious as he had ever been.

'What do you mean?' What could she do? She had to go back to England. She had a return ticket. And there was Philip and the promise she had made to him. Elisa dipped the corner of her bread into a pool of guava purée. Duardo was like a fantasy. This whole situation couldn't be real, and yet it was. She had slept with him in the back of his car and they had made love – not once, but twice. She still loved him, she realised. It was as she had thought – nothing had changed.

'Will you stay here with me in Havana? That is what I am asking you. Please, Elisa? *Por favor?*'

She had been awake half the night, lying twisted against him in the back of his car, with only this thought on her mind. Could it still be possible? She couldn't see how. She sighed. 'I would if I could,' she said. If she had saved her own money to come here, if she were not beholden to Philip, if she had not made him a solemn promise to come back and marry him. All these were very big 'ifs'.

'Why can't you? What could stop you?' He played with the fingers of her free hand. He was gentle but she could still feel the brooding strength of him, that seriousness of intent. She had almost forgotten about that, during those years in England. It was that intensity of his that had brought him to her for their first rumba and that same seriousness of intent which had taken him off to fight in the revolution. It was that intensity which had made her first fall in love. And which made him impossible to forget.

'Duardo,' she began, 'you're not free. Neither of us are free.'

'We are more free than most,' he said.

He had always been good with words, especially words about freedom. But Elisa was older now and had become practical. Words must have a meaning, a real meaning. 'What about the woman who lives with you?' she asked him. 'What about the mother of your son?'

'I told you.' He held her hand more fiercely now. 'She has a lover. She doesn't care for me.'

'Yes.' Gently, Elisa extricated her hand. She couldn't think straight when he was touching her. 'But she lives with you. Where would she go?'

He stared at her. 'I would fix that.'

'How?'

'I don't know. Not yet.' She saw the frustration in his eyes. 'But I would do it, Elisa. I would do it and we could marry.' His eyes burned. 'Imagine,' he whispered.

For a moment, she did. She saw them sleeping together and eating together, making a life together at last. But then she saw Duardo forcing Federico's mother out of the house. She saw Federico hating her for this. She saw Duardo's pain. And she saw his mother, Rosalyn. 'What about your mother?' she asked him.

He was taken aback. 'Where I am, my mother is too. Naturally,' he said. 'I must look after her now.'

'And how do you think she would like it?' Elisa hated to say this but she had to make him see. 'If you and I were living together? If her family had to go through all that disruption? How fair would it be to her?'

'She would accept it.' But she saw the truth behind his words. He was remembering just how much his mother had always opposed their match and the reasons why. He was remembering how they had been forced to run away together when his father had been alive and Duardo had been young and headstrong with no family responsibilities of his own.

Now he must look after his mother, as he had said. Now he had a son, and a woman whom he was responsible for too – however she behaved and however little she loved him.

'It's too late, Duardo.' Elisa said this, though her heart was screaming the opposite. If only, she thought, if only it were possible. If only it were not too late.

'How can it be too late? It's never too late. You're wrong.' His voice grew fierce. 'I can make it work, Elisa. I can make it right.'

'And there's something else.' Slowly, she stirred her coffee although it had already gone cold.

'Something else?' She saw him waver.

'There's a man in England,' she told him. 'I told you. He's given me the money to come here to see my aunt before she dies, the money to help the family too. Remember that I told you she was ill – that's why I came back to Havana.'

'Who is he?' he growled.

'His name's Philip.'

'And do you love him?' He seemed hardly able to utter the words.

'Not in the way you mean,' she said quickly. Though she was fond of Philip and grateful. Neither emotion could compare to the way she'd felt in the back of Duardo's Chevrolet last night or the way she'd felt when they danced the rumba. But until last night she had considered it enough, she reminded herself.

He spread his hands. 'Then, why?'

'I made him a promise.' She picked up her cup and forced

herself to take a sip. She was determined not to let Duardo see her pain; she was determined not to cry. If she cried, she thought, she'd be lost.

'A promise to another man,' he said. 'What is that to me?' He thumped his fist hard on the table. She winced. 'Once, I came first in your life.'

You still do. You are everything. But she didn't say it. 'I couldn't hurt Philip like that. It wouldn't be fair.' She looked down. She couldn't keep looking at him. If she kept looking at him, he'd make her change her mind, she knew it. And there was a part of her that wanted that so much. 'Just as you can't hurt those who are close to you.'

'A promise . . .' He leaned back in his chair now, looking up to the heavens as if this was impossible. 'What is a promise to me? What about what we promised each other, Elisa? What about what you promised me?'

Elisa didn't want to think about those promises. 'I've told him I'll marry him,' she said. She held herself tense waiting for the explosion.

But he only laughed, harshly and without humour. 'Because he has money?' he asked.

She met his gaze. 'For many reasons,' she said. 'Because he's lonely and so am I. Because I've grown fond of him. And because of Grace.'

'Grace?'

'His daughter.'

'Ah.' His brow furrowed. 'The one who depends on you.'

'Yes.' Elisa remembered Grace's face the day she left, the

expression in her grey eyes. 'You will come back?' she had asked. The poor girl had lost so much after all; she must think that wherever she loved she risked losing all over again. 'I will come back,' Elisa had reassured her. 'Don't worry, Grace.' And she had held out her arms to the girl who would be her stepdaughter.

'So you are leaving me again?' For a moment his eyes searched hers. And then he leaned further away from her. 'You are leaving me for a girl who is not your daughter and to marry a man you do not love?'

Put like that it sounded crazy indeed. 'I don't feel that I have any choice,' she said. 'Can't you see, Duardo? There's so much against us. How can we –'

'There has always been so much against us, Elisa.' He watched her. 'But the question is – is it too much for love to overcome?'

She couldn't answer him. She felt as if she were in an impossible situation. And there was no right answer. Because she and Duardo were not living in a vacuum. There were other people, other situations to think of. How could they be so selfish to just think of love? What was the right thing to do? She wished she knew. 'I'm sorry,' she whispered.

'What are you sorry for?' He got to his feet and shook his head. 'Are you sorry for what has happened between us?'

Miserably, she shook her head. She could never be sorry for that.

'Are you sorry for leaving Cuba before? Are you sorry for leaving now?'

Elisa gritted her teeth. All she wanted was to fling herself into his arms. To say – yes, we can do it. We can overcome the obstacles. We can be together. Love can conquer all.

'I hoped I had got over you, Elisa,' he said, 'and then when I saw you, I knew I never had.'

She nodded. 'I felt the same.'

'I waited to feel different from the man I once was – when we talked, when we danced, when we made love.' He paused. Elisa was silent. He bent his head close to hers. 'But there it is. My feelings never changed, you see.' And there was so much pain in his voice, such a tenderness in his eyes that she began to wonder. Could she walk away?

'Mine neither,' she said. 'Mine neither.'

'Then . . . ?'

Elisa grabbed his hand. 'I would never have left, Duardo,' she said, 'if your mother hadn't told me you were dead. I swear it.'

'My mother? What do you mean? I thought it was Francisco who came to you?'

Elisa had not meant to say this; it had slipped out in the heat of the moment. The last thing she'd intended was to cause more trouble after all these years. But she hated him thinking she had not waited when there was any doubt about his survival. 'I would have waited,' she said, 'but your mother was certain. She told me so. She told me to make a new life without you. To forget you. She said that she felt your death deep within her. That there was no doubt . . .' Her voice trailed away because of the way he was looking at her. Not with love any longer, but in fury.

'How dare you,' he said. 'How dare you try to blame her?'

'But –'

'I will not hear it.' He shook his head. 'I will not stay and listen to you insult her. How can you do that? She is old and she has only me to defend her.'

'Duardo. I didn't –' Insult her, she was going to say. But one glance at his face stopped her.

'If you could have admitted that you were wrong,' he said slowly. 'If you could have shown that now you have more courage . . .' He didn't finish what he was going to say.

It was her last chance, she knew it. Elisa longed to shout – but I do. If you are willing, then so am I. But he looked so cold and forbidding, that she found she could not. She couldn't think of the love they shared. She could only think of Rosalyn's hatred. Philip waiting in England, that poor sad man. And Grace, pretending to be tough, but really so vulnerable; the girl who had lost her own mother, whom Elisa now thought of as her own. The girl who was depending on her to return.

She had been on the brink of turning her back on the people she loved in Bristol. She had wanted Duardo to persuade her that love really could conquer all, that all those practical obstacles could be overcome if they faced them together. But in the end, she had watched him walk away.

Later that day at the airport, part of her was still watching for him, still half hoping that he would appear at the last moment, to stop her from leaving. That he would sweep her objections aside and take her back to where she belonged. But he never did. He would never even know how much she had wanted it.

Elisa saved the document and shut down the laptop. Enough. She knew what she had to do now. She had to go to Grace. She must talk to her. She had to stop this madness, before it was too late.

CHAPTER 25

When Grace opened her front door to let out one of her rare early-afternoon clients, she saw Elisa standing by the steps to the quay, holding on to the railings. She looked as though she had been there some time.

'Do not shut that door,' Elisa said sternly, so that the client, still in the process of saying goodbye, looked round in surprise.

'Thank you.' Grace waved her off. She turned to face her stepmother. 'Hello, Elisa. Why would I?' Elisa had left two messages on the answerphone earlier, both asking when it would be convenient for her to call round.

'Because you don't seem to want to talk to me, that's why.'

'Don't be silly. Come on in.' There was no point in discussing it on the doorstep. Grace went back into the cottage. She pulled off her white cotton tunic and changed back into jeans and a shirt. 'It's been a busy morning,' she said. Which was sort of true. She'd had two clients and she'd been doing a lot of thinking. About Robbie, about Theo and yes, about Elisa too.

Elisa grunted as she followed her inside. They exchanged their usual kiss on both cheeks and a quick hug.

'Anyway, why wouldn't I want to talk to you?' Grace had come to the conclusion that Elisa couldn't possibly know about her and Theo – at least, she couldn't know for sure.

Elisa's eyes narrowed. 'You're not avoiding me then?'

'Course not.' Although actually Grace would quite like to avoid everyone today – her father certainly, Elisa, Robbie, even Theo. He hadn't contacted her. She knew he'd be waiting for her to make the next move.

Elisa wagged a finger at her. 'You can't protect anyone by putting yourself in a bubble,' she said. As always, horribly near the truth.

Grace shrugged. She led the way into the living room. 'It's not a bubble exactly,' she said, 'I just want some time to myself.' She wasn't in the mood for this, she realised. Elisa was going to speak out and Grace didn't want confrontation. It was her problem and she'd deal with it her way. She was at least trying to think things through. And perhaps Theo was doing the same.

'I know about Theo,' Elisa said without further preamble, 'so you need not pretend with me.'

'What about him?' So she thought she knew. Still, Grace was determined not to make it easy for her.

'I know that you're seeing him.'

'Seeing him?'

'Grace.' Elisa closed her eyes as if gathering strength and then opened them again. 'I know that you are in love with him.'

Grace looked across at her, this small, indomitable woman who had become so much a part of her life. She couldn't lie to her. What point would there be? 'Yes,' she said. 'I know it sounds crazy, but –'

'It *is* crazy.' Elisa slammed her palm on to the wooden table.

Grace flinched. She had never seen her so cross. Her small frame was rigid with anger and her dark eyes flared.

'There is no doubt of that,' she added for good measure.

'It just happened, Elisa.' Grace sat down at the table but Elisa did not sit down opposite her as she had expected her to. 'I didn't intend it to happen. I wasn't looking for it.'

'*It just happened*,' mocked Elisa. 'In my experience, things like that do not just *happen*.'

Grace frowned. What did she know about it? What could anyone know?

'And now what?' Elisa demanded. 'What will you do now that this thing has . . . happened?'

'I don't know.'

'What about Robbie, for a start?' Elisa paced over to the window and stared out. 'What about your life together, eh? What about your husband?' She turned back to face her. 'Have you thought of that?'

'Of course I've thought of that.' Grace fought for control. She didn't need this. She felt bad enough about Robbie as it was. Didn't Elisa know that? If not, she bloody well should do. 'I never meant to hurt Robbie,' she said. 'We never meant to hurt him.' But that was how things started. You didn't always look forward to the consequences.

'Theo is Robbie's best friend.' Elisa paced back to the table.

She was glowering at Grace with undisguised hostility now and Grace was shocked.

'I know.' But shouldn't Elisa be on her side? Grace knew she hadn't been the easiest of teenagers. She'd had the occasional unsuitable boyfriend and she'd been grounded after flunking her exams. But whatever she'd done wrong, Elisa had been the one who had talked to her reasonably and calmly as if she were an adult, not a child. Elisa had always defended her to teachers and to her father. She had never lost her temper with Grace before.

'Robbie will be devastated,' Elisa said. At last she sank on to the chair opposite Grace. She shook her head sadly. 'How could you?'

'Do you think we don't know that?' Did her stepmother imagine she was taking this lightly? Did she really know Grace so little?

'Oh, it's "we" is it? You and Theo?' She leaned closer towards her. Her dark eyes betrayed how angry she was. 'How sweet. How cosy.' And she took a deep breath. 'You're a fool, Grace. You have so much. How can you even think about throwing it all away?'

Grace snapped. 'What gives you the right to come round here yelling at me?' She got to her feet. She was fed up with being under fire. Robbie had been in a 'no sex bad mood' earlier, still nothing from Theo and now this.

'Someone has to.'

'Why you? What do you know about it?' she shot back at her. 'Has this ever happened to you?

'What do you mean by that?' Elisa's voice was dangerously quiet.

Grace wasn't exactly sure what she did mean. But she sensed she'd hit a raw nerve. 'Was it this man you knew before my father came along? Didn't he love you enough? Did he play around – is that it?' She remembered how Elisa had looked when she'd talked about the baby she'd lost. It had almost seemed . . . 'Did you risk throwing it all away?' She was breathless now. 'Was that it?'

Her stepmother stared back at her. 'No, Grace,' she said, 'I didn't.' She looked down at the table now, her shoulders bowed.

For a moment, Grace felt sorry for her. But she'd gone too far; they'd both gone too far. 'I don't want to know,' she said. 'I really don't care. Whatever happened to you, you have no right to come round here acting all holier than thou.' She waited for her stepmother to reply but she didn't say a word. 'You have no idea what's going on between me and Theo,' she continued. 'But whatever your other failings, I would have at least credited you with a bit more bloody imagination . . .' Grace's words trailed away. She was breathing heavily. And there was more. Some old acrid resentment was curdling inside her and she couldn't stop it – not now. All the stresses and strains of the past weeks seemed to be rising to the surface and Elisa was here in the firing line.

'My other failings?' Elisa spoke quietly. Her hands were folded in her lap. She looked up at her. 'What other failings, Grace?'

'Your need to control.' Grace met her steady gaze head on. She leant on the back of the chair. She felt as if she were trying an argument out for size. And yes, it fitted. 'Your need to organise everything, to fix everything, to make us aware of just how broken we were and how proficient you were at repairing us.' The words sounded good, sounded right.

Elisa had sunk a bit lower in her chair and she was looking at Grace as if spellbound. She didn't speak, didn't attempt to defend herself.

Grace knew that she must stop now. It was unfair; Elisa didn't deserve it. Grace's words had been cruel and unnecessary. She didn't even know what dark well they'd risen up from. But all she could think of was her mother, her mother run down and dying out there in the road that Grace had to keep crossing and walking down every time she went back to King Street; her father's voice: 'I pushed her into this.' The woman, the scent of lily of the valley. The brittle clip of her high heels on the pavement. How could he have done it? How had he loved another woman? How had he had an affair and how could he ever have allowed Elisa to replace her? The fact that Grace too was having an affair just seemed to make her more angry, more resentful towards her stepmother. It didn't make sense, but nothing made sense. She wasn't even sure why she was behaving this way. Was she losing her mind?

'I had no idea that you felt like that,' Elisa said stiffly. 'I've only ever wanted to advise you, to help you –'

'You're not my mother,' Grace broke in. She hadn't finished yet, it seemed. 'You never will be. And I don't need your advice. You have no right to tell me how to run my life. No right at all.' But she couldn't look at Elisa now. She couldn't see her crumpled and old like this. Grace knew that she had gone too far. She couldn't believe what she had said to her.

'I see.' Slowly, Elisa got to her feet and Grace heard her walking along the hallway, heard her open the front door and shut it behind her.

What had she done? Grace stared into the distance. She had behaved appallingly. She was no better than her father, and Elisa had been right. She was risking throwing everything she had away. It was so easy to apportion blame. And now she had hurt the very person who had helped her make sense of her life, who had always been there for her, whom she loved so dearly. She had hurt her – perhaps irreparably. Could things get any worse?

Grace buried her head in her hands and wept.

CHAPTER 26

Havana 2012

Duardo looked around the dinner table. He would make his announcement to his family tonight, he decided. It was the right time.

He couldn't help but feel proud. His life had not always run smoothly. There were some things he had lost because of the decisions he had made, but he had learned to accept this. He took another forkful of stew and looked to his left, at Jaquinda, the woman he lived with. Had he ever loved her? He had cared for her, yes, especially when she was pregnant with their son; he had wanted her certainly – in the beginning when he had been without a woman for so long and she had drawn him in with her teasing smile and the toss of her brown, shiny hair. And he had felt the deepest gratitude when Federico was born and Duardo watched his son sleep in her arms wrapped in a white cotton shawl. But how could he love her when his heart had always belonged to another?

He watched her picking at her meal, the meal made by his mother and his daughter-in-law, Benita. Why did she always do that? She would not cook and yet she picked at what was cooked for her, a sullen kind of criticism in her eyes. Duardo hated that. Even so, she was here, he reminded himself. He drank from his tumbler of water. She was here and she was the mother of his son, so he must be tolerant and make the best of it. She was here and equally she was not here. She would far rather, he supposed, be eating with Felipe, a few blocks away. If he were not married. If he were not, like Duardo, living with his entire family in one apartment. Trapped.

He forked up some chicken and rice. Better not to think of such things. He had learned to accept because he had fought for their right to live this life. He had fought with the rebel army and even marched with Guevara, God rest his soul – through hard and flooded terrain infested with swarms of mosquitoes, drinking water from swampy rivers, weak with hunger. He had endured the noise, the smoke, the blood . . . But it had been worth it. Along with all the other men, their *companeros*, they had achieved freedom for the people of Cuba from the yoke of America. Duardo had fought because it was the right thing to do – though Elisa had never understood that. He had fought because he could not have lived with himself if he had not.

Next to Jaquinda sat Federico, who had never quite lived up to what Duardo had hoped and expected of him. Duardo watched him fondly though – of course he loved him, he was his son. Federico was swigging from a bottle of beer and laughing at something his wife, Benita, had said. He was lazy; his mother's son was what he was, and nothing Duardo had ever said could make a jot of difference. When Federico was young he had messed around in the streets and backyards near their home and when he was a teenager he'd messed around on the *malecón* and further afield. Now that he was an adult with a grown son of his own, he messed around still. He spent time down at the harbour, he played cards and dominos with his cronies in the local bars and when there was no beer he drank the hooch that was distilled locally and made brown with burnt molasses. He lazed in the sunshine in the afternoons and occasionally strolled around the city of Havana on the pretext of looking for work. He had been a musician when he was younger and he still played sometimes, but mostly, he didn't bother these days. The best two things he had done in his life were marry Benita – a hard worker if ever there was one – and sire his son, Luis, the apple of Duardo's eye.

Luis now . . . Duardo ate a spoonful of black beans and smiled down the table at his grandson. He was a chip off the old block indeed. He was twenty now and had gone to university. He was tall and upright and had his dark curly hair cut very short to his scalp, which revealed the strong shape of his young head. Like his grandfather Duardo before him, he had a mission, he had drive. He would get somewhere and be someone. Duardo knew it.

From a young age Luis had been interested in cars – specifically his old grandfather's Chevrolet – and from a young age, Duardo had fostered that interest, determined to turn it into a passion. It had worked. When he was six years old, Luis was helping clean and polish the 'taxi Parisien' as Duardo sometimes called the car to make the tourists smile; by the age of seven he had mastered some of the more simple mechanics. By eight he would have cheeky but endearing conversations with some of Duardo's clients. He learnt to say: 'Afternoon, ma'am and sir.' Sometimes he even came along for the ride.

Duardo continued to enjoy his stew, half listening to the conversations going on around the table. His mother was complaining to Benita about the produce from the fruitseller and Jaquinda and Federico were debating whether or not Alfonso who owned the bar they both frequented was starting up an affair with Zelia, one of their neighbours. Luis was unusually silent. Often he sat at his grandfather's right hand and as they ate they would discuss aspects of the business and how much money had been taken that day, but today he had retreated to the other side of Duardo's mother as he sometimes did to allow her to sit next to her son, good boy that he was. In the corner of the room the big-screened television with its habitual orangey picture blared, but no one paid it any mind.

Duardo was proud of many aspects of the regime, though even he had to admit that there had been some failures too. He was proud of their health service, but most especially of their educational system. Now, his countrymen were literate, had access to good health care and had enough to eat. This was what they had fought for. Federico couldn't see the point of keeping the political posters up around the city, but Duardo knew that they needed to remember. Because Raúl Castro was old and they must not let it happen again.

America must not be allowed to move in and take over. Cuba was poor, workers were underpaid and the people lacked the material goods that some craved. But Cuba was free. And everyone deserved to be a free man.

Federico had not gained much from the education system – he'd bunked off from school half the time and what he did learn he soon forgot. But Luis now . . . He was a bright boy. Duardo smiled at him down the table and his smart, bright-eyed grandson smiled back. He could be anything.

Duardo had started Luis off with English. He'd learnt a lot himself over the years and he made it his business to teach his grandson. 'It's not just the language or the grammar,' he told him. 'It's not the vocabulary, the amount of words you know. It's the way you say it.'

'How d'you mean, *abuelo*?' Luis was curious and he learnt fast.

'You're part of the experience,' Duardo told him. 'People want to go home and tell everyone that they talked to the real people of Cuba. They want to think they know us – how we operate, what we talk about, how we live. They want to listen to us talking about our country, about Castro, about the revolution. To do that we have to learn their languages. English, German and French.'

'And will they tell us about their lives?' Luis had asked him.

Duardo laughed. 'Oh, yes, kiddo, they'll tell us. All we have to do is ask the right questions.'

'And then?' Luis asked. 'What then?'

'Well, then we get paid for our trouble,' Duardo said. 'We

work in the tourist industry, Luis, and it's an industry that's going somewhere. Folk will always want to come here. And folk will always want to thank us for making their visit more pleasant for them. In a way you could say that we're representing our country. We're the people that the tourists speak to; through us they learn about the real Cuba. It is a big responsibility. Not a job to be taken lightly.'

Of course, Luis had learnt lots of other things at school. But as luck would have it, not only was the boy a good linguist, but he was a fine mechanic in the making too. He had the feel. He could tell where something was going wrong with the car and he had enough inventiveness to think of a way to put it right. 'Necessity is the mother of invention,' was a phrase that could have been coined for Cubans – how many of their neighbours had re-enamelled old baths with car paint for example? When you had nothing to work with, you had to make something from what you could find around you. Luis could do that. The boy had a brain and he had practical hands. He couldn't go wrong.

The Chevy, Duardo's other pride and joy, had a 405 Peugeot engine now of course. It had a Mitsubishi drive shaft and he often got her going with a machete. Needs must. The bumpers were riveted together and the chrome had been polished so much that it was down to the base metal in places. There were LED lights on the dashboard, pictures of his family stuck all over, and music which could be played through the large speakers fixed on the back shelf. One door didn't open from the outside – a minor issue that Duardo hadn't yet managed to fix – and he had to use coathanger wire to open one of the others. But it was still a comfortable car. The leather was cracked but intact, he hadn't – sensibly – gone for the cheap plastic tint on the windows that some of the guys had done (tourists hated this; they couldn't see out) there was plenty of legroom and she was a smooth ride. Even better, he had now saved enough money in tips to buy another American car.

Between Luis and Duardo, sat Duardo's mother, his rock. If not for her, Duardo knew he couldn't have achieved what he had. If not for her, he would be a broken man. She had stood by him and supported him through thick and thin, she had picked him up when he was defeated and imagined he'd lost everything. And he knew she always would. Duardo felt tears come to his eyes. That was why he'd had to defend her when Elisa had said what she had said. His mother always had his best interests at heart. It was simple as that. And now . . . It was time to make his announcement, he decided.

He banged his knife on the table. 'If I could have your attention, you rowdy bunch,' he said.

He was pleased to note Luis look up immediately. The boy had respect for his elders, which was good. Duardo's mother too was watching him, waiting expectantly, and he didn't doubt she already knew what it was he was going to say. Federico and Jaquinda though had taken no notice and were still eating, drinking and gossiping about other people's lives as though nothing had happened.

Duardo cleared his throat. '*Bueno*. I want to say something.' He spoke quietly but firmly. This had the desired effect. He had all their attention now. Even Jaquinda was quiet.

'I'm not a young man any longer,' he began.

'C'mon now, Papi,' Federico laughed, but Duardo waved his comment away.

'And the time has come for me to take stock.' He assessed his audience. His mother was nodding faintly and Luis was looking interested now. Jaquinda, Benita and Federico were all watching him. 'I've worked hard,' he said, 'in a business which has paid good dividends over the years.'

More nods from Benita and his mother.

He laid his palms flat on the table. 'But I don't have the energy I once had. And I don't have the heart.' This was quite an admission. Several times over the past months Duardo had thought he'd had enough, but the time hadn't been right and so he had forced himself to continue. There were others he had to think about now. He had to think of continuity and the future well-being of his family.

'So I want to let you know that I am officially retiring from the business,' he said. 'It's over. I've done my bit. It's time to hand over the reins.' He glanced at Luis and caught an expression on his grandson's face that he couldn't quite identify. Fear perhaps? The boy had nothing to be scared of. He was up for the job. Duardo would help him at first, of course, for as long as he was needed. But he had no doubts now that the boy had finished his education that he'd be able to take over where

Duardo left off – yes and develop the business too, in his own way.

'I thought you'd never stop working,' Jaquinda said.

Duardo shrugged.

'What will you do?' Federico frowned. 'I can't see you just sitting around all day.'

He should know what that felt like, thought Duardo. 'I will have my projects.' He smiled at them all. 'I'll find things to do, don't you worry.'

'And you deserve a rest, son,' his mother put in. 'You've worked so hard. You've built that business from nothing.'

Duardo smiled modestly. It was true. He had been fortunate in the beginning, of course. When Francisco had said that he was leaving the country, when he told Duardo he could have his old dog of a car for nothing . . . 'If you can make it go, you're a better man than I'll ever be.' He was aware that this had been a perfect opportunity. Nevertheless, he had worked on that car like crazy. He had begged, borrowed and stolen to find parts, to adapt parts, to invent parts to make that baby go. All a man needed was an opportunity. Where he took it was up to his own sense of ambition. He glanced at his son. Or lack of it.

'What do you think, Luis?' Duardo asked.

Luis glanced up as if shocked at being spoken to. 'I don't think you should, *abuelo*,' he said. 'At least not yet. You'll get bored without the business. It's your life.'

Duardo laughed. But the boy knew what he was talking about. It *was* his life. Time was when his life had centred around a woman. Time too when the revolution had been the driving force. But the woman hadn't worked out and the revolution . . . Some said the revolution hadn't worked out either, more fool them. 'It's a big part of my life, yes,' he conceded. 'And don't you worry – I'll stick around for a while and see that all progresses as it should.'

He saw Luis shoot a discomfited look towards his father. What now? Did Luis imagine that Federico would be upset at being passed over for his son? That was ridiculous. Federico wouldn't be in the slightest bit interested in the business – he never had been. 'I need it to be in good hands,' he said. 'That's all I ever wanted. Someone who holds it dear, who understands me and the way it works. But someone who is young, who has his own ideas of how to take things on to the next level for the next generation.'

He nodded. He'd said his piece.

'That's wonderful, son,' said his mother. She put her arm round Luis and gave his shoulders a squeeze. 'Isn't that wonderful, Luis?'

'Luis?' asked Federico. 'Are you talking about Luis taking over the business?'

That boy could be dense sometimes. 'Of course I'm talking about Luis,' said Duardo. 'You've finished studying now haven't you, Luis?'

'*Sí, abuelo.*' Luis was looking down at his plate.

Duardo hadn't expected him to leap up and throw his arms around his old grandfather. But he had expected a little more exuberance. And after all, hadn't he always told them that this was his intention, that this was what he wanted for the boy?

'Tourism,' said Federico. 'You'd think in this day and age there'd be a better occupation for an educated boy.'

Duardo glared at him. 'It puts food on your plate.'

Federico remained unfazed – he always did. He was so laid back that if he relaxed any more he'd be unconscious. 'I know that,' he said. 'But do you think it's right that boys who could be doctors or engineers say, end up being chefs in fancy hotels instead? Pandering to rich tourists?'

'I'm not saying that.' Duardo was the first to want the best for their young people and for Cuba.

Benita laid a hand on her husband's arm. 'Your father is giving our son a wonderful opportunity,' she said in her quiet voice. 'Don't forget that.'

'I know.' He took another swig of beer. 'I'm not blaming him. I'm just saying – look at our country. Castro tried to make us equal but we're as unequal as we ever were. It's just a different sort of inequality.' He shot his father a defiant look. 'And Cuba deserves better.'

'Since when did you become a politician?' Duardo frowned and pushed his plate away. He had the feeling that the conversation had been turned away from him, that now he had, once again, to defend the Castros and what they had done. And he was tired of it, frankly. Even he had to admit that however much good he had done in the first place and however well-intentioned he had been about freedom and social justice, Fidel Castro had become seen as something of a tyrant.

Duardo's disillusion had begun during the special period when no one had food to eat or work to do. Back then entire families had virtually thrown themselves into the sea on makeshift rafts made from wood or even the rubber tyres from lorries, heading for the US coastline, knowing that once they had their feet on American soil they could stay. They were desperate. The government had said they could go, so go they did. Once the police would have arrested them; now they were waving them off and wishing them luck for the journey. Some said the Americans were generous to allow this wet foot/dry foot policy to go on – because those captured at sea got short shrift from US officials and were returned from whence they came. Not everyone got there. The American coast was not far away – but it was too far to swim.

Still, Duardo reminded himself, the shortages of food and other problems were not the government's fault. With the fall of the Berlin Wall in 1989, help from the countries of the Socialist Bloc had, of necessity, dried up. Cuba had to find different strategies for survival. And yet land remained unploughed and unsown. Power cuts, *apagones*, could last for up to twenty hours a day. The currency changed and convertible currency was craved by all; families sold gold and silver and anything else they had, to obtain it. Men didn't work because there seemed no point – they got so little back in return; they could not further their careers like he had.

Because tourism had been encouraged. Foreigners were allowed to invest in the country, hotels were renovated at the expense of social housing and exclusive tourist resorts grew up around the most stunning beaches. Tourism became more important than even tobacco or sugar. And Duardo was ready to take advantage of the situation. Things had changed – he had proved that and they would change still more. Besides, let Federico talk to his grandmother – she would tell him how 'good' things had been before the revolution. In the 1940s there was the biggest gap between rich and poor. Their family lived in a slum. At least now people were fed, at least now they were equal.

'So what do you say, young Luis?' asked Duardo. They all looked at the boy expectantly.

Poor kid. It was a bit much for him. He was overwhelmed. Duardo got to his feet and clapped him on the shoulder. 'Say nothing,' he said. 'That's my advice. Say nothing and don't bother to thank me either. I'm just glad that I have you to leave the business to. I don't except you to run it the way I always have, mind – you'll have your own ideas. I couldn't stand the thought of leaving it to some stranger, that's all.'

Luis got to his feet and embraced him. 'Oh, *abuelo*,' he said. 'Oh, *abuelo*.'

'That's all right.' There were tears in the boy's eyes and Duardo felt his own emotions rising. 'There, my boy,' he said. 'There, there.' It was a lot for him to take in. But of course it would be all right in the end. Because even when the worst things happened . . . And Duardo thought of Elisa, he couldn't help but think of Elisa. There was always family to help you through.

CHAPTER 27

As Elisa left Grace's she almost wondered if she could walk at all. She felt attacked, berated, bruised; all the energy had been drained from her. And the worst thing was that the person who had done this was Grace.

She must go home. But first, she would sit for a moment and collect herself. She got down the steps to the wharf and made her way cautiously to the nearest bench, situated right by the water's edge. Ah. She lowered herself on to it with a sigh. She needed to rest. *How could she?* she thought. How could Grace have said all those things after everything Elisa had tried to do for her? Yes, after the choices Elisa had made. Some of those choices had not been easy ones. She thought of Duardo. How close she had been to staying with him in Cuba that time. But she had felt responsible for Grace. She had loved her as if she were her own daughter.

Elisa watched a fleet of swans glide along the water. Listen to yourself, she chided silently. Grace was right. Elisa had been so full of herself, so sure that she could repair what had been broken between Grace and her father. Had she been so desperate to be needed?

There must be eight swans at least, so elegant and queenly.

Their feathers were white and glossy and they held their heads high as they enjoyed the afternoon spring sunshine. They must sense that now spring was really here. Perhaps soon there would be cygnets joining the group; that would be a treat. Little ones always were. Elisa sighed. There was much to sigh about. On the one hand were Philip and his promises – the chance of a better life, companionship with a man she could learn to respect again. And on the other the bombshell of learning about Grace and Theo. And now this.

Elisa loosened the scarf around her neck. She felt as if it were choking her. Spring had indeed been late coming this year and at last it was sunny, yes, but there was still no real warmth in the air. If only she could go back, she thought, go back and feel the real warmth, the warmth of Cuba. Because she still didn't seem to belong here with these people, even after all these years. She had been wrong to imagine she did. She was still a foreigner and would remain so for the rest of her life. They were very different from her – Philip, Grace, even Theo, although he was her compatriot. She thought of how he had talked to her about everyone's disapproval and of how she had thought of Duardo and told Theo to follow his heart . . .

Follow his heart. *Dear lord* . . . She had virtually given him permission to seduce her stepdaughter. Elisa shook her head.

On the other side of the canal were some modern apartment blocks and the façade of an old warehouse. Just the façade – the rest of it was gone – narrow bricks and arched windows all held in place by some steel splinting. Elisa felt a bit like that herself – only she'd lost her steel for the moment. She supposed the building had been saved from being knocked down for aesthetic reasons; it was one of the many architectural quirks and glories that made Bristol what it was. The British, at least, were good at preserving history. Not in the nineteen sixties and seventies perhaps, when they had built some of these monstrous office and apartment blocks, but certainly in latter years.

Yes, she had been thinking of Duardo when she spoke to Theo, thinking of him as she so often did. In the park just up the pathway here was a tree in blossom. She'd gone up closer to it once to look at the name, for there was a plaque. But it was simply labelled 'Bob's tree'. *Gone but not forgotten*. Just like Duardo. That tree made her think every time she passed it.

Grace had been rather near the mark in the other things she'd said to her too. *Did you risk throwing it all away?* Her step-daughter must have guessed that Elisa had experienced something similar before she met Philip, although she hadn't got it right because of course she couldn't know. The fact was though, that Elisa had been no more loyal than she. What right then did Elisa have to judge, to tell Grace that what she was doing was so wrong?

Elisa gazed across the water. She had the right of not wanting Grace to suffer loss as Elisa had suffered loss, of not wanting Grace to make the mistakes that Elisa had. Only that right. She had that right because she'd always loved her. She still did. But was Theo the love of Grace's life as Duardo had been Elisa's? Was she trying to stop Grace doing what Elisa in fact had longed to do – throw convention to the wind and trust in the power of that love?

Elisa had come back from Cuba as she had promised Philip and Grace she would, although once again her heart was breaking. That Duardo had been alive all these years and she had never known . . . It was almost too much to contemplate. Nevertheless, she married Philip as she had vowed to do. And a few weeks later she had realised the truth. She was pregnant.

A little red and green boat was approaching, chugging towards the bridge. Elisa watched it. She had been overjoyed at first. She visited the doctor, she received the confirmation and then she was forced to face the truth. It was the dates. She was married to Philip and she was expecting Duardo's baby. According to the dates there could be no doubt. The prospect of having Duardo's child filled her with wonder and strange delight, such as she had hardly experienced before. A love child, a special child, a child who would be part of them. But she was married to the wrong man . . .

Two lovers approached, walking down the steps, hand in hand. 'Look,' the woman said to her companion. She pointed towards the little boat. 'That's sweet,' he agreed, laughing at her enthusiasm and pulling out his mobile phone to take a picture.

It was so easy nowadays, Elisa thought, to capture any moment, to keep it for ever.

She followed the direction in which they were looking but the boat was almost out of sight. A moorhen sat on a little island beyond the floating harbour with her chicks, the male swimming self-importantly around to collect bits of twigs and other material for their nest, part of which seemed to have been washed away by the wake. He was very industrious. Little ones, again.

Elisa smiled. She just couldn't help it. She had cared for Grace as if she were her own, but Grace was right. Elisa was not her mother and even if she were, what was to stop Grace lashing out at her just as Elisa had once lashed out at her mother when Mami had refused to understand about Duardo? She had been much younger then. Much younger than Grace was now. Grace wasn't a child, not even a young woman and Elisa out of everyone knew what could happen to a woman – of any age – when she fell in love.

The couple moved on, walking past her as she sat on the bench, barely noting Elisa's existence, she guessed. The woman was smiling up at the man but his gaze was skimming the park beyond. He was with her, but not entirely with her, and Elisa recognised that look since Philip had often looked that way. He had taken his time before he looked at Elisa as if he meant it. The man's gaze scoured the grass and the distant trees and now, even passed over Elisa as she sat there watching. When we are young, we see the old as old, she thought to herself. But as we grow old – we still feel so young inside.

She was expecting Duardo's child. What could she do? She

could tell Philip, break up their marriage and return to Cuba. It was what she wanted. She and Duardo could manage all those obstacles; she knew that he would still want her if he knew she was carrying his child. But what of Grace? And what of the man she had married who now seemed to need her more than ever? Philip had not been overjoyed at the news of her pregnancy, and she had already discovered how much he was drinking. She could make the baby go away – but everything in her shrank from this option; it was a repulsive thought; she simply could not even consider it. She could lie to Philip and pretend it was his baby – it would be easy to fudge the dates and even if the baby had a darker skin than might be expected, it wouldn't be so surprising. Or she could tell Philip the truth and then decide.

Night after night, she rolled these options around in her mind, trying to find a solution they could all live with. She stayed awake thinking, and kept her hands on her belly as if she could protect the child within. She considered contacting her cousin in Havana, getting a message to Duardo. She tried to think of a way to get the money together for a flight to Cuba.

And then she miscarried.

She was doing some light housework at the time – nothing strenuous – and she felt the warmth between her legs, the rush of blood. She cried as if her heart would break. This was her punishment, for what she had done – to Philip, to Duardo. And when Philip attempted awkwardly to comfort her, when he told her that everything would be all right, that she mustn't upset herself so . . . Well then, she hadn't been able to stand the dishonesty any more.

'You don't understand, Philip,' she had cried.

'Oh, but my dear, I do.' And his blue eyes held an expression of deep regret.

'It wasn't your baby,' she whispered. 'When I went back to Cuba . . .' And she told him about Duardo, about their reunion, about how she had thought her lover was dead.

She had expected him to be angry. She had expected him to be shocked. But at least there was honesty between them now. At least she had done what she could to make things right because most things had gone horribly wrong and some god somewhere whom she had once scorned had carelessly done the rest.

'And you chose us?' Philip had seemed moved by this. 'You came back to Bristol and chose us?'

She couldn't reply to this. It wasn't so simple. Nothing was. 'But the baby . . .' she began.

He patted her hand. 'I knew it couldn't be mine,' he said softly. 'After Grace was born . . . Nancy had such a hard time of it. She wasn't cut out for childbirth, you see, so . . .'

She stared at him, trying to understand what he was telling her.

He nodded. 'She didn't want to go through it again,' he said, 'so I agreed to have a vasectomy.'

So all the time he had known.

Elisa sat back on the bench and closed her eyes. What she should have done today, was talk calmly to Grace instead of losing control of her emotions like that. Her stepdaughter must be at her wit's end. She was not unkind or disloyal by nature. Whatever had happened between her and Theo must have happened for a reason and Elisa should have tried to find out what it was. Of course Grace would have thought of Robbie. She was not so insensitive. What she needed now was a friend with whom she could talk things through, not some half-demented mother-figure letting rip. Really. After all her experience, Elisa had handled this delicate situation very badly. And she knew the reason. It was because of what she herself had done. She sighed. Because of Duardo.

She pulled her mobile out of her black patent bag and called home. Robbie was right. A mobile phone was very useful after all.

Philip answered almost immediately.

'I need you,' she told him. She could not have said this while he was drinking. But she was beginning to allow herself to lean on him at last – just a little. She was proud of his determination to turn the corner, to face up to his responsibilities, to accept what and who he had become. 'I'm in Castle Park near Grace's. Can you come and pick me up?'

'Of course I can.' He sounded bemused, but, ah, how good it was to hear him sober. 'Whereabouts in the park are you? Are you all right, my dear?'

'Yes.' Though she was glad that he hadn't asked her exactly what had happened. 'I am almost directly below the old church. Sitting on a bench by the waterfront right opposite the warehouse that has no body.'

'No body,' he echoed. She could feel him absorbing the information.

'You could park in Queens Street or Grimes Lane,' she suggested. Not Passage Street; she did not want to return to Passage Street. 'I'll stay here and watch the moorhens.'

He chuckled. 'Right you are. I'll find you. I'll be fifteen minutes.' And he was gone.

True to his word, in little over fifteen minutes, Philip sat down beside her on the dark turquoise bench. He no longer wore his black heavy overcoat. Instead, he was wearing a navy fleece that made him look younger somehow.

She took his arm. 'Thank you for coming,' she said. She leant over, to rest her head briefly on his shoulder. It was still bony, but the padding of the fleece was thick and comforting.

'I was glad to.' And he looked glad. He looked happier than usual, more self-assured. 'It's a long time,' he added, 'since you asked me to do something for you.'

This was true. But you had to cut the man out of your life who was drinking. You couldn't depend on him. She had never really been able to depend on Philip.

'I have something else to ask you,' she said.

'Yes?'

'You said that you wanted to talk to Grace.'

'Yes.' He nodded. 'I tried phoning her but she never called back.'

Ditto, thought Elisa. Grace clearly had other things on her mind.

'I know it hasn't been long,' Philip was saying, 'but I'm determined not to go back to how things were. I need to tell her. I'm not going to start drinking again.'

Dear Philip. Elisa patted his arm. 'And when you talk to her,' she said. 'I also want you to tell her about her mother.' He had said he could not tell his daughter the truth, but Elisa needed to persuade him otherwise.

'What's happened?' he asked her. He put his arm around her shoulders. 'You went round to see Grace, didn't you?'

She nodded. 'We argued.'

'Oh, Elisa.' He squeezed her shoulder. 'What about?'

Elisa decided she would have to tell him. It was not her secret, but it was the only way. 'Grace is involved with someone,' she said, 'and I found out about it.'

Philip was shocked as she knew he would be. He stared out over the water and didn't say a word. Elisa guessed that he was thinking of Nancy.

'You must tell her what happened, Philip,' Elisa said. 'Not because it might stop her blaming you for Nancy's death at long last, but because everyone deserves the truth.'

He gave her a long look and again, she knew exactly what he was thinking. 'And you think it might persuade her to break off her own affair?' Philip asked.

She nodded. 'Perhaps. It's seeing the damage an affair can do. To a marriage. To a child. To a family.'

He didn't seem convinced. He frowned and stared out towards the waterway once more. There was the yellow ferry boat approaching now. 'Is it fair to Nancy though?' he said.

'Nancy is dead,' Elisa pointed out.

'But is it fair to her memory? Yes, she's dead. So she doesn't even have a voice.'

'Which is why you have to do the talking.' Elisa nudged him. 'And if you cannot do it for Grace or for yourself, then do it for me.'

'For you?' His eyes widened.

'Yes. Because that girl hasn't forgiven me for taking you away. She might think that she has, but she hasn't. Not deep inside. She can't understand how her father could have married another woman so soon after he lost her mother.' Elisa paused to allow this to sink in and as she did so, the sun disappeared momentarily behind a cloud. Elisa shivered. 'She doesn't believe you really loved Nancy,' she went on. It was important to make him understand. 'She thinks you're responsible for her death.'

At this, Philip nodded and Elisa had the awful feeling that he was about to cry. But he composed himself and she continued, 'She's confused because nothing fits and nothing makes proper sense. Lies never will.' She shook his arm. 'And that is why you must talk to her. You need to put her straight. She's thirty-nine years old, Philip. But she is still your daughter.'

It was a long speech and Philip seemed to consider her words for an awfully long time before he replied. She could see him mulling it over. Could he undo a decision he had made thirty years ago? She hoped so.

'Very well,' he said at last. 'I'll talk to her if you think that's the best thing to do.' He sighed. 'I'll tell her everything.'

He rubbed his hands together. 'But I'm taking you home first. You're cold. You're tired. You need a nice hot drink inside you.'

Elisa blinked at him. 'You're going to talk to her now?' she asked. There was a new, almost steely determination in Philip's blue eyes, in the set of his jaw.

'That's what I was thinking, Elisa,' he said. 'I'll just go round there. There's no time like the present.'

CHAPTER 28

Cuba 2012

'Tomorrow I will take you to Cayo Levisa,' Duardo had said. 'You've never been there, Mami. It's a taste of paradise.'

'Cayo Levisa?' Was it her birthday? In all her years in Havana, Rosalyn had never been there, though she'd heard it was a beautiful island. Once Duardo had started making a success of his taxi business, he had taken her to all sorts of places she had never been to before; Rosalyn was flattered and she loved to spend time with him, wherever they were. But truth to tell, she wasn't bothered about travelling, and less so as she grew older. She was quite happy going about her own business at home in Havana. She knew that fuel was expensive – a super-tax, some said, on people like her son who ran a car as a taxi business – and so she couldn't see the point of haring about here, there and everywhere. She went with Duardo though because it seemed to please him.

'Very well. If you insist, my son.' She understood what he was telling her although she didn't need to be told. She knew how well he'd done for himself. Besides, Rosalyn wasn't sure that she was ready to taste paradise – time enough for that, if she should be so fortunate. Tacito would be there for sure if such a place existed. She wondered what her son wanted to talk about; there must be something.

Cayo Levisa was just as Duardo had promised. They took a ferry boat over the smooth turquoise sea which deposited them on a makeshift platform set in a small mangrove plantation. A wooden walkway led to the beach, a long stretch of white powder sand backed by scrub grassland and palms. The sea was calm; the sunlight catching the dimples and ripples of the tide. They settled themselves on sunbeds under little canopies thatched with woven palm leaves. It was hot, but there was a light breeze and so Rosalyn was comfortable. And she had to admit that the place certainly was tranquil – and very different from Havana. She sat back and felt the warmth of the sun on her skin, smelt the salty tang of the sea air – fresher here than in the city – combining with the acrid tang of seaweed and dry shells.

Duardo was restless though. He got up, ran across the white sand and dived into the glittering blue sea – as if he thought he could be a boy again. Rosalyn clicked her tongue indulgently and got out her embroidery. There was a good light here, she'd say that; for once the work wasn't straining her eyes.

Duardo emerged from the ocean minutes later as slick as a seal. He grinned at her ruefully, towelled himself dry and went to fetch them fresh pineapple juice from the beach bar nestling amongst the palm trees behind them.

Rosalyn shook her head when he brought it back. 'I brought us something to drink,' she chided. 'I told you.

There's lemonade in the bag over there. I made it myself this morning.' She eyed the glass of pineapple juice suspiciously. 'How much did you have to pay for that?' And it had straws – as if they could not drink from the glass like normal people, as if they were children, or tourists.

'Relax, Mami,' he said. 'Just sit back and enjoy. It is *nada*.'

Rosalyn tried to do as he said. But the juice was chilling on her teeth and besides, she could never relax where money was concerned. Who could when they'd ever lived through a time of having none?

'And what is the problem?' she asked him as he put down his glass, lay back on the sunbed and closed his eyes as if he might sleep. No chance of that. She'd rarely seen him so ill at ease.

'Problems,' he said. He sat up and let out a hefty sigh. 'Always, there are problems. Look at that dinner the other night.'

'Dinner?' Though she knew the dinner he meant. Duardo's announcement of his forthcoming retirement had not been met as her son had expected. Federico had looked at Luis and the boy had looked back, guiltily almost, as if they shared some secret . . . They had all been pretty quiet about it. This didn't sound much like any Cuban family; it certainly didn't sound like Rosalyn's family.

'I expected more from him.' Duardo frowned.

From Luis, he meant. She knew that Duardo wanted Luis to take the business to the next level, taking on board all the changes that were taking place in the country and all the change that was to come. It was a great opportunity. He had expected Luis to say something . . .

'He was probably in shock,' Rosalyn suggested. 'He probably couldn't think how to thank you enough.' She made a mental note to talk to Federico. He knew. He would open up to her – if she handled it right. Time was, Rosalyn had known everything going on in her household; there were no secrets. Now they thought her too old to be trusted. But not Duardo. He still wanted to talk to his old mother about his problems.

Duardo brightened up at her words. 'In shock, yes,' he agreed. 'You're probably right. It's a lot to think about, a big responsibility for the boy.'

Rosalyn pushed that guilty look from her mind. Later. She would deal with it later. 'And what else?' she probed.

Duardo looked uncomfortable. 'Jaquinda,' he said.

'Ah.' Well, that was no surprise.

'We don't sleep together any more, you know,' he remarked casually.

Did he imagine she was stupid? Of course she knew.

'She has another man. She has done for years.'

Rosalyn knew this too. 'Do you care, my son?' she asked him.

'I used to think it didn't matter.' He adjusted his straw hat which was balanced at the usual angle over his forehead, protecting him from the sun.

'And now?'

'It seems dishonest, that's all.'

Roslyn shrugged. 'She's Federico's mother,' she said. That's how things were in Cuba. Where else would she go? Their lives had improved, they had more food and Duardo could drive his mother to the seaside in his American car. But they still had to live with people they did not love. They still didn't have the freedom they craved. And when they had that freedom? When men and women could travel freely all around the globe, when they could buy whatever goods they desired from wherever they liked, when they could discard a woman or a man as easily as dropping the peel from a papaya fruit; what then? Would they be happy then? She eyed her son carefully. She'd always believed in straight talking. 'But you must want a woman?'

'Sometimes.' The hat slipped further over his eyes.

It was Rosalyn's turn to sigh. She shifted her embroidery on her lap. It was natural for a man to want a woman, but sex was better when combined with love. Like a good home-cooked meal with chicken, white rice and black beans, it was far more satisfying. And he'd had the best role model. Tacito had never wanted another woman and she had never wanted another man.

'Perhaps you should have married her,' she said, 'at least then she'd have more respect for you.'

Duardo swung his legs over the side of the sunbed. Good, strong legs, she thought. Once, she'd liked to dance, and Duardo took after her in that department too. Tacito now, he could shimmy and *cha cha* with the best of them, but he wasn't a man for always getting to his feet when the music was playing. Duardo though . . . Even as a boy he'd been unable to resist; it was in his blood, buried deep in his soul.

'You know why I couldn't do that,' he said.

Her again. Rosalyn gave a brief shrug and returned her attention to her work. Elisa Fernandez-Garcia. The only woman who had ever posed a threat to Rosalyn. The only woman who could have taken her son away – and who had, at least for a while.

Abruptly, Duardo got to his feet and walked off, towards the sea again. Rosalyn could, if she almost closed her eyes, let the sparkle of the sun on the rippling water take her drifting back in time, let her imagine him as a little boy once more. How she had loved that boy. She would have given him everything. Tacito knew. He even warned her about it, but she didn't listen. She should have. She should have held back from giving Duardo every square inch of her heart.

Rosalyn adjusted her scarf and leaned back a little so that the sun was not in her eyes. She understood his disillusion. She understood that he was an all or nothing sort of person and that he expected the same feeling in return. But at least Duardo had worked hard and had bettered himself. Look at him now – bringing his old mother to Cayo Levisa and buying her fresh *pina* juice. And besides . . . There was still time for him to find love – he could have twenty years left in him, or more.

She continued to watch him as he walked into the ocean, plunged beneath the waves and then swam out to sea. Further out, the turquoise of the water deepened like the centre of a gemstone and in the distance the horizon was a grey, bruised purple. All she could hear was the curl and crackle of the waves on the sand and the shells, the draw of the water, and occasional birdsong.

'Turn around,' she whispered. 'Don't go out too far.' It wasn't that she wanted to hold him back; she'd never do that. She simply wanted him to respect his roots, to remember what had gone before and to be safe.

Time drifted. Just as she was about to shout out to him: *Duardo! Come in now. Please come in!* he turned. Rosalyn realised that she was already halfway out of her sunbed, tense as an alley cat. What was wrong with her? He was a grown man.

He emerged from the water, brown as Cuban coffee and dripping, his skin gleaming in the sun. Still a fine figure of a man, she thought – just like his father. And oh, she was proud of him.

He walked up the beach and grabbed a towel, still blinking the water out of his eyes.

'You never told me,' Rosalyn said, 'why she didn't stay.'

'Eh?'

'That second time. When Elisa Fernandez-Garcia came back here to Cuba. Didn't you want her, my son?' Because of course, this was what Rosalyn wanted to hear.

He towelled his hair. His dark curls were turning grey but his hair would still be soft and Rosalyn wished she could run her fingers through it.

'I wanted her.' His voice was low. 'I tried everything I could to make her come back here.'

Once again, Rosalyn clicked her tongue. Well, then. The girl had been given a second chance and still she'd thrown it away. Which vindicated what Rosalyn had done, surely? 'She wasn't interested I suppose?' she asked. 'Found a better life in England, had she?'

He put the towel down and looked at her. 'I don't think she had, no.'

Rosalyn had not expected to hear this. 'It shows how little she thought of you anyway.' She couldn't help it. It was cruel and how she hated to hurt him, but the bitterness was still rolling around inside her and it kept emerging on her tongue.

Duardo eyed her with what she was terribly afraid was pity. 'It wasn't like that, Mami,' he said.

It certainly looked like that. What did he mean? Rosalyn continued with her needlework. 'People leave,' she said, in a tone meant to placate him. 'People have always left our country.'

'She thought I was dead,' said Duardo.

'And you believed her?' Listen to her. Listen to what a mother would do for love.

'I did.' Was it Rosalyn's imagination – or was he scrutinising her more closely?

Rosalyn bent forwards over her embroidery, giving it more attention than it merited. 'But once she saw you were alive . . .' She let the words hang. No need to say more.

'She'd already made a promise by then.' Duardo's voice was bleak now and Rosalyn regretted bringing the subject up. Whenever they talked about Elisa she was always wrong-footed, she always said things she hadn't meant to say.

'To another man?' she guessed.

'To another man and his daughter. The man had given her money for her family. That's why Elisa had to go back to England. It wouldn't have been fair not to.'

'Hmm,' Rosalyn tried to make this sound sceptical, but in point of fact she was conscious of a rare stab of admiration for Elisa. She'd shown integrity at least.

She tapped the watch that Duardo had given her for her last birthday. 'We must go and catch the ferry,' she told him. There were chores to be done at home and dinner to be prepared. And after dinner she would take Federico aside and she would talk to him. Secrets were all very well but Rosalyn would not allow any to be kept from her in her own house. And she wouldn't be dwelling on her own secrets either.

She looked out to sea. The waves seemed to be whipping up the turquoise water now and there was a pinkish light deepening into charcoal on the horizon. Rosalyn shivered. She could feel change in the air. And she didn't like it – not one bit.

CHAPTER 29

Grace looked at her father standing at the door. He was wearing a fleecy hooded jacket she hadn't seen before, and he wasn't smiling that fake smile of his that drove her crazy. In fact, he wasn't smiling at all.

'Hello, Dad.' She knew her voice was wary. She hadn't seen him since the last time she'd gone round to King Street – several weeks ago now – which was partly intentional and partly thanks to Theo. Who had been, she thought guiltily, almost the only thing on her mind.

'Hello, Grace.'

She hesitated.

'Can I come in?'

'Yes, of course.' Had he spoken to Elisa? He must have. So what was this? The second line of attack? Grace needed to talk to her father about as much as she'd needed that lecture from her stepmother.

It was only the second time he'd been round here. The first was when Grace had cooked a family Sunday roast to celebrate her and Robbie moving in. Her father had drunk too much, started slurring, then mouthing off about something on the news, and Elisa had ended up calling a taxi to take them home.

Never again, Grace had thought. Not until he stopped drinking so much anyway. At least when she visited her father and Elisa in King Street she could escape when she needed to.

She led the way into the living room. 'I've got an appointment in half an hour,' she said. So any lecture would have to be a quick one.

'Someone coming here?'

She nodded. 'For a treatment.' She braced herself, but he didn't respond as she'd expected.

'I could wait.' He glanced at her. 'If that's all right?'

Grace could hardly say no. It was only a half-hour appointment for a foot massage. Besides, he seemed more determined than usual. More composed. More sober, she thought. She straightened her back. 'Are you here because of what I said to Elisa?' she asked him.

He seemed to consider this, head to one side, watching her. 'You could say that. Sort of.'

Grace sighed. 'I shouldn't have said those things to her. I know that. I went too far.' She moved towards the kitchen. 'Tea?'

'Please.' He took off his jacket and put it on the back of a chair. 'Anyway, that's between the two of you.' He sat down. 'I'm sure you'll sort it out.'

But would they? Grace had been shocked at herself, at some of the things that had emerged. She didn't know what had got into her. Lately, she'd been doing a few things that had shocked her. It was almost as if she were turning into a different person – or perhaps admitting at long last what kind of a person she was. She put the kettle on and put cups on a tray.

'I'll apologise to Elisa, of course,' she said as she came back into the room. Elisa had done so much for her. Perhaps she'd earned the right to tell Grace what to do. 'I was angry with her,' she admitted. 'She didn't seem to even want to understand. She just came round here laying down the law.' Even so. 'But I was totally out of order,' she admitted.

He shrugged. 'I'm sure Elisa can take it,' he said. 'After all, I've been totally out of order to her for years.' And was Grace imagining it – or was there a glimmer of a smile touching his mouth, his eyes? A real smile.

'I can't take back everything that I said though,' Grace told him. It might have come from a dark place, but some of it, at least, had been true.

'No. But you can go forward from it together.'

Grace glanced across at him. 'You look different,' she said. He sounded different too.

The kettle boiled and she returned to the kitchen. She dropped tea bags into the mugs and poured on the boiling water.

'I'm not drinking,' she heard him say.

She glanced through the hatch and saw him sit up straighter. 'That is, I've stopped drinking.'

'Ah.' Grace continued to watch him speculatively. That's why he seemed different. He'd tried before. Not that he'd ever acknowledged the extent of the problem – as far as she was aware. She supposed that most addicts were in denial;

that was part of it. 'How are you doing?' She kept her voice noncommittal; added milk to his tea and stirred. There was no point getting her hopes up. She had accepted what he was a long time ago. But she still wanted him in her life, that was the thing. She blamed him for her mother's death and sometimes she hated him. But she couldn't quite let him go. She returned to the living room and put the tray on the table.

'It's early days.' He took the cup of tea she gave to him. 'Thanks. I've joined AA,' he added. 'I'm even seeing a counsellor.'

'Great.' That surprised her.

'And I've changed my routines, you know?'

She nodded. Perhaps that was what she needed to do. Change the routines she'd established with Theo, to cure her of her addiction to love. 'How much did Elisa tell you?' she asked him.

'Enough.' He sipped his tea. 'I'll admit I was surprised, Grace,' he said. 'But it's your life. You're the one who has to live it.'

And take the consequences, she added silently. She sat down opposite him and picked up her own mint tea. In a way her father's calm reaction was even harder to take than Elisa's outright anger. 'And yet, you're here, aren't you?' she pointed out. If it wasn't about Theo or Elisa, then what was it about? 'Elisa must have asked you to come.'

'She did, yes.'

Grace shook her head. She'd thought as much. 'Well, you're right,' she said. 'It is my life. And if the only time you can be bothered to come round here and talk to me is when my stepmother asks you to, just because I'm doing something she doesn't approve of for once . . .' She could feel it again – the sap rising. 'Even though –' She stopped herself just in time. She was about to say – *even though she's probably done the same thing herself*. She was about to tell him something she didn't even know was true.

'Even though?' he asked mildly.

'Nothing.' She buttoned up.

Her father took another slug of tea. 'You're right to be angry with me,' he said.

Which made her angrier still. She didn't want him to agree with her, damn it. 'So don't think you can come round here telling me what to do, any more than Elisa can,' she said. 'You lost that kind of authority a long time ago.' Yes and she had grown up a long time ago – supposedly.

'That's not why I'm here, Grace,' he said. 'I told you that.' His voice had grown a fraction cooler but other than that he seemed unaffected by her outburst, merely continuing to drink his tea. Grace felt more of a child than ever.

'Why are you here then?' she muttered.

He looked her squarely in the eye. 'I wanted to tell you that I'd stopped drinking,' he said. 'I left you a message.'

'Sorry.' She had been ignoring messages that weren't work related; avoiding them all. 'So why did Elisa ask you to come?'

'She asked me to come and tell you the truth,' he said, 'about what really happened when your mother died.'

★

The truth, Grace thought, as she worked on her client, gently mobilising the ankles. That was a biggie. The scent of rosemary was deeply infused in the oil she was using this afternoon. It didn't smell like fresh rosemary though, it was more camphorous; as an essential oil, it was supposed to be both stimulating and invigorating, and was intended to impart energy and confidence to her client. Grace had done her usual pre-massage consultation and grounding session; there were rituals which were both professional, such as leaving the room while a client got ready for the treatment, and personal – such as Grace taking a moment to steady her breathing, still her body, stand straight and mentally prepare herself for this work. Talking to her father and speculating on what he was about to tell her, was not an ideal preparation. But hopefully in half an hour's time she would be able to sort this out with him once and for all.

'Why now?' she had asked him.

He heaved a deep sigh. 'Because Elisa – and I – think you need to know. Because it feels like part of the clean slate, I suppose.' He shrugged. 'There's no point in being honest in one part of your life if you're not honest in another.'

Like some awful cliff-hanger in a soap opera, at that precise moment the doorbell had rung and Grace had only had time to shoot him a look, before going to let her client into the house.

Grace steadied her breathing once again as she performed the stretching strokes across the top of the foot. Touch was instinctive but she wasn't properly present right now and this irritated her. She had found her rhythm, and her hands were working well, but part of her mind was still with her father in the living room. He hadn't really answered her question of 'why now?' And what did this have to do with Theo? Because she was pretty sure it had something.

As she worked her knuckles into the sole of the first foot, stretching and mobilising, Grace thought of her father and she thought of the past. Had she loved him? What did love even look like? In her mind's eye an image began to form – blue twinkly eyes, a stubbly jaw, the cool cotton fabric of a shirt against her cheek when he held her safe in his arms. Sandcastles, summer picnics and laughter.

Grace performed the usual toe pulls and circular movement just below the toes, completing the massage with a figure of eight along each foot and a sliding sandwich hold to finish. She hadn't thought of such things for a long time. She supposed that was love.

When she returned to the living room, her father was still sitting at the table. 'Fancy a walk?' she asked him. 'I've been stuck in all day.'

'Oh.' He seemed surprised. And, it had been a long time, she realised, since they'd done anything ordinary like that together. Walked. Talked. Just spent time with one another really. 'Yes. I'd like that.' Slowly, he got to his feet.

He was getting old, Grace realised. He had lost some colour from his face and his cheeks were sunken, his eyes hollow in the deep sockets of approaching old age. His skin was creased, his white-gold hair more sparse even than it had been the last time she saw him. She had lost most of her time with him already. And now he wanted to confess about what had happened when her mother died. Well, there was no need. She already knew.

'We never talked much about your mother after she'd gone,' he began conversationally as they set off towards the bridge and the floating harbour.

'No, we didn't.' Grace remembered that he hadn't really wanted to. Part of the attraction about going to stay with Aunt Mag in Madrid had been that she was her mother's sister, that Grace could talk about her mother, even pretend that she was still in England, patiently waiting for Grace's return.

'I suppose we both grieved in our different ways. But . . .' He glanced across at her. 'I think we could have been stronger together.'

But I blamed you, Grace thought, but didn't say. *I blamed you and I hated you.* She wouldn't have listened to anything he'd had to say about that time.

They walked along past the Hole in the Wall pub which, true to its name, had a small spyhole in the wall through which sailors used to keep a look out for customs men searching for smugglers or press gangs collecting drunks for service in the royal navy. How things had changed, thought Grace. Now, groups of young people sat drinking beer and wine at the wooden tables outside so they could get a better view of the river.

Grace sneaked a sideways glance at her father. She was

surprised that the rhythm of their step was so in synch as they strolled on towards the brick-built Mud Dock. With Robbie she always had to hurry. With Elisa she always slowed her pace a little. With Theo . . . She looked up towards the colourful terrace of Georgian houses that sat high above the river looking down. She loved those houses.

'That's how it often is when you lose someone.' Her father rubbed at his chin, pulled his fleece closer into him against the spring breeze. 'Sometimes you can bear it together. Sometimes you break apart.'

Grace cast him another covert look. Did he not know how she had felt about him? 'Did you feel guilty?' she asked.

'Guilty? Oh, yes.' He hesitated for just a moment and his stride wavered. 'Grief and guilt are a potent mix, I've found.'

They paused on the swivel bridge, looking down the wide waterway. There was a good view from here of an elegant old schooner on the river, a red and black tugboat, the old cranes and the colourful houseboats, the church spire in the distance, and by the bridge, a black cormorant calmly spreading its wings.

'And is that when you started drinking?' Grace turned to face him. She had always supposed so.

'Grief certainly had a lot to do with it,' he said. 'Your mother was my life.'

'Really?' Grace was unable to keep the scepticism out of her voice. He certainly looked as if he meant it. But looks were deceptive, she'd found.

They walked on down the wide walkway, looking, she guessed, like any other father and daughter out for an afternoon stroll. Only they weren't any other father and daughter. What was he going to tell her? That he'd loved her mother so much he'd been forced to have sex with another woman?

Grace breathed more deeply. She tried to relax and admire the way the sun gleamed and glittered on the gently rippling water, the soft sway of the boats on the quayside as though they were warming up for a slow waltz, as much as she usually did. But this wasn't a usual situation. Far from it. She knew she was the pot calling the kettle black. But Robbie had never been her life. He was her husband and she loved him. If he had been her life, she would never have looked twice at Theo.

'My life,' he repeated. 'Along with you, of course.' He turned to smile at her – another real one; a sort of long-lost smile. Shocking herself, Grace found herself smiling back.

'But then I don't understand,' she began. 'Why did you . . . ?'

He shook his head. 'That look in your eyes, Grace,' he said. 'You were only a child. I didn't know what the hell to do. You looked at me sometimes as though you couldn't stand the sight of me.'

Oh, God. As Grace walked along the cobbles, she realised that he had answered a different question to the one she'd been going to ask. She was silent for a moment. What would that feel like? she wondered. To have your child look at you that way? She didn't want to imagine.

At last they reached the flamboyant Ostrich Inn, another

old harbourside pub used by sailors and dockside workers in centuries gone by, but now smartened up with cream and black paint and red parasols outside.

They lingered by the bridge. 'I started drinking because of grief,' her father said, 'and because I felt so alone.' He turned to face her and the pain in his eyes made Grace feel bad. She had to remind herself again of what he had done, of the reason why.

'I tried to be strong for you, my darling,' he said sadly, 'but I knew the truth. I'd let my wife down and I'd let my daughter down – so much so that she hated me.'

Grace was unable to meet his eye. She looked down at the ground. She didn't think they should go any further. It was time to turn back.

He followed her lead and they turned around, retracing their steps. 'I never meant to drink so much,' he said, after a moment or two. 'It crept up on me, you see, Grace. It does that.'

She nodded.

'It was a way to forget.' He took a deep breath. 'And before I knew it, it was the only way I could get through another day.'

Grace wasn't sure what to say. He'd never talked like this before. He'd never been so open. And she could see how it had happened and even how they had moved further apart. *Now that I've had an affair myself*, she thought bitterly. *Now that I can't take the superior stance any longer.*

'Would you like a cup of tea, my dear?' he asked her. They

had reached the Riverstation. 'Or coffee?' He hesitated. 'Or something?'

Grace glanced at his face. He looked pretty pale and washed out and she guessed this was taking its toll. The truth and the not drinking. 'Of course,' she said. 'If you like.'

'It's better than going to a pub.' He grimaced.

'Yes.' And Grace guessed that the clean and chrome modern lines of a place like the Riverstation would never be his first choice. But he was trying, she'd give him that.

They chose a table on the terrace overlooking the river and ordered Earl Grey for him and green tea with lavender for Grace.

'What was she like?' she asked him, as they waited for their tea to arrive. 'My mother?' Now seemed a good time to ask. 'Sometimes I feel as if I hardly remember her.'

'She was lovely,' he said. His eyes misted and he settled back on his seat. 'I loved her from the first moment I saw her.'

Grace smiled. 'Where was that?'

'At a local tea shop.' He chuckled and his face suddenly seemed younger and less grey as if he were living the memory once again. 'I asked her if I could share her table.' He laughed out loud this time.

It was a nice sound, thought Grace, and the awful thing was that she couldn't remember the last time she'd heard it. 'And did she let you?'

He nodded. 'It was very old-fashioned of us,' he said. 'But she was young and a bit of an innocent and I . . .'

'Yes?' She leaned forwards.

'I wanted to look after her,' he said simply.

Which was ironic, Grace thought, given what happened later.

The waitress brought out their tea and Grace busied herself arranging it on the table. Her father continued. It was as if he had a story in his head and he had to let it out. 'We started seeing one another and it got serious quite quickly,' he said. 'Courting, we called it then. She was young, but I sensed she wanted to get away.'

'From her parents?' Grace had never known her maternal grandparents; they had died when she was a baby. Her paternal grandparents she'd seen from time to time – they lived in southern Ireland – but they too had died in their seventies and had seemed distant in manner as well as geographically.

'I suppose so.' Her father frowned. 'I don't think she had an easy childhood. She always said that Margaret was the favourite daughter. But who knows?'

Grace thought of Aunt Mag; remembered how much she had wanted to live there after that visit to Spain; how determined she'd been to be somewhere different, someone different. 'I wanted to leave home too – as soon as I possibly could,' she confessed. 'That's why when Robbie came along . . .'

'You took the chance.'

She nodded. 'I loved him.' She corrected herself. 'I love him. I do. But yes, I took the chance.' Grace poured out her tea and indicated her father's cup. 'Shall I?'

'Please.' Her father was watching her closely, but he didn't seem to be in judgemental mode. 'I never quite made that connection,' he admitted, 'but, well, your mother did the same. I asked her to marry me and she accepted. My uncle Mervyn had already died and left me the house. I had a decent job and no money worries. So she took the chance as well.'

Grace pushed his cup towards him. What was he trying to tell her? 'Didn't she love you, Dad?' she asked him gently. 'Weren't you happy?' She'd never been able to accept this possibility before. But now, since Theo, she had learnt how complicated relationships could be.

'I believe she tried,' he said firmly. 'Physically, well . . .' He shot her a look. 'I won't go into that. But it was difficult for her.'

'She had me.' Grace laughed. It couldn't have been that difficult.

'Yes. And she tried to be a good mother.' His gaze drifted down to the waterway and the canal boats.

Grace took a sip of her tea and gave him the space to continue. She knew there was a lot more that he wanted to say.

'She *was* a good mother, Grace.' He was looking at her as if she'd denied it. 'But she was a human being with flaws, as we all are.' He picked up his cup and took a gulp of hot tea. 'And she had different needs.'

Grace raised an eyebrow. Different needs? What did he mean by that?

'Perhaps it was my fault.' He put his cup down and then

picked it up again. 'Perhaps there was something she needed, that I couldn't give her.'

'What sort of something? What sort of needs?' Grace leaned closer. 'What are you talking about, Dad? Does this have something to do with how she died?' The story was getting more confusing by the second. What exactly was he trying to tell her?

But he shook his head. 'There were problems between us,' he said. 'We'd had the odd row in the past, but your mother simply couldn't cope with that.'

'No one likes confrontation,' Grace murmured, though of course this probably wasn't true.

'She'd get over-emotional, hysterical almost. I learnt not to upset her. It wasn't worth it.'

Grace stared at him. 'Then you went a pretty funny way about it,' she said. Committing adultery probably wasn't the ideal way to deal with your wife's insecurity and emotional frailty.

'But I did try.' He frowned. 'Don't you remember? Anything?'

Grace shook her head. She too looked out across the waterway at the boats and the bridges. It was growing cooler now; they should get back. Only her father hadn't told her yet. She frowned. What did she remember? She remembered tears; she remembered shouting. Who had been shouting? Who had been crying? Her mother? She finished her tea and refilled her cup. The green tea was refreshing, the scent of lavender drifting through it like a faintly remembered scent of summer afternoons. Most of her memories were of her father, she realised again; her mother didn't really seem to be there. And yet Grace had been nine years old when she died. Why couldn't she remember things more clearly?

'Did she love me?' she asked him. She pushed her cup away. It suddenly seemed terribly important to know.

'Of course.' He smiled across at her. 'We both did.'

'But . . .'

'The thing is, Grace. Your mother was what she was.'

What was he talking about? 'What was she?' Grace whispered.

But at that moment the waitress reappeared asking them if they'd like to order anything else. They told her no and Grace's father groped in his back pocket for his wallet. He extracted a crisp fiver.

'Thanks, Dad.' They both got to their feet.

Her father looked round and then he leaned towards her, his voice low. The waitress had gone inside for change. 'When I came back early from work that day . . .' he began.

'What day?' Grace was more confused than ever now.

'The day she died, Grace.'

'But you were at home.' Grace found herself flailing around in her memory for . . . What? Whatever it was, it was something she couldn't quite grasp. 'Wasn't it Mother who came home and . . .' Her voice faltered. She couldn't say it. Something was wrong with the story, but she couldn't work out what it was.

The waitress came back with her father's change. He left

299

her a tip on the saucer and she smiled her thanks. 'Have a good evening,' she said.

'You too,' said Grace.

They left the terrace. 'She was at home,' her father said softly as they rejoined the waterfront path. There were more people around now; they were leaving town, finishing work. Robbie would be home soon, Grace realised. This was the time she was usually rushing back to the house after seeing Theo. But they hadn't arranged to meet today and Grace hadn't heard from him. She knew that he was waiting for her to get in touch, to decide.

'She was always at home.' Her father was still speaking. 'She didn't go out much. She didn't work.' His voice was quiet but the words seemed to drive into her. 'Don't you remember, Grace?'

Grace nodded. Because now, she did. She could picture her mother talking and laughing on the phone. She remembered her lying on the sofa reading a book. She saw her in the kitchen cooking meals that Grace and her father both pretended to like while trying not to look at each other and laugh. Grace stared at him. She stopped walking. She remembered.

'You were having tea with your friend Amanda, do you recall that?'

'Of course. Amanda felt sick. Her mother . . .'

'Brought you home, yes.' He paused. 'Well, I knew you would be at Amanda's because you'd been talking about it at breakfast, so I went home early that day. I wanted to have a chat with your mother – about things. I knew she wasn't happy. I even thought perhaps . . .'

He hesitated. Grace waited.

'That we should call it a day.'

Again, she stopped walking and stared at him.

He raised his hand. 'I know what you're thinking,' he said. 'How could we have split up when we had you? But she was so unhappy, you see, Grace, and . . .' He sighed. 'To tell you the truth I didn't know what the hell to do.'

So you had an affair, Grace thought. Just like she had.

He ran his hands through his white-gold hair. 'So I went home that day and I walked into the house, and . . .' He grabbed Grace's arm. 'I'm sorry. I never wanted to tell you this. I told myself I never would.'

'And what?' Something lurched inside her. But she wanted to know. Even after all these years, she wanted to know.

'There's no easy way to say it, Grace.' He sighed. 'She was with someone. She was seeing someone. I hadn't suspected a thing. I walked in on them and I . . .' He shook his head. 'I lost my temper.'

'She was seeing another man?' Grace was finding this turn-around difficult to believe. For so many years the story had been so different in her head. 'Then, who . . . ?' Who was that woman who walked out of the house? The woman with the brittle heels who smelt of lily of the valley and of funerals? The woman she'd always assumed had been with her father in the house that day?

'Your mother was seeing a woman, Grace,' her father said

sadly. 'I had no idea. But after that, it all made sense. She didn't like men, you see. Not in that way. That's why . . .'

They had so many problems. Grace looked at him for a very long moment, and then she continued walking at a faster pace. Her brain was trying to compute what he'd told her. They reached Welsh Back and headed towards Passage Street. Grace knew her father had come to the house by car; she'd seen the Volvo parked down the road on Counterslip when they'd left the house.

The roads seemed to be getting busier by the second. She heard the familiar sound of a siren wailing. 'Are you telling me the truth?' she asked at last. But she knew that he was. It all fitted. Of course her mother wouldn't have walked in on him that day – he was at work; he was always at work at that time of day. He wouldn't have been with anyone at home. Her mother was the one who was always at home. Grace couldn't believe that such an obvious fact had eluded her. And the woman. She was her mother's lover. Yes, it all made perfect sense. Perfect, but almost unbelievable sense. Grace tried to let her brain absorb these new facts.

'Yes, Grace,' he said. 'I am.'

'Poor Mum.' She gripped her father's arm as they crossed the busy road by Bristol Bridge. They were just two people who should never have been together. 'And poor you.' They walked in silence for a moment until they reached Castle Park. 'But why didn't you tell me sooner?' Not while she was still a child, of course, but once she was old enough to understand. Then, he should have told her.

'I didn't want to spoil your memory of her,' he said. 'Losing your mother at nine years old is bad enough, without losing your memories too. It wasn't her fault she chose the wrong life.'

'And it wasn't yours,' Grace said sharply. They descended the steps towards the floating harbour. 'But why did she rush into the road like that?'

He looked crushed. 'That was my fault,' he admitted. 'When I charged in and ordered that woman to leave my house . . . They laughed at me. I was ranting and raving a bit, I know I was. Your mother got upset. She started crying, screaming about how she couldn't stand living in a cage.' He sighed. 'And then she ran out of it.'

'I see.' He had already explained how upset her mother used to get, and now, with an awful clarity, Grace remembered that too. Her mother crying if they hadn't appreciated her cooking, stalking out of the room if they spent too long talking or laughing together. And she remembered her mother's arms. Her fierce hugs. *If anything happened to you, Grace, I'd die*. So dramatic. But, yes, she had loved her. Grace had often had to choose between them, because they were never together, not really. She hadn't understood it at the time. But no wonder she had blamed her father all these years. She had never chosen. The choice had been taken away from her when her mother died.

They climbed up the steps that led to the house. 'Come in for a bit,' she urged him.

He shook his head. 'I need to get back to Elisa. If you're all right, that is?'

'I'm all right.' She smiled weakly. Bomb blasted, but all right. It had been a hell of a day. First that dreadful row with her stepmother; now this from her father. And her memory seemed to have woken up. Images and scenes from the past were pedalling furiously through her brain. Perhaps that was what trauma did to you – it forced you to forget.

'I'll be off then.' He hesitated, standing by the gate, looking a bit lost.

'Thanks, Dad.' And before she knew it, Grace was in his arms, somewhere she hadn't been for an awfully long time.

'For what?' His voice was choked.

'For telling me.' She held on tight. He smelt of old-fashioned shaving cream but not alcohol. 'And thank you for not drinking,' she said. 'I know how hard it must be. Thank you for trying.'

'I'm sorry, Grace.' He let her go at last. 'For everything.'

She nodded. And she thought of Theo. 'I'm sorry too.'

CHAPTER 30

Havana 2012

Duardo was surprised to see the tall familiar figure of his son sauntering along the pavement towards him.

He finished polishing the headlamps of the Chevy. As bright and shiny as a mirror they were now. It was strange to think that soon he'd no longer be doing this; soon the Chevy would not be his to lovingly cherish, to service, to clean and best of all to drive – hands on the leather-clad steering wheel, back supported by the comfortable old familiar red leather, now cracked and lined with age. And weren't they all . . .

'Hey.' He acknowledged his son's presence. 'What's up, Federico?' Because Federico had never had anything to do with his father's taxi business – he'd made a point of it. So he certainly wasn't here to lend a hand.

'Hey, Papi.' Federico clapped him on the shoulder. He had a grin on his face as usual, but Duardo could tell he had something on his mind. His step wasn't quite so jaunty, his hat wasn't perched at such a precarious angle; there was a faint furrow of a frown on his brow.

'What's up?' Duardo said again.

Instead of answering, Federico ran his palm along the smooth surface of the Chevy's wing.

Don't smear it, Duardo wanted to say. Customers want cars that shine; it was part of the allure. But he kept quiet.

'Business been good today?' his son asked.

Ah, so that was it. He was checking up on Luis's inheritance. He wanted to know the figures; the ins and outs.

'Not so bad.' Duardo narrowed his eyes. He'd learnt to be cagey where Federico was concerned. 'You're lucky to catch me. I did a Trinidad run today.' The town of Trinidad was in Central Cuba, in the province of Sancti Spiritus; it wasn't a short trip.

'Trinidad?' Federico seemed to be mulling this over. 'How much do you charge?'

Duardo named a figure. 'That's standard. If I charged more, they'd go somewhere else.' There remained plenty of imports of the Soviet era in the cities and towns of Cuba – Moskviches and Ladas; by now you'd think they too might be evocative of another vanished world – but people still wanted the American classics. And some might think that, given his views, Duardo would prefer the relics of the Soviets to the Americans. But he had always been pragmatic. And in some ways the Cubans had never been on the same wavelength as Russia. The Soviets were a chilly and introverted race; Cubans warm and outgoing. Besides, the American Chevrolet was a lovely thing to behold. And you couldn't put the blame for a rotten system on a car.

'And the tip?' Federico frowned.

As if it was any of his business. 'Five CUCs,' he said. It could be anywhere from half a peso to ten – which was more than two weeks wages for most people.

Federico whistled. Had he only just clocked how well the business was doing?

Duardo repressed a sigh. He thought of the couple today, posing beside the Chevy for photos. One of her opening the door and climbing into the passenger seat. One of him in the driver's seat. (As if.) One of them both in the back, arms outstretched along the red leather seat back in a pose of proud ownership. *I own it,* he'd wanted to remind them. You can pretend. But it's mine.

'I earned it,' was all he said to Federico. His son knew nothing. Luis now . . . But that was another story.

'Sure you did,' said Federico.

'Do you need a loan?' This was almost the only reason his son would be here asking these sorts of questions.

Federico shrugged. 'Not specially.'

'Why are you asking about the money then?' Duardo threw the polishing cloth back on the pile in the garage. He was done here for today. He'd go back home, grab himself a beer, relax for once. Pretty soon, he reminded himself, he'd be doing a lot more relaxing. He'd have to think about what those projects he'd mentioned to his family might be. For a moment, he felt a dull sensation in his belly. But why should he be afraid? He wasn't losing anything. He'd still have a life; he was sure Luis would allow him to keep his hand in.

'No reason.'

Duardo glanced across at him. Federico might be his son, but he was a taker; something Duardo had never been. 'If you want to know how much Luis is gonna be earning . . . If you're thinking you deserve some of it –'

'He won't be.' Federico leaned against the Chevy. But not in his usual confident style. He seemed ill at ease, upset about something. 'And I'm not thinking that, no.'

Slowly, his words sunk in. 'What d'you mean, "he won't be"?'

'I mean he's not gonna be here.'

'Not going to be here when?' Duardo groaned. So Luis was going away to do more studying, was he? Goddammit. Why couldn't he just stay where he belonged? Time was, he'd always been hanging round the garage. Now Duardo went for days hardly seeing the boy. He paused as he reflected on this. He hadn't been in denial exactly. He'd just assumed Luis was busy with other things – studying maybe, or even a girl. But inside, he knew that Luis's neglect, his uncharacteristic disappearance from Duardo's right-hand side, had influenced the timing of his announcement the other night. Duardo needed to reel his grandson back in.

'He's not going to be here when you retire.' Federico fished in his pocket for a cigarette.

Once again, Duardo swore under his breath. 'I can wait,' he added. 'I'll just keep going for a few more months on my own. It's not a problem.' This explained Luis's reaction to his news. He must have been wondering how to tell his old *abuelo* that actually he wasn't going to be around for a while.

'That's the thing,' said Federico. He lit up, inhaling deeply as if he needed it.

'What's the thing?'

'It ain't gonna be a few months.'

'What are you talking about?' Duardo was conscious of an uneasy feeling creeping along his veins. Why wouldn't it be a few months? Sometimes his son talked in riddles.

'He's going away,' Federico said. He flicked ash from the cigarette.

'You said that already.'

'For a long time.'

Duardo stared at him. The uneasy feeling solidified into something more tangible; a real fear, a black fear. 'How long?'

Federico shrugged. 'Could be for ever,' he said.

For a moment, Duardo felt physically ill. He had not felt like this since . . . For a long time. He sensed the black fear that the uneasy feeling had become, creeping further into him, threatening to engulf him completely. He took a deep breath and focused on Federico's mouth, on the words he was saying. He tried to make sense of them. 'It can't be true. *Por Dios* . . . It can't be true.'

'It was a bombshell to me and Benita too.' He took another deep drag. '*Mira* . . . He just came in one day and told us about this job offer. In Spain. Some sort of tour operator.'

'Tour operator?' Duardo's first instinct was not to believe him. Tour operator? Maybe he'd got it wrong. Luis couldn't leave, he just couldn't. Not after everything Duardo had done, everything he had hoped for. It couldn't have all been for nothing. And as for being a tour operator . . . Duardo had taught Luis that job already – so that he could be a tour operator in Cuba. So that he could represent his country as Duardo did, so that he could take over the business and build on what Duardo had started. Not to go to . . . 'Spain?' he heard himself shouting. 'Why the hell is he going to Spain?'

Once again, Federico shrugged. 'Search me. It was a German guy he met. A German guy living in Madrid. This guy was impressed with Luis and he kept in touch.'

Despite everything, Duardo noticed the note of pride in his son's voice.

'This guy ended up talking to his people and offering Luis a job.' Another drag. 'A good job. He'll be sponsored by the company if he moves to Spain.' Federico moved away from the car. One hand holding the cigarette, one hand looped in the pocket of his jeans. He seemed casual enough, but Duardo knew that he wasn't feeling it.

He shook his head. *A good job?* Wasn't Duardo offering him a good job? He was offering Luis his own business in his own country, for Christ's sake. *Sponsored by some company in Spain?* What the fuck kind of tinpot job was that? 'Where the hell did he meet this German guy?' Duardo growled. He realised that his fists were clenched and he did nothing to unclench them. He'd fight that bastard if he walked into the yard right now.

'In your taxi.' Federico nodded towards the Chevy.

'Shit,' said Duardo. He eased open his fists. Who did he think he was? His days of fighting were long gone. He thought of his little speech around the dinner table. Christ. Had they all been laughing at him? He felt the burn of humiliation. 'How long have you known?'

'Only a couple of weeks,' Federico said.

A couple of weeks . . . 'Why didn't someone tell me?'

Again, Federico shrugged. 'Guess we were all too scared. Thought you'd hit the roof.'

And they were dead right. 'Still, you let me do the whole retirement speech, didn't you?' He glowered at his son. 'You could have spared me that much.'

Federico had the grace to look ashamed. 'I had no idea you were gonna do that,' he said. 'I knew someday you might, but –'

'*He* should have told me.' Duardo felt a cold fury rising inside him. A cold fury against the boy he had nurtured, loved, groomed to take over from him.

'Yeah.' Federico met his gaze head on. 'I told him he should.'

'But he didn't have the nerve,' Duardo finished for him. Was he so terrifying? He'd only ever wanted the best for Luis.

'That's right.' Federico raised an eyebrow. 'He didn't want to disappoint you.'

Duardo considered this. Disappointed wasn't the word. He was devastated, that's what he was. 'But you had the nerve,' he said, glancing at his son.

'Someone had to.' Federico stubbed his cigarette out under his shoe. 'It had to be said. Now it's up to you what you do with it.'

Duardo stuck his hands in his pockets. What should he do with it? 'Any chance of changing his mind?' he asked.

'Would you want to?'

Again, Federico had surprised him. Duardo considered. 'No.' The boy was old enough to make his own decisions and stick by them. He didn't want him if he'd only got him by threats or emotional blackmail.

'When will he be gone?' he asked Federico.

'As soon as they get the paperwork done, I guess. Visas and stuff, you know what it's like. Even with a sponsor it's still not easy.'

Duardo nodded. He recognised the sadness in Federico's eyes. This was his son he was losing. If Luis went to Spain he wouldn't come back – at least not frequently. And he'd probably never come back to his homeland to stay. He'd have a different life, be living in a different world; he'd become a different person. *Like Elisa,* some small voice reminded him. 'You'll miss him too,' he said.

'Yeah.' Once again, Federico clapped a hand on his father's shoulder. It was a gesture of condolence, but of camaraderie too, of understanding. 'I'll miss him too.'

Why did everyone he loved leave the country he loved? Duardo climbed into the driver's seat and edged the Chevy carefully into its garage – a shack really – which kept it under cover in a country where being exposed to the elements could bring on rust and erosion quick as a spark to a flame. It was a blow.

He rested his palms on the steering wheel, closed his eyes and thought of Elisa. How he had cherished that girl. Every day trudging through the mountains, every night making up a camp, loaded with ammunition with the horses too tired and weak to carry a thing, and not knowing where the next meal would be coming from during those long weeks and months in 1958 – he thought of her more often than he liked to remember. The thought of her was the one thing that had kept him going. Elisa. Their future. In a country very different from the one they'd grown up in, where the rich lorded it over the poor, where Americans filled the bars of Havana and his family lived in little more than a slum. *Hastra la victoria siempre!* Ever onward to victory . . . They could be part of that new vision together.

But in fighting for their future, he'd lost it; lost her. While he was fighting for their future, Elisa was running scared – first back to her parents and then out of Cuba, away from him, to a land he hadn't seen and had no knowledge of. A land where she made her home, when she should have been with him in Cuba. And where was she now?

Slowly, he got out of the car. Oh, she'd explained her point of view that time when she came back, when he'd honestly thought she'd come back to him. And he'd tried to understand. He'd forgiven her of course – because she was still his Elisa and he had little choice. But ultimately, he still felt betrayed. She'd never accepted why he had to go and fight. For the love of God . . . There were boys of fifteen fighting in the revolution. How could he not?

He retrieved a bottle of water still nestling in the footwell of the back of the car from today's trip. Couldn't help remembering that back seat and that time with Elisa . . . That night in La Cueva when once again they had danced the rumba – he'd thought they'd already danced it for the last time. The rumba. Their last dance in Havana. It meant a lot to Duardo, did the rumba. He knew that the dance had evolved on the sugar plantations of Havana and Matanzas, that it was originally an Afro-Cuban fertility dance, and that in the seventeenth century it formed the basis of ballroom – with the influential Cuban *son* music as a starting point. But more importantly, he knew that the rumba was part of him, part of Cuba and part of Elisa – and that they were all intertwined with the echo of the music in their souls. That was why he would never dance it with another woman. That was why the music still sometimes brought tears to his eyes.

He'd thought she would stay. If he could forgive, if he could take up where they had left off, then surely she could come back to him? But, no. His mother was right in what she had said to him. Elisa hadn't loved him enough for that.

His life had gone on, of course, and it would go on now. Luis was his grandson but he still felt the loss as keenly. He thought of the afternoon he'd spent with his mother on the beach at Cayo Levisa. She hadn't known, he was sure of that. She, of everyone, would never betray him.

Could Duardo forgive his grandson? He thought of the hours they'd spent together working on the car like comrades. The hours he'd spent coaching him in the languages that had since created a fluency which had presumably got him that job in Spain. The hopes he'd had. The dreams. Sometimes, thought Duardo, there was just too much to forgive.

CHAPTER 31

'I was thinking, Gracie.' Robbie came up behind her and wrapped his arms around her waist. 'How about we go out for dinner this evening?'

'What are we celebrating?' Grace felt her body tense as she tried not to wriggle out of his embrace. It had been quite a day and she was still trying to get to grips with it. And yet . . . in a way she did feel like celebrating. It was the first time in years that her father had talked to her – really talked. It was the first time in years she'd let herself truly remember. Grace felt as though the veil – separating present from past, thoughts from memories – was finally beginning to lift and it was showing her something rather surprising.

'Do we need to be celebrating anything?' Robbie turned her round to face him. His expression was concerned. 'You're feeling better, aren't you?'

'A bit,' she agreed, refusing to think about Theo. 'I've got a lot to tell you.'

'Sounds ominous.' He narrowed his eyes and put his head to one side, still holding her lightly by the arms, watching her. 'Good news or bad news?'

'Good.' She hoped. 'Dad's given up drinking.' She caught

his look. 'Again, I know. And I know what you're thinking. But this time . . .' She touched his arm and moved away, busying herself putting away some mugs and plates from lunchtime and tea with her father. 'He seems different.' She closed the cupboard door.

'Different how?'

She turned back to face him. 'He seems serious about it, Robbie. As if . . .' How could she explain? 'As if he's made the decision himself instead of everyone nagging him to do it. As if he's reached a turning point, you know?'

Robbie nodded. He went back through to the living room and picked up the coat he'd flung on the chair when he came in. 'I hope you're right though, Gracie,' he said. 'We all know it's not the first time.'

She stood in the doorway, arms folded. 'And he talked about my mother,' she added. That *was* the first time.

'Yeah?' He looked up. She could tell that his mind was half occupied with something else. Where they might go for dinner perhaps or what he needed for work the following morning.

Marriage, she thought. When did you stop listening, really holding on to everything your partner said as if it were precious, as if it might tell you something more about them? When did you imagine you knew them so well that you didn't need to listen to what they said any more? She thought of some of the conversations she'd had with Theo over the past weeks. About his life in Florida, about his parents. About why he'd begun practising magic and why he spent time at the children's hospital. Would there ever come a time when they too stopped listening to one another? She didn't know — and it seemed unlikely she'd ever get to find out.

Nevertheless. 'He told me how he felt about my mother. What happened when she died. And my memories . . .' She couldn't think how to describe it. Robbie still had that half-listening look on his face and now he was holding his iPad as if he were just waiting for her to finish talking before he switched it on. She wondered if it would come any easier if she were telling Theo. Damn it, she wanted to tell Theo. 'The memories just came flooding into my head.'

'Is that a good thing?' Robbie frowned.

Perhaps she was doing her husband an injustice. He cared, didn't he? That was the main thing. But he was so black and white. Things weren't always so clear cut. There were rather a lot of shades of grey. She shrugged. 'I think so.'

Wasn't it good to get your childhood back? Grace knew that it would take a long time and that this was just a first step. You couldn't undo thirty years of resentment with just one conversation and a hug. And then there were the readjustments she'd have to make about her mother and who she was . . . Grace came into the room and tidied the table, stacking the place mats, moving the small vase of early daffodils back into the centre of the table. Just their small burst of sunshine cheered her.

Her understanding had made her feel confident for the future. It had made her want to try. And something else. She had known when her father talked about her mother and why she'd run into the road that it would never have happened if she hadn't been deceiving him, if she hadn't been having an affair. She glanced at Robbie who was hanging up his coat on the hook by the door and thought about what her father had said about honesty. What she and Theo were doing wasn't honest; it wasn't a way Grace wanted to live. It caused hurt and anger and betrayal. And she didn't want to hurt or betray the people she loved.

She sat down heavily at the table. So she would end it with Theo as she'd tried to do before – and this time she would do it with a real determination in her heart. It was a pact. If her father could give up drinking, then she could give up Theo. She had to give him up. She couldn't go on like this – none of them could.

'Something to celebrate then,' Robbie said, almost as if he'd been following her thoughts. He sat down opposite her and switched on the iPad.

'Yes.' Grace decided not to tell him about the row with Elisa. That would be getting a bit too close to the subject she wanted to avoid. She watched him switch his attention to the tablet in front of him. Had the increased use of technology made the divorce rate go up or down? There were several ways of looking at it.

'So where shall we go?' she asked brightly.

The phone rang as if in response to her question. Grace went to answer it.

It was Elisa.

Grace took a breath. She slipped into her therapy room, shutting the door behind her. 'I'm so sorry, Elisa,' she said. 'I don't know what came over me this afternoon. You were only trying to help. I shouldn't have said all that.'

She heard Elisa sigh. 'You and me both, Grace, my dear,' she said. 'But I haven't called you about that. We can talk properly another time.'

'Of course we can.' Grace was relieved. 'So, what is it?' She went to the window and drew the blind. Evenings were getting lighter though. Summer was on its way.

'It's your father,' said Elisa.

'What about him?' Grace wanted to thank her for encouraging him to come round and talk to her, but she sensed that this was not on Elisa's agenda either. She sounded worried.

'Is he still with you?' Her stepmother's voice wavered.

'No.' Automatically, Grace glanced at her watch. 'He left a while ago.' She tried to think. It had been before Robbie got home. 'An hour ago, at least.'

'I see.' She heard her stepmother's breath catch.

'He hasn't come home yet then?' Grace frowned, 'he said he was going straight –' She stopped abruptly, realizing the implication of her words. 'You don't think . . . ?'

'Can you tell me what happened between you?' Grace sensed Elisa was trying hard to keep her voice level. 'Was he upset? Angry?'

'No.' Grace thought about it. 'He seemed fine. We had a really good conversation, Elisa. I've just been telling Robbie. We went for a walk and Dad told me everything – about my mother, about their lives together . . .' Her voice trailed.

'And you weren't upset?' Elisa asked her. 'I'm sorry to ask,

my dear. But you didn't say anything to make him feel . . .'
She hesitated. 'Bad?'

'No.' Grace held the phone closer to her ear and tried not
to sound defensive. Of course Elisa had to ask. 'Definitely
not. It was nice.' She could hear the wistfulness though, in
her voice. 'When he left, we hugged, and . . .' And she'd
hoped; she'd really hoped.

'Thank you. I'm so relieved to hear that. It's just that he
seemed so determined. And he was doing so well.' Her voice
broke.

Grace knew what she was thinking. No. 'I'm sure he hasn't
been drinking,' she said stoically. 'Honestly, Elisa, I am.
There're so many places he could have gone instead.' Only
she couldn't think of any. 'It's only been an hour.'

'I wish I had your confidence, Grace,' Elisa said sadly, 'but
you know as well as I do that when you're an addict . . .' She
sighed. 'It has such a hold on you. You try to escape it. And
yet it pulls you back.'

'Yes.' Grace thought of Theo. But this didn't change anything. He wasn't pulling her back this time. 'Will you call me,
when he gets in? Either way?'

'Of course I will,' Elisa told her. 'Goodbye, my dear.'

Grace put down the phone and went back into the living
room. Robbie was still checking his emails. She touched his
shoulder. 'Do you mind if we stay in tonight?' she asked him.
'That was Elisa. I'm worried about Dad.'

'Oh, no.' Robbie stared at her. 'He hasn't lapsed again
already, has he? I'm sorry, love.'

He got to his feet. But as he held her in his arms, Grace thought about it. She'd been so sure her father wouldn't start drinking again — at least not so soon. She'd felt so strongly that this was a new start. And it seemed impossible that she could have been so wrong.

Grace reheated the spaghetti Bolognese she'd planned for tonight and she and Robbie ate it, not saying very much at all. Grace's head felt stuffed full to bursting with everything that had been happening, new information to assimilate, new feelings to embrace, which at least provided a distraction from Theo. Where was her father? Elisa hadn't rung to say he was back safely, which could only mean one thing. After their heart to heart, after telling her the truth about her mother's death, after that rare moment of closeness between them . . . Her father must have given in to temptation and gone out drinking. Grace didn't even feel anger. Just sadness.

The phone rang just as she was stacking the dishwasher. Grace ran to answer it.

'Yes?'

'Grace.' It was Elisa, but it hardly sounded like Elisa.

'Is he back?' she whispered.

'No, said Elisa. 'Grace, he's not coming back.' Her voice broke and Grace thought she heard a muffled sob.

'What's happened? What do you mean?'

Elisa was clearly trying to get her emotions under control. 'The police were here,' she said.

'The police?' Grace felt a dip of panic. So . . . what? He'd hurt himself? He'd been found drunk in a gutter somewhere? What?

'There has been an accident, Grace,' Elisa whispered. 'A car accident. I don't know how else to tell you. Your father – he died before they even got him to hospital.'

Died? Her father had died? Grace was silent. She stared at a spot just above the mirror that hung over the fireplace. Her gaze dropped. She saw a woman, tall, serious, frowning. Unable to take it in. 'I don't understand,' the woman said stupidly. 'How can he be dead? He was here, this afternoon.'

In a few strides, Robbie was beside her. 'What's happened?' he hissed. 'Is it your father?'

She managed to nod. But in truth, she couldn't think, could hardly breathe. She felt numb. 'How?'

'He had a heart attack while he was driving, they think,' Elisa said. 'He almost didn't stop at some traffic lights. There was a woman walking across the road . . .'

My mother, thought Grace. What had happened? Had he been so deep in his thoughts that he hadn't seen the lights change? Hadn't he seen her step out in front of him? Grace could only imagine.

'Was she OK?' she asked sharply.

'Yes.' And Grace guessed that Elisa's thought pattern was running along the same lines as her own.

'It's not fair,' Grace said.

'No, it is not,' Elisa agreed. She stifled another sob.

It was supposed to be a new start – for him, for all of them. 'Stay there,' Grace said, 'I'm coming over.'

CHAPTER 32

Havana 2012

Duardo walked into the apartment that evening looking a broken man. Rosalyn started – she had been sitting on Tacito's favourite twine chair, by the open window, half asleep if truth be told, dozing in the late-afternoon sun. Tacito had made that chair himself, twisting and winding the twine so that it made a flat seat on a broken wooden chair that would then be made good again. He had, she thought, repaired so much that was wrong with her life.

'Hello, my son.' As usual, the door had been left open for ventilation and she hadn't bothered to lock the wrought-iron grille. Rosalyn struggled to sit up, to get back to the present and away from the half dreams and half memories that both plagued and comforted her.

'Hello, Mami.' But he barely looked at her.

'Want some coffee? A beer?' Slowly, she got to her feet. She couldn't do anything quickly these days; it seemed incredible how she had once darted around the apartment doing the chores. '*Para comer?* Something to eat?'

He grunted. 'Just beer. I'll get it.'

She gently pushed him aside and towards the chair she'd

vacated. It was a small thing but she still wanted to be able to do these small things for him.

She took the can from the noisy Russian fridge in the kitchen and went back into the living room. She handed it to him.

'Thanks.' He flipped the tab and drank greedily.

What could have happened? Rosalyn remembered her resolution on the beach at Cayo Levisa and Luis's guilty look at dinner the other evening. She had tried to talk to Federico and then Benita, but neither of them would say much. Federico had given his lazy shrug. 'It will come out soon enough,' he said. 'It is not for me to say.'

'What?' Rosalyn had asked him. 'What is not for you to say?' But he had only shrugged again and walked away.

Benita had not been much more forthcoming. She had stifled a sob and turned her face. 'It is the way of the world,' she had said. 'The new way.'

It was frustrating for Rosalyn. She had always known what was going on in her household and it seemed the reins were indeed now slipping from her grasp. Did she have the strength to hang on to them? She feared not. But she sensed that she would know the truth soon enough.

What could have happened? Was it Federico? Was it Luis? Rosalyn hung onto the counter. She had not seen Duardo like this, with such a blank look about him, since, well, since that day when he'd finally come back from the mountains and discovered that the life he had been fighting for was gone. Elisa Fernandez-Garcia was gone. Rosalyn had desired that outcome, she could not deny it, but she'd never forgive Elisa for succumbing so easily.

'Are you all right, son?' Rosalyn looked around her but Jaquinda wasn't here, and anyway, what could *she* do? More and more, she wasn't here – Rosalyn wished she would just walk out altogether. Could it be something to do with her? But no – Duardo would not care enough. 'What's happened?' Federico and Benita weren't around either, nor Luis. She and Duardo were alone.

Duardo drained the last dregs of the beer from the can. He got up, stomped over to the doorway and threw the empty can into the kitchen sink. Rosalyn jumped. His eyes when he turned were black with anger.

'All we have fought for,' he muttered, 'all I have worked for.'

Rosalyn waited, though she felt she could hardly stand. 'What?' she whispered. And she was glad now that she did not know. This was worse than she had feared.

Duardo came closer. He put his hands gently on her shoulders and looked into her face. 'Luis will not be taking over my business when I stop working,' he said stiffly. 'He has no interest in it.' He let go of her and walked to the window.

Rosalyn frowned. Since when? From a young boy, Luis had doted on his *abuelo*, followed in his grandfather's footsteps, lovingly polished the red and white Chevrolet until it shone. And in return, Duardo had taught him all he knew. Duardo had taught himself, of course. But they both knew that his grandson could do it even better. He was young, he was charming. So what could have gone wrong?

'What will he do then?' Rosalyn whispered. She couldn't imagine.

Duardo clenched his fists. 'He will leave us, Mami,' he said. 'I thought he was our bright star and yet he will leave us.' And he looked out of the window to the street outside as if he could see Luis on his way already.

'Leave us?' What was he saying? But Rosalyn remembered Benita's stifled sob.

Duardo stood up straighter. 'My grandson is applying for a visa to leave our country,' he said. He turned towards her once more.

'Oh.' Rosalyn was stunned. For many years it had been all too easy to leave their country – and then it had become impossible. It still was difficult, she knew, with red tape and bureaucracy and long waiting times. But Raúl Castro had relaxed the laws a little. And now . . .

'But where would he go?' For her part, Rosalyn could not understand why anyone would want to leave Cuba. Things were hard, yes – though not as they had once been hard. But when all was said and done, it was home.

'Spain.' Duardo practically spat the word. He moved from the window, back towards her.

'Spain?' Rosalyn felt dizzy. She put out her arm and held onto the back of a chair. All she could think was of her grandmother and the stories she told of the plantations and the Spanish owners. In Cuba, in the beginning, there were the Indians. In 1492 Columbus came and he conquered them. But so many Indians died from war and from diseases brought into their country that new workers were needed for the land – for the tobacco and for the sugar. And so they looked to Africa. Rosalyn's and Tacito's families were Yoruban African. They came in slave ships where men and women were chained, tortured and thrown overboard if they became too ill. They came to work for the Spanish. There were good Spanish and bad Spanish. Good masters and bad masters. The races mixed over time and now they were all Cuban. It was how the world operated. Power. War. Integration. First Duardo, she thought, and now Luis. But what could he say to the boy? He was his grandfather and he too had fought for the right to be independent. He couldn't now take that right away from Luis.

'How can he go to Spain?' she said. 'It is still not so easy. He has no money to speak of. No job. His job is here, with you.'

'He's been offered a job,' Duardo said, 'with someone he met in my taxi.' He slammed his palm on the table beside them and swore colourfully.

Rosalyn didn't flinch. 'Who?' she asked.

'Does it matter?' he snapped. 'The guy was impressed with his manner – which I taught him. He was impressed by his language skills – which I encouraged. He was impressed by everything – including my damned car.'

'So he offered him a job? Just like that?' It was a strange world indeed, thought Rosalyn.

'He turned the boy's head.' Duardo sighed. 'He talked to him about travelling the world as a tour operator. He told him he was wasting his skills living here with us, working with me and earning some pittance.' He shook his head. 'He told him how much he could earn, where he could go, what he could see.'

Rosalyn nodded. Now she understood. The world was changing and now it was Duardo who was being left behind. But Luis was young; he was part of the new world. 'It would be a wonderful experience for him,' she said, almost surprising herself.

Duardo stared at her. 'What? What are you saying?'

Rosalyn smoothed her skirt and held herself upright. Yes, she had always supported her son, but now her loyalties were being pulled two ways. Duardo would always come first, but she was old enough to see that he would be hurt even more if he tried to hold Luis back, if he did not give him his blessing. Luis was a lovely boy. He reminded her so much of Duardo. 'It was something not possible for you or me,' she said. 'Not even for Federico. But Luis is young. Maybe he deserves this chance.'

Duardo shook his greying head. 'I cannot believe you are saying this, Mami.' And when he looked at her, she felt that she had betrayed him.

She spread her hands. 'Nor me. I cannot believe it either.' She smiled, and after a moment, Duardo smiled too. She patted his hand. 'I know how you feel and it is hard. But he will be back. We will not lose him.' She was very sure of this. 'Cuba is in his soul.'

'And meanwhile, what about the business?' Duardo still looked very glum. 'It has all been for him, you know.'

Rosalyn shrugged. 'We do things for our family without asking first if they want it. So we cannot always expect to be thanked, you know.'

Duardo gave her a sharp look. She wasn't sure what he was thinking. But he sat down at the table and she stood by him, smoothed his hair as she had longed to when they were at Cayo Levisa, as she had done so often when he was a child.

'When did you get to be so wise, Mami?' he asked her.

That was easy to answer. 'When I got to be so old.' She patted his shoulder. 'You will work until you stop, and then you will sell the car and the business,' she said. 'You have done well. I am proud of you and your father would have been proud too. And you have given Luis the best start any grandfather could give his grandson. Now he can take off and fly.'

'What would I do without you, my dear Mami?' Duardo's words were muffled in his fists. 'You are the only one who has not left me.'

But Rosalyn did not reply to this. She had the feeling that it would not be long before he found out.

CHAPTER 33

Elisa didn't know what to do with herself in the days that followed Philip's death. There were so many thoughts in her head, so many *if onlys*. If only she had not asked him to go round to see Grace that afternoon, if only he had left sooner or later, if only that woman had not walked out into the road at that precise moment. But as Grace had told her when she came round that evening, when she stayed with her overnight and the next day too, when they sat and talked it out and through until there was nothing more they could say . . . there was no point in being haunted by *if onlys*. Life was made up of them. If you knew what was round the corner you might never leave the house. You had to live, you had to hope and you had to deal with life's blows and tragedies.

And Elisa knew, from the losses that had gone before, that she was a survivor. What else could you do? So she bustled around in her kitchen, talking to the food, the fridge, herself; keeping herself busy, not giving herself too much time to think. There was plenty of time already for thinking in the small hours when sleep was elusive and yet it seemed too early to give up on it.

Tonight, Grace was coming round for supper and Elisa had

decided to cook *Moros y Cristianos*. It must originally have been a Spanish dish, she supposed, but no other meal represented Cuban cuisine better than this; it was a traditional staple. Elisa needed comfort food, and she suspected that Grace did too. How galling it must be to resurrect a long-lost relationship with your father, to finally have the hope that he could fill the role as you'd always wanted him to, that he could give up his addiction and live a normal life . . . only to have it snatched away from you before it even became a reality.

Elisa shook her head. That was hard. Grace had been right in what she had said that night. It wasn't fair. Elisa checked the black beans simmering in her large stockpot along with the garlic, onion, smoked ham hock and spices. Life wasn't fair.

As for Elisa . . . She leant against the counter for a moment for support. Philip's drinking had been a heavy burden. But. She had been offered a brief and tantalising second chance of contentment in this marriage, which had been snatched away just as cruelly. All she could tell herself was that perhaps it was meant to be.

The doorbell rang and Elisa wiped her hands on her apron and roused herself to answer it. Grace stood on the doorstep looking wan but attempting a smile. 'Come in, my dear,' she said. 'How are you feeling?'

'All right.' Grace kissed her and followed her inside.

'Let me take your coat.' Elisa waited as Grace slipped off her jacket. She hung it on the hook by the door. She was almost sure their relationship was as good as it had ever been before Grace's outburst on the day Philip died. In many ways she thought it was better. There was more honesty between them. But not, she reminded herself, complete honesty. Not yet.

'And you?' asked Grace.

Elisa nodded. 'I'm making *Moros y Cristianos*,' she said, although this hardly answered the question.

Grace smiled. 'Sounds good.' She had always enjoyed Elisa's cooking; always been happy to try anything that was different, even as a child.

'And how's Robbie?' Elisa asked more carefully. She led the way back into the kitchen and lifted the lid of the pan to check the stew. It emitted a gush of fragrant steam. She picked up a fork and gave an experimental prod. Everything seemed as it should be.

'Oh, well, you know, he's fine.' Grace had followed her into the kitchen and stood watching her.

Evasion, thought Elisa. The rice was soaking in a large pan of water in the sink. She drained it and put on more water to boil.

'Smells good too,' Grace said, sniffing appreciatively.

Elisa shook the sieve energetically. 'I take it he didn't want to come tonight,' she said.

Grace was staring out of the window now. Not a good sign. She turned. 'I didn't want him to come,' she said.

Oh, dear. 'But he's helping you? Supporting you?' Elisa couldn't imagine Robbie not doing this. He was the supportive kind. But that was in an equation that did not include Theo.

'Oh, yes.' Grace spoke quickly. Too quickly. 'He's being very good. But what can you say to someone whose father has just died?'

Elisa knew what she meant. Someone who was outside the circle of suffering, like Robbie, couldn't share the grief, not really. He could murmur platitudes and be there for her; he could hold her in his arms and he could empathise. But he would never be able to step inside the circle himself.

'I just need . . .' Grace shrugged, 'to be on my own sometimes.'

Elisa nodded. Time alone was a necessary part of the grieving process. Time to reflect and remember. Time to mourn. It was also good to be with someone who was grieving too. She lifted the ham hock from her stew and set to work removing the bones. She took a deep breath. 'And Theo?' she asked, with a quick glance behind her to gauge Grace's reaction.

'What about him?' Grace had flushed at the mention of his name. But if there was to be honesty between them, Elisa thought, then there would be honesty.

'How are you feeling about him now?' The meat slipped off the bones very easily and Elisa gathered it in her cupped hands and dropped it back into the stewpot. She rinsed her hands under the tap.

'I miss him.' Grace glanced at her and then looked quickly away.

She seemed raw, Elisa thought. 'But?'

'But I haven't changed my mind.'

Elisa noticed that her fists were balled. That bad, was it? Oh, dear.

'I made my decision when Dad came round that day — before that even,' Grace said. Her eyes filled. 'Nothing since then has changed.'

Apart from your father's death, thought Elisa. 'I see,' she said gently. But what she could also see were the expressions on their faces. Theo and Grace. Not together — she had never seen them together — but separately, when one was thinking of the other. And of love. Elisa sighed and turned back to her cooking. She hoped that Robbie would help Grace; that they could eventually be strong enough to get over everything together, and that this feeling for Theo would pass . . . But she knew the feeling only too well. After all. She had never forgotten that final rumba with Duardo.

Elisa tasted her stew, added seasoning and the vinegar and put the rice on to boil.

'And what about you?' Grace asked her. She had recovered her composure. She came over to the cooker and peered into the stewpot which Elisa had left simmering and uncovered for the final fifteen minutes of cooking. 'Are you managing?'

'Of course.' Elisa realised that her answer had also emerged somewhat glibly. As if these things were easy. They exchanged a wry smile. 'You know, your father and I never had much of a chance,' Elisa said. 'What would you like to drink? Water? Wine?'

'Wine?' Grace's eyebrows raised.

Elisa shrugged. 'These days, I'm allowed to have alcohol in

the house, I think,' she said. 'A little of what you like does you no harm, I'm sure.'

'In that case, it would be rude not to join you.' Grace opened the kitchen cupboard and got out the glasses. 'Robbie said he'd pick me up at ten.'

'Perfect.' Elisa gestured. 'There's some white in the fridge.'

Grace went to fetch it. 'Why didn't you and Dad have much of a chance?' She returned to their previous conversation. 'Because of the way he felt about Mum, do you mean? Or because of the way she died?'

'Both.'

Grace poured the wine and passed a glass to Elisa. They clinked glasses and exchanged a sad smile. 'And then because of his drinking?' Grace suggested.

'Yes,' said Elisa. She took a sip of wine and then another for courage. 'And also,' she said, 'because of Duardo.'

'Duardo?' Grace sat down at the table, which Elisa had already laid before she'd arrived. 'Who's Duardo?'

Now there was the question. Elisa checked the rice. It was done. 'You were right,' she said, 'there was someone else for me too. There always has been.'

Grace stared at her.

'Yes, it is true.' Elisa nodded. She drained the rice, taking her time to recover herself as she forked it into fluffiness. She served it on to two plates, dishing up the soupy beans separately so that Grace could help herself.

'Elisa? You don't have to tell me, you know.' Grace put a hand on her arm.

Elisa nodded to her to help herself. 'But I want to.' Honesty, that was the thing.

'It's none of my business, really.' Grace helped herself to beans, spooning them on top of the fluffy white rice. 'I said all those things that day because I was tired and stressed and because I didn't know what to do – about Theo.'

'I know.' It didn't matter. Not now.

'So . . .'

Elisa put a hand over hers. 'I want to tell you, Grace,' she repeated. 'You see I was very young when I first met Duardo.' She smiled at the memory. 'It was in Havana in a bar called La Cueva. He came up to me and asked me to dance the rumba . . .'

By the time Elisa finished talking, they had eaten their meal and each drunk another glass of wine. Elisa had cleared away their plates but they remained seated at the table, heads together. Elisa had told Grace about how she and Duardo had run away to Matanzas, how he had gone off to fight, how she thought he was dead and didn't find out the truth until she returned to Havana in 1985, by which time both Philip and Grace had become a part of her life. Finally, she told her about the baby, Duardo's baby, whom she had lost even before she had the opportunity to make a decision about him. Philip had always said that he forgave her, but when he finally told Elisa about his first wife and the affair she'd had, Elisa had been left to wonder. How much of her behaviour had contributed to her husband's drinking? Just how had he felt – being betrayed again?

'I knew there was something,' Grace said at last. 'Or someone. Even before you told me about your miscarriage.' She put her hand on Elisa's and squeezed gently.

'How?' And Elisa thought she had been so careful not to give anything away.

'When you talked about Cuba.' Grace shook her head. 'It was an expression in your eyes.'

'Ah.' Elisa knew that expression rather well.

'And will you ever go back there?'

'To Cuba?' Elisa was shocked.

'Of course. After all, he may still be alive.'

Elisa considered this. 'Yes, he may,' she conceded.

'Don't you want to find out?'

Elisa was aware that she could find out whenever she wanted to. She still had family in Havana – not her Aunt Beatriz of course who had died many years ago, but her cousins. It would not be difficult. But she had made it a point of loyalty not to. That time was gone. She had made her decision and she had returned to Philip, determined to make her marriage succeed – although whether she had achieved this aim, she wasn't sure. But now . . . 'I don't know,' she said.

Grace seemed to have the bit between her teeth. 'You could go back now,' she said. 'There's nothing to stop you.'

Elisa eyed her sorrowfully. There was still Grace. There were still the responsibilities of her life here. And she was no longer young. She was tired. She'd had the best of her life.

'You must have thought about it,' Grace said.

It seemed disloyal to admit this. With losing Philip so

recently, and with that new promise there had been between them. Elisa had never loved him in the all-consuming and passionate way she had loved Duardo. Nevertheless, with Philip, there had always been something; a small spark, but something that could perhaps have been fanned into a flame. But. 'Yes,' she said, 'I have thought of it. But Grace, my dear, even if I could bring myself to go back there, it is certainly much, much too late.'

CHAPTER 34

'Let's go away for the weekend,' Robbie had said. 'We need a break.'

Grace was in that sort of mood where you just go with the flow, as if you're waiting for something or someone to happen to snap you into action or reaction. So, 'All right,' she said. 'Why not?' She didn't want to be here in Bristol. Every time she went out she kept catching glimpses of men who she thought were Theo. She thought she'd seen him yesterday in the supermarket – but when she got to the end of the aisle he wasn't there, then she thought she saw him in Castle Park later that day when she'd gone out for some air and a walk around. A tall man, a dark-haired man, an olive-skinned man who could melt into any background he chose. A man who could be there and not be there. A man who could click his fingers and produce a coin in the palm of his hand. Where was he? Did he know about her father? What was he doing? She longed to know.

They drove down to Dorset, to a place called West Bay where ginger-coloured cliffs were stacked high against the spring-blue sky, and where real fishing tugs collected in the small harbour, seagulls dived crazily for pickings and children went crabbing with their nets and their buckets by the harbour wall. There was a tea room on a now unused station platform, a seaside café and brightly painted kiosks selling fish and chips and candyfloss. There was an old chapel, some new flats and fishermen's cottages from more than a century ago. It felt like a real place, thought Grace; a good choice.

The breeze was brisk as they took a Saturday morning stroll along the pebbly beach beside the golden cliffs; it was early, so they pretty much had the place to themselves. Grace took Robbie's arm. He felt solid and reassuring. They walked in an easy rhythm, steady and slow enough to take in the landscape. Grace felt her shoulders lose some of the tension she'd been holding. The past weeks hadn't been easy – trying to juggle work with helping Elisa sort out the administration following her father's death, trying to stay positive in the wake of what had happened, trying not to miss Theo. Robbie had heard nothing from him either. Perhaps he had gone away? Grace didn't dare ask Elisa, although she guessed that she would know.

Rather to her surprise, Robbie had dropped the subject of finding him. He'd gone round to Theo's house once or twice, increasingly half-heartedly, and a couple of times he'd said, 'I just don't understand it, you know, Gracie.' But that was about it. Grace was surprised; it had been a long and close friendship and she was pretty sure she wouldn't have given up on it quite so easily. But she knew Robbie had been busy too – a new contract at work, a colleague to train up, not to mention looking after Grace's wellbeing following her father's death. It was what they all needed, she supposed, someone to watch over them.

But what did it mean? Did Theo's silence mean that he planned simply to vanish from their lives as if he were performing one of his magic tricks? Did it mean she could stay here in Bristol and not go to live under the wing of Robbie's family in Sussex? She hoped so. Sussex became less appealing by the day. She was building up a good client list. And there was even more reason now, to be with Elisa, to stay.

'It feels good, doesn't it?' Robbie patted her arm. 'To be somewhere different.'

'Mmm.' Grace looked up at the tall cliffs, at the gulls climbing to the grassy summit, swooping down to perch on the ledges, behind which their nests were tucked into little sandy caves and crevices. Any part of this rock face might crumble into the sea at any moment, so eroded was the sandstone coastline.

'And you know, we'll be all right.'

'Yes,' she said. Now the funeral was over, there was a sense of relief and release. She had said her goodbyes to the man she'd hardly known for most of his life, whispered an apology too. For judging him. For not communicating with him. For being unfair. Was it enough? She gave a mental shrug. It would have to be. She had a feeling that her father – her real father, the man who was not an alcoholic, but simply a man trying to do his best for his family and the people he loved – would understand.

'We should go away more,' Robbie was saying. And it was

true that they both seemed more relaxed than they had been of late. Robbie was wearing jeans and a loose shirt, and his hair had grown into a more casual style which suited him. When he was away he smiled more often and checked his emails less frequently; she had a glimpse of a more easy-going and laid-back man, a more confident self who often stayed in the shadows.

They passed a lone fisherman who had erected a small blue tent next to where he stood in his green waders, legs apart, body balanced, as he held the rod, about to cast his line into the ocean. Grace wondered if he had been there all night.

'There's nothing to stop us,' Robbie added.

'No.' But what had stopped them before? Nothing. Certainly not her father.

Grace's feet sunk deeper into the soft bank of tiny pebbles and sand. Ahead of them, Chesil Beach appeared to go on for ever, although the high golden cliff gradually grew lower in the distance, until it met the beach on the same level. They had walked so far that they had reached a caravan park. A family appeared from behind one of the mobile homes, the parents holding hands, the boy and the girl running ahead. Grace felt Robbie's step pause, his rhythm change. She glanced across at him, followed his gaze. He was staring at the children. The look on his face startled her; it was a look of pure wistfulness.

But he recovered almost immediately. 'And this is a great place to bring the kids,' he said, as if they already had a few up their sleeve. *Up their sleeve* . . . Grace thought of Theo.

Couldn't help but think of him. He'd disappeared from her physically but it wasn't so simple to banish him from her mind.

What kids? She wanted to say. But she knew what kids. The kids they were supposed to be having. The kids Robbie wanted. The kids he deserved.

The children, who were about five and seven years old, she guessed, ran down to the water's edge and then screamed and raced back as the tide came in. 'Careful,' called their mother, but she was laughing.

Grace tried to imagine being that caring, laughing mother. Could she do it? Could she be her?

'Let's sit down for a minute,' Robbie said, and dropped down on to the stones.

Grace sat next to him and hugged her knees. She would have rather kept on walking. She'd found this was happening to her a lot lately. She couldn't stop doing or moving. It was as if she were scared to stop. As if she didn't dare to. Stopping meant you had time to think.

The parents of the children sat down too, just in front of them and over to one side so they were in their sightline. The father was skimming stones into the sea. Pretty soon he was joined by his children and they all had a go, except the mother who simply lay back on the stones and stared up at the pure blue sky. Grace guessed she didn't have too many times when she could do just that. Grace wanted to do the same. She wanted to just lie and stare up at the sky and . . . and what? She simply had no idea.

'Have you had enough time, Gracie?'

For a moment, Grace thought she'd imagined this question. Once she knew it was real, she couldn't understand who could have said it or what it meant. 'Time?' she echoed. Her mind was a blank.

'Time to think,' said Robbie. She heard just a note of frustration.

Grace realised he was still gazing at the family, that look on his face. She sighed. How long had it been? Weeks? And her father had just died, for pity's sake. 'Now, Robbie?' She stared at him. 'Do we have to talk about it now?'

He shrugged. 'I know it's not a good time for you.' He took her hand. 'But new life can be a comfort at a time like this.'

It sounded like a platitude. Life and death, thought Grace. Her father had died. It didn't sound like the best reason for having a baby. Was Robbie so desperate that he would turn everything that happened into a reason for starting a family?

'And it's your birthday soon.'

She turned away from him at that. Watched the inexorable roll of the waves on to the shore. They curled and foamed and the tiny bubbles burst as the tide drew back from the wet shingle. Nothing would stop them.

'Gracie?' It seemed as if nothing would stop Robbie either.

'For God's sake,' she hissed. 'Life doesn't stop when you're forty.'

'But some things stop, Gracie.' He jumped to his feet. For

344

a moment she imagined he was going to go charging off in a temper, but he held out a hand to her instead. She took it and he pulled her up. 'Fertility decreases for a start.'

Grace glanced at the little family of four. The father had got up too and was playing with the children down by the water's edge. The woman was still lying with her face to the sky, eyes closed. 'I know,' she said.

'Well, then.' He shrugged as if that was all there was to it.

Grace didn't want to argue. Not now that the morning sun was lighting up the blue tints of the waves and the gulls were cruising effortlessly on the thermals and everything looked so fresh and new. Later, she thought.

Later, was when they were having dinner in a seafood restaurant by the harbour. Grace's first course of scallops with pea-shoots and cumin, was delicious; the sweet softness of the scallops complemented by the edgy spiciness of the cumin and the crunch of the shoots. Robbie had chosen prawn kebab with chilli.

He speared a prawn. 'I don't know why you're so resistant, Gracie,' he said conversationally, as if they were discussing which movie to go and see. 'What are you scared of?'

'Do I have to be scared of something?' Grace dipped her scallop into the cumin foam.

Robbie considered her words, a faint frown on his brow. 'I think so,' he said at last. He munched on another prawn. 'Women are supposed to get broody at a certain age, aren't they? Isn't it supposed to be a biological urge?'

'If it is, I've never felt it.' Although this wasn't quite true. Grace remembered a friend of Elisa's coming round one afternoon with her baby. She remembered holding him – wanting to hold him and yet being frightened to. So much responsibility. The baby had seemed so tiny, so vulnerable and frail.

'Pretty robust things, babies,' the friend had said, and Elisa had smiled and agreed. She'd looked more than a little wistful too, come to think of it. The baby had smelt of milk and creamy freshness and something about holding him had opened something up inside Grace. It was a kind of special baby smell that defied description but seemed to have a direct connection with part of her, deep inside.

'And anyway, this isn't one of your computer programs,' Grace added. Because it had only been a temporary sensation that biological urge. There had been something else that made her much more unwilling to start a family, and that had been by far the stronger pull.

'What do you mean?' Robbie looked hurt.

'It isn't an exact science,' she said. 'It's personal, subjective. Complicated.'

'Complicated?' he echoed.

Honestly. 'And children are a huge tie.' She finished her starter. 'You have to be one hundred per cent committed.'

'But I am.' Robbie too pushed his plate away and grabbed her hand.

Grace couldn't help smiling at his enthusiasm. It reminded her of when he'd proposed to her. 'Already?' she had said. 'Are you sure?' Because they'd only been seeing each other for two months. 'Already,' he had told her. 'And I am sure. I was sure the night I met you.'

But now she had to be honest. 'You're not the problem,' she said, 'or at least you are . . .'

The waitress came to clear their plates and Robbie poured them more wine. 'What if I went part time and helped look after the baby?' he said. 'Would that help persuade you?'

Grace wiped her lips with her napkin. He just didn't get it. He thought she was scared of the amount of work a child would entail, of what she might lose. 'Let me ask you a question,' she countered.

'OK.'

'Why is it so important to you for us to have children?' She put her elbows on the table, leaned forwards and looked into his eyes. 'Is it because your family expect it? Because your sister's done it? Because you think it would make us complete in some way? Or is it a deep primeval longing that tells you to be a father?' She leaned back in her chair again and sipped her wine.

He too picked up his glass. He seemed thoughtful. 'All those things,' he said. 'And more.' His eyes softened behind his glasses. 'I want a boy I can play football with, Gracie, or teach science to and stuff. A girl I can take swimming or to dancing lessons . . . I don't know.'

'All the clichés,' Grace teased. 'All the stereotypes.' But inside, she was shrieking against it. She couldn't help it. It just didn't seem right. For her, it didn't seem right.

'Probably.' The waitress brought their main course and

they thanked her. 'I'd give them whatever they needed.' Robbie's eyes were serious now. 'I'd give them anything, Gracie.'

She bowed her head. He was making this so difficult. She knew he'd be a great father. That was the trouble. 'And if I don't want to . . .' Her words trailed.

She saw him stiffen. He didn't reply, just picked up his fork and started eating his sea bream with fresh mint and rocket. She hesitated, picked up her own knife and fork, still watching him.

'Don't you?' he asked, after a few minutes had passed. 'You always said you just needed time.'

Grace looked past him and out towards the harbour, in darkness now. The boats had been emptied and cleaned, the fish crated and sent out to retailers and restaurants. The lights around the harbour wall were beaming down on to the gently rippling water. 'I'm not sure that I do,' she said. 'I'm not sure that I ever will.'

Robbie clenched his fists. 'What's wrong with you, Gracie?' he muttered.

Grace looked across at him and raised an eyebrow. Perhaps here wasn't the place.

He cut almost savagely into his fish. 'You marry someone, you have children. That's the deal.'

Grace put her knife and fork back on the plate. Her plaice with asparagus in a white wine sauce was light and delicious but she seemed to have lost her appetite. 'It wasn't a deal I ever agreed to,' she said softly. She sipped her wine and gazed back at her husband. What had she agreed to? To love, hon-our and obey? To cherish? To be faithful?

Robbie shook his head in despair. He too pushed his plate away and the waitress came scurrying across to check every-thing was okay. 'It's fine,' he said tersely. 'We may as well get the bill.'

Oh, hell, thought Grace. They had come away for a break, and she had so hoped that things might get back on an even keel, that she might start feeling the right things again. But here they were arguing. About babies. Again.

'Is it because of your childhood?' he asked her as they left the restaurant and walked back towards the beach and their hotel. 'Is it because of your mother dying when you were so young?'

It was the scientist in him that always assumed there was an answer – that one simply had to dig deep enough in order to find it. But Grace wasn't so sure there was an easy answer. 'I don't know,' she admitted. 'I used to think so. It's terribly hard, losing your mother at such a young age.' She stuck her hands in her pockets.

'Because people die.'

Grace winced. Did he think she didn't know that?

'They just do. It's sad for them and it's sad for the people they leave behind. But it happens.' He grabbed hold of her arm. 'You can't let it ruin your life,' he said. 'You have to move on. You're not going to die. You're not ever going to leave our children.'

'There won't be any children.' She spoke so quietly that for a moment she wasn't even sure she'd said it out loud.

'What?'

Grace took a breath. She looked out in front of her towards the deep, dark ocean. There were clouds hiding the moon. It was only fair. 'There won't be any children, Robbie,' she said. 'Not for us. I'm sorry.'

'But . . .'

'There won't be any children.' She stopped walking, turned to face him and eyed him steadily. 'And you deserve better than that.'

'What are you saying, Gracie?' In the darkness his features were blurred, but his eyes behind his glasses were clear. He still didn't seem to understand what she was telling him.

'You know what I'm saying.' Grace took a breath. Listened to the rush of the tide as it pushed relentlessly onshore, the hiss on the pebbles as it drew back. She was wrong to stop Robbie having children, she could see that now. He deserved to have them. He'd be a brilliant father. Being a father would enable the background Robbie to shine through. She could see it. He'd play with them, he'd teach them, he'd give them everything, just like he'd said. They would adore him in return. And Robbie would become the laid back and confident man she'd almost seen on the beach this morning. That was his destiny and it was up to Grace to help him fulfil it. But not in the way he wanted her to.

'Is it about moving to Sussex?' He took hold of her hands. 'Because you know we don't have to do that. I never meant —'

'No.' She stopped him.

'Then we won't have any kids.' He turned away, still

350

holding her hand, leading her closer towards the sea. Their footsteps scrunched in the pebbles. 'What does it matter? Lots of people don't have kids. We'll save one hell of a lot of money too.' He laughed and swung her hand, but the sound was hollow and it was echoed by the tide.

If they did that then Grace knew that there would come a day when he would never forgive her. She looked up into the night-time sky and saw the clouds scudding gently past to reveal a beam of light. It was a full moon, and as Grace stared, it seemed to emit an aura of serenity that touched her. 'You need someone else, Robbie,' she said. She couldn't believe she hadn't seen that before, that this clarity had only come on a summer evening in Dorset on a darkly golden beach with a full moon spotlighting the water.

'Someone else?' he echoed. The waves seemed to take his words and roll with them.

'Someone who will give you what you want,' she said. She had been so wrong. It had never been a choice between Robbie and Theo. It had always been a choice for her. What Grace needed after what had happened – her father's revelation, his death, what she had learned from Elisa, and Theo . . . was to be alone. How could she have a life with someone when she hadn't even learned to be alone?

It felt as if they were the only people on the beach. They were surrounded by wind and tide and moon and something that took Grace's breath away. You fell out of love, didn't you? It happened. It was better and more honest to acknowledge it than to pretend.

'Are we breaking up, Grace?' Robbie's voice was thin and unsure. He sounded as though he simply couldn't believe it. 'Are you breaking up with me?'

Grace turned to him. 'I love you.' She took hold of his hand and she held it between her two hands. 'But I'm not right for you. I've treated you badly. I haven't given you what you need. And I can't, because if I did, it would be for all the wrong reasons.'

'But –'

She saw that she would have to say more. 'Theo,' she whispered, 'he left us because of me.' Because what difference did it make now? Their friendship was over. And it would do the job. It would make him hate her.

'Theo.' That was all he said. He seemed to look through her and inside her, just for a moment, as if understanding something for the very first time. Then he turned into the darkness and walked away.

CHAPTER 35

Elisa walked round to Grace's for her massage. She had gladly agreed to being one of her stepdaughter's original guinea pigs and since losing Philip she'd appreciated her regular visits even more. Growing older, she concluded, as she walked through Castle Park, which was blooming with geraniums and flowering shrubs now that summer was truly here, was overrated. Wisdom and experience were all very well, but one lived in one's body and she was fed up with un-cooperative joints, stiff limbs and aching muscles. Grace's therapeutic hands once a fortnight were heaven. Grace's touch was heaven.

Grace opened the front door and kissed her hello. 'Come in, Elisa. How are you feeling?' She was wearing the white cotton tunic she always wore for work and her feet were bare. Her dark hair was tied back in a ponytail and she looked ridiculously young.

'Thankful for the sunshine.' Elisa followed her into the therapy room. It was light, bright and smelt faintly of rose oil.

Grace smiled. 'Does it remind you of home?'

'A little.' It was funny, Elisa thought, they both referred to Cuba as her home. What was England then? What had it been all these years since she had moved here as a girl of eighteen?

She took off her coat and put it with her handbag on the chair by the door.

Grace picked up her clipboard and immediately took on a professional air. 'Any aches and pains to report? Any injuries?'

'You would be the first to know,' said Elisa. She was confident that they had become closer since Grace's split with Robbie. Shocked at first, Elisa had also understood her reasons, and respected Grace's honesty. Grace had come round to the house in King Street after their weekend in West Bay and it had all spilled out – her discussion with Robbie about how they both felt about starting a family, Grace's realisation of what Robbie needed – and what she needed too. How she had told him about Theo. A week later Robbie had moved out and Grace hadn't tried to stop him.

'Do you want to take off your things and lie down for me? Face down in the cradle as usual and here's a nice warm drape to cover yourself with. I'll be back in a few minutes.' Grace smiled and left the room.

Elisa slipped off her red blouse and put it on top of her summer jacket, stepped carefully out of the purple skirt she was wearing and removed the vest she wouldn't do without until August probably – if then. She gave a quick glance of satisfaction towards Grace's framed certificate of qualification and nodded at the books on massage and anatomy in the bookcase. She pulled a silly face at Grace's small skeleton, Angus, who stood on a shelf in the corner. She lay face down on the massage table, covering herself with the cosy brushed cotton drape. The room was already warm; Elisa knew that Grace turned up the heating for her before she arrived.

There was a light knock on the door.

'Come in.' Elisa heard Grace softly enter the room. She approved of her stepdaughter's professionalism; she wanted to be a client rather than a stepmother when she was lying here and she liked the fact that their relationship never got in the way of her therapy. Probably, it even helped it.

Grace went straight over to the table in the corner and started preparing the oils. She had a large glass bottle filled with the oil she used for massage – usually an almond base – and small vials with essential oil to add. 'Would you like lavender and thyme or something different?' she asked.

Elisa sighed. Lavender and thyme was her staple and lavender was good, Grace had always said, for maintaining a calm state of mind. But . . . she couldn't get the scent of mariposa out of her head. It was sweet and delicate with a hint of ginger. The white butterfly, or mariposa was the national flower of Cuba. And Grace had been right. That was home.

Grace glanced across at her. 'How about rose?' she asked gently. 'It's already in the room. I could soon clear it with a citrus candle and some fresh air, but it may help you sleep better. And it's very good for grief.'

'Why not?' Was she grieving? Was that it? Grace was good at her job, thought Elisa. She was alert to mood, to what someone might need at any given time. 'It is a very pleasant scent,' she conceded. Nevertheless, it was not mariposa. The white butterfly ginger would not grow here in Bristol; it was a tropical plant, it needed plenty of sun to thrive. Elisa smiled, remembering how the zun zun birds had always flocked to the heady mariposa rather than to the roses or jasmine. And she thought of how she had loved to wear the white flower in her hair when she was a girl.

Elisa wriggled to make herself comfortable, felt Grace adjust the drape so that the heat seemed to seep into her once more. Ah. She closed her eyes. Grace had turned on the soft classical music. And now she was beginning. She laid her hands first on top of the drape before gently pulling it up a little. Elisa felt the warm oil seeping into her skin, the firm confident touch of Grace's hands as she moved from her first reassuring hold, which seemed to establish a note of trust between them, to working on Elisa's legs with long, sure strokes that were already imparting a sense of wellbeing. Oh my goodness, thought Elisa. How she would have loved this in her dancing days.

At first, they were both silent as Grace got into her rhythm, pressing and kneading; teasing out the knots and tangles of the muscles and sinews beneath the surface, as she focused on first one part of her body and then another. The soft background music filled Elisa's senses, along with the sweet fragrance of the rose oil. Weathered old skin, she found herself thinking. But a good massage made you forget all that. Age was no longer an issue. Human touch was healing in itself. And this was so much more. It made Elisa feel pampered and cared for.

'Would you turn, please?' Grace asked when she'd finished

Elisa's back and shoulders. 'Can I help you?' And she held the drape up to preserve her dignity, as Elisa turned, giving her the other arm to help ease her over. 'A bit lower this time, please, so that your head is on the couch.'

Grace rearranged the drape and began to work on her arms. This was Elisa's favourite part; she loved the way Grace smoothed her hands over the wrists and elbows, the attention she lavished on each knotty finger. She sighed again – a good one this time. She knew Grace had struggled with her studying on occasion – the course had been more academic than she'd been expecting, and her confidence levels had veered alarmingly at times – but it had been so worth the effort. Look at her now. Such a professional. So good at her job. Doing something that was so worthwhile.

'Any news on the house?' she murmured. It was on the market, she knew that much. Grace was planning to buy a smaller place. 'It's just me and my therapy table now,' she had joked to Elisa, and of course she would have to share any profits with Robbie. Even so. Elisa saw the sadness in her eyes. She knew it had been a difficult decision for her. None of this was easy.

Grace rubbed and pressed into the palms of her hands. It was exquisite. Elisa exhaled.

'I've had a few people round,' she said, 'and one second viewing. No definite offer though.'

'And Robbie?' Elisa knew he had moved out. But where had he gone? And what was he planning to do? 'Have you seen him?'

Grace didn't answer immediately. Elisa could see that a lot was going through her mind. Perhaps she shouldn't ask so many questions, perhaps she should leave her be – especially when she was focusing on work. But Elisa had brought her up, in part, and old habits died hard.

'He's decided to live in West Sussex,' Grace said at last. 'He wanted to get right away.'

Elisa raised her eyebrows. 'Will he live with his parents?' she asked.

'Only until this place is sold and he finds something else.' Grace covered her once more with the cotton drape and moved up to her neck. 'It's where he's always wanted to be,' she added. 'Close to his family. And luckily for him there's a London office, so he can commute.'

Elisa pulled a face. She wouldn't fancy that sort of a commute herself. Life was too short. But then again, things were different now. If you travelled by train you could do so much – get some work done on your laptop, have dinner, catch up with friends and family, surf the net. It wasn't as if he would have a wife to come home to. She wondered though how long it would be before Robbie moved on. Not long, she guessed. That man needed an uncomplicated woman who simply wanted a good man and a lovely family. She would make him happy and he would do the same for her. A man like Robbie didn't need her amazing but wilful stepdaughter. She was far too complex. But what did Grace need?

Grace finished in her usual way with a sweep and a cradle, holding Elisa's neck in both her hands and staying still for a few beats, signalling closure. Elisa heard her breathing change, felt her stepdaughter's touch linger and then leave her. It was almost as if, Elisa thought, she had been unravelled, treated and then tied back together again.

'You're done,' Grace informed her. She covered her gently with the warm drape from chin to toes. 'How are you feeling?'

'Wonderful.' And it was true that Elisa felt relaxed and yet energised; a potent combination.

'Good.' Grace was over at the basin now washing her hands. 'Well, take your time getting up. There's a glass of water on the table.' She turned to throw her a smile. 'Can you stay for a cup of coffee?'

'Of course – if you have the time.' Slowly, Elisa sat up. She watched Grace thoughtfully. What Grace needed . . . Could it still be Theo? 'And what about Theo?' she asked – though she almost didn't dare to. 'What are you going to do about him? Have you decided?'

Grace swung around, drape in hand. She looked defenceless suddenly. 'Nothing,' she said.

'Nothing?'

'I'm not going to try to see him again, if that's what you mean.'

'Why not?' Elisa began to get dressed. She thought of that look of love. It seemed such a waste.

'It's over between us.' Grace slipped out of her white tunic and pulled on a casual summer dress. This symbolised her transition, as Elisa was aware, from massage therapist to stepdaughter, acquaintance or friend. 'It was impossible back then and it still is. It's . . .' She shrugged. 'Complicated.'

'Too complicated to explain?' Elisa asked. Though she knew from her own experience that love often was.

'I need some time on my own,' Grace said. 'Theo was a sort of madness.'

'I see.' Elisa wondered if she had been mistaken.

'And I don't want Robbie to be hurt even more.'

Elisa nodded. 'Has Robbie seen him?' She picked up the rest of her things.

'I don't know.' Grace looked sad. 'I've hardly seen Robbie myself to be honest. He just wants to keep right away.'

Elisa couldn't blame him for that. He was grieving for his loss just as she and Grace were grieving.

'But does Theo know?' she asked Grace. 'About you and Robbie splitting up?'

'I have no idea.' Grace's voice was different now, more brisk. 'I told you, Elisa, it's over. I chose Robbie. There's no going back. I'm on my own now. And that's fine.'

'Very well, my dear.' Perhaps it was for the best.

Elisa followed her into the living room. 'But you will stay in Bristol?' She eased herself down into a chair at the table. She was zonked, so relaxed she could almost drop off to sleep right here and now.

Grace was filling the coffee maker in the kitchen. She switched it on and came back into the room. 'Oh, yes. I couldn't let down all my clients for a start.'

Elisa smiled. 'We are all dependent on you,' she agreed.

'And it should be easy enough to find a smaller place.'

Elisa wondered how well off she would be after the sale of this cottage. Maybe Grace wouldn't be able to afford even a smaller place. 'You could always come and live with me,' she suggested.

'No.' Grace spoke so quickly that Elisa was rather taken aback.

'I only meant for a while,' she said. 'If it would help in any way.'

'It's so kind of you, Elisa.' In seconds, Grace had crossed the room and was beside her. She sank down to her knees and took Elisa's hand. 'And I really didn't mean it to come out like that.' She pulled a face. 'But I want to be independent, you see. It feels as if it's the first time.'

'I know.' Elisa nodded. 'I understand perfectly.' Living with her stepmother would be going back. And she thought that she understood too about Theo.

The coffee was gurgling in the pot and Grace got to her feet and returned to the kitchen. She had been badly affected by the break-up with Robbie so soon after her father's death, Elisa reflected, but she seemed to be moving on from it in a positive way. It had been her decision, of course, but Elisa hoped she didn't regret it. Sometimes, you did or said things on the spur of the moment – and then regretted them for the rest of your life.

'And what about you?' Elisa realised that Grace was beside her, giving her a probing look. She held a small mug of coffee in each hand.

'Me?' She was a little confused.

'Yes. Have you decided what you're doing?'

'Not really.' Elisa took the mug she offered her. 'Thank you, my dear.' She sniffed the brew. It wasn't as rich as her own brand – Grace preferred the more mellow flavour of Italian coffee – but it was fresh and smelt inviting.

'I was wondering if you'd thought any more about visiting Cuba,' Grace said.

Ah. 'I could not afford that sort of holiday,' Elisa said. 'Even if I wanted to.'

'That sounds a bit defeatist.' Grace came and sat opposite her. She sipped her coffee. 'You could always get a loan against the house.'

'Mmm.' Elisa supposed that she could. There was no mortgage – thank the lord – though not much in the way of savings apart from the house in King Street itself. That big pile of a place – she had always hated it and the influence it had had over Philip. It had contained Nancy's ghost and Grace's unhappiness. It had been built on the profits from slavery. And yet now it was about all Elisa had.

'Or you could sell it.' Grace had a twinkle in her eyes now. Elisa suspected that she knew quite well how Elisa felt about the family home.

'Yes, I suppose I could.' If she sold it, she found herself thinking, she could downsize and help Grace out too. It was her stepdaughter's family's home and yet Philip had left it in trust to Elisa.

'So you could go to Cuba. For a holiday. To see your

family. To stay as long as you wanted to.' Grace paused. 'Maybe even meet up with your Duardo again.'

Elisa snapped a look across at her, but Grace was all innocence, sipping her coffee as if nothing important had been said. 'Yes,' she said. 'I had not thought.' Only she had. Constantly.

'I think you should go.' Grace put down her mug and fixed Elisa with a determined stare.

'Oh, you do, do you?'

'Yes, I do. Because if you don't . . .' Grace let her words hang. 'Then you'll never know.'

Then I'll never know, Elisa thought when she got home that lunchtime. She made herself a quick sandwich and then prepared her *pollo de coco* for dinner, frying off the chicken, garlic, onions and peppers in her skillet and adding the coconut milk so that she just had to put the skillet in the oven later. And then she looked up a number in her address book and dialled it on the house phone.

He answered on the third ring.

'Theo? It's Elisa.'

'Elisa. How are you?' Friendly enough, she thought, but with a wariness to his voice.

'Getting through,' she said. 'Though it's been hard.'

'Of course.' He hesitated. 'I'm so sorry. Is there anything I can . . . ?'

'Yes,' she said firmly. 'It's been far too long and I'd like to talk to you about a certain matter. I wondered if you could call round? Or better still perhaps you could come along to the meeting this afternoon?'

She heard him hesitate.

'It's not about Grace,' she said. Because it was always best to come out with it. 'There's something else.'

'Very well then.' There was a pause. 'In that case I'll come along to the meeting. We can have a chat afterwards if you like.'

'Excellent.' Elisa put on her jacket, picked up her black patent-leather handbag and set off along Welsh Back for the church hall. It was always a good thing to make plans for the future, she thought. One must have something to live for, after all.

Theo had seemed more subdued than usual, but the meeting had gone well and the profits from the crafts and cuisine day had been good, even after their expenses had been taken off.

At the end of the meeting, she took him to one side. 'What will you do, Theo?' she asked him gently, for he had a bruised look about him. 'Are you planning on staying in Bristol?'

'Now that Grace and I aren't together?' He raised an eyebrow but she could see his hurt. 'Now that she and Robbie have split up anyway?'

'I'm sorry.' She couldn't blame him for being bitter. He had lost his two best friends and it must seem as if it had all been for nothing.

'I did go away for a while,' he told her. 'It wasn't just that I was avoiding you.'

Elisa smiled, relieved to hear a glimmer of his old humour. 'And now?'

'Now, I have to think. Shall I stay or shall I go?'

Elisa studied his face. He had lost a bit of weight, which someone as lean as Theo couldn't afford to lose. But there was something else that was new about him – a kind of hardness. Life's blows, she thought. It wasn't pleasant to be rejected, to be made to feel second best, especially when you'd risked so much.

'And like I said on the phone, I'm so sorry about Philip.'

Elisa acknowledged this with a nod. 'Theo,' she touched his arm, 'I hope that we are still friends?'

'Of course. And if there's anything I can do for you at any time you only have to ask.'

'Thank you.' But that was not what she had meant. 'I have a proposition to put to you. That's why I wanted us to meet.' Elisa wasn't sure where it had come from – her idea – but it seemed like a good one. She just hoped that Theo would agree.

CHAPTER 36

Havana 2012

'Did you know?' Duardo demanded of Jaquinda. He was aware that she was about to go out – she'd applied more lipstick after dinner and a spray of perfume which had left its cloying smell in the air. She was wearing a low-cut orange T-shirt and black cropped trousers. She was younger than him but not twenty years younger. How could he respect a woman like her?

'Know what?' Jaquinda was sorting through her bag. She seemed unaware of what he was feeling, of how he'd felt since that conversation with Federico in the garage.

'About Luis. About this job he's been offered in Spain.' He could barely bring himself to say the words. 'About the fact that he's leaving Cuba.' She would know, of course. She was hardly ever here and yet she seemed to know everything.

'I do now,' she said, 'Federico told me yesterday.'

'And?' She seemed very calm about it.

Jaquinda straightened for a moment to look at him. She shrugged. 'It's a shame. We'll all miss him.'

We'll all miss him. Was that it? She was Luis's grandparent too. He shook his head in despair.

'What?' Her eyes narrowed.

'It doesn't matter.' He had long ago given up expecting anything different from her.

'Tell me.' Her hands were on her hips now. She had a confrontational look in her eye. She wanted a fight, he realised. All right. Let her have one.

'You don't seem to get it,' he said. 'The business I run, the way I feel about Luis, the fact that I worked so hard because I had him to hand it over to.' For the past twenty years anyway. Before that he had nurtured a vain hope that his own son might turn out to be interested. But Federico had no more ambition than his mother.

'Not get it?' she screeched. He hated it when she screeched like that. It was so unbecoming in a woman. He was sure that Elisa would never screech. Shout, yes, if she was angry; she had plenty of fire about her and there was nothing wrong with fire. But she wouldn't screech. There was something piercing and bitter about it that he hated.

'Of course I get it. Haven't you talked about little else for years?'

He blinked. Had he? It had often been on his mind, but he wasn't aware he'd been such a bore.

'Didn't you give us all the big speech about your retirement?' She paused for breath. Her chest was heaving. 'Of course I get it, you idiot.'

Duardo winced. But let her throw insults around if it made her feel better. 'Then you'll know how I'm feeling,' he said shortly.

'So?' Clearly, she wasn't finished yet.

'So, as the woman who lives under my roof, a man might expect some compassion at least.' Perhaps he was feeling sorry for himself. Who wouldn't? Even his mother had not sided with him as he had expected. He recognised her wise words, but still he felt dissatisfied. Yes and wronged. He had given Luis so much.

'Compassion?' Once again her voice rose. 'When have you ever shown me compassion? When have you ever thought of my feelings? Eh, tell me that.'

He looked at her, at the full red lips with the lipstick bleeding into the creases around her mouth. He looked at her eyes – hooded these days but still black with make-up, often smudged, just as it was now. He looked at the far-too-tight T-shirt and leggings, the bulges of her stomach and thighs. 'I've given you a home,' he said quietly. 'I've given you food on the table and a roof over your head at least.' But the question she had asked remained unanswered.

Jaquinda snorted with disgust. 'And I'm supposed to get down on my knees and thank you for that, oh bountiful master? The mother of your son and you're patting yourself on the back because you allow me to live in your home and eat at your table?' Her mouth curled into a sneer, a sneer that he had grown to know very well over the years.

'I'm sorry if I haven't give you what you wanted,' he said. Which was inadequate. But there, she hadn't given him what he wanted either, so he supposed they were quits.

'No you certainly have not.' She altered her position, stuck out one hip. 'But then, you didn't come to me a free man, now did you?'

He didn't reply. He knew what she was about to say.

'Elisa this, Elisa that –'

'I didn't talk about her,' he broke in. 'Not to you.' And he didn't want Jaquinda to talk about her either – even now.

'You didn't have to,' she snapped. 'It was obvious. We all know who you wanted. We all know who you loved.'

'*Mira* . . . Look, I didn't want to . . .' Love her, he was going to say. He didn't want to keep thinking of her. He had wanted a fresh start with Jaquinda. There had been some chemistry between them when they first met. He'd hoped it would be enough, always hoped it would be more. Until he finally realised it was never going to happen. 'I tried . . .' He started again.

'To make it work between us?' she jeered. Her eyes were like dark flames now. She walked right up to him and she slapped him hard across the cheek.

He was so surprised at this sudden physical attack that it took him a moment to react. When he did, he grabbed her wrist hard. 'What was that for?'

'It was for all these years,' she almost spat. She tried to shake him off but he was too strong for her. 'It was for what you didn't give me.'

'I tried my best.' His cheek was stinging now. He still had hold of her and her eyes were full as if she might cry. Duardo tried to feel sorry for her. He had never meant to scorn her, but she felt, it seemed, like a woman scorned. She was right, he supposed. He had never shown her compassion. It had gone wrong because it had never been right. And it was his fault, as his mother had always known. He had chosen Jaquinda too quickly, too desperately, wanting only to forget Elisa rather than taking the time to search for a woman who he could love. It wasn't Jaquinda's fault. She was quite correct. He had never been a free man.

She was shaking her head now. 'Never hard enough,' she said.

Duardo was silent. He knew that he could have done more, should have done more. She shouldn't have had to stay here until he despised her.

'And your best stinks,' she hissed. 'Your best is less than useless. You always expected me to be someone other than the person I really am – is that trying your best?'

He shook his head. He was hypnotised by her almost. This was the first time that she had really told him what she thought. It shocked him.

She moved closer. Instinctively, he let go of her wrist. He could smell the perfume more strongly now. It made him feel sick. 'You don't even care that I go out and sleep with Felipe,' she said. 'You don't even care that your woman fucks another man whenever she wants a body to hold her.'

'I do care about that.' Duardo stood straighter. He hated it.

'Then why don't you say anything? Why don't you try to stop me? Why don't you go round to Felipe's house and have a fight with him like a normal man would? Why do you let it go?'

'Because . . .' He couldn't quite work out how to answer this question. What was the truth anyhow? 'I don't think I have the right to stop you.'

She nodded. 'Too damn sure you don't.'

'So . . .'

'The truth is, you only hate it because I'm humiliating your manhood. And you don't stop me because it means you don't have to pretend.'

'Pretend?' he echoed. But he knew what she was saying.

She got closer still. She reached out and stroked his face, raking her long red nails over the cheek that she had already slapped. Duardo winced. 'If I'm with another man, you don't have to pretend to love me,' she whispered. 'You don't have to pretend to want to sleep with me, make love with me. You don't have to pretend to want to hold me.'

Duardo was silent. She was right – again. Dear God. She was making him feel a monster.

'Isn't it true, darling?' she murmured. She reached up and kissed his lips. He couldn't respond, but he knew she wasn't expecting him to.

'What do you want to do?' he asked blankly. Well of course they were living a lie. Felipe too. What else could they do – in Cuba?

'I'll tell you.' Abruptly, she spun away from him. She grabbed some clothes from the makeshift rail and started packing them haphazardly in her carpet bag. 'I'm going to move out of your house so I don't have to listen to your sermons any more. I've had enough. Finally. I can't stand living here with you and your family a second longer. I'm going to move out and Felipe will find us a place.'

'Where?' Duardo knew that this was just a bluff. Jaquinda had done it many times before. The truth was that Felipe didn't have the money to find a place. And what about Felipe's wife?

'I'd rather sleep in the streets than live here any longer.' And she moved on to the contents of the chest of drawers; stuffing tops, leggings and underwear into the bag. She was like a woman possessed.

'Your son lives here,' Duardo reminded her. He sank on to the single chair beside his bed. She'd be back in the morning. She always was.

'My son can do as he likes.' Fiercely, she shoved the drawers shut. 'My grandson can do as he likes.' She straightened and glared across at him. 'And the sooner you and your mother realise that and stop trying to control everyone's lives, the better for this family.' She tipped the contents of her jewellery box in the bag after the other stuff and scooped up some shoes.

Controlling people's lives? Duardo stared at her. Did he do that?

'Goodbye, Duardo,' she said. And she picked up the carpet bag and flounced out of the room, slamming the door for good measure behind her.

That night, as Duardo tossed and turned on his narrow bed, he dreamt of his African forebears working on the sugar plantation. There were no tangible images in his head when he awoke in the middle of night, but the essence of the dream remained with him. His forefathers and so many others too had suffered and then they had been freed and they'd continued to suffer – because they were still ill-used and still hungry. But at least they were no longer enslaved now they were all Cuban. It was a matter then, he knew, of fighting to improve their social conditions, of fighting for a different sort of freedom – this time for their country.

Even so, even though Duardo had always thought of Elisa Fernandez-Garcia as his equal, there was something about her, something elusive that he looked up to, that he craved.

When his mother had first asked who he was seeing, when he said Elisa's family name and saw his mother's expression change, her eyes widen, her mouth opening to a silent gasp of horror . . . 'No,' she had said. That was all she had said at first. 'No.'

'What is it? What's wrong?' Duardo forgot the pride he'd been feeling two minutes before. *She cares for me. I know that she cares for me. And when I hold her I feel I'm alive* . . . He was all concern for his mother. Was she unwell? Should he fetch his father?

She didn't scream or shout. '*Mi madre,*' she said softly. *Mother mine* . . . 'You cannot go on seeing her. It's impossible.'

Duardo stared at her. 'But why?'

And so his mother had sat him down and told him quietly, who they were, what they meant to her, to his family. 'They were a well-known Spanish landowning family,' she said, 'and they were our masters.'

'Our masters?' He frowned.

His mother sighed. 'You know that our forefathers were slaves, my son. The sugar plantation they worked on was owned by her ancestors. You cannot see the daughter of this family.' She repeated the words. 'It's impossible.'

Impossible . . . The word resounded in his head. It couldn't be. Now that he had found her he couldn't lose her – and over something that had happened centuries ago. But . . .

His mother had sat up straighter. 'You have your dignity,' she said. 'You have your freedom. You got nothing to thank them for.'

'But I love her.' The words had tipped out of him without thought.

She turned on him then. 'More than you love your family?'

He stared at her, not even knowing the answer. 'No, but . . .' How could you compare different sorts of love? There was the love you had for those closest to you, those you lived with, who had brought you up and, in his parents' case, brought you into the world. And then there was passion. And what a passion . . . It was something Duardo had never felt before. It was all-consuming. It filled his every waking moment. The image of Elisa filled his every waking moment.

'Then you know what you must do.' His mother nodded. 'She's just a girl,' she said. 'There will be other girls, my son.'

Other girls, thought Duardo, but none like her. None

whose hair was black and shiny as a blackbird's wing, whose body could make him feel on fire when he held her close, when they danced the rumba, when he kissed her. None whose lips tasted of pomegranate and whose hands flew about when she was happy or excited, whose dark eyes held a gleam of indigo blue. None who could mesmerise him, who could charm him, who could make him want to protect her from the world.

Even so, he was his mother's son through and through and so he came to a painful decision – to forget Elisa. That night when he went to tell her, he thought that he might die from the pain of it. 'I can't see you any more,' he said. 'My fore-fathers were slaves – on your family's sugar plantation.' And he used his mother's word. 'It's impossible.'

Elisa had reared up as if struck. 'Nothing's impossible,' she said regally. 'Our family is Creole. We're Cuban-born Span-ish and colour is of no consequence to us. Now and back then. We're not racist, you know. We are as Cuban as it's pos-sible to be.'

He marvelled at her bravery. In some strange way she even reminded him of his mother, who would fight for what she wanted and believed in. But he shook his head sadly. 'My mother would not be able to stand it,' he said.

'In time . . .'

'You don't know her as I do.'

Elisa considered this. 'But you love me?'

'You know I do.' He grasped her shoulders.

'It matters more than anything that we should be together?'

'You know it does.' Already his mother's voice in his head was fading. All he could see was Elisa, the girl he loved.

'Then it depends if you are brave enough to live in the present and dismiss the past.'

He tried to kiss her then but she pulled out of his arms. 'Come back to me when you know what you want,' she said. And she ran.

For three days Duardo had moped around the house, unable to concentrate on any activity, hardly eating, barely speaking to his parents. And then he went back to Elisa. He had decided. Her parents too were against the match; they said that Elisa and Duardo were too young. But Elisa and Duardo were not their parents. They *were* young yes, and they wanted to change the world. Things had moved on. They were not responsible for the sins of their forebears – they had not even been born. It was not their fault that even in their parents' day black Cubans had held the lowliest jobs and were bellboys, shoeshiners or street cleaners. Elisa was right, this was not the attitude of the Spanish Cubans; it never had been. And besides, whatever had happened in the past, people must move on. If there was ever to be change, then people must move on.

Duardo and Elisa had been forced to run away from their parents' disapproval; it was the only way they could be together. But his mother, he thought now, had not moved on. She was glad when things didn't work out between Elisa and Duardo, glad when Elisa left the country and she didn't have to worry about her any more. Even so, his mother had been right in what she had said to him yesterday. Luis was the one who was young now. Duardo had helped him all he could, but now perhaps it was time to let him go his own way, to make his own decisions and find his own path. It would be wrong to try to stop him. He did not want to control Luis's life as his mother had tried to control his. Duardo should be proud of Luis, just as Federico was.

He got up and went over to the small porcelain sink, ran some cold water and washed his face with the thin slice of soap. What had happened to that girl who had once been so brave? As he dried his face with a threadbare towel he looked around the small room, less than half the size it had once been before he repartitioned it to accommodate his growing family. Without Jaquinda's bright and colourful dresses, it looked drab and bare. But that was how it should be, he realised. He thought of Luis and then he came to a decision. It was the right thing too that Luis should go his own way. Because once again, it was happening. Things in Cuba were changing. And there was a change that Duardo must make too.

CHAPTER 37

4 months later

From her sitting-room window on the first floor, Grace watched Robbie walk along the street towards her new flat. She had to admit to feeling a small pang. You couldn't be married to someone for all those years and not feel a pang, surely? The pavement was busy – it always was because now she was living on the corner of St Nicholas Street in the Old City, a vibrant and bustling area just fifty metres from the indoor market and the Corn Exchange. But still she spotted him. He was looking at the numbers on the houses and shops. Frowning. And carrying a box of stuff – her stuff.

She went down the stairs to the front door of the building and opened it. 'Hi.' She smiled. He was wearing his faded weekend jeans and a navy sweater and his hair was much shorter than it had been when they were together. Otherwise, he looked reassuringly familiar.

'Hello, Gracie.' He smiled back – a good sign – and gave her a long look as if he were carrying out a similar kind of assessment.

'Come in.' She led the way upstairs to her flat.

The box of her things was the reason for his visit. 'We got

some of the boxes mixed up,' he'd said on the phone a few days ago. 'I've got one of yours.'

'Ah.' She had tried to think which one it might be. She'd finished most of her unpacking; it hadn't been easy to fit her possessions – although some had been divided up between the two of them – into this flat, but she'd managed it. It had one decent-sized bedroom, and a smaller room which would be Grace's therapy room, with just about enough room for her books, her massage table and Angus the skeleton.

'I could bring it over at the weekend,' Robbie had said.

'Oh. You're coming back to Bristol?' Why? she wondered. Just to see her? Or was he by any chance back in touch with Theo? She couldn't imagine what or who else might bring him here. She hadn't seen Theo – though she still saw the ghost of him from time to time and she knew from Elisa that he was still around. Bristol, it seemed, was a big city. Theo's ghost though was little more than a shadow. Grace saw it sometimes when she glanced in a shop window – behind her shoulder, there one moment and gone the next; she saw it flicker briefly from behind the trunk of a tree in Castle Park or Queens Square and then melt into nothing, and she saw it glimmer over the water when the sunlight gave the canal an iridescence that made you think you could see right to the very bottom.

'Just for the day.' He didn't fill her in any further. 'Will you be around? Can I drop it in?'

'Well, if you don't mind . . .' And she'd given him the address.

Now, it felt weird though, inviting her husband over her new threshold. She supposed she should be thinking 'ex-husband' but she hadn't quite got that far yet. Independence, she had found, was a slippery thing. You thought you had it at times; other times it simply crept through your fingers and you realised you weren't quite there.

'Thanks.' He came in and put the box down on the floor.

'What's in it anyway?' She went over to take a look, kneeling down, easing back the packaging.

'Books,' he said.

'Ah, yes.' Grace could see her John Donne peeping out of the top opening. D. H. Lawrence was there as well. 'Poetry books.' She used to read a lot of poetry; it was something she had determined to rediscover. 'Thanks.'

'So this is it?' He looked around the sitting room and open-plan kitchen.

'It's small,' Grace found herself wanting to defend the flat, 'but I like the location.' She walked over to the window which sported 1930s narrow-paned windows and blistered white paint. She liked being in the centre of things; enjoyed the buzz surrounding the market and the quirky shops and loved the Elephant pub which was practically next door.

He nodded. 'It's a nice place.'

'And you? Have you found somewhere?' Should she offer him tea? Grace hesitated.

'Yeah, I have. Just outside Brighton.' He winced. 'It's whacked up the mortgage a bit, but it's closer to London.'

'And you're enjoying working in the new office?' Goodness,

thought Grace, this politeness was killing her. Any second and they'd be talking about the weather.

'Yeah, it's pretty good.' He smiled and Grace saw something. Just a glimpse, but . . . He's moved on, she thought. He'd met someone else – maybe even at his new office – and he'd moved on. Which made her pleased for him and also a bit sad. Perhaps because he'd found it so easy.

'Would you like a cup of tea?' She half hoped he'd say no, spare them both this conversation. On the other hand, she was curious. Robbie had been in her life for so many years. You couldn't just switch off the caring.

'Uh, all right.' He sat down at the table. 'Thanks.'

Fortunately the downstairs space was virtually open plan. Grace went through to put the kettle on and recalled the last time she'd seen him – when he'd left the house on Passage Street, tight-lipped and angry. If he had moved on perhaps he had also forgiven her? She hoped so. They had never talked about what had happened with Theo; he had never asked for an explanation or hurled abuse at her for what she had done. They hadn't argued or cried or discussed. They had just broken up. Grace glanced back at him as he sat at the table waiting for his tea. She missed the Robbie who had been her husband, and yet she felt free. Which was terrifying but good.

'How have you been?' Robbie asked her from the other room. 'Have you got plenty of work? Are you managing financially?'

Grace hoped he wasn't about to offer her a handout. 'Fine,' she said brightly. 'We all know moving is stressful, but I'm more or less sorted. And I've got plenty of clients.' Which was true enough – as far as it went. She wasn't well off, but she could manage and Elisa was in the process of selling King Street and was determined to give her a share.

'How's Elisa?' Robbie asked, as if he'd followed her train of thought. He stretched out his legs in that way she remembered.

'About to go to Cuba.' Grace smiled at Robbie's expression. She had been surprised too, despite being the one who'd tried to persuade her stepmother to go.

'Permanently?' Robbie asked. 'Or for a holiday?'

'For a holiday, she says.' Though Grace had her own theories about that.

'And please don't think that this has anything to do with you,' Elisa had added when she told Grace of her plans.

Grace frowned. 'How do you mean?'

Elisa had reached up to put her hands on Grace's shoulders. 'I'm going with Theo,' she said.

Grace supposed it shouldn't have come as quite such a surprise. Elisa wasn't as young as she once was and it would be helpful for her to have a travelling companion. Her stepmother had always been fond of Theo and they were both Cuban after all. Theo had no memories of Cuba, and Grace guessed he'd be more than happy to get away, to visit the land he'd been born in and even meet some of his parents' friends who might still be there perhaps. Even so . . . there was something about her stepmother's plan that gave her a twinge of sadness every time she thought of it.

★

'You'll miss her,' Robbie said.

Grace nodded. 'I will. But I'm glad for her sake.' It was about time Elisa started living her own life instead of other people's.

The kettle boiled and Grace made the tea and took it over to the table. She sat opposite him so that she was what seemed to be the right distance away. What should they talk about now? Awkwardness seemed to be sitting in the room right beside them.

Robbie cradled the mug between his hands, looking everywhere except at her. 'Are you seeing anyone, Gracie?' he asked at last.

She shook her head. She hadn't been expecting that.

'Not Theo?'

So he hadn't come here to see his old friend. 'Not Theo,' she said. Most definitely, not Theo. Of course she missed him more than she could have guessed. Not just the Theo who had been her lover, but the friend she'd had ever since she first met Robbie. She missed their closeness, the intimacy they'd shared so briefly, the gleam of his eyes and the magical touch of his hand. But she had let him down when he'd asked her to make a commitment to him and there was no going back with a man like Theo. She'd chosen Robbie and Theo was far too proud to accept second best. Not that he had ever been second best. Grace sighed. But as she had told Elisa – it was complicated.

Robbie nodded, as if satisfied.

'Are you?' she asked. 'Seeing anyone, I mean.'

He looked at her over the rim of his cup as he sipped his tea. 'I have met someone,' he said.

She'd thought so. Grace nodded encouragingly.

'Which was why I wanted to see you today,' he added.

Grace raised an eyebrow. So he hadn't been coming here anyway; he'd made a special trip, her box of poetry books being the excuse. But why?

'I suppose I wanted to see you again,' he pushed his glasses up his nose, 'before I . . . could move on.'

Grace nodded. She could understand that.

'I wanted to make sure we were doing the right thing,' he said. 'It's a drastic step – to break up a marriage. Children or no children.'

'Yes, it is.' Grace sipped her mint tea. She had been surprised how painful it had been. She reached out and took his hand. 'But it's OK,' she said. 'We have done the right thing, even if I didn't go about it in the right way.' The strange thing was that their break-up had come almost as much of a surprise to Grace as it had to Robbie. It was almost as if what had happened – Theo, her father's death and all the emotional turmoil that followed, had opened her up and made her see things more clearly. She knew that this was best for them both.

'Is she nice?' she asked. Though she knew she would be.

'Yeah, she is.' He laughed. 'I could show you a picture.' He hesitated. 'If you don't think that's inappropriate?'

'No, I don't think that.' Grace tried not to smile, and waited as he fished out his mobile from the pocket of his jeans and brought up an image on the screen. She leaned closer. She was fair haired and smiley. Yes, she looked nice. 'Children?' she asked him.

'One boy of three.' He scrolled across.

A cheeky face grinned back at Grace. Goodness, she thought, they'd only been together for five minutes and yet Robbie already had her son's picture on his phone. He was a fast mover all right.

'And ready to have more?' she teased. And thank goodness she could do that. She'd married Robbie for all the wrong reasons – she could see that now. He was a problem solver and somewhere inside her she'd imagined he could solve all hers. She'd left home too soon to be with him because he was safe, grounded and reliable. She understood him; he loved her and he was predictable, which was exactly what she'd needed. Then. Grace smiled at Robbie; the man, rather than the husband. Sometimes you needed to be your own problem solver, to trust in your own judgement, to develop your inner strength and to learn to be independent. And after you'd managed to do all those things, the very person who helped you . . . well, he didn't seem to be the right person any longer.

Robbie shrugged. 'It's early days,' he said. 'But yes, it's what she wants.'

'Then you're right to move on.'

A look of relief crossed Robbie's features; it was, Grace thought, almost as if he'd needed her permission before he could take the final step of commitment.

They chatted about other things and after half an hour he got up to go.

'It's been good to see you,' Grace said, realising that she meant it. Could they still be friends? Perhaps.

'You too.' He kissed her on the cheek and that felt right as well. 'And about Theo . . .'

'Yes?' Grace was wary.

'If it happened. It would be OK.' He gave her a long look and walked out of the door.

Grace smiled to herself as she watched him heading off down the street. He must know that it could never happen now. But for the first time, she realised, she was taking control of her own life. She had lost her father and she had lost her husband. But she had her business and a few close friends and she was managing alone, learning who she was, finding her own truth. And perhaps that was the most important thing of all. She had that even though she no longer had Theo or Robbie or her father. She had fought for it. It was hers.

CHAPTER 38

Havana 2012

Rosalyn walked her usual route towards the Plaza de Armas and the fruit stall on Obispo, wishing that her steps could feel more certain. It was not yet ten in the morning but already the sun was hot on her head. She stumbled slightly on a broken paving stone. They had done much restoration in the city, yes, but the streets of Havana were still pockmarked with potholes, crumbling pavements and cracked cobbles that could send a body flying.

Once again, she was beginning to feel a little dizzy. She often felt dizzy in the mornings these days, though she tried to hide it. But she was happier. Yes, indeed. Things were much better now. A thorn in her side had been removed.

That night of what she called their final argument, that night when Jaquinda had left the apartment, Rosalyn had known something was different. The raised voices had gone on and on, drumming through the thin walls. Rosalyn had tried to sleep but it was hard to shut them out. Part of her longed to get up, go in there, tell Jaquinda exactly what she thought of her. But she knew she could not. It was Duardo's life, not hers. It was not her concern. And eventually, she must have slept.

The following morning, however, she had got up as usual. 'Where is she?' she had asked Duardo.

He had shrugged. 'Who knows?'

'But she will come back.'

'When she does,' Duardo said, 'we won't be here to see her.' And his expression was grim, his face closed.

'What do you mean, my son?' Rosalyn blinked at him.

'I mean,' he said, 'that I have had enough. I have money – Luis won't need it now. And there's no point in buying another car.'

'What are you saying?' Rosalyn was confused. Why would he buy another car? Though she seemed to remember that had once been his plan.

'I am saying that we can afford to rent another apartment,' Duardo said. 'You and me, Mami. The rest of them . . .' he gestured to the place that had been home for so many years, 'can stay here. But I am not living with Jaquinda another second. That's all.'

'But . . .' Rosalyn wasn't sure what to say. She couldn't imagine leaving here. And yet – why not? Another apartment could be pleasant enough. There would be no Jaquinda hanging around the place doing less than nothing, no Jaquinda cheating on her son while she ate the food he provided and slept under their roof. Mother of Rosalyn's grandson she might be, but in Rosalyn's eyes Jaquinda was little more than a lazy whore. 'Very well, my son,' she had said.

She had pottered around making breakfast, fresh mango

juice and coffee, slicing papaya and the ripe water melon she had carried back from the fruit stall the day before.

'It's my fault as much as Jaquinda's,' Duardo had said. 'Once, I thought it might get better. But now . . .' He sighed.

Rosalyn turned and held him, just for a few moments, in her arms. Now was when things would get better, she thought to herself. 'It was not right,' she murmured. 'You mustn't blame yourself.' Truth was, it had not been right for a long time. *And you still have me . . .* But she whispered this silently to herself.

'Do you think it's my fault that Luis is leaving?' he asked as he drew out of her embrace.

Rosalyn pulled back in surprise. 'How could it be?'

He shrugged. 'Perhaps I've spoiled him, made him think he can be better.'

Rosalyn considered this. It was true up to a point. But if people didn't think they could be better, how could any lives be changed? If Tacito had not come for her, she would have stayed in the bars of Havana plying her wares. If her grand-father had not wanted to save himself from slavery, he would never have run away. 'It's not wrong,' she said, 'to make someone think they can have a better life.'

Rosalyn trudged on towards the plaza. It might not be compatible with the politics of the regime, she thought, but the regime was her son's dream, not Rosalyn's. And Duardo had not been content with his lot; he'd always been ambitious and keen to better himself. The irony being that ambitious men were likely to be the frustrated ones in Cuba.

So now Rosalyn lived with Duardo in a much smaller

apartment in the next block and Benita, Federico and Luis still lived with Jaquinda as before. No one seemed much affected by the new living arrangements. Benita came round to help with the cooking and often they ate together. Now, though, Rosalyn had her son all to herself.

But Duardo seemed almost a shadow of his former self. Rosalyn guessed this was more because of the loss of Luis than Jaquinda. Paperwork in Cuba took a long time but Luis's exit visa had finally come through and now he was busy making his plans to leave. Rosalyn watched Duardo watching Luis and it was heartbreaking. What could she do?

She scrutinised the fruit and vegetables in the fruitseller's cart. Some fried plantains perhaps? They had always been Duardo's favourite. What he needed was something to buck him up, something to make him feel happier about his place in the world. She checked the quality between thumb and forefinger and began to haggle. Food was as good a place as any to start.

'Rosalyn?'

She heard her name being spoken. For a moment it sounded as if it had come from a long distance away – from way back in the mists of time perhaps? She stopped talking and put down the fruit.

'Rosalyn?'

Her blood ran cold. Her mind went into freefall. She could feel herself breathing more heavily and she tried to calm herself. But it wasn't the dizziness; this was something quite different. This was what she had always feared. Slowly, she turned. She knew that voice. Even so, she just had to be sure.

CHAPTER 39

Havana 2012

When she had left the last time, when she had parted from Duardo after dancing that last rumba in La Cueva, after spending the night with him in the back of his Chevrolet, Elisa had believed she would never return again to Havana.

What was there to come back for? Her aunt had died, she had all but lost touch with her cousins and she had refused Duardo. Surely, he would never give her another chance? And now she was so much older, too old some would say. But Grace had persuaded her that she should try, 'otherwise you'll never know'. And Cuba was her homeland – which was certainly something to come back for. So.

Philip's death had seemed like another turning point, a now or never sort of moment. So she had decided that, yes, she would come back – for a holiday at least. Forget pride – where Duardo was concerned, she had none. She would offer herself to him one last time. All or nothing; the way she had never been free to offer herself to him before. And if he said 'no', then she had done all she could. If he said 'no' then she had the option of returning to Grace and her little community in Bristol and, as Grace had said, at least she would know.

Elisa did not, however, go to see Duardo immediately; she forced herself to wait. First, she must show Theo around Havana, she must see her family, and then . . . Elisa rather hoped she would run into Duardo by chance as she had run into his son before. She knew what it was like here in the old town. News trickled and spread down from balconies and spun along narrow streets – so maybe he would hear that she had returned.

But she had been in Havana a week and had seen neither Duardo nor his son, despite spending much of her time close to their neighbourhood. Things hadn't changed so much. The place was still noisy: dogs barked, kids shrieked, men shouted and musicians played on every street corner. Buildings were still crumbling, the road was still pitted with potholes, sunlight was still slanting across the washing hung on balconies.

It had been something of a relief to travel here with Theo although now they had gone their separate ways. He wanted to explore the island and, after spending a few days here in Havana, had set off on an itinerary of his own.

'It's remarkable,' he had said, the night before he left as they sat outside a small café off Obispo Street. 'To be in the country where my parents grew up, where I was born.'

Cuba, she realised, was having a profound effect on him. He had lost the bruised look he'd had before they left Bristol. Now, he was busy finding out everything he could about Cuban history, drinking it in as if it could tell him something important about himself and his family, his roots. It made

Elisa think about all those Cubans who had left since the revolution. They must have felt that to leave would be the best thing for their children, and perhaps materially, it was. But what about the deprivation of their roots, their culture? Many migrants would feel a strong sense of displacement, she was sure, in this world of exodus from people's homelands.

'Where will you go next?' Elisa asked him.

'Trinidad. That's where my family lived, you know.'

'And how long will you stay?' Elisa was thinking of Grace. She couldn't help but think of Grace, couldn't help but think she had deserted her rather.

'Until I run out of money.' Theo grinned.

But Elisa wondered. Theo too had come to a turning point in his life. If he was ever going to return to his homeland, now would be the time.

And so Theo left Havana heading east and Elisa ran into the very last person she wanted to see – Duardo's mother.

The old woman was buying bananas and papaya from a fruit and vegetable stall near the Plaza de Armas. Or at least, she was arguing with the fruitseller about the fruit she might or might not be buying. Elisa stared at her. She was flinging her arms around to make her point, picking up one piece of fruit and then another, squeezing them between thumb and forefinger, replacing them on the stall with a gesture of disdain. It was definitely Rosalyn. She was a lot older, of course, but apart from being now wreathed in lines and creases and a little stouter, she didn't look so very different. Her hair was still black although marbled with white and she still moved and spoke with the same confidence although she must be a very old lady indeed.

Elisa listened as she criticised the over-ripeness of the bananas, the size of the mangos, the price of the goods on offer. Her voice was the same too though more brackish with age, and her manner as she dealt in no uncertain terms with the fruitseller took Elisa right back to the time when she was just sixteen and Rosalyn commanded her son to have nothing more to do with her. It was so unfair, the young Elisa had thought then, frankly terrified of the diminutive woman who seemed to threaten her destiny. But she saw now the pride of her instead; the pride of the woman whose ancestors had been enslaved. That was something no one could take away from her.

'Rosalyn,' she said quietly. 'Rosalyn?'

It was hardly loud enough for her to hear, but the old woman turned as if by instinct. She frowned – a deep furrow in her brow. Elisa could see that her eyes were old too – brown and milky and slightly glazed as if she could no longer see too far in front of her.

'It's me. Elisa,' she said.

'Elisa!' Rosalyn reared back as if she had been struck. 'You,' she said.

Elisa nodded. 'How are you? It's been a long time.' She held out her hand.

Rosalyn glared at it with distrust. 'What are you doing here?' she demanded. 'Causing trouble? Again?' Which sounded very much as if she knew this wasn't the first time Elisa had returned.

'I hope not.' She smiled. Duardo's mother didn't frighten her as she once had. After all, Elisa too was older. She was certainly too old to be intimidated by an elderly lady in the Plaza de Armas.

Rosalyn put her hands on her hips. 'Why come back then?' she muttered. 'What do you want this time?' Or *who*, she might have added.

Elisa eyed her squarely. 'This was my home once,' she said.

'But you left.'

'Because my family left. Because I was young. Because I thought your son was dead.' As if Rosalyn didn't know the reasons why . . .

'Pfaf.' Rosalyn snorted. Although she did at least have the grace to look slightly ashamed. 'A better woman would have waited to be sure.' She turned back to the fruitseller and plucked a bunch of bananas from the stall which she thrust at him to be weighed. To this she added two mangos and three papayas.

Elisa waited patiently while she got out her purse and completed the purchase. She was not going to slip away and she was not going to argue with her. Anyway, it was a fair point. 'Perhaps you're right,' she said, when Rosalyn had finished, given the fruitseller a curt nod, and moved away from the stall. 'But I was very young.'

'And a better woman would never have returned to torment him again,' Rosalyn added for good measure. She adjusted the weight of her shopping bag on her arm and stepped away from Elisa, heading for Obispo Street.

Elisa stayed with her. Rosalyn hadn't changed. She was still as unreasonable and narrow-minded as ever. 'I'm tormenting no one.'

Rosalyn shook her head as she walked on. 'He couldn't help himself,' she said. 'That's how it is for some men. You were always like a drug.'

Elisa wanted to laugh out loud at this. Her – a drug? Well now she was almost seventy and she couldn't be accused of that any longer. 'I've always loved him,' she said.

Rosalyn glanced at her sharply. 'But you left a second time,' she said. 'I know all about that. You left and then you married some other man in England. Is that what you call love?' She stopped walking.

Yes, you know it all, Elisa thought. Or you think you do. She guessed that Rosalyn didn't want her to walk any further with her. She certainly wouldn't want her near the family home. 'I had made that man and his daughter a promise. I felt I had to go back.' She bowed her head. She wouldn't tell Rosalyn that she had argued with Duardo, that she had been within an inch of agreeing to stay. And she wouldn't tell her that she had often regretted it, especially when she had found herself pregnant with Duardo's child.

'Well then.' Rosalyn frowned once more. 'Maybe my son is fed up with you running away, eh?'

'I never wanted to run away.'

But Rosalyn seemed unconvinced. 'Leave him alone, will you?' she asked. 'For me? He is very content without you.' And once again, she took a step forwards as if to move on.

Elisa blinked. Why would she do anything for the sake of this woman who had tried her level best to prevent her from having all that she had ever wanted? 'Tell him I'm here, will you?' she returned. She touched Rosalyn's arm. 'If you care for your son and his happiness – just tell him I'm here if he still wants me – that's all.'

'You're here.' Rosalyn looked her up and down. 'But for how long? And what about that other man, that husband of yours?'

'He died, Rosalyn.' Elisa clenched her fists and then unclenched them again. She was an old lady. She was his mother. Elisa must be calm. 'If Duardo wants me to, I'll stay this time,' she said. 'Will you tell him?'

Rosalyn seemed to consider. 'I'll tell him.' But her eyes gave nothing away.

'I'm staying at my cousin's *casa*. He knows where.'

Rosalyn gave a brusque nod and turned away.

Would she tell him? Elisa had no idea. But she was here and she had to put her trust in someone. She had been led to him before. If it was meant to be, then she would be led to him again.

CHAPTER 40

Havana 2012

Duardo managed to catch Luis early one morning in the old apartment before he had the chance to slope off somewhere. His grandson had been avoiding him and he hated that. He could even almost accept Luis's decision, but not the fact that he, Duardo, was apparently so terrifying that Luis couldn't talk to him about it.

'I want to take you somewhere,' he told him. Before he knew it Luis would be gone. And there were things that had to be said between them. He had never been as close to his son as he was to this boy. That had to mean something.

'This morning?' He saw Luis frown as if trying to think up an excuse.

Duardo nodded. 'It's important.' And then when he didn't reply. 'We've got to talk about it sometime, Luis. Or were you planning to just disappear one day without saying goodbye?'

The boy almost crumpled in front of him. 'No, of course not, *abuelo*. I . . .'

'Don't get upset now.' Duardo patted him on the shoulder, shared a complicit glance with Benita, who was standing behind him by the sink. Luis was young after all, he must make allowances. 'Not here,' he said, 'not now. There's somewhere else we should go.'

The boy nodded.

'Come on, then.' And Duardo jangled the keys in his pocket. 'Let's do it.'

It was a while since Duardo had been to Santa Clara. Occasionally he drove tourists there, but most didn't bother with it. They went the other way to the tobacco plantations at Vinales, to the coastal strip at Varadero or further south and east to Trinidad. Which was sad, Duardo thought as he drove the car down the half-empty highway, because Santa Clara was Che's town, and it would all have come to nothing without Che. Shame that so many people seemed to have forgotten.

The hoardings and posters reminded them though as they approached the industrial outskirts of the town. They were not just of Che either, but Fidel Castro, the Venezuelan Chavez and Nelson Mandela, freedom fighters all. And what they had fought for . . . Could it have all been in vain?

'We're going to the memorial at Santa Clara,' said Luis, though it was obvious by now. They had seen it from the highway; it was on the southern edge of town a good twenty-minute walk from the centre.

Duardo nodded. 'Don't worry, I'm not trying to change your mind.' Though he probably would if he thought there was the slightest chance he could. 'I just want you to see.'

That wasn't quite right though. Luis had been here before. He had seen. Duardo tried again. 'I want to see it with you.' Through his grandson's eyes? Was that what he meant, what he wanted?

'I know though,' Luis said. 'And I've thought it through. All of it.'

'So why didn't you say anything to me?' Duardo was surprised that his voice sounded so casual. He had come a long way, he told himself. Somewhere along the line he must have got good at pretending.

'I was going to,' Luis began. 'At first I thought nothing would come of it. People say things, don't they?'

'Yes.' The complex had been set up on a slightly raised mound and they drove up the incline and parked under a line of tall trees to the right. The statue and mausoleum were to their left. Duardo put on the handbrake and turned to face his grandson. 'People say things,' he agreed.

'And then it happened so quick. And I couldn't work out when to tell you – or how.'

Duardo nodded. He could see that. But. All the family knew how much Luis meant to him. They'd all known his intentions too – more fool him. Jaquinda had been right – Duardo had become controlling. It had happened without him even realizing it; thinking he had the right to run other people's lives. Who did he think he was? 'Come on,' he said again, more briskly. They could talk about it later.

This was the Plaza de la Revolución. The Conjunto Escultorico Comandante – the monument to Che – had been built in 1988 to commemorate the thirtieth anniversary of the revolution and Duardo had come here to see it many times since. It was a homage. The large open-air space was paved, landscaped and flood-lit and dominated by the towering bronze statue of the great man himself. Dressed in combat fatigues, his arm was in plaster – it had been broken in a previous battle, and such details told anyone who cared to think about it, a great deal about the courage of the man. Just standing in the plaza looking at the figure against the backdrop of the blue Cuban sky always gave Duardo a feeling of awe and remembrance, as he recalled those hard days and nights in the mountains, the marching, the fighting, the noise and stench of the battle. Nowadays, people collected here in the plaza for rallies and concerts, but this hadn't diluted the space for Duardo; it still meant as much as it always had. Beneath the statue was a bas-relief depicting scenes from the battle and on this were carved the historic words that Che had written in his farewell letter before leaving for Bolivia.

Duardo looked up at one of the hoardings. 'We want to be like Che,' he read.

'Did you want to be like Che?' Luis asked him. He seemed to have recovered his equilibrium. He seemed genuinely curious.

Duardo couldn't help but smile. 'Of course,' he said. 'He was a hero.' *Our hero*. He surveyed the stone terracing, the massive blocks of granite and relief sculptures and the huge statue. Che and their Cuban flag – fluttering in massive glory. Which said it all really.

'We don't all want that though,' Luis said, 'no matter how many times we're made to say it.'

Duardo nodded. He knew that. He even understood. Some men's dreams were simple and there was no room for only a simple dream if you followed Che Guevara. 'I haven't brought you here to make a point about your plans to leave the country,' he said, 'or even to discuss politics.'

Luis raised an eyebrow.

'Well, maybe a little,' Duardo conceded.

'It's not that I don't appreciate everything.' Luis made a gesture which included the statue, the entire plaza in fact. 'But what use is education if you don't have freedom of thought and action, *abuelo*?'

Duardo said nothing. But he thought of *Granma*, the paper they all read, the paper that was nothing more than an endless repetition of the party line. He knew it. He'd always known it, but until now he hadn't acknowledged it even to himself. It was easier to blame the Americans and the US embargo for everything that had happened, for all that had failed to happen for Cuba. And it was true – the US had done some terrible things to his country. But they couldn't be blamed for everything, because there were other countries to trade with and there were other ways to govern.

'When Papi told you what I was doing' asked Luis, 'I bet you were pretty mad?'

Duardo couldn't deny it. 'I was angry at first, yes. I had so many hopes. So many dreams.' He shook his head, felt the emotion well up. Fantasies, he supposed you could call them.

He had known it would be like this coming here. Luis and what he had decided; Che Guevara and what he had achieved for their country. Though it should be the other way round. Because they had not fought so that young men would leave.

'I'm sorry, *abuelo*.'

Duardo acknowledged the apology with a slight nod. But he was pleased to see that Luis was holding himself erect, standing up for his beliefs and his decision. He didn't want the boy to be cowed and apologetic; that wasn't what he wanted at all.

'Why did you bring me here?'

Duardo registered the usual armed guards and high level of security, which was as it should be. This was a special place and as such it must be protected. Underneath the terracing were the burial tombs and the eternal flame. Duardo had thought, when the fighting was over, that this brave new world they had created would grow and get stronger, that the Cuban people would be free and independent and thankful. But this had not been the case. It wasn't just his grandson who was looking elsewhere. Why had he brought Luis here? It was a good question.

He took his arm. 'It was a long time ago,' he said quietly, 'the fighting and the changes; the start of Fidel's regime. We had lofty ambitions, you might say, fierce dreams. But in the event . . .' He sighed. 'I brought you here because I wanted to remember how it should have been and I wanted you to be here to remind me of the reality.' Something like that anyway.

Luis nodded and gave him a long look. 'Do you want me to tell you why I'm leaving?' he asked.

'If you like.' Though Duardo thought he knew already. Luis was leaving because his homeland could not give him the opportunities he craved. He couldn't earn a lot of money here and his ambitions would always be thwarted by the system. He couldn't be free to make certain choices. None of them were. Though things were changing. Since Raúl, the regime had not been so strict – which was precisely why Luis was able to go.

'I want to travel,' he said. 'I want to see something of the world. And I want to make a difference.'

'Do you think that the rest of the world is so much better?' Duardo asked him.

His grandson spread his hands. 'I don't know. But I want to find out. I want to discover that for myself.'

Duardo couldn't help but see the clarity of Luis's intentions. This was why they were losing their young people. They were expected to tread in the paths of their forefathers, to expect nothing more. But that wasn't the way of the world. The way of the world was change and evolution and, as he'd already told himself, as his mother had tried to tell him in her own way, he had to be man enough to see that, to accept it.

'Shall we go in?' Duardo asked. The memorial was a quiet and sacred place; they must prepare themselves for the experience.

Luis nodded. Duardo could tell he was affected by the place. They walked through the imposing wooden door into the dimly lit chapel-like tomb, a cavern with niches containing ossuaries. There were the remains of thirty-eight comrades interred along one wall, along with Che's remains, brought here from Bolivia. Each tomb was decorated with a cameo-like head of the fighter and a red imitation carnation and at the end of the room was a brazier housing the eternal flame. Duardo closed his eyes as a mark of respect and whispered a silent prayer.

Once outside, they went through another door to the museum. Duardo had been here before too, of course, but he never tired of examining the artefacts that had made up the life of Che: from baby photos to his doctor's coat, from letters he wrote to the pistol he used. There was his pipe, his watch, his beret – Che Guevara's equivalent of the crown of thorns – and the telephone he used during the campaign of Santa Clara along with his binoculars, camera and his transmitter for the pirate radio 'Rebelde' set up in February 1958. There was even the container from which he used to drink *mate* tea. There was a chronological reconstruction of his life too which made it possible to chart the development of his revolutionary ideas and a black and white reel of film which brought tears to Duardo's eyes.

Handsome and charismatic, Che was the archetypal tragic and romantic hero gunned down in his prime. He summed up all the new ideals. A doctor and intellectual, he had an instinctive sympathy towards the downtrodden. He had been a thinker, Duardo reminded himself, as much as a fighter. But Duardo couldn't argue with Che's belief that the only way to be liberated from an oppressive regime was through armed revolution. And then to be brutally executed in the way he had been . . . It was no surprise that he had become a cult figure, a martyr and a man of his time – not just in Cuba, people often told Duardo, but all around the world. In the 1960s many teenagers had a Che Guevara poster on their bedroom wall; Duardo had been told all about this by tourists in his car. Imagine . . .

'What do you feel when you come here?' Duardo asked Luis. He supposed he just wanted to reassure himself.

'Proud.' They were at the back of the memorial now, in another garden of remembrance with more graves and dedications and another eternal flame.

Duardo nodded. He knew, like everyone, that schoolchildren not only still recited 'We want to be like Che' every morning, but that they were also still brought here to this complex in Santa Clara to be inspired. But he wasn't interested in brainwashing or thoughtless incantations. He wanted to know what Luis really felt, in his heart. He wanted to be reassured that although his grandson was leaving Cuba, it hadn't been for nothing after all.

'I know what he did for us,' Luis said. 'I know what you all did.'

It seemed a long time ago now. Standing here in this serene and manicured garden, the battles, the hardship, the hunger seemed so far away that sometimes it was hard for Duardo to believe that he had ever walked barefoot through Oriente or swum across the Jobabo river. 'Even so,' he said. And he remembered how he had felt, barefoot in the mud of southern Camaguey with Che and the other men, their brothers. *All for one* . . . Che's chronic asthma has slowed them down as much as enemy ambushes and Batista's airforce, but now it was almost impossible to believe that he hadn't been invincible.

By the time Duardo had left Elisa and joined the men in the Sierra Maestra in the early summer of 1958, the guerillas had consolidated their military position; they occupied a considerable territory and were in a state of armed truce with Batista. Rations were meagre from the start. They subsisted on locally grown vegetables and occasionally chicken soup or pork, provided by local sympathisers, the *campesinos*, and they had built a network of communications as well as hospitals to tend to the sick and wounded, and industrial areas in which to manufacture weapons. Thus their power grew during that spring and summer. Informers could be weeded out and any army presence quickly identified. More importantly, the ordinary people were turning to them. Morale was so low in the enemy camp that they began to issue pardons to the revolutionaries should they decide to give up their struggle. But there was no way that would happen, and the skirmishes continued as the revolutionaries tried to gain ground. But they knew what was coming. Something had to change. Batista's army was on the march. Its encirclement and annihilation offensive was beginning. Fidel, Che and the others constructed their final strategy.

'You fought your battle,' Luis said now, 'for things to change.'

'Yes.' And they had won. Things couldn't become perfect overnight – and what was perfect anyhow? Che had once said that revolutions were made from passion and that they could never be perfect. But they had broken the tyranny and they had won.

His grandson turned to face him. His eyes were dark and inscrutable, his jaw was strong and firm. He had grown up, Duardo realised suddenly. With this decision of his, he had become a man.

'And now some of us want to fight our battle in a different way,' said Luis.

'By leaving our country?' Duardo blinked at him. It was hard to see the logic in that.

'Our battle may seem more individual,' Luis said.

'Or selfish.' It certainly wasn't the communist way.

Luis conceded this with an inclination of his head. 'Or it may be more long term,' he said. 'Think about it, *abuelo*. Is it good for our country to be living in the dark ages with none of the benefits of technology, business and trade? Is that the way forward for Cuba?'

Duardo wasn't sure how to answer this. He thought of the latest superpower that seemed to be creeping into their lives. Now in Cuba there were Chinese buses, Chinese trains, Chinese energy-saving light bulbs . . . And he thought about what had happened at the end of December 1958 when the rebels' Molotov cocktails had forced the men out of the armoured train. 'Shall we go on to the Tren Blindado monument?' he asked.

Luis laughed. 'Of course, *abuelo*,' he said.

They headed across town past the main square, Parque Leoncio Vidal, which was, Duardo always felt, surprisingly elegant with its fine buildings, flowering trees, and wrought-iron benches and lamps. In stark contrast though was the green tower-block hotel, which might be hideous, but was in a way, he felt, more real, since it still bore the bullet holes from the fighting. Another memory, another battle.

They reached the place on the line to Remedios, where it had happened and once again got out of the car. Duardo looked around. He fancied he could still hear the splatter of rifle fire, smell the stench of blood and death, see the charred bodies of men who had died in that last fire . . . And then the light of hope. The triumph. On 28 December 1958 with the help of only three hundred men, mark you – of which Duardo was proud to have been one – Che had finally captured the town, overcoming ten times that number of Batista's soldiers. The next day he derailed a train right here on this spot, a train of twenty-two carriages carrying ammunition, anti-aircraft and machine guns, rations and soldiers on its way to be used to fight the rebels. They took the power station and the north-west of the city. They went on air to announce that Santa Clara was in the hands of the revolutionaries. This event turned the tide of the revolution in their favour, there was no doubt it had been the best of days.

Duardo and Luis walked around the plinth, where the yellow D6 caterpillar bulldozer that had been used to break the rail tracks in order to derail the train was stationed, the red boxcars arranged at higgledy-piggledy angles alongside concrete spikes. This was the real thing – restored, of course, but the original bulldozer, paused as if at the point of drama and derailment. Inside the boxcars were photographs, maps and artifacts recreating the sequence of events of the raid. Side by side, Duardo and Luis examined these.

There was, of course, more fighting after the victory at Santa Clara. There was the skirmish where the barn was bombed and so many of Duardo's brothers were killed – the time when he and a few others fled back to the mountains, not knowing that the rebels were so close to victory. Duardo had been badly injured then. He had been half crazy and close to starvation. He'd stayed on a farm miles from anywhere, unaware that it was all over, nursed back to health by the kindness of the farmer and his wife. It was a time that had cost him dear.

But Fidel Castro had triumphed. Yes, thought Duardo. And he had only been in power for six months before the US began plotting to oust him. Or worse. When they failed . . . they severed diplomatic relations in 1961 and imposed the embargo a year later. And so.

'I understand that you want better living conditions,' Duardo said after they had been silent for a while. 'I understand that you want all the things that money can buy. You're young. That's normal. It's how things are in the rest of the world, or so they tell me.' And I tried to give it to you, he thought to himself. It was what he'd always wanted for Luis. Through his business, through tourism, he had wanted Luis to be a young ambassador for their country. He had wanted so much, it seemed. Too much.

'But I want more than that,' Luis said.

'More?'

'I want us Cubans to take our proper place in the world.'

Duardo stared at him. He tried to take in what his grandson was telling him.

'And to do that,' he said, 'we have to get out there and be in it.'

Grace peered out of the porthole window and checked their progress on the sky map. She was almost halfway there. Story of her life.

'You've been through so much,' Elisa had said to her when she phoned from Cuba, 'you need a holiday, my dear.' Cuba was an awful long way away but she sounded as if she were in the next room. 'Has the money come through yet?'

'Ye-es.' The house in King Street had sold quickly and Elisa had insisted the proceeds be divided equally between the two of them. 'You'll get the rest when I'm gone,' she'd promised. In point of fact, she had tried to make Grace take the lot, which was plainly ridiculous; Elisa must have something to live on and Grace's father would have wanted her to be looked after for the rest of her life. So did Grace, come to that.

'And can you take some time off?'

'I've got some bookings. But I could rearrange them, I suppose.' She was thinking about it. A holiday sounded appealing. Maybe the Canaries. It would still be warm there in November. She could try to catch some winter sun. Relax. Recharge.

'Then come to Cuba,' said Elisa.

'Cuba . . .' She hadn't considered Cuba. It seemed so distant, so . . . well, so complicated. She couldn't imagine relaxing in Cuba. When she thought of Cuba she thought of Theo – she couldn't help it.

The last time she had seen him – properly seen him, not just his shadow – was that final afternoon in Gorse Lane the day before her father had died. She thought of the note she'd sent him a few days later, ending things between them; ending what should never have begun. She'd lacked the courage to go round to see him. Feeling fragile and grieving for her father, she couldn't risk the temptation of folding herself into his arms and just staying there. But she couldn't end things by phone call or text, so she'd written it and she'd posted it. Theo had never replied.

And now? Grace still missed him. But she had lost her chance and she had made her choice. She knew it was over.

'Won't you be coming back to Bristol soon?' she asked her stepmother. Elisa had been cagey about this so far. 'You and . . . ?' It was hard, she found, to even say his name.

'Theo's decided to stay a while longer.' Elisa's tone was matter of fact. 'I wouldn't be surprised if –'

'If what?'

'Oh, nothing.' Grace heard her take a deep breath. Did that mean he was staying in Cuba? Could he – stay in Cuba? He had said he'd have to go away, but she'd assumed he meant to another town, not another country halfway round the world.

'And as for me . . .'

'Yes? Have you seen him? Duardo?'

'Not yet.'

'So?' Grace held the receiver more tightly. Although she had encouraged Elisa to go, although she felt more independent than she ever had, she still couldn't quite imagine life without her stepmother on a day-to-day basis.

Elisa sighed. 'I'd love to show you Cuba, my dear,' she said, 'and I think you know that even if I never see Duardo, I will stay.'

'It still feels like your home,' Grace murmured.

'Exactly. I left Cuba when I was eighteen, Grace,' she said, 'but it is in my blood – it always will be.' She paused. 'It's so warm here, you know. But it's not just the sunshine, it's the people too. In Havana most people know most people. There are stronger connections. For a woman living alone . . .' Her voice trailed.

'I understand.' Grace saw how hard it must have been for her stepmother here in England, wilting like a hothouse flower left out in the rain.

'We all have to follow our own hearts, my dear, I hope you can see that.'

'Of course I can.' And she did. But all of a sudden, Grace felt terribly alone.

'But I miss you so much. You know I do. So will you come for a visit? Please?'

Grace made a rapid decision. She could go to the Canaries anytime. But Cuba . . . 'I'll try to book a flight right away,' she said. Because it meant so much to Elisa and Elisa meant so much to Grace. And because Grace wanted to see it

414

too – this country that was so close to both Elisa and Theo. Things were changing, she had heard on the news. Embargos with the US were being lifted, the two governments were beginning to discuss future talks. Gradually, Cubans were becoming more free.

'Wonderful.' Elisa sounded triumphant. 'I'll call you in a day or two and you can give me your flight details.'

And now, only weeks later, Grace was hurtling towards them – Cuba, her stepmother, Theo.

It seemed like an eternity before she stepped into the arrivals section of the airport, having ploughed through a noisy security that was stricter than when she'd left the UK, past the stern-looking women in their short skirts and fishnets and men frowning and beckoning from behind desks and screens, taking an age before stamping her passport and her visa. And there was Elisa, looking different somehow – brighter, warmer. At home, thought Grace.

'Grace!' she said. 'How lovely to see you, my dear. But, oh.' She drew back for a moment and then pulled her close again. 'You're looking far too thin.'

Over Elisa's shoulder, Grace looked for Theo, but of course he wasn't there.

For the first few days, Elisa showed her round Havana. 'We'll do all the tourist things,' she said. So they strolled down the tree-lined Paseo del Prado, a picturesque boulevard leading from the harbour up to the grand Capitolia Square, where Moorish architecture jostled with fancy baroque and half-derelict mansions. 'Back in the day, this was one of the wealthiest streets in Havana,' Elisa told her. '*Paseo* was the daily carriage ride – an important social ritual.'

Grace laughed at Elisa's slightly sceptical tone of voice. This wasn't a Cuba that her stepmother would have experienced as a child growing up in Havana. There was always something to see. Every few yards motley bands of musicians played them on their way with music – a mix of Spanish roots and the drums of Africa with a few Cuban evolutions thrown in. Artists sketched at easels capturing the essence of the place in wild, bright sweeps of the brush, dusky-skinned children played ball and tag in the shade. The people were so colourful. The men reminded her of Theo; they seemed to possess the same air of easy confidence. The women wore skimpy tops and tight leggings or jeans and were justifiably proud of their generous curves on show.

After this, they wandered through all four of the squares in the Old City. Grace loved the air of tranquillity in the cobbled Plaza de la Catedral – despite the tourists – and the majestic off-white baroque façade of the cathedral, which, according to Elisa, had once been described by a Cuban author as 'music set in stone'. Grace wouldn't argue with that. She also loved the narrow, cluttered Obispo Street ('Where the bishop used to live,' said Elisa. 'Really.') now crammed with markets, historic pharmacies in the massive foyers of old colonial buildings, bookshops and cafés. And she adored her breezy ride in a classic American car – a red and white open-topped Chevrolet – which Elisa had insisted on.

'Every tourist does it,' she said. Grace saw Elisa looking – but apparently there was no sign of Duardo in the line of drivers using every art of persuasion at their disposal. Elisa had said that it was the best way to see Havana, and Grace had to agree, as she made her choice and they left behind the grand buildings of Parque Central and swept along the Malecón to Vedado and the west of Havana where steel sky-scrapers dominated the cityscape. Not only that, but it made you feel like a 1950s movie star.

After the heady car ride they drank Cuban coffee in Ernest Hemingway's favourite old hang-out, the Bodeguita del Medio. 'It was literally a little food shop in the middle of the road,' Elisa told her. 'In the 1940s they started serving drinks and before you knew it, the place became a haunt for artists, writers and intellectuals.' The walls were plastered with graf-fiti, old photos, and the autographs of famous patrons such as Nat King Cole and good old Hemingway himself. It was crowded, thought Grace, and loud.

When they were exhausted from walking round the city, Elisa took Grace to the Hotel Ambos Mundos to relax on the roof terrace with a cocktail. There was a refreshing breeze up here, pretty mosaic tiles on the walls and it had the best views of the city. Grace leaned on the balustrade. She could see the cobbled rooftops below, the people strolling down Obispo, the blue shuttered windows of the Hotel Santa Isa-bel, the Generals' Palace – complete with two towering royal palms in the centre of the courtyard – the fort on the hill, the Malecón and the sea. Plus – almost inevitably, thought Grace, consulting her guide book – Hemingway had given Hotel Ambos Mundos his seal of approval by staying here when he began to write *For Whom the Bell Tolls*. This afternoon however, things were more down to earth. Sort of. Men balancing precariously on wooden seats attached to ropes, were repainting the pretty peach and white façade and here on the roof terrace a band of musicians were playing 'Que sera sera'. And giving it some.

Grace turned around. 'What about Duardo?' she asked her stepmother. 'How come you haven't seen him?' She knew that he wasn't the only reason Elisa had returned to Cuba. She missed the warmth and the culture and Grace understood that her stepmother wanted to spend the rest of her days in the place where she'd grown up. But . . .

'So much time has gone by, Grace, my dear.' Elisa sipped her mojito, apparently unfazed at the direct question. 'We're getting old and it is of course much too late.'

'You haven't tried to see him then?'

'No. I thought I might run into him. But I haven't – not yet.'

Grace went to sit down opposite her at the table. 'Why don't you just go round to his house and talk to him?' she asked. 'The worst that can happen is that he'll tell you he's not interested.' She picked up her own rum cocktail. 'At least then you'll know,' she reminded her.

'It's not so simple.' Elisa sighed. 'He will still be living with the mother of his son, even if they are not really together.' She leaned back in her chair. She looked tired, thought Grace. 'But perhaps they are together again now. And, anyway, I can't just barge in there after all this time. Especially after leaving him twice before.'

Grace thought of Theo. Where was he? Elisa hadn't breathed a word. 'But if Duardo doesn't know you're here,' she said, 'then you're not even giving him a chance.'

'I have told his mother I am staying for good,' Elisa said. 'So if it is meant to be . . .' Her voice trailed. *Que sera sera* indeed.

Which was all very well, Grace listened as the musicians on the terrace changed tempo, but sometimes you had to give 'meant to be' a helping hand. Fate was always more effective that way.

All the time they were exploring Havana, Grace half-expected Theo to materialise from behind some colonial balustrade or jump out from behind a golden statue on Obispo Street. But he didn't. And she wouldn't cross-question Elisa. He must know she was here and he'd obviously decided to stay out of her way. This hurt, but Grace had too much pride to risk having her nose rubbed in it. Perhaps Elisa did too. The two of them seemed to have more parallels in their lives than she had ever realised before.

On her third day, Elisa took Grace to the chocolate museum to sit outside and drink cold chocolate with honey and milk, the most delicious thing Grace had ever tasted. And suddenly she could stand it no longer. 'So where's Theo?' she asked.

Elisa raised an eyebrow. 'Three days,' she marvelled. 'You're so stubborn, Grace. Your father would be proud of you.'

Grace continued drinking her chocolate. It was slightly grainy and not too sweet. 'Perhaps he isn't on my mind as much as you think he is,' she countered.

'Perhaps.' But Elisa shook her head and smiled.

'So?'

'He's in Trinidad.'

'Trinidad?' Grace stared at her. 'What's he doing there?'

Elisa shrugged. 'It's very beautiful. Historic colonial buildings, lovely scenery, remains of old sugar plantations . . .'

'Did he go there to avoid seeing me?' What other conclusion was she supposed to come to?

Elisa gave her a long look. 'I did tell him you were coming out, but he was already on his way round the island. Trinidad is where his family originated. Some of his parents' friends and family may still live there.'

'Right.' Grace felt bleak. She had been so nervous about seeing him, but now it seemed there was nothing she wanted more. She was probably wasting her time. But she wanted to at least talk to him, to find out how he felt, to discover . . . if they could still be friends. 'Do you think he'll stay here in Cuba?' she asked.

Elisa's dark eyes were sympathetic. 'I don't know, my dear, but I do think that Cuba has had quite an effect on that young man. You should be prepared.'

So she'd been right. He might not even be coming back. Grace let this thought filter through her. She might never see him again.

'Tomorrow, I'd like to take you to Vinales,' Elisa went on, 'it's a unique landscape. A bit like a lost world.'

A lost world. It sounded, thought Grace, exactly what she needed.

It was true that Vinales was a unique place. The *mogotes* were large plugs of ancient limestone rocks covered in thick vegetation that seemed to rise straight up from the vibrant green tobacco fields and red earth of the valley, creating an otherworldly atmosphere. Grace and Elisa walked through the rusty paths of the Valle de Vinales watching egrets following the oxen and plough as the red earth was prepared for planting. They explored the caves and grottoes, wandered into tobacco-drying huts whose roofs were made of leaves from the royal palm, watched expert *torcedores*, cigar rollers, in action and drank enough coconut juice to fuel a cruise ship.

But it was no use. Grace couldn't get Theo out of her mind.

'Elisa,' she said to her stepmother after dinner one night, 'do you think I should go to Trinidad?'

Elisa watched her for a long moment and then placed her hand over hers. 'Do you love him, my dear?' she asked. 'Is he everything to you?'

And Grace thought she saw the sadness in her stepmother's heart. She nodded. 'I think so.'

Elisa nodded. 'Then, yes, you should go to Trinidad. And you should tell him.'

CHAPTER 42

Rosalyn began the slow trudge home. Since she had seen Elisa that day at the plaza, she worried each time she went out that she would see her again, that Elisa would approach her just as she had approached her before, and ask her if she had given her message to Duardo.

The answer was no, she had not. Oh, that day . . . She could barely bring herself to think of it, although some nights she thought of little else. She could hardly believe who it was who had spoken her name, who it was she was seeing. Her. Elisa Fernandez-Garcia, or whatever she might be called now – back here in Havana after all these years. It was not just a matter of who she was, of her family and the fact that Rosalyn's own ancestors had been owned by them. It was not just the fact that she had taken Duardo and had had so much power over Rosalyn's son that she had seduced him into running away with her. It was not just how she had treated him, how she had let him down. She had always been Rosalyn's secret fear. Power was not just about ownership, it seemed. She was the one woman who could take Duardo away from Rosalyn – in every way that mattered.

She could imagine how it would be. Elisa would creep

back into his life. Elisa would have his confidences. Elisa would have his very soul. No longer would Duardo come to his mother to discuss the problems and high points of his day. She would be left out in the cold and forgotten; she might as well be dead. And for this to happen now when Rosalyn was living together and at peace with her son at last . . . It must not be. How could the woman even dare to ask her to speak to Duardo on her behalf? After all the pain and loss she had put him through? As if he'd ever forgive or forget. Did Elisa think she was crazy? Rosalyn would not do that to her son. Elisa would have him over her dead body.

Just thinking of all this, put Rosalyn into a panic. She took some deep rasping breaths. She needed to stay calm and she needed to be in a place where she could breathe more freely, that much she knew. Since their meeting, Rosalyn had been unable to quash the feeling that fate was working against her. Punishing her perhaps for what she had done.

She had never been a religious woman – not for her the rituals of *santeria*, the worship of the gods and goddesses who were supposed to keep them all safe; what use had they ever been to anyone? Though she understood that people – especially hurt or oppressed people – needed something to believe in and the Africans had simply tried to hold on to something of their own. Sometimes it was all they had. Her father had kept a shrine tucked in a niche in their living room and he had often made offerings and prayers to African gods, mumbling to himself as he did so. As a young girl, Rosalyn had frequently eyed the offerings of a perfectly ripe banana or papaya with some resentment, since the family often had so little to eat, and so it was no surprise that she, like her mother, had grown up grounded in practicalities. You could only depend on yourself and on your family. That was all. And even your family would sometimes let you down.

She paused at the ring of a bell to let a cycle-taxi overtake her on the cobbles. Downtown Havana, she thought, overrun by tourists as far as the eye could see. Once again it almost seemed as if the city was no longer Cuban. She shook her head and returned to her previous train of thought. Look at Luis. Not that he had let Duardo down, exactly; the boy had merely chosen his own way. But Duardo felt betrayed, that was sure enough.

There had been an awful sense of timing about that meeting with Elisa that made it seem as if it had been meant to be. It was only a few months since Jaquinda . . . but no, it was a coincidence, nothing more. Rosalyn had to believe that.

In the square, the same boys were playing ball, the same gleam in the eye of the tall, skinny one in the baseball hat. Unusually, there weren't many people around, perhaps because it was past noon. Rosalyn decided to take a shorter route than usual. She was tired, always tired these days.

One of the boys kicked the ball, hard. Rosalyn saw it coming. She moved deftly and it passed by. Rosalyn grimaced and shifted the weight of her shopping bag on to her other arm. *You see*, she felt like shouting. She was not so old. She was not so decrepit . . . Pouf!

The ball came from nowhere – or at least from behind her – and it caught her firmly on the back of her right shin. She tottered, just a little, and turned around to release a torrent of angry abuse at the boy who had kicked it. What did he think he was playing at? Didn't he have eyes in his head? Didn't he have anything better to do – like helping his father or doing some chores in the house – rather than behaving like a good for nothing street urchin, blocking the square so that decent folks going about their business couldn't get past without having a ball kicked at them? Time was that young people had more respect for their elders.

Rosalyn drew breath. It was the boy with the gleam and the baseball hat. But she realised it too late. Saw his toothy grin too late. Saw the gleam turn into something more malevolent.

'Hey, you wanna join in our game, Gramma?' he called. 'Is that a water melon in your bag? We could sure use one of those.' The rest of them laughed loudly.

He sounded American. Rosalyn shuddered. It came back to her, clear as day, that first night in the bar when the fat balding American with the cigar had grabbed her round the waist and plonked her on his knee. When she had first realised: *I have no choice. This is what I will have to do.*

And then the dizziness came again and she felt herself going, slipping . . . She heard voices in the background – the boys' voices – sounding somehow both strident and scared. Then she heard footsteps as if they were running away. Perhaps they were scared that they had really hurt her. *Holy*

Mary, Mother of God, she sent up a silent prayer. Perhaps she was badly hurt. Dying even.

For a moment – or more, she could not tell – everything went black.

She awoke to another voice – a soft, elderly female voice. 'Are you all right? Let me help you. Can you lift your head? Carefully now.'

Rosalyn realised she was lying on the hard cobbles and lying at an awkward angle too. She had fallen then. She blinked. Her head was still swimming. Gingerly, she moved a leg, then an arm. There was no pain. Miraculously it seemed that nothing was broken. The woman gave her water from a cup, held her head gently while she sipped. Rosalyn sat up, opened her eyes, saw the kind face of the woman who was helping her – and her fruit and vegetables all over the cobbles of the plaza. She moaned.

'Be still.' The woman seemed to have fetched a man and together they helped Rosalyn sit up. They waited a few more minutes and then got her to her feet and led her to a nearby bench.

'How silly of me,' Rosalyn murmured. 'Those boys . . .'

'Should know better,' the woman said.

Rosalyn didn't argue with her. She sat and felt some strength returning, but in truth she still didn't feel herself, not remotely herself. What was happening to her? Was she so old that she couldn't even venture out into the city any more?

'Come to my *casa*,' the woman said decisively. 'It is very close by. Can you walk if you lean on my arm and let me take your weight? You can rest there until you are ready and then I'll take you home.'

Rosalyn didn't have the strength to object. Besides, where else could she go? She was still feeling at a loss, still a little dizzy and certainly unsteady. She even thought that she knew this woman from somewhere, but she couldn't dredge the memory from the recesses of her mind.

So she allowed herself to be gently led to a nearby apartment. It wasn't large and it wasn't smart, but it was cosy and comfortable and rather reminded her of her own home. The woman sat her down in a chair and said she was going to make lime-blossom tea. Rosalyn allowed herself to relax.

'Thank you so much,' she said, when the woman returned with a tray of hot drinks. 'The ball, that boy . . . I merely felt a little dizzy . . .'

'You were carrying a very heavy bag,' the woman said. It sounded as if she understood the situation completely, 'and it is very hot outside.'

'Yes.' This made Rosalyn feel better. The woman seemed to be suggesting that it could have happened to anyone. 'But so kind of you,' she added.

The woman smiled and shrugged. 'It was nothing. I was glad to help.'

Something about her face. Rosalyn blinked. At last, everything came into focus. Of course, she knew her. She had been busily ignoring her for a very long time.

'I have often seen you,' the woman said. 'My family knows your family. Do you remember?'

Rosalyn looked at her and a wave of shame passed over her. Because she had been so kind to her, this woman whom Rosalyn had so often ignored, simply because she was a cousin of Elisa's.

She closed her eyes. 'I remember,' she whispered. What a proud fool she had been, she thought. What a proud fool she had been for love.

CHAPTER 43

Grace didn't start to get nervous until they left the *autopista* and entered the province of Cienfuegos. Her driver was still talking – he had talked non-stop most of the way, while Grace tried to relax and enjoy the countryside as they swept by. At the waterfront and docks of Havana they lurched past trucks of all shapes and sizes, in front of them a hazy vista of palm trees beckoning them on. After the industrial area, they joined the *autopista* – Alex explaining at great length why he must keep to a speed of 100 kilometres per hour, otherwise he'd exceed the government petrol allowance and have to fork out the difference himself. Such a different life, Grace reflected, listening to him; so few of the freedoms that she and most people she knew, took for granted.

As they drove past the checkpoints separating province from province, Grace remarked on the number of hitchhikers on the road. 'I can't pick anyone up,' he said. 'They might be carrying beef.'

'Beef?'

Beef smuggling, it transpired, was common in Cuba; beef was a highly restricted commodity. 'Cows are working animals in this country,' Alex explained. 'We need them for dairy. A vet must certify that a cow has died from natural causes. To kill a cow is a criminal offence resulting in up to fifteen years imprisonment.'

Goodness. Grace responded with a couple of anecdotes about British traffic jams, petrol prices and road rage but mostly she just let him talk. It was easier that way, to think.

'In Cuba, it is very different,' Alex said frequently. He explained why some number plates had a blue section with a 'B' as the first letter (these were private taxis) and why a Cuban bank would never lend money to an ordinary man like himself (most Cubans owned almost nothing). 'In Cuba, a qualified engineer or a vet will earn twenty-five CUCs a month,' he said, 'which is why it is better to be a taxi driver.'

Tips, she thought. So, yes, in Cuba it was very different. How would Theo manage to live here if that was what he decided to do? She couldn't imagine that accountancy skills were any more in demand than those of a magician.

'What's going on over there?' Grace pointed. A car had apparently broken down in the centre of the freeway. It was surrounded by the driver and five passengers, all circling the vehicle and examining the engine, apparently oblivious to oncoming traffic veering to avoid them.

Alex shrugged. 'They must discuss the problem,' he said. 'Someone must fix it. Until then . . .' In Cuba apparently, it was easy come, easy go. There was no AA or roadside assistance. 'In Cuba we live for the moment,' Alex clarified. 'It is different here.'

They passed the turning for Matanzas, its roadside

hoardings plastered with political slogans. Grace saw a poster of a beaming Raúl Castro in army cap and glasses. *Unity means strength and victory* . . . It had been a while since the revolution, thought Grace, but Che's and Fidel's legend lived on and was celebrated still – at least on the outside. She was about to quiz Alex about the revolution; she sensed that he wouldn't hesitate to give his opinions, but his mobile went off and he began talking in a fast Cuban Spanish that was hard to follow. Grace didn't care that he was using his mobile while driving – there was hardly any traffic and even less at the weekends, Alex had informed her. She supposed only government-owned trucks, taxis and tourists could afford to travel at all. No wonder then that there were so many hitchhikers lining the roads.

The landscape became increasingly arid as they passed banana plantations, orange groves and bony humped-back cattle grazing; broad-winged turkey vultures gliding across the expanse of clear blue sky. Alex finished his call and began showing Grace the pictures on his mobile.

She leaned forwards to look. He had five children, though he hardly looked old enough, and a souped-up ancient red Lada, of which he seemed equally proud. 'I have more than many people in Cuba,' he told her. And Grace had seen plenty of evidence in Havana to know that he was right.

In Cienfuegos province they turned off the *autopista* and the fields became more cultivated and the lanes more rural as they drove along past ancient tractors, horses and carts and rattling old bicycles, occasionally stopping to allow stray cows, horses or chickens to cross the road. The houses were made of wood or thatch, the roads edged with deep ditches and lined with fields of densely planted, lime-green sugar cane. Grace could see only too well what back-breaking work it must have been to cut them down.

She settled back in her seat. OK, she thought, so when she saw him, what would she say to Theo? And how would he react at the sight of her? No one liked being rejected – though she'd had good reason. Grace wasn't expecting him to welcome her with open arms, she wasn't even expecting to be able to have a relationship with him again. But she longed for his friendship and she hoped that he might forgive her – eventually. If she could just talk to him . . . She hoped that she might be able to make him understand.

They arrived at the coast and began to pass wide rivers – the Danjo and Solado – the mouths of which had created small local beaches with a few lonely thatched parasols and the occasional run-down bar. Then the road took them away from the coast again and as they approached Sancti Spiritus province, there were more mango plantations and more sugar cane. They were getting closer and Grace could feel her trepidation growing.

Alex asked her if she wanted a break.

'No, thanks.' Grace just wanted to get there as soon as possible. 'What about you? You must be tired.'

He laughed and shook his head. 'I will drive straight back to Havana,' he said. 'I will meet some friends for a beer, maybe listen to some music.' He shifted his hips as if in readiness. 'And whoever has some money will pay.'

'How does that work?' she asked. And what if no one had money?

He smiled at her in the driver's mirror. 'If we have no money we stay at home,' he said. 'It is simple. This is what we do in Cuba.'

Tonight. Grace wondered what she would be doing tonight. It probably wouldn't be simple. But Cuba wasn't simple either. Some of the people seemed happy despite their lack of freedom and money – because at least, as people kept telling her, they had food to eat, a free health service and education; others hated the Castro regime and the dictatorship it had turned out to be. Some hated America, some wanted nothing more than to live there. Some people wanted to work to improve their lot, others were content doing very little. Everyone had something different to say about the past and everyone had different expectations of the future. What would happen to this country? Grace wondered if Theo had any more idea than she.

When they eventually arrived in Trinidad, Alex asked at least half a dozen people for directions to her hotel and Grace began to suspect that he simply liked the sound of his own voice. Never mind, finally they found it – *La Ronda*, painted pink and white, flags flying, and inside, comfortable basket-weave chairs and a wonderfully cool courtyard interior.

'*Gracias*, Alex.' Grace pulled out her purse and took out a note to tip him with. She was never sure how much to tip, so she usually overdid it just in case. At least he'd be able to buy the beer for his friends tonight, she thought.

Alex bent and kissed her hand. 'I hope you find what you are looking for,' he said.

Grace watched him leave as the hotel receptionist handed her a cool drink of fresh guava juice. 'Thank you so much,' she told her. How on earth had chatterbox Alex known that she was looking for anything?

Once she'd checked in and had a shower, Grace decided not to waste any more time. She'd go and find him. It was the reason she'd come here, after all.

Armed with a rather inadequate street map given to her by the hotel, she left *La Ronda* and turned right, heading for the historic centre and the hostel where Elisa had told her Theo was staying. She passed a bank with a long queue of people waiting outside and a group of men sitting on low stools on the pavement selling *Granma* newspapers and muttering 'Che Guevara', in hopeful voices to every tourist who passed by. Elisa had told her that the newspaper was named after the yacht *Granma* which carried Fidel Castro and other rebels to Cuba's shores in 1956, thus launching the revolution. 'Many people,' she had said, including her Duardo by the wistful expression in her dark eyes, 'will ensure that they never forget.'

Trinidad was a bustling and pretty place. The houses were charming – painted pink, turquoise and mint green – and telegraph poles leaned precariously across the narrow streets; tangled with wires and doubling up as street lamps. And the people were colourful too, thought Grace as she passed a mobile fruit stall – piled with juicy ripe mangos, oranges and papaya – and one of the supply shops which Elisa had also pointed out to her in Havana. She turned right at the bakery at Simon Bolivar Street, the sweet scent of baking bread reminding her that it was after one and that she hadn't had lunch.

She approached the cobbled area of the old city. Here, hat shops, leather craft stores and art galleries lined the streets, but it was difficult to walk on the smooth and slippery cobbles, so Grace took to the larger stones in the centre of the road, avoiding the horses and carts and bicycle taxis when they appeared behind her, ringing their bells and tooting their horns. In this town, she found herself thinking, was Theo.

The art was as bright as the rest of Cuba, she noted as she passed the galleries showing Picasso-esque figures, flamboyant depictions of old American cars, huge-breasted naked women or Che Guevara. That was about it really. There were also craft shops located in private houses – some roomy with large shady courtyards, some dimly lit, cramped and apparently sharing the limited space with a bed and a dining table. Grace had already learned how hard it was to make money in Cuba, so why not paint? Even if they sold only one picture a month it would be something. Markets spreadeagled out from the main drag, but Grace resisted them and focused on getting to the end of the street where would be – she hoped – the place she was looking for: Maison del Regidor.

And suddenly – there it was, a small building painted ochre

with simple white and turquoise wooden balconies, the front door wide open, a sunlit courtyard visible beyond it. Grace crossed over. She took a deep breath, straightened her shoulders and stepped inside.

There was a good deal of polished mahogany furniture in the reception room, pictures of landscapes hung on the walls and a charming frieze of red, yellow and turquoise spanned the room. An ornate glass chandelier hung from the ceiling, and to the right she could see a dining room with tables already laid. A young woman dressed in sunshine yellow was washing the old terracotta tiles. '*Hola*,' she said cheerfully.

'*Hola, senorita.*' Grace smiled back at her, though all her senses seemed to be churning. 'I'm looking for Theo Cantos.'

'Theo?' Was it her imagination or did a look of fondness cross the young woman's expressive features? 'Ah, Theo, *si, si.*'

'Is he here?' Grace looked past her to the leafy courtyard beyond. A table and two chairs were positioned to get full sun but no one was around.

'Not now, no.' The woman shook her dark head and began to elaborate in a stream of fast Cuban Spanish.

Grace tried to follow. '*Gracias*,' she said. 'I'll come back later.' But her stomach dipped with disappointment. She stepped back outside again where a man sat on the pavement, a chicken on his head.

'*De donde?*' he growled through missing teeth.

'*Inglaterre*,' she replied. It was a question she'd had to answer many times since she'd arrived here. He nodded approvingly and flashed her a gappy grin while the chicken fluttered its wings and resettled. Grace had to laugh. Alex had been spot-on. Things were definitely different in Cuba.

She walked towards the main square, pausing every few moments to take in her surroundings. The historic centre of Trinidad was so breathtakingly beautiful that it almost didn't seem real. Ahead of her was a mushroom-coloured church with a neo-classical facade and surrounding the plaza several grand mansions of blues, creams and buttermilk yellow, with frescoes, murals and wooden balustrades. She had already read that the city had been founded in 1514 and had been restored and maintained as a World Heritage site, and now, Grace could see why. The cobblestones and colonialism made her feel as if time had stood still. *If only* . . .

The plaza was made up of four symmetrical squares. Each one was surrounded by white railings and lined by tall royal palms with a low hedge of red flowers and decorative, green and cream ceramic urns. She sat down on one of several elaborately wrought white metal benches in the centre of the square opposite a white statue and a cross of dusty flagstones. Some young boys were playing tag and Grace watched them careering around the pathways and spinning around the ornate lampposts, the youngest and smallest always being 'It' for the longest time. She took a swig from her water bottle. It was, she thought, the way of the world.

So where would he be? Grace looked round her, past the colonial-style building painted dark turquoise to the church behind her and to the apricot and green bullet-shaped little convent bell tower which must be symbolic of Trinidad as she'd seen the image quite often, even in Havana. The historic centre of the city wasn't huge, but Theo could have gone off for the day — to the mountains, to the old sugar plantations, or the beach. He could be anywhere.

Music drifted towards her — it was never far away; music and Cuba seemed to be inseparable. It rippled in the breeze along pavements and throbbed from the very ground beneath. It tipped out of upstairs windows, echoed through walls and poured from bars, restaurants, cafés. Curious, Grace got to her feet and followed the seductive salsa rhythm past the church and round the corner towards a vast set of high cobbled grey steps where tables had been set up. At the top, a band was playing: a drummer, a guitarist and two percussionists — one shaking the maracas and one scraping a wooden serrated instrument to produce an unusual rasping sound. Grace smiled and watched.

People had drifted out of the *casa de trova* and, in front of the musicians, the dancing had begun; couples were shifting their bodies to the salsa music, holding hands, stepping out and back, the women shaking their breasts, grinding their buttocks and whirling to the beat. Skirts rode up over polished knees, arms whipped in the air, hips shook and circled, limbs seemed almost to be made of elastic. All ages, all sizes; no one seemed self-conscious, even the men — who moved with a sure and sensual grace of their own. A black woman wearing a hot-pink dress came down the steps doing a shimmy, beads of sweat gathering between her breasts. Grace found her feet tapping; she let her shoulders go and allowed the music to shake up her senses. It was fast and it was strong. It was almost impossible to listen and not move.

And then she saw him. He was sitting on the steps near the front, staring ahead, almost as if he was waiting for her – which, under the circumstances was obviously wishful thinking.

'Theo,' she breathed, though he hadn't seen her. 'So there you are.'

He looked very different and yet the same – his body seeming to be still and relaxed but also alert. It was a quality Grace had always noticed about him; as if he were for ever poised in readiness for something to happen. His hair was a little longer, he was wearing jeans although it was a warm day and his pale-blue short-sleeved shirt was collarless and unbuttoned at the neck. Grace watched him for a few minutes while the musicians played on. And then, just as she was about to go over and touch him gently on the shoulder, he looked across and saw her.

He was wearing shades, but they didn't hide his surprise, swiftly followed by a look of sadness, and then – a cool smile as he got to his feet. Oh, dear. Coolness, Grace thought, was awful. She took a few steps towards him and he too moved towards her.

'Hello, Grace.' He stood, arms hanging loose by his side, watching her. Body-language defensive, she noted. The free flow of music and dancing in the background provided a stark contrast. 'I didn't expect to see you here.'

She tried a casual shrug, but it felt wrong. Casual was

apparently as inappropriate as cool. 'Elisa encouraged me to come,' she said, 'to Cuba, that is.'

'Elisa's not here in Trinidad?' He looked around as if he expected her to be dancing on the steps above.

'No, she's not. I came alone.'

'Ah.' He took off his shades and scrutinised her more closely – that black gaze. Grace almost baulked at the sight of it. But she stood her ground. She was here now. She had to give it a go.

'I came to see you,' she said. Though he would know that already.

'Long way to come, Grace.' But he was almost smiling and this gave her courage. It was just a small twitch of his lips, but thankfully Grace knew him well enough to recognise it. Or, at least, she had done.

'I felt I had to.' Which sounded awfully lame, but she was struggling.

He looked at her for a long moment. She didn't, however, know him well enough to be able to tell what he was thinking. She couldn't even tell if he was glad to see her, or not.

Abruptly, he looked away, breaking the spell, glancing up towards the dancers still shimmying and sashaying above. 'Dancing is their freedom,' he said.

Grace followed his gaze. It seemed to be true. Cuban people looked so happy when they were dancing – she had never witnessed such a pure *joie de vivre*, such a passion for the music, and such a natural rhythm. It was as if they had all been born to dance. She nodded.

'How long have you been in Trinidad?' she asked him. It was small talk but this was a refuge. Big talk had always come naturally to Grace and Theo – but that was before.

'Several days,' he said. 'I'm getting to understand the place.'

Grace steadied her breathing. 'Would you show me around?' she asked.

Again, he watched her for a long moment before he replied. She noticed the fine lines at the corners of his eyes and mouth; he seemed older than he ever had before. 'Of course I will,' he said after what seemed a lifetime.

Yes, but do you want to? she wondered. And once again, she wondered if she shouldn't have come. She hadn't expected to fall into his arms – of course she hadn't, but she had expected something. Theo had always been elusive, but he had also been warm. Now, he was almost looking at her as if she were a stranger.

'Coffee?' he asked.

'Lovely.' They walked side by side away from the music to a courtyard café just round the corner from the plaza. Grace tried not to think of those other coffees in Bristol. She was conscious of the closeness of him – and of the distance he was creating between them. Was that because she had hurt him? Or did he simply want her to leave?

The café was small and colourful, its rough wooden tables and chairs and marble-topped benches part-shaded by a red, flowering poinciana tree and a date palm; on the far stone wall a small fountain was set into the centre of bright mosaic patterned tiles. It seemed an oasis of calm.

Theo spoke to the waitress in rapid Spanish. Grace watched him. Despite everything, she was happy to see him here in Cuba, the land he'd been born in. A part of him I've never known, she thought. And a part she'd probably never get to know, she reminded herself.

'How did you feel coming here?' she asked him when the waitress had gone.

'Good.' She saw him take a deep breath. 'It felt healing, Grace, if you want to know the truth.'

Grace bowed her head. 'Look, Theo . . .' And she reached out to put a hand on his.

'No, Grace.' He snatched his hand away. 'You look –' he broke off abruptly as the waitress appeared with their drinks. '*Gracias*,' he said to her. 'Best coffee in Trinidad.'

'I'm sorry, Theo.'

He picked up his spoon and stirred the coffee slowly, not looking at her. 'Is that why you've come all this way to see me,' he asked her, 'to tell me that you're sorry?'

She shrugged. 'I suppose so.' Though they probably both knew that wasn't true. She tried a small smile and once again caught the answering gleam in Theo's eyes. It was a beginning at least. They were talking. He hadn't told her to go. He was opening up – a bit. She could see glimpses of the old Theo. He was still there. Grace picked up her cup and took a sip. He was right. It was good coffee.

'I've made contact with a few of my parents' old friends,' he said, changing the subject. 'We've talked about the old days, why my folks decided to leave Cuba, why some people would never have dreamt of leaving. It's been a revelation, Grace.' And for a moment his black eyes were as warm as they ever were.

'Why did they leave?' Grace supposed it was the obvious reason. They wanted a different life, a better life. They'd had enough of poverty and struggling to live the way they wanted to live.

'For me,' he said. 'They had a chance and they took it – for me. For my future, I guess you could say.'

Grace nodded. 'Do you think it was the right decision?' she asked. His reply might give her a clue as to how he was feeling now about Cuba, about his future.

But Theo eyed her over the rim of his coffee cup. That black gaze. 'We can't play that game, can we, Grace?' he said.

'What game?'

'The "what if" game?'

Grace drank her coffee. She tried another casual shrug. He'd see through it though – he always had.

'How do we know what would have happened if we'd taken another pathway?' He leaned towards her, eyes glittering. 'How do we know how better – or worse – things would have been?'

Grace knew he wasn't just talking about his parents and their decision to leave Cuba. 'Theo, I –'

'Why have you come here?' He pushed his dark hair back from his forehead but it immediately flopped back into place. 'The truth now.'

'I told you, I . . .' But of course she hadn't told him, not really. It was true that she had wanted to apologise, but it had been more than that. She was on her own now. Everything had changed. She knew it was over between them and she knew how she had made him feel – it was becoming increasingly obvious. But a small part of her had still wondered. Would it be possible?

'Look, Grace, I made it easy for you. I got out of your way. Right out of your way.' He leaned back in his seat, as though he were going to tip the little chair right back and go toppling to the floor.

Grace sighed. 'I didn't want you to be out of the way.'

'You did once.'

'That was different.' And she had never wanted it, not really. It was just that she had been married to Robbie. It had been the hardest decision she'd ever made.

'Different.' Once again, he scrutinised her. During the time they had been lovers she had grown used to the Theo scrutiny; the intense gaze that seemed to take in every detail, leave no stone unturned; the gaze that went through to the other side, did a somersault and then returned the way it had come. 'Different because back then you had Robbie, and I was a complication you didn't want or need? Different because now you're alone?'

'Yes.' He knew how to cut to the quick, she thought. He always had. Even so, he had a fair point. 'But you know it wasn't like that,' she said. 'He was my husband.'

'And I was his best friend.' Theo finished the last of his coffee and pushed the cup aside.

'And mine.' Grace was stung. This was all going hopelessly wrong. But she had known how proud he was, how hurt he would be. She should, she realised, have expected it. She tried again. 'I loved you, Theo. You must know that.'

His dark eyes flickered and, for a moment, she saw his pain. 'I loved you too, Grace. You were everything. If you hadn't been everything I could never have done that to Robbie.' He pulled his wallet out of his pocket and signalled to the waitress. Briefly, he leaned towards her. 'But that's in the past now.'

Grace let the words sink in. She hadn't wanted to hear them, but she'd guessed they'd be said. Even so, they still hurt. 'Can't we even be friends?' She risked another glance at him.

'Is that what you want?' His voice was low. He was leaning close towards her again, his black gaze as intense as it had ever been.

She found that she couldn't reply. Yes, it was what she wanted. But she hadn't come all this way to restore their friendship. She had come to tell him that she had never stopped loving him. She had come to tell him that she had been forced into making the wrong decision back then. She had come to tell him that she was sorry but she would do anything if they could try again. In the past months she had learned an independence that she had never known before; she had found out who she was and what she wanted. With her father's revelation, she had realised how long she had been pretending – about her mother, about her childhood, about what she had lost and what she wanted. Once she had allowed the memories to resurface she had found the truth she'd always denied before. Her truth. Her mother's sexuality meant very little to her, but her parents' happiness did. She didn't just need someone to look after her. She had lost her mother and she had lost her father too, but she had found a way to be.

The waitress came over to their table and Theo handed her a note, waving away the change. He turned back towards Grace. Grace willed herself to say something, but she couldn't see how to bridge this new distance between them.

'I'm not sure that we can still be friends, Grace.' Theo got to his feet. 'I'm not sure that it's possible. We overstepped that mark, I guess.'

'If we could go back . . .' Her voice trailed. She was losing him – she could feel it. Maybe she had lost him before she even got here.

'There's no going back.' And now his voice was gentle, almost as if he were talking to one of the children at the hospital he used to entertain with his magic tricks, she thought. 'That's not how it works at all.'

Grace followed him out of the courtyard. It was hopeless.

He turned to face her as they reached the cobbled street. 'I have to go, I'm afraid,' he said. 'I've promised to meet someone this afternoon.'

She looked straight into those black eyes and tried to convey how she was feeling – as truly as she could. She was still here. She shouldn't give up. 'But tomorrow,' she said, 'will you take me to the old slave plantation at Valle de los Ingenios?'

He seemed surprised. 'Why?'

'Because it's important.' She had talked to Elisa about their family backgrounds and the slavery that had been part of the lives of both their forefathers. And she had seen in her guide book that the Valle de los Ingenios was the place to visit to find out more. Perhaps it would help her understand a part of Cuba's history. Perhaps that might help her understand this man.

He seemed to consider. And then the glimmer of a smile returned. 'I'll take you,' he said. 'And, yes, it is important.'

'Thank you,' she said. He might be a lost cause. But she had come all this way. And Grace couldn't give up quite so easily.

The morning after her dream, Rosalyn returned to the woman's apartment to thank her. In the dream, her old *abuela* had come to her, talking in her sing-song voice about her days of slavery on the sugar plantation. She told Rosalyn again about the back-breaking work, about the games, the dancing and the songs of freedom. *There are many ways,* she said, *of enslaving a body.* Which Rosalyn knew about, for sure. *And many ways,* she said, *of ensuring a man is not free.*

Rosalyn had to think about that one. It seemed to her that her *abuela* was touching on a different subject here, one rather close to Rosalyn's heart. Was she also guilty of such a thing? Had she stopped Duardo from being free?

In the woman's apartment was Elisa, standing at the kitchen sink peeling vegetables and looking very much at home. Rosalyn wasn't surprised. Since her fall, since returning to her own apartment, she had been doing a lot of thinking. The privilege of the old, she thought now. *It is all that is left to us. When that is gone, heaven help us all.*

So she greeted Elisa with a smile and a nod. '*Hola,* my dear,' she said.

Elisa turned from the sink and stared at her for a long

moment in surprise – understandably, for when had Rosalyn ever called her 'my dear'?

'*Hola*, Rosalyn,' she said, recovering remarkably quickly. 'How are you? I heard you had a fall. I hope you're feeling better?' And the curious thing was, that even after everything that had happened between them, Rosalyn sensed that she meant this. Unlikely though it was, Elisa cared for the welfare of a woman who had lied to her and possibly ruined her life. She cared for her simply because she was Duardo's mother. It was more than Rosalyn deserved. It was humbling.

Rosalyn began to realise that she had been right in some of her more recent reflections. People should not be blamed for the behaviour of those who had gone before. All people were individuals, responsible only for their own actions. And no one could decide where they would fall in love. Elisa was a young woman no longer. When she was young, she had been beautiful and Rosalyn had been blinded by this; imagined that Duardo had been blinded too. But whereas Rosalyn had assumed Elisa's beauty to be only skin-deep; assumed too that under that pretty cover, she was deeply flawed, deeply suspect; controlling perhaps, manipulative certainly, stupid probably . . . Duardo had seen an inner beauty, an inner worth. He must have, because he'd never forgotten her. He'd loved her still when she was forty and no longer in the bloom of youth. And he'd love her now.

Rosalyn had been slow to see Elisa's qualities. And even when she'd sneakily admired her loyalty and integrity in returning to the man who had helped her family . . . even then she had not allowed such facts to sway her from her path of blatant hostility. Duardo, she saw – and her *abuela* too – had been so much wiser than she.

'I came to thank your cousin,' Rosalyn told her. She turned to the woman. 'Ramira, isn't it? I am very grateful for your help the other day.' And she brought out from her bag a little box of star-shaped biscuits which she had baked earlier that very morning with the help of Benita.

Ramira accepted the gift with a gracious nod and a beaming smile. 'Stay and have coffee with us,' she urged.

Rosalyn refused. 'I will come back for that another morning if I may,' she said. And she knew that she would. She looked around the neat apartment, at the bright embroidered cushion on the rocking chair, the potted plants and ornaments on the shelves and the family pictures on the wall. This family was a Cuban family just like her own. What's more, she knew that here, in Elisa's cousin Ramira, she had a new and unexpected friend and ally.

She turned to Elisa. 'You are still here in Havana then,' she remarked. Because she had wondered.

Elisa nodded.

'And you're going to stay, are you, this time?'

'Yes, I am,' she said.

She looked straight back at her woman to woman and Rosalyn could see that she wasn't scared of her in the least. Elisa was a good match for her all right. Rosalyn gave her a half smile. 'Then I expect I shall see you again soon,' she said. '*Hasta luego.*'

★

Duardo was at home when she got back, for it was a Sunday. Not that this usually prevented him from tinkering with his blessed car at all hours, but much of the heart for this task had gone out of him since Luis's announcement. Besides, Rosalyn had asked him to take her out this afternoon. 'I have something I need to tell you,' she had said.

And so after lunch they drove along the Malecón until they reached the Boulevard Paseo del Prado. Rosalyn had always loved this street. It was, she believed, the most picturesque in Havana with its wide walkway, bronze lions, and restored porticoed buildings originally built in the late nineteenth century, she supposed, when her family had been poor and living in a slum, and city aristocrats had driven their carriages along the boulevard to the Morro fortress on the waterfront.

Duardo parked the car on the Malecón. This part of the city had once been so chic – Rosalyn remembered. Now it was shabby and she recognised the prostitutes and their *jineteros* loitering and waiting for business. Prostitutes and pimps; people for sale. She had seen more than enough of that in her lifetime. But never mind. Duardo helped her out of the car and across the road. That was better. The multi-coloured marble pavement of the boulevard was decorated with geometric shapes. People sat on marble benches – Cuban and tourists alike – watching pedestrians pass by.

'So what is it, Mami?' Duardo's voice was gentle; he was even more tender with her these days since her fall. 'Is it about Luis?'

'No,' said Rosalyn. Although she knew that in a week or so Luis would be gone.

'What then?' He slowed his pace to match hers and squeezed her arm which was tucked into his. 'I have come to terms with Luis leaving, you know. I was looking at things from a selfish point of view. I see that now. How proud I would be if I could give him my business built from next to *nada* but a clapped-out American car, how much I would have achieved in the face of our common Cuban adversity.' He laughed. 'I wasn't thinking of Luis and what he wanted, though, was I? I wasn't remembering how passionately I felt about things when I was a boy, when I went off to fight.' He shook his head and sighed. 'I lost sight of that, Mami. And you . . .' again, he squeezed her arm, 'you helped me see.'

Rosalyn nodded though she had not intended to have him thank her for anything. As for his passion – she remembered that only too well. And passion . . . Now there was a starting point. 'I have done the same thing, my son,' she said, 'but no one stopped me. No one said – you are being selfish, think of the boy . . .' Her voice trailed away, because she was remembering that actually Tacito had said something. He had tried to stop her. *Do not love him too much,* he had said. *Give him space to grow.* How could she have forgotten that? What a stubborn old fool she had been.

'What boy?' said Duardo. And when she didn't reply: 'You mean me?'

Rosalyn paused to take in a particularly dilapidated building on her left which had not yet been restored. It was supported by steel girders, had no roof and a huge pile of rubble filled the centre of its frame. Heavens, but what a job that would be. 'Yes.' She squeezed his arm back. 'I mean you.'

He grinned and his step seemed to become more jaunty. 'But you have always put me first, Mami,' he said. 'There was never a time when you didn't think of me. Don't you realise that I know that?'

Love and possession, thought Rosalyn. The boundary sometimes could blur. It was too easy to slip from the first to the second without even knowing what you had done. Human beings would usually take the selfish path. She looked to her right. Noted the high tenement building with flaking paint and brittle balconies; some of the occupants were leaning over these, looking down on the street life below.

'It was a long time ago,' she said. 'A time when I came close to believing that I had lost you.'

'What was a long time ago?' he asked. 'What are you talking about, Mami?'

She took a deep breath. 'I told your Elisa that I knew for certain you were dead.' There, she'd said it. Now let him hate her. The thing she'd dreaded since she'd first said those words to the girl.

He stopped walking but he didn't drop her arm. 'Elisa,' he said softly. And she heard the tenderness in his voice. 'What exactly happened, Mami?'

Rosalyn sighed. They continued to walk along the boulevard, but more slowly now. 'When Francisco came back and told me you were missing . . . I couldn't believe it. I didn't want to believe it. He said you were presumed dead, but that you might have fled to the mountains since your body had not been found. I knew you were not dead. I did not feel it.' She hit herself lightly on the chest with her fist. 'I didn't feel it in here,' she whispered.

Duardo turned to face her. His eyes were grave. 'And you were right,' he said. He drew her closer in and they continued to walk along the Prado, for all the world like any ageing mother with her son out for a Sunday afternoon promenade along a fancy boulevard in Havana.

She acknowledged Duardo's words with a small nod. 'But that's not all. Francisco said he was going to see Elisa, to tell her what had happened in all the fighting that day. I . . .' She gulped. She felt as if she could not get enough air but she was determined not to stop walking. 'I told him it would be kinder to make things more certain for her.'

'More certain?' Duardo's eyes were still gentle, still loving. Rosalyn couldn't bear it if that were to change.

She nodded. *Let her have no doubt,* she had said to Francisco, placing a firm hand on his shoulder when he looked unsure. *I will hold the hope. I am his mother. She is young. You can give the girl her life back.*

She waited for Duardo to make the connections, to realise what she had done.

'So he told Elisa I was definitely dead and gone,' Duardo seemed to find this interesting rather than awful, 'which is why she didn't hesitate to leave Cuba when her family did.'

'Yes.' They were passing the Centro de Danza now and a

blue baroque building that made her think of the icing on a wedding cake. Rosalyn wondered if she needed to tell Duardo the rest, but she'd decided on honesty so she would have to stay with it. He deserved to know it all and this might be the last thing she could do for him before they parted for good. She didn't know exactly when it would be – but it wouldn't be long. 'I knew her family wanted to leave Cuba,' she said. 'I even hoped they would go – and her with them. I did not expect her to, but she came to me.'

Duardo stopped walking for a moment and looked at her once more. 'So Elisa did come to see you,' he repeated. 'I did wonder . . .'

For years he must have felt rejected by the girl, Rosalyn thought, for years he had thought she simply didn't care enough. And Rosalyn had fostered that feeling all she could. She hadn't considered her son's wellbeing at all.

She took a deep breath and continued. ' "Do you really think he is dead, Rosalyn?" she asked me that day. Her eyes were wild, desperate.' Rosalyn paused, remembering those eyes. It was as if Elisa recognised that Rosalyn would know the truth. "In your heart," she said. "Do you feel it?" '

Duardo increased the pressure on her arm just slightly. 'And what did you say to her, Mami?' he asked.

Rosalyn fixed her eyes straight ahead. 'I lied to her, my son. I chose not to feed that desperation, I chose not to give her that hope, even though I had heard just a few hours before that there was a band of men living in the mountains and that you might be among them.'

'What did you say?' Duardo asked her again.

Rosalyn couldn't even risk a glance at him. ' "I feel it," I told her. "I know in my heart and in my mind that it is true. I am certain that we have lost him." ' She exhaled, waited for the explosion.

'Ah.' They walked on past more blue and pink porticoed buildings, the branches of the trees that lined the Prado stretching across the boulevard, practically meeting each other and providing patches of much-needed shade.

Clearly Duardo was still digesting what she had told him. But that didn't mean there wouldn't be an explosion – eventually.

'She was young and frightened,' Rosalyn said. 'I have been a selfish woman, my son. I have never been fair to her.'

Duardo still seemed in a reflective mood and not angry in the least. 'I always thought that she would wait for me,' he said. He stopped walking and gently turned them round so that they were once more facing the ramparts of the *castillo*. 'We should go back,' he murmured.

Rosalyn said nothing. What more could she say? They walked in silence for a few minutes, but she could no longer enjoy the sights of the architecture or the children playing with their string and their spinning tops.

'Why did you do it, Mami?' he asked her at last. 'You wanted me to be happy, didn't you?' And for a moment he seemed like her little boy again, slightly confused, very serious and dependant on Rosalyn for his entire world.

Why had she done it? *Honesty now.* 'I thought it was for the

456

best,' she said. 'I didn't think she was right for you.' They walked on. 'At the time.' Rosalyn was still wondering how to say it. 'Truth was, I hardly knew the girl.' She paused for breath. 'But I knew her family and I knew ours.' She glanced across at Duardo but his face was set and provided no clues of what he might be thinking. 'I'd spent my entire childhood listening to those stories of how our family was enslaved. I couldn't bear the thought that you –' She broke off. Was that the entire truth? 'I loved you too much, son,' she said. 'I thought she would take you away from me again and I couldn't bear the thought of that.'

'So you tried to break us up? You tried to set her free so she would run, and so that I would always blame her for not waiting?' His words were bitter, but he had not yet dropped her arm. Rosalyn hung on to this thought. He had not dropped her arm.

'Yes,' she said. 'I was wrong and I am sorry. I thought that you would meet a nice girl and be happy. I thought that you would forget her. But you didn't. And then . . .'

'She came back and she left again.' He led her over to a marble bench, gestured for her to sit down and rest for a few moments. He sat down next to her and leaned forward. 'So should I blame you, Mami? Or thank you?'

'I don't know,' she whispered. She sat back against the cool stone, which was hard against her spine. 'I only know that I held hatred in my heart for much too long. Now that I have seen it, now that I have recognised it for what it is, all I can ask is for you to forgive me.' She realised that her face was wet with tears. And if he did not, or could not forgive her? What then?

'Mami.' He turned to face her, pulled a small cotton handkerchief from his pocket and gently wiped her tears away. 'Don't get worked up like this. I always knew how you felt. I always understood. And besides . . .' He looked out over the Prado, at the people promenading, at the children playing. 'It's all so long ago. It's much too late to be worrying over such things. It is done and she has long gone. Stop your crying now, please.'

'So you forgive me?' she whispered again.

'Of course I do.' He took her tenderly in his arms right there on the bench in the middle of the Prado. 'You don't even need to ask such things. And now let's go.'

Rosalyn drew away. He got to his feet and took her arm to help her up.

'And it is not too late, Duardo,' she said as they walked on towards the Morro fortress. It stood grey and sturdy, a symbol of protection and security for the city.

'How so?'

'You're not old, not old as I am old. And she is here in Havana. Your Elisa. You should go to her. She wants you. She has come here to see you. And she will stay this time.' *And when I am gone . . .* She didn't say this. But someone had to look after him when Rosalyn was no longer around to do it.

He stared at her. 'What do you mean?'

'Exactly what I say.'

'But . . .'

She saw him struggling to come to grips with this information. 'She no longer has ties to England. She is free for the first time.' Rosalyn nodded. 'Believe me, it is true.'

'You have seen her?' he whispered.

'I have.' She wagged a finger. 'So you should go to her. Now. Before she flies off again thinking you no longer want her.'

'It's much too late, Mami.' And she saw the pride in his face, the pride she had always fostered.

Rosalyn stopped walking. This would be hard but it must be done. She turned him to face her. 'Forgive her,' she said. 'Be strong. Like you, she's never forgotten. Trust me. Your father loved your mother in the same way. Take it. Enjoy it. Listen to your mother who has been such a fool. It's not too late.'

CHAPTER 45

The following day Theo picked Grace up from La Ronda. She'd half thought he wouldn't come, and was relieved to hear a horn sounding from a dusty red Kia and to see Theo's long rangy figure at the wheel.

'Morning, Grace.' There was even a smile – a real one. Grace realised that yesterday she had taken him by surprise. Today, he seemed calm and very much in control.

'Hello, Theo.' She restrained herself from leaning over and kissing him on the cheek. She knew the feel of his skin so well and it seemed odd to be having no physical contact after the intimacy they'd shared. But she had to give it time.

He drove in a north-easterly direction towards Sancti Spiritus to a nearby look-out point and they got out of the car.

'Come and look.' He began to climb some steps leading to what looked like a small café at the top.

Grace went after him, but more slowly. Beyond the occasional wooden shack, the palms and mango plantations, she could see the fertile plain and in the distance, the blue curve of the ocean. Slowly, she followed Theo to the top. 'Wow!' The entire valley of Los Ingenios was laid out in front of them – green and verdant with fields of sugar cane and towering royal palms, the Sierra del Escambray mountains forming an elegant backdrop behind.

'Just think, Grace.' His voice was low. He was standing so close to her that she could feel the heat from his skin. 'One hundred and four square miles and seventy old *ingenios* – sugar mills.'

That was, she thought, an awful lot of slaves.

They walked along the back veranda. Grace could smell the scent of herbs – basil and something lemony.

'Do you know what tree this is, Theo?' she asked him.

'Lychee.' He pointed. 'And this one's breadfruit.'

'You've been doing your homework.' She kept her voice light. But she'd been right yesterday in her first impression. This Theo was a very different man from the one she'd known in Bristol, and she didn't quite know how to be with him.

'Yes.' He looked serious. 'I thought it was about time.'

And what else did you think? she wanted to ask him. *What did you think about us?*

On the other side of the road stood a typical squat wooden house with a tiled roof and a dusty garden. There was a little plot for vegetables, some chickens and a goat, all fenced in. Some people, Grace thought, had carved a simple, rural self-sufficiency out here in the Sancti Spiritus countryside.

From the look-out point, they drove on to a disused sugar plantation now in ruins. 'This isn't the one all the tourists go to,' he said to her. 'I found this one by chance.'

Grace nodded. It was more authentic, she thought, to be

away from the tourist trail. She preferred it like this. Just her and Theo was absolutely fine.

'This,' Theo went on, 'is one that still has the feel.'

The feel . . . They got out of the car and Grace stood at the entrance of the plantation for a moment. She understood immediately what he had meant. There was a sense of stillness that seemed almost to hang tangibly in the air, dense and heavy with the grim events of the past. She couldn't help but imagine . . .

The manner in which slaves had been brought from Africa, the way they had been treated, was such a time of darkness in world history. After Grace had left Theo yesterday afternoon, she'd bought herself a sandwich and then visited Trinidad's history museum, where, among other things, she'd seen examples of some of the instruments of torture used to keep slaves under control. She guessed the nature of the work on the plantation had also been torturous. And yet today the place seemed so peaceful, you'd hardly know. It was as if nature had healed the land, but the memories still remained.

Grace looked around as she followed Theo further into the old *ingenio*. The royal palms grew straight and true aiming for the heavens and the lush planting of bananas and guavas lined narrow, dusty pathways of brick and red earth.

'Look.' Theo took her arm and pointed.

She stopped in her tracks, more than aware of the touch of his hand. A tiny bird with iridescent blue-green feathers and a long pointed beak was perched on the branch of a tree just in front of them. Even as she watched, it fluffed up its feathers and was gone in a flash, wings whirring. 'What was it?' she asked him.

'A bee hummingbird,' he told her. He had already taken his hand away. '*Zunzuncito*.'

'This is an amazing place,' Grace said. It wasn't quite the right word, but she hoped Theo would understand what she was trying to say.

'I came here the first day I was in Trinidad,' he told her.

She glanced at him. Today he was wearing loose cotton shorts and a faded T-shirt. He was beginning to look less and less like the accountant cum magician she'd known so well in Bristol. And more at home.

'I'd hired the car and I just wanted to get out here, into the real history of the province. I guess I just wanted to see what I could find out for myself, you know?'

Grace nodded. She knew what he was saying. The colonial buildings of historic Trinidad were picture-postcard perfect and had been restored in every last detail – but this was more real. She looked up towards the plantation-owner's house, another large colonial-style building now in a state of disrepair, almost a ruin.

Theo followed the direction of her gaze. 'The house had to be higher than the main plantation,' he said. 'It was a power thing – symbolic of the social status.'

'Practical too,' Grace added.

'Exactly. They could keep a watch for slaves running away or not working hard enough. Can you imagine? Talk about lord of the manor.' He pointed to a tall tower built on several levels and shaped like a piece of sugar cane itself. At the bottom there was an old bell which must have tolled to signify their working hours, Grace supposed. 'Though they could watch from this vantage point too. That was the point of it – it's even higher. Want to go up?'

It seemed like a challenge. 'OK.' Grace followed him into the tower and up the steep and rickety wooden staircase. It was open to the air but still claustrophobic. Grace wondered just how safe these stairs really were. She concentrated on her breathing, matching her step to Theo's rhythm as he climbed just above her. Yet another reminder, she thought sadly; close, but not close enough. But it was worth the climb. When they got to the top they had a panoramic view of the surrounding countryside, including the plantation itself. Grace was silent, thinking about the runaway slaves, about where they might have run to and how desperate they must have been.

Theo pointed out the cooking area of brick pits, where the crystallisation of the sugar would have taken place.

'When was the harvest?' Grace asked him.

'Between December and June. They burn the field apparently to get rid of the outer leaves and then out comes the old machete for the harvesting.' He mimed the action of cutting the cane.

'A machete? Not still in this day and age?' Grace was surprised.

'In the hills, yes.' He looked towards the mountains. 'I guess they use machinery in the plains though.'

'And how tall does it grow?' Grace wanted to know these

things, but she also wanted to listen to him. When he was talking about Cuba and its history, his voice was natural and ran free. She could hear how glad he was to have this opportunity of being here, in the land of his forefathers.

He shrugged. 'Taller than me. A lot taller than me. Up to about fifteen feet I should guess.'

'That high?' She tried to visualise it. 'No wonder it was such hard work.'

He nodded. 'Eventually they built a rail network so they could use steam trains for transporting the sugar and molasses. These places became like huge factories stuck in the middle of nowhere generating huge wealth for the owners. But before that . . .' His voice trailed. 'There's a steam train that still runs from time to time from Trinidad.' He shaded his eyes from the sun. 'But like most things in Cuba it's what you might call unreliable.'

Grace laughed. 'Did you come here with a tour guide?' she joked. He was pretty knowledgeable for a man who'd been here less than a week.

Theo pulled a face. 'You know me, Grace.'

Did she? She would have liked to think so.

'I've made it my business to find out, that's all. I've been reading up and talking to people. I can't be doing with tour guides. You stand there listening to the same old spiel, it goes in one ear and out the other and you forget nearly everything. Worse than that.' He shot her one of his dark looks. 'You forget to feel it.'

Grace nodded. 'I know,' she whispered. It was quite an

experience – to stand at the top of this watch tower, to walk through the plantation where the sugar cane had been grown, cut, harvested and cooked; where slaves and masters had trod, stirred, carried. She could only imagine the heat, the sweat gleaming on black bodies, the chanting and the singing, the unending work and the pure desperation. But when you came here that's what you had to imagine, and like Theo, Grace didn't want too many facts to cloud her experience. Even so, she couldn't envisage Theo ever forgetting to feel.

They made their way back down the tower in silence and continued walking around; beside each other but not touching. Not easy, Grace found herself thinking. No longer easy with one another as they had once been. That was what they had done to themselves.

'This was part of my history,' Theo said, 'Cuban history.' It sounded as if he could hardly believe it. 'That's why it's so important to me to find out everything I can, I guess.'

'And is it good that it's on the tourist trail?' Grace was half speaking to herself. 'By restoring these places and bringing in the public, are they trying too hard to bring back the memory of something that's died?'

Theo stopped walking. 'People need to be reminded.'

Grace realised that he was probably right. 'Did your parents talk much about Cuba?' she asked him as they walked on.

'Not much. My mother missed it, she said. My father . . .' He shook his head. 'He always said he'd been one of the clever ones to get out while it was still possible.'

'I suppose he was.' Grace thought of Elisa. It didn't seem

right that so many people had felt compelled to leave. But who could blame them for wanting to?

'By the time they left, things were pretty bad,' Theo said. 'Fidel's new regime didn't live up to its promises – I expect you've heard people saying that?'

'Plenty.' Grace thought of Alex and some of the people she'd talked to in Havana and Vinales. Elisa had talked about it too – and she was in a position to see it first hand, rather than from a tourist point of view.

'But Pop never even spoke about all this sort of stuff,' Theo added. 'About slavery.'

'It wasn't just happening in Cuba,' Grace reminded him. 'Most of the world was making use of African slaves. It was the way things were.'

'A bad way,' said Theo.

'Yes.' She couldn't argue with that. 'A bad way.' And she was aware that over a century ago her ancestors had been guilty too. Wasn't her father's house in King Street built on the money made from slavery? Grace shivered. Theo was right. It had been the way of the world but it needed to be remembered.

She looked at him now, at the coffee-coloured skin she'd always taken for granted and at the dark hair that swung onto his forehead in a small wave. He was a fusion all right. Since coming here, she'd realised just how mixed the races were. Theo had the cheekbones of a Spaniard, the dark eyes of an African and a mouth that was somewhere in between. Their multiracial history had produced Cubans with a special jumble of good looks; a fascinating mix of features and creamy coffee to chocolate-coloured skin. From Spanish conquistadors to American plantation owners – they had probably all used and abused their power and position. Or maybe they'd just fallen in love.

'Look at this.' Theo pointed to a shallow pit that had been fashioned out of the brick at the top of a dam where water must have been collected.

'What is it?'

'Exactly what it looks like.' He reached down and ran his hand along the edge of the structure. 'It's a bath. The slave owner would have come on down for a bathe, waited on by a dusky maiden or two, I'd bet.'

'It couldn't have been all use and abuse.' Grace spoke her thoughts out loud.

'It never is.' Theo straightened up and glanced across at her. 'There's always room for romance, Grace, for caring and protection. Not to mention love.' He was echoing her own thoughts.

Yes, she thought, not to mention love.

They paused by the remains of the *barracones*, the slaves' quarters. 'And these guys were smart,' Theo said, 'they got everything they could out of the sugar and all they could out of the slaves too.'

Grace nodded. 'They domesticated the Africans, didn't they in these places?' She'd read about it in her guide book. In the *barracones*, African slaves were encouraged to build a community and make babies – which meant more workers as soon as the children were old enough. When the plantation owners bought them they would be looking for strength and good health; they would buy from different tribes to reduce the chance of an uprising. It wasn't just the sugar that was being farmed and harvested, it was also the African slaves.

'I should have come to Cuba before now,' Theo was saying. 'I often used to talk about it with Elisa, I knew it was a gap in my life that one day I'd want to fill, but . . .'

'Why didn't you come then?' Money, she supposed. It wasn't a cheap destination and while Theo had always made a reasonable living, he wasn't exactly wealthy.

'I was doing other things.' He shot her a look. Yes, and she knew what things. 'I wasn't taking life seriously. I was messing around.'

'You worked at the hospital,' Grace protested. 'What about all those kids you practised your magic tricks on?' She had always admired him for giving up so much of his time for that.

'That was just an ego boost.' He shrugged. 'Don't get me wrong. I was glad to help those kids feel a bit more cheerful. But it was one hell of a buzz, performing for them. Kids are a lot less critical than grown-ups.'

Grace laughed. 'There's nothing wrong with feeling good about your work.'

'Except you can hide behind it.' He led the way up a narrow path between some palms.

'Were you hiding?' She watched him walk in front of her,

thought about how simple it would be to reach out and touch him. Simple and yet forbidden. She sighed.

He turned to face her. 'We were both hiding.'

Were they? Grace thought of her newfound independence, her feeling that she had always needed to be looked after. 'Yes.' Her gaze locked onto his.

He moved closer towards her and rested his open palm against her cheek. She felt the warmth of his skin, thought of what he'd said to Robbie when he did that ridiculous card trick of his. How he kept the lady in the palm of his hand. She closed her eyes. The chemistry was still there. She could feel it zinging between them. In a moment, she knew, he would kiss her.

'Why did you break up with Robbie?'

Her eyes flicked open.

He put his other hand to her face, his other palm on her cheek so that he was holding her. 'After . . .'

He didn't need to finish the sentence. *After giving me up for him* . . . And she supposed that he had a right to know – if she could put it into words. 'I thought I could make it work,' she said. She watched his expression. His eyes were searching. He really didn't know. 'I thought I could stop the deception and give him what he wanted. A family . . .' She tailed off. Because it wasn't just about Robbie wanting a family, was it? It wasn't just about Grace not being ready to have children. It was about growing apart from someone, no longer wanting their touch. It was about the way you shifted as a couple so that your partner was no longer the centre of your universe. It was about falling out of love. 'But I didn't love him enough,' she said. 'Theo . . .'

Theo was still watching her closely. 'Wouldn't you ever want children, Grace?' he asked. Around them the vegetation was lush and thick, the air so still. All she could hear was the occasional sound of an insect, the faint trill of far-off birdsong.

'I don't know.' Perhaps now that she had grown up, she might be ready to at last. She wished she could talk to him about what her father had told her the day he died. But now wasn't the time and perhaps there would never be a time, not for her and Theo at least. 'I just didn't want that life,' she said. 'The life that was right for Robbie.'

He nodded as if perhaps he understood. And Grace had the feeling that he had always understood more about her marriage than she had — even back when they had first begun.

He reached up to catch a stray tangle of hair and smoothed it from her face. 'I've missed you, Grace,' he said.

'Me too.' She put her hands on his shoulders. He felt familiar and dear. 'So . . . ?' Surely, he would kiss her now.

'But it's like this place,' he said.

'This place?' She looked around and shivered.

'We can revisit the past. We can hold the memories. We can even hear the voices.'

Grace listened and thought she heard it — soft and sing-song. Perhaps it was just the breeze in the trees, the whirr of the wings of the bee hummingbird. Or perhaps it was the echo of the old voices; the chanting, the music of those who had been enslaved.

Theo shook his head. 'We should look to the future now.' Abruptly, he let go of her and for a moment Grace thought she would fall. 'We should go,' he said. And turned around and continued along the pathway.

Grace sighed. 'So what were *you* hiding from, Theo?' she asked. Once a magician, always a magician. Once, she had got past the enigma that was Theo. Now, she just didn't know.

'Love.' He threw the word back over his shoulder. 'Commitment. Feeling trapped – in a job, in a relationship. You name it.'

Grace stopped walking. She thought of the relationships Theo had had when all three of them were friends; the women who had never had the chance to enter their charmed circle. 'So I was a safe bet,' she said.

'Grace.' He spun briefly around to face her. 'You were never a safe bet.' He carried on walking. 'The truth is, I was scared,' he said.

'Scared?' Grace couldn't imagine that somehow. She'd never put fear and Theo together. He'd never shown fear. Even when he initiated an affair with the wife of his best friend.

'Yeah.' His voice was quiet now; he was walking ahead of her again so she couldn't see his face. There were trees on either side of the path so it was still single file only. 'I was scared of letting anyone in.'

And then you let me in, she thought.

'And I was scared to come here.'

'Why?' At last, the pathway opened up into a clearing and Grace saw that they were back near the entrance of the plantation.

'I think I was scared of what I might find.' He gave a small shrug. 'Scared of how much I'd like the country maybe.'

Grace's breath caught. This was it then.

'And . . .'

'And?'

Once again, he met her gaze head-on. He always had. 'And it wasn't the right time to leave,' he said.

When Grace stopped seeing him, she thought. For Theo, that had been the right time to leave.

CHAPTER 46

Elisa had decided to throw a party to say goodbye to Grace. It had been lovely to have her stepdaughter here in Cuba and she was sad to see her go. She looked out of the open door to the communal backyard of the apartment block behind Plaza de Armas where neighbours, friends and relatives were beginning to cluster. Grace was there and Theo was there, but they were not standing anywhere near one another. And she could admit to herself, if not to Grace, that certain aspects of her plan hadn't come to fruition in quite the way she'd hoped.

That was what happened when you tried to matchmake, she told herself sternly as she lifted the chicken pieces from the marinade and put them on to the grill pan. She had thought that coming to Cuba might somehow bring Theo and Grace together in a way that living in Bristol had not. She had imagined them rekindling their love affair under warm Cuban skies, to the background of a salsa rhythm playing in the square. And when Grace went off to Trinidad to tell him how much she cared . . . let's say Elisa had been quietly confident of the outcome.

But when Grace had returned from Trinidad the day before

yesterday, she had been awfully quiet. Yes, she had seen Theo, she told Elisa. They'd gone to one of the old sugar mills. Yes, they'd talked about how he felt about Cuba, about Robbie, about what had happened between them.

'And?' It sounded good so far, she thought.

'And nothing,' Grace replied. 'Theo's not interested in rekindling any past relationship. He's looking to the future now.'

'The future?' Did she mean what Elisa thought she meant? Had Theo decided to stay in Cuba? Elisa opened her arms and her stepdaughter walked right in. She stroked Grace's hair. That was the one thing she had been concerned about. Their country had this way of reclaiming its own. And it just went to show — life was not a romantic novel; life always had a few surprises in store.

Elisa stood in the doorway for a moment. Outside in the yard, a wood-fired barbecue was already raging and a band of street musicians were playing a motley array of instruments ranging from a handmade drum and a pair of wooden sticks to a guitar. The woman who lived next door had decided to be the *artista* of the night. She was wearing a close-fitting, silver-spangled dress which ended above the knee to reveal plump black thighs, and which was cut low to show off her other assets. Fake gold jewellery gleamed at her throat and wrists and she was crooning into the evening air as if she'd like to make love to them — to all of them. Elisa smiled. Her cousins often made fun of Vinita but she was at least getting the party off to a good start.

Elisa took the tray of chicken out to the barbecue and

passed it over to Vinita's husband, Rudi, who was supervising the cooking, shouting to people over the music and performing the odd shimmy and salsa step to get everyone in the mood. Not that they needed it. The yard was filling up with folk – they didn't even need to have met her stepdaughter, that was immaterial. In Cuba, a party was a party and free food was free food. Fortunately, there was enough for all.

Elisa checked on Grace who was sipping a rum cocktail and chatting to Ramira and her daughter in one corner of the yard. She seemed distracted though and every so often she glanced over to the far side where Theo was talking to a small group of men. Hmm. Elisa wiped her hands on her apron and went back inside.

'And who can blame him?' Grace had said to her at the tail end of their previous conversation. 'There was always too much against us, Elisa. Comes a time when you have to just accept it.'

Elisa thought about this as she finished preparing the rice. It was strained and rinsed and was now just finishing cooking in its own steam so that it would be fluffy when she forked it up, ready to serve. There had been many obstacles for her and Duardo throughout their lives so she knew exactly what Grace was saying. Sometimes there were opportunities too; times when you must grab happiness even when it seemed too foolhardy, too risky. But you had to grab it because otherwise that happiness would run away without you. You could chase it down the street for the rest of your life, but happiness was an elusive thing. If you gave it away too often . . . it might never give you the chance to catch it again.

She thought of the baby she had lost. Duardo's baby. If she hadn't lost that baby when she did . . . she paused and felt the dull pain that had never quite gone away – what might have been? Would she have stuck with Philip and brought the child up in England? Or would she have returned to Cuba and Duardo? She had never had the chance to find out. Philip had forgiven her for conceiving another man's child, but would Duardo ever forgive her for losing it? She longed to talk to him about it nonetheless. She had never shared her grief about losing her baby and if she ever had the chance, she would tell him. She would trust him to understand.

She took the rice outside, passed it to Rudi and laughed as he grabbed her round the waist and twirled her round to the rippling beat of the percussion. She pushed him away and gave the black beans a quick stir. Lots of people were dancing. Neighbours had brought beer, rum and bottles of local hooch and contributions of food. They were determined to have a good time.

Elisa looked round. Theo and Grace had both moved, she noted, and were standing in two different groups that were beside each other. It was like a dance, Elisa thought. Moving forward, moving back. Moving closer, moving away. Much like the rumba. There was a pull to it, a sense of magnetism. This gave her an idea.

As the band struck up a salsa, she eased her way between them. After all, what did it matter now? She may as well throw caution to the wind.

'Grace, Theo,' she called. She clapped her hands. They

both looked at her, slightly startled. 'Grace, you can't leave Cuba without dancing the salsa,' she declared.

'Oh, but . . .' Grace spread her hands and laughed. 'I don't know how.'

'Theo.' Elisa reached for his hand. 'You must know how to salsa.' Every Cuban man knew how to salsa – even if they'd been brought up in America. And you could lose yourself in a dance. When you were dancing, it no longer mattered who had said what or done what; who had chosen who or where you were going in the future. The dance was about the present and the dance was about the rhythm. Nothing else mattered. If dancing didn't get these two together, then nothing would.

She felt Theo hesitate. And before she knew it Rudi was there in front of them, his feet already moving to the salsa beat. 'I'll show her how,' he shouted. He grabbed Grace's hand and pulled her into the dance.

Grace threw a quick look of regret towards Theo. But already her feet were moving. She shrugged and laughed. Elisa could still see in Grace's eyes, just as she'd seen it before, that time back in Gorse Lane, the look of love. It was something you couldn't pretend not to recognise. It would always get you in the end.

'Just follow me,' Rudi yelled above the music. 'Listen to the rhythm and let go. That's all you have to do. Let go.'

Elisa sighed. But Theo grinned. He was watching Grace shift her hips and be spun around by the human livewire that was Rudi and he was clearly enjoying the spectacle.

'Is there a chance, Theo?' Elisa asked him. 'Please tell me.'

'You never give up, do you, Elisa?' He chuckled.

She had given up – once. But she wouldn't give up for the girl she thought of as her daughter. Grace was still young. There was still time – for dreams, for love. For everything really.

Theo turned to her. 'I'm so grateful to you, Elisa,' he said. 'Coming here was one of the best things I've ever done. It's been great. Really great. But . . .'

'But?'

His gaze darkened. 'I can't go through it again,' he said.

So that was that then, she thought.

Back in the kitchen she prepared the salad, helped by her cousin Ramira and her cousin's daughter, Seleste. It had been kind of Ramira to help Rosalyn that day when she fell – though Elisa had been shocked to see Duardo's mother at their door when she came to thank them. *Hasta luego*, she had said. See you later. Did that mean that there was no longer a battle between them? Elisa hoped that was the case although she guessed the reason why. Rosalyn no longer had anything to fear from Elisa. Duardo knew she was here in Havana and yet he had kept away. Elisa had missed her opportunity for happiness too.

Nevertheless, she would be staying in Cuba, probably for the remainder of her days. Not just because of Duardo – though it was true that she felt somehow more content simply knowing that at last she was near him. But also because of her family – she had left them once too often, she felt. Most importantly, she was staying for herself. She would miss Grace, of course, but now that the house in King Street was sold, she could afford to go back to Bristol from time to time and visit.

It was her time now. It was hard living here in Havana, not as comfortable as she was accustomed to. You couldn't always find the things to buy that you needed. But there was human warmth, spontaneity and sunshine and there was a street band playing on every corner. Music was in the air that she breathed, and that was the air she wanted.

She looked round the kitchen. Everything had been done. Ramira had taken out the salad, the music was louder and faster and she must go out and smile, talk, dance and play the hostess. Slowly, Elisa untied her apron and hung it on the hook by the stove. She smoothed her dress – a yellow dress – and rearranged her hair, adjusting a few of the hairpins without bothering to use the cracked old mirror by the door. She was old, but she still knew how to party.

She threaded her way through friends and neighbours laughing, chatting, dancing; bodies bumping, grinding, swirling, sweating, until she reached Grace's side. True to form, Theo had disappeared from sight; Grace was talking to Elisa's cousin Pueblo's daughter. She turned when she saw Elisa. 'Look what Isabel has given me,' she said.

Elisa looked down at the flowers in her palm. The Cuban national flower, the butterfly plant, the white ginger mariposa.

Isabel smiled shyly and then a young man pulled her into the dancing and Grace and Elisa were alone.

'You should put it in your hair.' Elisa took one of the flowers and threaded it into Grace's brown hair. She was wearing it down tonight so Elisa plucked a pin from her own hair and fastened it in place on the side. She stood back to admire the effect. Her stepdaughter looked beautiful.

'Thank you, Elisa,' she said. 'For everything.' Grace took the second mariposa flower and pinned it carefully in Elisa's greying hair.

'Goodness.' Elisa laughed. 'I think I'm too old for flowers in my hair.'

'Never too old.' Grace held on to her for a moment, her grey eyes steady. And then another neighbour came to whisk her off into the dancing and in a sudden flash of blue, just like the zun zun bird, she was gone.

Later, after Elisa had talked to almost everyone – yes, and done her share of dancing too, the band slowed the tempo and she let out a small sigh as she realised what was coming. You couldn't get away from it in Cuba. The rumba. It would always be there at every celebration, every party; in every bar and on every street corner in Havana. A reminder. She put her hand up to the flower in her hair and gently touched a petal with her forefinger. The scent of the mariposa was as sweet and heady as the memory of that last dance with Duardo in Havana.

CHAPTER 47

Grace poured herself some iced water from the jug in the kitchen. She drank thirstily and then splashed some on the back of her neck. It was way past midnight but the party was still in full swing and the night outside was warm and humid. Cuba, she thought, had been quite an experience. But where did you go in Havana when you simply wanted to think?

She slipped through the other open door which led up some steps, down a passage and out on to another courtyard and the street beyond. A man stood by the gate and he jumped as she approached.

'Good evening,' Grace said in Spanish. 'Sorry to disturb you.' Because he had clearly been deep in thought.

'Good evening.' He touched his hat. 'And you are not disturbing me.' He smiled.

'Are you looking for the party?' He didn't look as though he was. Perhaps he lived here and had just come out for some air, or perhaps the noise was disturbing him? Not everyone in Cuba could be a party animal.

'No,' he said. 'And you? Are you escaping from the party perhaps?' Again, he smiled. He had a nice smile, she thought.

'I just came outside for a minute to think about things,' she said. There was something about this place and the darkness of the early hours, with the music playing in the yard next door and the chatter and laughter drifting past in the night air, that made confidences acceptable.

'I see.' He nodded gravely. 'You speak Spanish but you are English, I think?'

'Yes. I came here for a fortnight's holiday,' she said. Although it hadn't been at all the kind of holiday she'd been expecting. Somewhere along the way she had lost them both – Elisa and Theo. From now on, Grace would be on her own. It would be a challenge but she had to believe in her own strength.

'Ah, a holiday. You are a tourist then.' He nodded.

'Sort of. I'm staying with my stepmother. She lives here. But I'm leaving tomorrow.'

In the darkness his expression was inscrutable. 'Your step-mother you say?'

'Yes. Her name is Elisa. Perhaps you know her?'

'And what do you think of our country?' he asked. 'What do you think of our city Havana?'

She heard the pride in his voice. 'It has so much life,' she said. 'I can see how hard things are sometimes, but people smile a lot. You're all so warm and friendly.'

He gave a short laugh. 'That's true I suppose,' he said.

Grace wondered if she had said the wrong thing. 'Are you going to go to the party?' she asked him.

'I doubt it,' he said. 'I haven't been invited, you know.'

'Oh, that doesn't matter.' Grace shrugged. 'I'm sure you'd

be welcome if you live around here.' She laughed. 'Or even if you don't.'

'Grace . . .'

She heard her name being called and looked over her shoulder. Theo's voice. 'Out here,' she called. She glanced at the man she'd been chatting to and felt herself flush.

'Well, goodbye, Grace,' he said. 'Have a safe trip home. *Hasta luego*. It was nice to meet you.'

He held out his hand and she put her hand in his. It felt warm and strong. And there was something about him. 'You should go to the party,' she said. 'You might enjoy it. You never know.'

She watched as he lifted his hand in a salute and sauntered away.

'There you are,' said Theo. 'Were you running away?' He came to stand beside her, close beside her, so close that his arm was almost touching her arm, his hip almost touching her hip, so close that she could smell the scent of him. It hadn't changed. Red apples and pepper, something vaguely Caribbean and coal-tar soap.

'No, I wasn't.' She looked up at him. 'I just needed a few moments alone.' A few moments away from the party, from the people; a few moments in which to collect herself and prepare herself for leaving.

'What will you do, Grace?' Theo asked her.

She could feel his mind on her wavelength. Probably he was worrying about her now, feeling guilty that he'd rejected her. She knew he was still fond of her. Theo wasn't the kind

484

of man who could love like that and then simply forget. 'You needn't worry,' she said. 'I'll go back to Bristol. Carry on building up the business. Build up my life. Since Robbie left I've already begun.'

'I know.' His voice was low. She could feel his breath grazing her cheek.

'How do you know?'

'I've been keeping an eye on you,' he said. 'Don't look so scared.'

Was she? Grace thought of all the times she'd imagined she'd seen him. 'I'm not scared,' she said. At least not any more. 'And what about you?' she asked. 'What will you do here? Will you be able to find work?'

'I don't think I'll have time for that,' he said. He was even closer now. Somehow, he had taken hold of her hand.

Grace was confused. 'Why not? What else will you be doing?'

'I'm flying back to the UK tomorrow.'

Tomorrow. Grace struggled to make sense of this. In the courtyard next door the party noise had abated for a moment and she was aware that the band had slowed down the tempo. But her heart was beating fast enough to more than make up for it.

'Over here, Grace.' Theo led her to the back of the little terrace by a small poinciana tree. From here they could actually see the party with a bird's-eye-view of the musicians. 'This is the best place to be,' he said. 'We can see them, but they can't see us.'

Once a magician, always a magician. Grace looked. She could see Elisa. She was standing slightly apart from the rest of them in her yellow dress with the mariposa flower in her hair. And behind her was a man – the man Grace had just been talking to. She saw the man lean forward and say something to Elisa. She saw Elisa spin around. She saw them stare at each other. She saw them begin to dance, slow and swaying, eyes locked to the rhythm of the music. 'Duardo . . .' she murmured.

'Duardo?' Theo frowned.

'Nothing.' Grace shook her head. She stared at Theo. 'So after all that you're not staying in Cuba?'

'No. Did I ever say I was?' He took both her hands in his. 'I'll probably only have time to dance the rumba,' he said.

'The rumba?' He wasn't making much sense. But Grace wasn't worried. She felt more calm than she had ever been. This was Theo, enigmatic and obtuse. The sense was somewhere; she'd trust that he and she would find it.

'Apparently it's just a matter of timing.' They were facing one another. He put his right arm around her, letting his palm rest on her left shoulder blade.

'I believe so.' She put her left hand on his shoulder.

'And for us, Grace, the timing wasn't great first time around.'

'No, it wasn't.' Grace tried to refocus. She heard the beat of the percussion. What was he saying? What was he telling her?

'And this time.' He drew her free hand up to meet his, like

486

a wave. 'Are you sure this time? Because I couldn't go through that again. Losing you, I mean.'

'I'm sure.' She stepped in so close that her body was pressed against his. She liked that feeling; she always had. 'But I was always sure, Theo. You know that.' He was the magician, wasn't he? And Grace, she hoped, was the lady in question.

'So will you dance?' And then he leaned down towards her and she leaned up towards him and she didn't know if they were dancing and kissing or kissing and dancing. But whatever it was, it was the sweetest thing.

ACKNOWLEDGEMENTS AND THANKS

First thanks go to everyone who has read this book. I really appreciate your lovely comments and your continued support so much.

Right from the start, Cuba was way outside my personal experience, so writing this novel was full of challenges. To help me on my way I read lots of books about the country – its culture, its history, its geography and so on – watched films and documentaries, scoured the Internet for interesting blogs and articles and, of course, talked to as many people as possible when I visited the country. Some of the most useful books and films on my Cuban journey were: *Biography of a Runaway Slave* by Miguel Barnet, translated by W. Nick Hill, published by Curbstone Press; *Reminiscences of the Cuban Revolutionary War* by Ernesto 'Che' Guevara, published by Harper Perennial; *Enduring Cuba* by Zoe Bran, published by Lonely Planet; *Memories of Underdevelopment* by Thomas Gutierrez Alea, published by Rutgers University Press; *No Way Home* by Carlos Acosta, published by Harper Perennial; *Waiting for Snow in Havana* by Carlos M. N. Eire, published by Scribner; *Our Man in Havana* by Graham Greene, published by Vintage Classics; *7 days in Havana* (DVD) directed by Benecio del Toro; *Buena Vista Social Club* (DVD) directed by Wim Wenders; *I am Cuba (Soy Cuba)* (DVD) directed by Mikhail Kalatozov.

Fascinating work, all. Any mistakes are, of course, my own.

Big, big thanks to my wonderful editor Stef Bierwerth, to my other wonderful editor Kathryn Taussig and the rest of the lovely team at Quercus Books, who are just an amazing group of people to have behind you! Equally massive thanks to my super and supportive agent, Laura Longrigg, at MBA – it has been such a pleasure to work with you this past year, Laura. And as for Sophie Ransom and Eve Wersocki at Midas PR – I can't thank you enough for your unflagging energy and enthusiasm. I am so fortunate to have all these clever and motivated people onside . . .

Other thanks go to Diane Fullerton, MTI, for discussions about massage therapy (and for the massage!) and for her time and generosity in sharing some of her own experiences and putting me right when I went horribly wrong; Olivia Chapman BSc (Hons), MIFPA, ITEC for discussions about how massage can sit happily alongside aromatherapy (and for the massage!); Annie and Richard Kelly for their thoughts and memories of Santa Clara, for reading the Santa Clara passages and for educational and entertaining discussions on Cuba whilst in Trinidad; Dawn Dyer at the Bristol Reference Library for help with research; Anita Count dance expert for reading, talking and dancing; Alan Fish for being a valued early reader of the book and other friends for their encouragement – especially Wendy Tomlins who always does so much and who, along with her husband, Andy, is unflagging in her support of my books and events.

My family are incredibly supportive and gorgeous and so I want to give big love to them – to Luke and Agata and their new baby, Tristan; to Alexa – with special thanks for the help she has given me with design matters; to Ana with special thanks for help she has provided with design and social media; to my mother, Daphne Squires, who has always believed in me and my writing, and to my husband, Grey, who comes with me on every journey – whether it be to Cuba, to Bristol or from the start of one book to the day it's completed and ready to face the world. Thank you, my lovelies . . .